Praise for *Dance fro*

"Deeply drawn characters take you on a journey that will change their lives...and yours. Women's fiction at its finest."

~ Nikki Arana, award-winning author of *The Next Target*

"This is not my kind of book. So when I say it went deep into my heart, you'll know it's a story that will impact you no matter what genre you typically read. This novel will open your eyes. You'll start seeing the people around you in a vastly different way than you do right now. And you can't help but be changed by the three young women who Sleiman portrays with authenticity, penetrating insight, and well-crafted prose."

~ James L. Rubart, bestselling author of *Soul's Gate* and *Memory's Door*

"Dina Sleiman allows the reader to see the beauty hidden inside her characters, especially Layla the Muslim girl—the beauty hidden because of social and religious restrictions. The author captured this feeling in the book itself when she said through her college professor, 'This is the power of literature. It allows us to see the beauty in people around us. Gives us glimpses into their minds and their souls.'"

~ Brother Rasheed, host of the international television program *Daring Questions*, aimed at the Muslim world

"Well-written, thoughtful and engaging, *Dance from Deep Within* follows the lives and friendship of three young women as they learn about love, faith and truth. Fans of Dina Sleiman are in for a real treat!"

~ Ann Tatlock, award-winning author of *Sweet Mercy*

"Dina Sleiman has written a heart-gripping and mind-expanding novel about three young women, each in search of something deeper than the usual fare offered by the world. One is a Muslim, one a Christian, and one a former gypsy with no real spiritual roots at all. Yet, as their lives intertwine, they find they truly do have more in common than they would have imagined—though they also learn there can be a serious price required in fulfilling their quest for deeper meaning and wholehearted commitment."

~ Kathi Macias (www.boldfiction.com) is the author of more than 40 books, including *People of the Book*, set in Saudi Arabia.

"In *Dance from Deep Within*, three young women of vastly contrasting cultures—southern Christian, Lebanese Muslim, agnostic 'flower child'—walk into a classroom seeking very different ideas of truth, romance, and a happy-ever-after future. The friendship they forge is as unexpected as the twists and turns, danger and joy, and heartache and laughter they find. Their individual quests and mutual friendship ultimately confront each with a life-altering choice. This tale of love, faith, courage—and, yes, romance too—will leave Dina Sleiman fans laughing, crying, and reluctant to turn the final page."

~ Jeanette Windle, award-winning author of *Veiled Freedom*, *Freedom's Stand*, and *Congo Dawn*

dance from DEEP WITHIN

dance *from* DEEP WITHIN

D. L. Sleiman

WhiteFire Publishing

This is a work of fiction. All characters and events portrayed in this novel are either fictitious or used fictitiously.

DANCE FROM DEEP WITHIN

WhiteFire Publishing
13607 Bedford Rd NE
Cumberland, MD 21502

ISBN: 978-1-939023-29-2 (digital)
          978-1-939023-28-5 (print)

FOREWORD

Dear Readers,

My name is Sister Amani. I am a former Muslim woman and the host of the first Christian TV program directed to Muslim women. You might notice my name as you read through this book, because I am a part of the journey of the fictional character Layla in the story.

I have a deep appreciation for Dina Sleiman's understanding of the struggles of Muslim women. Reading through the story, I was able to see through Layla's eyes. I can identify with her impressions of the American culture and the relationships around her—with the battle between the freedoms she longs to have and the taboos she was taught. Dina brilliantly captured a glimpse of the free Layla that lives deep within yet doesn't dare to peek from behind that veil. She is a talented author with a heart that understands sisterhood beyond the boundaries of countries, religions, and cultures. To my surprise, I discovered through the friendship between these three young women that true freedom has a cost and requires a risk in any culture, not only my own.

The story uniquely bridges the gap between the Western culture and the Middle Eastern culture to reveal the beauty of both while not ignoring the problems and the darkness in either. I think the story eloquently speaks of the realities of Muslim families living in the west. It also illustrates true and simple ways that friendship can open the door for someone like Layla to understand that they have a choice and have been created with a purpose. A gentle theme of love and truth flows through the book, woven together with intense excitement as the story unfolds. It became clear to me that our author is speaking from a heart that has shared these sorts of experiences, and that she herself was given a heart of compassion for those who never had the freedom to "dance."

My prayers are for our Lord Jesus Christ to show his love to you as you go on this journey to find your own Dance from Deep Within.

Sister Amani
Host of the internationally aired program, *The Muslim Woman*

To my husband, Dani Sleiman.
He imparted his love for the Muslim people to me,
and without him this book would never have been written.

The contemporary dancer stretches and tenses,
bends and contorts, writhes on the floor all
in search of that fulcrum of human physicality.

That singularity in her abdomen she will strengthen
and hone to tighten her craft, to control each
turn, jump, and postmodern pose in a delicate

tango with gravity. It is the place of perfect
balance, the human conductor by which spirit
to flesh is conveyed. It must flow through and out

fingertips and toes. They are not held safe
in ballet's constraining outward shapes,
arms and hands curved into beautiful

nineteenth century artifacts.
For the postmodern dance, an electrical current
must fill the body, charging each cell,

creating power and immediacy.
The center of a man is higher up, in his chest,
beneath his ribs, nearer the heart to keep

his scales from tipping; but our dancer is reaching
deep in the bowl between her hips,
the halfway point of her entire being,

for that core, the stability, the consummation
of internal struggle, resulting in the dance

ONE

Four years' worth of anticipation gathered in her chest. A pounding she must quiet before stepping through that doorway. *It's just a door.* Layla Al-Rai glanced at the handle, and then back to her Old Dominion University schedule to review it yet again. *English 101 MWF 10:00 a.m. Batten Arts 205.*

Yes, this was the place. She had circled the hallway several times to be punctual but not early. *It's just a door,* she told herself more firmly this time. And the people beyond it were just students, like her. She could barely believe she was standing here—that her Middle Eastern mother had relented at long last. But years of patient persistence won her over.

Allah willing, her parents might even let her stay long enough to finish the engineering degree she dreamed of before insisting Layla marry. Surely stranger things had happened. She was only twenty-two years old. She should be enjoying her youth. And maybe she'd finally make friends with some regular Americans. Growing up in the Islamic section of Detroit had made it all too easy to stay immersed in her Muslim bubble.

If only her best friend Fatima were here, the day would be complete. She and Fatima had dreamed of this moment together, imagined choosing classes and buying textbooks. But for her devout Saudi Arabian neighbor, college could never be more than a bittersweet fantasy. For Fatima's sake, she determined to enjoy the experience all the more and to e-mail her every last detail.

Layla straightened her spine and smoothed her red knit

mini-dress over her modest black leggings and long-sleeved shirt. Reaching up, she adjusted her silky veil. The elegant crimson fabric draped about her head, covering her hair and neck but leaving her face exposed for all to see. She took a deep breath and attempted to relax her features into a casual expression. Then she willed her feet to move forward. Time to step into a new experience.

Entering the classroom, the pounding in her chest quickened. But she would not let the dingy walls and faint smell of mold dampen her spirits. Instead she focused upon the windows across the back displaying a bright golden sun, blue sky, and swaying green leaves.

As she gathered her courage and scanned the room for empty seats, she noticed that most of the hyperactive freshmen looked like they had mistaken the class for a keg party. But she spied one blond woman in the corner, her nose buried in a novel, quietly waiting for the lesson to begin. Almost the same image that met Layla every time she entered Fatima's bedroom. The sight comforted her, and she headed in that direction.

She drew stares as she crossed the room and hid deeper in the folds of her veil. In general, Americans were politically correct enough to be respectful of, although curious about, a Muslim female in their midst. But she'd learned the hard way that a few sick guys harbored twisted fantasies involving veiled women. Her uncle blamed the evil porn sites of the "infidels," but Layla chose not to use that close-minded term.

As she reached the desk in the back, the novel-wielding student looked up with a warm smile.

Layla smiled back. "Is this seat taken?"

"No, please." She pointed to the chair, and Layla lowered herself into it.

The blond returned to her book, but when a flying paper airplane came sailing onto her desk, she picked it up and smashed it, shooting a sassy grin to the perpetrators. Layla wished she could be so confident around men.

"Ugh," she said to Layla. "It's like going back to high school. Maybe worse. Probably wasn't such a bright idea to take eight years off before starting college."

"Me too. Well, only four, but it's been awhile."

"I'm sure you'll do fine. I'm Allie." She tossed the smashed plane to Layla. "Cute outfit."

If Layla's old-fashioned auntie had her way this morning, Layla would have left the house camouflaged from head to toe in an ugly gray overcoat. She grinned. With Auntie, she had to pick her battles, but this one had been so worth it. The red mini-dress ensemble was a success!

She tipped the crumpled paper in salute. "Thanks. I'm Layla." Placing the unusual gift on her desk for additional courage, she turned her attention to organizing her notebooks and supplies. She needed this class to go well and give her strength to face the rest of the week.

The instructor entered the classroom and situated himself at the '70s style teacher's desk. The middle-aged professor with his wool suit jacket and wire-rimmed glasses fit the role so perfectly, he could have walked straight out of her television set. He pulled a stack of papers from his briefcase and began a weaving journey about the room.

Layla examined Allie as the teacher handed out syllabi. The young woman's hair was pulled atop her head in a casual bun with tendrils escaping. Her slim lavender T-shirt flattered her slender, graceful figure and blue-eyed, blond coloring. The creamy tank top worn underneath gave the shirt a more modest cut.

Looking closer, she attempted to decipher the words on Allie's T-shirt. It was difficult from her angle until Allie shifted. *Your beauty should not come from outward appearance... it should be that of your inner self, the unfading beauty of a gentle and quiet spirit. ~ I Peter 3:3-4.*

Some sort of scripture? Christian, Layla guessed from the cross-like symbol substituting for the "T" on the logo. The verse resonated with her, and she loved the surrounding drawing of a young woman's face half concealed by a tumble of modern art swirls in place of her hair. But Layla's mind struggled to connect the sentiment to the brash girls from the Christian community in Lebanon.

The professor began the morning by introducing himself as Professor Robinson and giving the basic guidelines for the class. Then something in his demeanor altered. "This year I've decided to use a central theme for our writing assignments: Unity in Diversity."

He pushed up his glasses and crossed his arms over his chest. "A favorite poem of mine by Harlem Renaissance author Langston Hughes begins, 'I too, sing America.' He goes on to explain that while he is the darker brother sent to the kitchen when company comes, someday things would change. 'They'll see how beautiful I am and be ashamed,' he says, 'I, too, am America.'"

The brief quote stirred Layla with hope, but with confusion as well. She too was America—sort of—not quite. Her passport claimed she was a U.S. citizen. But what did that really mean? A part of her longed to feel more connected to this land of her birth.

"This is the power of literature. It allows us to see the beauty in people around us. Gives us glimpses into their minds and their souls. Our readings will come from various societies and focus on multiculturalism. It seems like we have a nice mix of students here." The professor gestured to the room.

Layla took in the faces staring back at him: mostly Caucasian, but interspersed with Asian, Hispanic, and African-American. Before moving here she'd been assured that, thanks to the local Navy bases, the Hampton Roads area had a better ethnic balance than the rest of Virginia. Although, Layla still appeared to be the only Islamic student in the bunch. Her nervous excitement reared again. What if she couldn't do it? Couldn't click with these people? Couldn't connect?

"But let's think further than skin deep about what defines our 'cultures,'" continued the professor. "The surfer and the jock, the artist and the businessman, the Christian and the atheist, the New Yorker and the Alabaman. In a moment I'm going to give you all a chance to mingle. I want you to find two to three students who in some way come from a different culture than your own. Ideally, you will find both similarities and differences. These students will become your diversity group for the semester, so choose wisely."

This was precisely what Layla desired, a chance to broaden her perspective. She tingled at the thought. But could she really do it? And what might it cost her if she did?

The professor turned on the overhead projector and pointed with his pen to a list of essays, creative writing exercises, and a final research paper. "Take a moment to glance over the assignments and then begin looking for your group members." He put the cap back on the pen. "Remember, the purpose of this project is to see past people's exteriors and get a peek at who they are deep within. I'll be around to help."

Oh, the class sounded too amazing to be true. Layla bit her lip to hold back a rare squeal and proceeded to skim the syllabus. Each lesson was designed to explore the beliefs of others. Their personalities. Their cultures. Contrasting viewpoints. The research paper tackled the subject of one aspect of your culture you would like to change. Her mind brimmed with ideas already.

As Layla reached the end of the list, the boy in front of her turned around and leered. "I'd sure be happy to get a peek at who you are deep inside, gorgeous."

Layla recoiled. Her anticipation about the assignment fled, and her fingers began to tremble. Barely into her first class, and already her auntie's worst fears were coming true. She had no idea how to handle such an uncouth male. What had she gotten herself into?

"Back off, scumbag. Layla's my partner."

Layla breathed a sigh of relief as Allie claimed her hand and held it firm in her own.

Allie whispered in her ear, "Don't worry, I've got this."

Layla's shaking subsided. Why couldn't she think of responses like Allie just delivered? But even if she could, would she dare speak so boldly to a man? Probably not. This was foreign territory for sure. More so than she had ever imagined.

The girls pushed their chairs together. Allie beckoned to

another twenty-something woman who had arrived mid-lecture and slid into the desk closest to the door.

The young lady mirrored Layla's relief as she came to join them. She appeared the Bohemian type in her Birkenstock sandals, raggedy pants, and loose tunic shirt with the strap of her patchwork bag cutting diagonally across the outfit. Her café-au-lait skin contrasted attractively with the ivory cotton of her hand-woven top. A tuft of golden-brown corkscrew curls framed her face.

Layla couldn't contain a welcoming grin. This girl would be fun to get to know. So different than anyone she had met before.

"Hi, I'm Rain," she said as she pulled up a third desk beside them. She settled in, eagerly leaning forward as Allie and Layla introduced themselves.

Allie peered at Rain. "You don't have a boyfriend with dreadlocks, do you?"

Layla gasped at Allie's audacity. Did she intend the comment to be derogatory? Hopefully Rain would not be offended. Layla so wanted this project to go well. Her college dreams flashed before her eyes, in peril already.

"Hey." Rain wagged her finger at Allie. "I thought we were moving beyond our stereotypes."

Allie smiled. "I saw you with him at McDonalds last night. You guys make an adorable couple. I remember because I was surprised that you ordered meat. Now that, I confess, was stereotypical. Hamburgers don't fit my image of the whole Bohemian vibe."

Rain laughed, and Layla restrained her sigh of relief.

"We lived on the streets for years," Rain said. "We worked and ate in a lot of soup kitchens. You don't get to be picky."

Streets, soup kitchens? Layla never dreamed of enduring such horrors. Compassion welled in her heart, a pleasant respite from the tension of the morning. "*Harum habibti.*" The whispered Arabic phrase of sympathy escaped Layla's mouth before she could stop it. "You poor thing. That's terrible."

Rain placed a warm hand on Layla's. "No. We were just experiencing the plight of the homeless. Raising our social consciousness. Stuff like that. I'm writing a book about it. That's why I'm here. To study writing. Virginia was the last place we established residency. Couldn't resist those in-state tuition rates."

"That's what drew me back too." Allie nodded. "I'm here for dance and business. What about you, Layla?"

"Engineering," she said. "Well, I guess the three of us will have no problem proving our case for a culturally diverse group." So much so that Layla's head threatened to explode on the spot. She tried to be open-minded, really she did, but this was almost too much to take in at once.

Rain glanced around the small circle. "So we've got our Middle Eastern Muslim. Classic white chick. Let me guess. Anglo-Saxon Protestant?" Her fingers swirled about expressively as she spoke. "Then there's me. Bi-racial, tree-hugging, social-activist raised by aging flower children. I guess my heritage is a little harder to pin down."

Allie raised an eyebrow. "Since you seem to have us all figured out, do you mind if I ask about your religion?"

"Hmm, my mother went through her pagan Wicca phase," Rain said. "It didn't really stick, though. I'm a spiritual person, but I find religion restrictive. I suppose I would describe my faith as...imaginative."

"Interesting." Layla wrote that down, although she had no idea what it meant. She might as well buckle up her seat belt and try to enjoy the assignment. She was in for quite a ride with this group.

Imaginative religion. Hmm. Allie Carmichael was hesitant to encourage Rain's New Age belief system, but she didn't want to blow an opportunity to befriend these women. She liked them already and always enjoyed meeting people with different perspectives. Tapping her hand against the fake wood of the desktop, she said, "Works great for the project. I'm sure we can get a lot of mileage out of that."

Allie took in the two girls before her. The fashionable veiled woman with her bright red lipstick. The hippie chick with fresh, clean skin shining in the sun. What a study in contrasts.

Rain folded herself cross-legged on her chair in an earthy manner. "So where do we start?"

Layla scribbled more notes into her well-organized binder. "According to the syllabus, we need to choose a neutral territory outside of school to meet and continue our discussion." Although she spoke perfect English with no discernable accent, a certain stiffness to her cadence caused Allie to suspect it wasn't her first language.

"So I guess a bar is out of the question." As Rain made the teasing suggestion, Layla's eyes popped wide open.

"For both of us." Allie wouldn't mind so much. She had visited plenty of pubs while touring Europe with her Christian dance company. But she had picked up a few tidbits about Muslims during her travels as well, and she didn't want Layla to feel uncomfortable.

Layla glanced from her to Rain and back again with dark, haunting, black-rimmed eyes over a slim nose and full mouth. Allie had noticed a number of trendy young Muslim women around campus. Although they displayed only the skin of their hands and faces, they managed to look even more stylish in their layered clothing and matching veils than the normal American girls.

"Don't you drink?" Layla squinted at Allie as though seeing her for the first time. "I thought most Christians did. That's the main way you can spot a Christian in Lebanon. Beer and bikinis." Layla sucked in a breath and bit her lip, as if she had said too much.

Pretty funny. Although Allie suspected her parents wouldn't find the assessment amusing. They would probably offer a lecture on sound doctrine and denominational differences. But Allie was nothing like them. She attempted a joke to lighten the moment. "Don't you know the three Christian commandments: thou shalt not drink, thou shalt not smoke, thou shalt not cuss?"

But somehow her attempt at humor fell flat. Allie twisted

her face in an ironic expression. True Christianity was so much more. She still could hardly believe she had come home to subject herself to such a legalistic mindset all over again.

"Seriously? Christians are that strict?" Layla pressed a hand to her mouth. "I didn't realize. Things are very different in Lebanon."

Allie didn't know what to say. She wanted to believe she was free of all that religiosity. She had felt free enough for the last eight years on the mission field. But since she had returned to Virginia, her family's belief system slowly wrapped itself around her like some sort of boa constrictor. She hated viewing herself through their eyes. Hearing their voices in her head. Now here they were again, threatening her conversation with these refreshing young women. Oh, how she wished she could afford college without her parents' help.

"No, those aren't the Christian commandments," Rain snickered. "She's being facetious. None of those are found in the Bible as far as I know, but they're all some Christians seem to worry about."

Allie couldn't help but wonder about Rain's previous experience with Christians. People like her parents, perhaps? "She's right. They aren't in the Bible. Not exactly, anyway. It's complicated."

"Or maybe just stupid." Rain pinned Allie with her gaze. Her belligerent tone spoke volumes.

"Maybe it is." Allie continued to meet the stare emanating from Rain's catlike golden-green eyes, hoping Rain could somehow see clear into her soul and understand that Allie carried wounds from that sort of judgmental thinking too. She suspected her own mother still questioned her commitment to Christ. Over what? A pair of cut-off jean shorts? Some alternative music? A belly piercing that chafed against her leotards and had grown shut long ago? Did her years spent sharing the gospel count for nothing?

Rain shook off the challenge. "So how about a coffee shop?"

"Coffee, yes." Layla sighed, brushing the fire-engine red fringe from her face. "I'm so sick of my auntie's syrupy Lebanese version. But can we make it after sunset? Ramadan lasts another week, and I could really use some good American coffee."

As the professor called the class to order, Allie shot Rain a questioning glance. What did Ramadan have to do with sunset? Rain shrugged, clearly having no clue either. Allie had much to learn about these surprising young women. She couldn't wait to start the project. Maybe this homecoming wouldn't be the disaster she dreaded after all.

TWO

Rain Butler-Briggs managed to squelch her distressing concerns for the moment. She sat across the dinner table from her boyfriend, James Allen. In companionable silence, they ate the lovely meal of field green salad dressed with lemon and olive oil alongside Spanish beans and rice. Since they'd gotten this small studio apartment several weeks ago, Rain had taken to preparing home-cooked dinners. Such a novelty after years on the road.

She supposed that made up for turning herself into a domestic servant. Her mother always insisted her father prepare half the meals, but truth be told, Rain enjoyed cooking, and she enjoyed serving James in this simple way. After all, he would be earning most of the money for the next few years while she focused on her writing. They were morphing into a cliché couple.

James munched his salad and offered Rain an appreciative grin. Warm tingles flooded her. Even after nine years together, he remained the handsomest man she had ever seen. He came from a mixed ethnic heritage as she did, his black and Native American. The resulting brown skin, deep eyes, and dark hair could have been Mexican, Islander, or any combination of races.

Today his dreadlocks hid under a three-toned knit hat, revealing a face any artist would love: strong lines, sharp cheekbones, angled jaw, straight nose, soft berry-colored lips, the scruff of goatee. His deep chocolate eyes looked straight into her soul, melting her.

He remained the one constant in her life during her years

spent as a roving gypsy. She would gladly marry him. A part of her longed for structure and stability, but people in their circles rarely did such orthodox things. Her hippie parents would not be pleased. That sort of convention was linked to the world of "the man." The "capitalist establishment." Rain snickered to herself.

"What's going on in that pretty little head of yours?" James's low, smooth voice caressed her ears.

"Just how nice it is to make dinner for my oh-so-handsome boyfriend."

"You're a great cook. Who knew?" He reached across the table and lifted her hand to his lips. James might not give much thought to convention and manners, but he played the gentleman out of his own sense of kindness, consideration, and natural charm.

Rain took note of her many blessings and smiled her gratitude to the universe. Their migrant farm work that summer had paid better than expected, supplying ample grocery funds.

"Do you think we're getting to be too 'normal'?" James laughed.

"No, it's a nice change. Maybe we can settle down and have a couple of rug rats." She wiggled her eyebrows at him, hoping against all odds that he might warm to the idea in this relaxed atmosphere.

"Not funny." James clenched his jaw.

The salad turned to paper in Rain's mouth. James refused to bring any innocent souls into this harsh, cruel world. What demons from his past reared their ugly heads at the very mention of children? Sometimes she felt so close to him. Other times she wondered if she knew the man at all.

She changed the subject. "Sorry. Bad joke. But I am enjoying settling down. Actually, I was thinking about organizing some kind of cleaning schedule." She looked around the room. They had cleared off their secondhand table and lit a ginger-scented candle, but her grandma would no doubt declare the surrounding room a pigsty.

"Not likely, babe." James curled his lip and shot her a look.

"Well, if we don't, I'm going to end up doing all the work myself." Now that they had a place of their own, she wanted it to look nice, homey. She had gone for so long without. Was that too much to ask?

"Sounds fine by me," James said in his too-cool tone of voice. "Clean if you want to clean. You know I don't do schedules."

It wouldn't hurt him to pay a little more attention to his school schedule. James wouldn't want to hear it from her, though. They never *judged* each other. They weren't into that. But Rain couldn't help thinking a little tough love might come in handy if she wanted to get him safely through pre-med and on to his physician's assistant degree. With that he could work as a doctor in most third world countries, and they could start a new adventure and a second book.

Rain tried a different route. "That doesn't sound very enlightened of you, letting the woman do all the housework."

"Now don't go and turn this into some feminist platform. I just think the person who feels like cleaning should do the cleaning. If I want a clean house, I'll pitch in. But right now, I really don't care."

Those words were the final straw. Tears filled Rain's eyes. "Do you care about me?"

She had no idea. The beautiful woman sitting across from James had no clue his whole world revolved around her. He reached over and took her hand in his, rubbing his thumb across her silken skin. Rain was his sun and his moon. His life meant nothing until she entered it. But he'd never admit that. He might scare her away. He couldn't bear to lose her. Nor could he bear the pain in her eyes caused by his thoughtless comment.

If only she knew. If only she understood why rules freaked him out. Worse yet, children. How could he ever explain? Rain came from a loving family.

James could never expose this innocent girl to the evil ghosts that haunted his soul. What he could do was change the world.

Make it a better place. Stop the hurt, starting right now with the hurt in her eyes. "Come on, babe. Don't take it that way. I'll tell you what. I'll try to help out, but no schedules. Fair enough?"

"Yeah, that's fair." Rain stared down at her plate and pushed her beans and rice around for a few moments.

Why did she worry about this stuff? After all these years, aspects of his woman remained a mystery. "What's bothering you now?"

"Do you ever wonder if there's more?" Although Rain took another bite of her food, she looked as if she could barely swallow it down.

He enjoyed a good existentialist discussion, but not with Rain in this mood. "More than beans and rice? Sure, all the time, but I keep coming up short."

"I'm serious, James. What if there's more to life than this ooey gooey, go-with-the-flow existence of ours? What if there's some actual greater purpose? What if there is a God? A real living God, not some sort of universal something or another?"

James quoted one of his favorite Taoist sentiments. "'Try the highest degree, travelling in the realm where there is no sign. Exercise fully what you have received from nature, without any subjective viewpoint. In one word: be absolutely vacuous.'"

"Well, you've certainly got the vacuous part down," she mumbled.

James chuckled. Rain was some smart *chica*. One of the many qualities he admired in her. "I think that multi-cultural assignment is getting to your head. The point isn't to change *you*. It's to show you a different perspective. Don't lose who you are." He reached for her hand again. "Who we are." He gave it a reassuring squeeze.

An adorable rosy blush flooded her cheeks. The soft, hazy look of a woman in love fell over her like a trance. "Well, when you put it that way."

Then unexpectedly, she quirked her lips and turned away. What had gotten into her today?

After dinner Rain scooped up the dishes and headed to the sink. She dropped them into the tepid water with a splash. To her relief, James followed and pulled out a flowered towel to help dry. She handed the plates and cups to him one by one.

As they finished up, he bent over and gave her a feather light kiss on the lips. "What now? Once I start that night watchman gig, you won't have me around in the evenings so much."

"How about ice cream? I'm starved." She snatched up the dish towel and wiped her hands.

James leaned against the counter. "We just finished dinner. Is this what domestication does to you, woman? I've never seen you eat so much in your life."

Rain's heart sped. James could be observant at the most inconvenient times. She moved to brush off the dining table, scooping crumbs into her hand and avoiding eye contact as she gathered her wits. "Come on. A walk to the store would be nice. It's beautiful out."

"Okay, cuteness. Whatever you want."

Surely with all the commotion of the move he hadn't noticed anything. She shouldn't be so paranoid. Rain tossed the crumbs in the trash, crossed to her man, and snuggled into his roughhewn side, breathing deep the scent of sandalwood. "Mm, you're so good to me."

They headed outdoors with James's arm draped around Rain's shoulders. Booming rap music rumbled through an open car window, followed by loud, angry shouts, but that didn't bother her.

Due to her bi-racial heritage, Rain received warm, Southern hospitality from the adorable grandmas of Norfolk, even if their children were busy working, and their grandchildren were... well, let's face it...a little scary. With strong and handsome James by her side, she felt safe enough.

They passed a man from their building. He lifted his chin and uttered a low-toned, "'Sup."

James raised a fist in the air. "Stay true, man."

Rain hated that stupid saying. Stay true to what? She shook her head and pressed deeper into his side.

They continued their journey through the decrepit old houses. Norfolk held interwoven pockets of rich and poor districts, originating from the time right after slavery when the white oppressors wanted to keep their servants nearby in separate ghettos. James knew all about these things and schooled Rain well.

Once at the store, James headed straight toward the freezer section. But as they passed through the aisles, Rain's gaze fell upon the tell-tale rack.

And there it hung.

Her eyes glued to it.

The early pregnancy test.

Mocking. Accusing.

Surely it was nothing. No point in worrying yet.

She tensed as she passed by the blaring package, careful to drag her eyes away from its mesmerizing pull before James noticed. How long could she put it off?

THREE

Layla picked up a strand of her dark hair to study it. Of course Uncle did not require the veil at home. Only in families such as Fatima's was such ridiculousness expected. She sat on the silky, pink comforter of her California king-sized bed with her new laptop splayed over her knees. Thankful for her American attire, she brushed a hand across the soft fabric of her jeans.

All week thoughts of her neighbor Fatima from Detroit had weighed heavily on Layla's mind. Each lecture at the college reminded Layla of Fatima's love for learning, of how much she would treasure an education. But her Saudi friend would never be afforded such a chance.

She stared at the computer screen through the shimmer of tears.

> *Dear Fatima,*
>
> *Oh, how I wish you could be here with me, my sister of the heart. This week has passed in a blur. My classes are wonderful. Physics, calculus, computer design. You would adore them. Yet despite your affection for science, I do believe the class you would enjoy the most is English. We managed to read little enough Western literature in our Muslim schools. And we're working on a fascinating project about diversity. It is just like we always dreamed. There's a whole world out there full of ideas and opinions.*

You should meet my group partners. A Christian ballerina. A New Age hippie chick. And me. What a mix. Perhaps we shall even grow to be friends. Remember how we longed to be friends with an actual blond American like Barbie? Ha ha.

Allie, that's her name, moves like a fairy princess, her gold hair glistening with sunlight, but she doesn't seem to notice. I suspect she sincerely believes in God, just as we do. Rain is the hippie. Can you imagine a more fitting name? She is hysterical. Anything that pops into her head flies out of her mouth with no filter whatsoever. What a pleasant contrast to the scripted niceties that substitute for conversation in our culture.

On the outside these girls are very different from me, of course. But I sense we all seek after the same thing. Truth. Reality. Authenticity. I can't express to you how excited I am about this opportunity.

Except, of course, that you are not here to share it with me. I picture you back home, hidden within the long folds of your thick black veil, faceless, expressionless. Like a phantom imprisoned in walls of dreary fabric. When you walk down the street, trailing behind your sullen brothers, I want to shout, "Please see her! She's a real live human being."

I'm so sorry, my friend. I know you do your best to follow Allah. As do I. I should not judge. But I know you. I see you. I wish I could share your beautiful face and heart with the world.

What can I do to brighten your day? I have an idea. I am attaching book lists from my classes. Good thing your father doesn't monitor your reading material, or we would have been

*in trouble long ago. I suppose there are a few
advantages to being invisible.*
*But know that I love you and would bring
you here with me if I could. I miss you so. Have
a wonderful week.*
Forever your friend,
Layla

Layla hit send, stood, and moped her way through the
enormous house and to the patio along the inlet. Out in nature,
she felt closest to God. The setting sun streaked the sky like an
artist's palette with paint strokes of blue, purple, and pink. She
watched the shadowed silhouette of a bird ascending toward
the heavens.

Oh, to soar free on the wind like that bird.

Her aunt joined her. "What's wrong, *habibti?*"

"I was thinking of Fatima."

Auntie knew the story well. "*En sha'allah,*" *Um-Wassim*
muttered and pressed her lips tight. *As Allah wills.*

Was that her answer to everything? If Layla heard that
ridiculous sentiment one more time, she might just scream.

The headlights of the Cadillac brightened the driveway.
"Come, help me set the table for *Iftar.*" Auntie ushered her
inside. "We don't want to keep *Abou-Wassim* waiting to break
his fast."

Layla's family religiously observed the fasting season, never
eating or drinking between sunrise and sunset. Allah forbid
she keep the patriarch from his esteemed dinner, especially
during Ramadan. But she was starving and near dying from
thirst herself, so she hurried after her aunt. Within minutes,
a spread of Middle Eastern wonders appeared on the center
island: chicken shawarma, labneh, kefta, rice, fried potatoes,
pita bread, tabouli salad, and of course the traditional *Iftar*
dates. The meal smelled of garlic, lemon, and cinnamon as
Lebanese food always did.

Aunt and Uncle were so excited to have her staying with
them. Their own children had grown and moved away. She

joined them for the ritual washing and the *Maghrib* prayer on their small rugs, then braced herself for a long night as they gathered at the table. At least there would be no guests today. Although Layla enjoyed company on occasion, she preferred a quiet evening.

They all began with a big glass of water to fend off dehydration and their three traditional dates to emulate the prophet. Layla nearly swooned at the sweetness after her long day of hunger.

"So, this has been a big week for you." Uncle winked at her and passed the pita bread.

"I know. I'm too excited. I can hardly sit still." Maybe that would win her a reprieve from a drawn out dinner. She stuffed a wedge of bread into her mouth to soothe her grumbling stomach.

"I don't understand your father sending you to school with all those wild American boys." Auntie bustled about fetching more food and filling glasses with soda. If she had her way, Layla would be helping out at the family restaurants and engaged to some nice Muslim man.

Layla pushed aside a twinge of guilt as she recalled the jerk from English class. Auntie didn't need to hear about that, and Layla was already learning to take care of herself.

Uncle ripped off a piece of bread and dipped it in the fresh lebneh yogurt. "We've been over this. It is her father's decision to make, not ours. He says she's an adult woman, a modern woman, and she wants a career. Not every girl can cook like you, *marti*. Old Dominion University has an excellent program in her field, and it's much safer than the schools in Detroit."

Layla grimaced, not sure if she should be insulted by the cooking comment.

Um-Wassim did more of her Arabic muttering. "If they knew she wanted to study, why didn't they send her sooner? She'll be an old lady when she's done, and all the decent men will be gone."

Yes, definitely an insult. She took a bite of her aunt's scrumptious potatoes. She'd have to be careful not to pack on the pounds while living here, or no decent men would be looking at her anyway. Hmm. That strategy might actually work.

Auntie noticed Layla's frown and came to sit beside her. She laid her hand on Layla's knee. "Don't worry, *habibti*. You are a good girl still. As my old grandmother used to say, someday you will find a man to cover your shame."

Uncle winced. Even he was Westernized enough to know how that traditional comment would grate against Layla's ears. "She wants to be an engineer. So leave her alone." He smacked the table, closing the issue. No doubt he dreaded listening to the women of his house bicker over the matter.

Auntie scooped food onto the plates. "Of course she will be an engineer. She will be an engineer, and she will find a man. Surely such a modern girl can do both. And have a baby boy while she's at it." She nudged Layla with her hip.

"Yes," Layla said. "And if I have a girl by mistake you can say, '*Allah yaateeki sabi*'."

May Allah bless you with a boy. The required Arabic response to the birth of a female. As if a girl were any less precious than a male child. Hot lava filled Layla's veins at the thought. Rain and Allie must be rubbing off on her.

Auntie looked confused. Uncle shot Layla a silencing glare. She wished her aunt could move out of her ancient traditions into the modern world. Her mother too, for that matter. The women were too much alike.

She took a moment to gaze out the patio doors at the flower-laden sitting area and the inlet beyond, glimmering with moonlight. Her auntie spoke too much truth. Before long Layla's parents would "recommend" a nice young man for her to marry, and like Fatima, Layla would endure. Perhaps the small chance existed that if she met "Mister Sunni Muslim Right," her parents might consider letting her choose her own husband.

No, the idea was too ludicrous. Why pin her hopes on such an improbability? She could only hope they would let her finish her degree before that fateful day arrived.

Uncle cleared his throat. "So, how were your classes?"

Layla swallowed down the parsley laden meatball.

"Wonderful. Everything I dreamed of. I'm learning so much already. I love being back in the world of math and science."

"Physics, calculus, technology. So silly. What can you do with those?" Auntie waved them away with annoyance.

"Uh...engineering." Layla forced herself to keep eating and avoid any disrespectful eye rolling or hand gestures.

Uncle grunted. "They sound interesting, *habibti*. And you have general ed classes too, correct?"

"Yes, English and Human Creativity."

"How are those?" Uncle handed his plate to Auntie for refills. She bustled back to the counter.

"Really good. I can tell that Old Dominion is an excellent university." She couldn't bring herself to talk about the English project yet. Especially in front of Auntie. It would be her secret for now. She could hardly wait for Friday night.

"Well, if you must have an education, only the best will do. I can't believe my little girl is so grown-up." A twinkle filled Uncle's eye. He raised his hands by his head. "*Hal seesan.*" He clicked his tongue and twisted his wrists, starting the beloved Arabic children's song.

Layla bit down a grin. "Absolutely not, Uncle. Don't be ridiculous."

He raised his eyebrows to her and persisted. "*Hal seesan.*" *These little chicks*, he sang and clicked again.

How many times had she begged Uncle to sing this song during her younger years? A hundred? More? "Fine, *sho helween.*" *So beautiful,* she responded, twisting her own wrists as he clicked out the percussion.

They both laughed. Uncle gave her hand a squeeze. Warmth filled Layla's chest. Her family loved her, she never doubted that for a moment. If only they could stop trying to run her life.

"*Majnoon!* Crazy!" Layla's uncle shouted, throwing an empty water bottle at the television in the media room and following the projectile with a stream of Arabic curse words.

Uncle's favorite new pastime was watching live call-in talk shows where former Muslims discussed their conversions to Christianity. Today's show, *Daring Questions*, never failed to evoke a display of histrionics. And Layla's favorite new pastime was watching her uncle watch the talk shows. If he hated them so much, why did he keep tuning in?

Layla pressed herself into the cool leather armchair as Brother Rasheed on the huge, flat screen TV took a caller. Ali, from Dubai, let loose a slew of insults much like her uncle had flung. The host sat patiently and listened. When the man stopped yelling, Brother Rasheed spoke with much understanding in his eyes. "I know, my brother. I felt this way once too. But I believe Jesus is knocking at the door of your heart, as he once knocked at the door of mine. Can you hear it? I say these words out of love. I long to speak the truth. Truth that was denied me for much of my life."

His gentle answer settled the caller, but Uncle grew madder than ever, stomping around the room and flinging his arms about his head in a full-blown tantrum.

Layla hid her laughter behind her hand. Forget the little chicks in the song, he reminded her of Grandmother's rooster.

Even in Lebanon, most everyone followed *Daring Questions* religiously. Love it or hate it, you simply couldn't ignore it. She found her uncle's displays amusing, but more than that, something in Rasheed's words resonated with her, vibrated deep inside her core. *I believe Jesus is knocking at the door of your heart. Can you hear it?*

As the host wrapped up the conversation and opened a new topic, Uncle swiped his hand in disgust and returned to his seat.

"Tonight we bring to you the story of Ameera, a nine-year-old girl from Saudi Arabia. She is petitioning the courts to save her from an arranged marriage to an abusive husband who is older than her grandfather."

Layla flinched at the harsh statement and crossed her arms tight around her middle. Rasheed spoke the words in Arabic. But they sounded equally horrifying in any language.

"Now, the courts have no real discretion in this situation,

and you all know why that is."

Knew, but never spoke of it.

"I will give you two words," Brother Rasheed said. "*Sharia* law."

What thoughts, what questions filled the minds of her aunt and uncle? Were they the same ones warring within Layla? Did it bother them to be reminded that the prophet himself married a young girl such as Ameera? That many experts in the Middle East claimed the *Qur'an* permitted, even encouraged a man to beat his wife for the good of her soul? Of course Layla's family didn't believe such nonsense, but still... Her stomach churned, and she pulled her arms in tighter. For the longest time no one said a word.

Then Auntie whispered her useless sentiment, "*En sha'allah,*" under her breath once again. *As Allah wills.*

Layla had so many questions, but she dared not voice them. Brother Rasheed not only spoke them aloud, he answered them honestly with wisdom and conviction. Yet, she hoped from the bottom of her heart his answers weren't true. They could turn her whole world upside down.

Once the show ended, her family would do their *wudu* cleansing ritual and mutter their rote prayers for the fifth round that day. As if that would make all of the negative aspects of their culture go away. Sometimes Layla enjoyed the quiet moments, kneeling still before her God. *Allah is the greatest. Allah is the greatest. I bear witness that there is nothing worthy of worship save Allah...* But all too often the words rang as vain repetitions.

Ugh! She must stop this line of thinking. Enough *Daring Questions* for her. She stood and headed through the kitchen, back to the moonlit patio. Her life, her friends, her values, everything wrapped around her Muslim identity. She could never turn her back on that. *Allah, speak to me your truth. Show me your way.* She whispered the words to the starry sky. Peace settled about her like a snuggly blanket.

Auntie approached, her sandaled feet scratching across the cement, and took Layla's hand in her own. "I forgot to ask how the Muslim Student Union meeting went today."

"Fine, I guess."

"Any handsome boys?"

"I don't know." Of course there were, but Layla would never admit it.

"We have some fine young men at the mosque. I can't wait for you to meet them."

"I don't need a man right now, Auntie. I need to finish school and get some experience working in Dad's office first." That way, once Layla could no longer hold off marriage and family, she'd be prepared to work part time from home.

Auntie's face fell.

Layla hated to disappoint the sweet lady. "But...the MSU has a beach party planned for next week after Ramadan. So who knows?"

"Oh, that's excellent. You've been longing to visit the ocean. This way you can feel comfortable in a group."

"We're heading to a quiet part of the beach, and we'll have a big picnic."

Auntie gave her hand a squeeze. "That sounds fun, *amar*." The moon, auntie called her, a favorite Arabic endearment.

The beach party did sound fun. The females could feel comfortable swimming with their modest clothing. Although she now lived in Virginia Beach, Layla felt too odd to visit the actual oceanfront, a veiled woman alone amidst the bikini-clad Americans.

She wondered what it would be like, just once, to feel the kiss of the warm ocean water against her bare skin. What would it be like to swim without gritty sand rubbing her arms and her legs, trapped inside layers of clothing? What would it be like, just once, to feel...*free*?

FOUR

Oh, what a relief to be back in tights and leotards. Allie missed dancing for hours a day with her old company, but it was time to stop flitting around the globe and get serious with her life. Her intermediate level lyrical class finished up their final combination, a quick series of pirouettes and leaps. The tween girls came and gave her moist hugs on their way out. The scent of deodorant and baby powder filled the air. She paused to offer each of them a special moment of encouragement. Katie on her flexibility. Brooklyn on her grace. Savannah on her hard work and determination.

The studio owner poked her head through the doorway. "Nice job, Allie."

"Thanks. I enjoyed it." With all the upper-level ballet classes at the studio being taught by professional Russian dancers, they had agreed lyrical would be the perfect niche for Allie. Thank God she had found this job so quickly. It gave her hope that she hadn't thrown her life away by returning home.

And Allie loved this contemporary style—less rules and more feeling—no pinchy *pointe* shoes digging into her toes. Lyrical lent itself to an organic means of dancing...and living. She looked forward to using worship music for her recital pieces like they did at her old dance company, *Alight*, although she already had in mind some cool, heavy metal versions. Several churches in the area supported worship dance ministries. Too bad her family's traditional pastor didn't believe dancing belonged in a sanctuary.

She popped her CD out of the player and snapped it into its case. The giant mirror in front of her reflected the entire room with its simple white walls and gray floor. This place had been her refuge for so many years while growing up.

Moving to the center of the floor, she flowed through a more advanced version of the combination she had given the girls that day. *Tombé, pas de bourrée, glissade, glissade, grand jeté,* finishing with a perfect triple *pirouette.* Bright white energy flowed from deep in her core, filling her with lightness and joy.

Moving to the *barre,* she brushed her toes in a soothing circular motion along the smooth vinyl flooring. Goodness, it's a wonder Pastor Jenkins hadn't talked her parents out of letting her dance altogether. But despite their ultra-conservative natures, Allie had to admit her parents wanted each of their children to pursue the gifts God had given them, even if they didn't understand Allie's passion for dance. For that matter, didn't understand Allie at all. She was forever twirling and leaping as a child. Standing still during the song service Sunday after Sunday had required every ounce of her self-control.

Allie's chest constricted and her airway began to close as so often happened when she remembered those days in her family's church, but she pushed the awful sensations away. She may have returned home, but she could never go back to that congregation.

Students for the next class filled the room and began stretching on the floor. She gathered her supplies and headed for the changing area. Allie pulled jeans overtop her wine-colored leotard and left on her wraparound pink dance sweater. She kept her hair safe in its bun, never liking the feeling of it against her neck. Her cell phone rang. She took it out of her bag. The display read, "Andy Vargas." Her chest tightened, and the constricting feeling struck her ring finger this time.

And another reason. Another reason to avoid that church. Allie needed to stay as far away from Andy as she could. She tossed the phone in her bag without answering it. Andy had been her first and only high school boyfriend. The relationship was enough for her then, but now she wondered how she ever tolerated him.

"Give it up, Andy," she whispered to herself.

Brooklyn eyed her curiously.

"Never mind. See you girls next week." Allie smiled to her students as she left the changing area.

On the way to the parking lot, Allie spotted a familiar face in the waiting room. She scanned her memory, attempting to place it. Of course, they took classes together as kids at this very studio. "Jessica?"

"Allie Carmichael. I heard you were back." Jessica opened her arms for a hug. "Good grief. You haven't aged a day."

"You look great too."

Jessica had traded her svelte dancer's body for plump curves, but earned in the bargain the most adorable little ballerina, who currently hid behind her legs.

"And who is this?"

"This is my daughter, Taylor. Taylor, say hi to Mommy's old friend Allie."

"Eddo," the little girl said and promptly stuck a thumb in her mouth.

Allie squatted down to Taylor's level, tilted her head, and raised the pitch of her voice. "I love your tutu. Pink is my favorite color." She touched the sweater on her arm to prove her point.

The girl removed her thumb and whispered. "Me too."

"You look just like a princess."

Taylor grinned.

"Tell Miss Allie thank you, Taylor," Jessica prompted.

"Tank you."

"Miss Allie is a teacher here." Jessica looked at her daughter with shining eyes and smoothed a few escaped hairs from the small redhead's beaded bun holder. Taylor scuffed the toe of her dance slipper against the carpet showing off her ballet *tendus*, then switched to an abbreviated *plié* by bending her knees.

"That is very good." Allie gave Taylor's belly a gentle poke. "I bet you're going to be a beautiful dancer when you grow up."

The child nodded.

"Do you think I can have a hug?"

Taylor studied Allie for a moment before she toddled toward her and threw chubby arms around Allie's neck. She buried her face against the child's hair. It sparkled like cherry candy.

She administered a kiss. Peeking up at Jessica she said, "Ohh, I want one."

"Talk to Andy Vargas. I'm sure he'd be happy to oblige," Jessica said with an ornery grin.

"Uh! Why Andy?"

"Why Andy? Because that man is still in love with you."

Good grief. Mom had been harping on the same issue ever since Allie came to town. Did everybody know? "I have no idea why he would be. We have nothing in common. I don't understand how we stayed together as long as we did." Allie let go of the small girl and stood.

"Duh?" Jessica made the expression to match the sentiment. "Because he was hot. And popular."

"Football players always are, but he was such a goody-good." No, she would never go back to Andy.

"Aw, show the poor guy some mercy."

Allie rolled her eyes. "You know, Jess, when I came back home I made myself two promises. One, I would not go back to that church." She shivered at the thought. "I can never get over the feeling that everyone is watching me and judging me."

Jessica nodded her head to the side, indicating the decision was reasonable enough.

"And two, I would not go back to Andy Vargas, a.k.a. the worst offender of all." Allie took a deep breath. "Now, can we talk about something else please? Looks like you've been busy."

"And you. So what are the big plans? Do tell." Jessica scooped Taylor naturally into her arms.

"Well, first the joint degree in business and dance. Then maybe open my own branch of the studio down by the beachfront." Allie shrugged her shoulders, hoping Jessica would like the idea.

"Oh, Allie, that would be awesome. I love this place, but the drive during traffic is a nightmare."

"Tell me about it." Allie shook her head. "I can hardly believe how much time has passed. It sort of flew by for me with all the traveling." How could Jessica be a mother already?

Jessica glanced at Taylor and back to Allie. "But it was worth it, I'm sure. You were living the dream."

Paris, Rome, Moscow, Beijing. Did any of them compare to the priceless treasure cuddling against her friend? "Yeah." Allie shook off a wave of emptiness. "I wouldn't have traded it for anything. I mean, that's what I always wanted, right? To dance full time."

"So why'd you stop?"

"I'm not sure." Allie rubbed her arms. "It was time to move on, I guess."

They chatted a few more minutes, but neither suggested a get-together. Too many years had passed. They were at different stages in life. Allie waved to students and staff as she headed toward the used red and black Mini-Cooper her parents had insisted on buying her.

For once she was happy to give in to their demands. She loved the car. Adorable and economical. But she longed to be financially independent and far from their grasp. Sharing a bungalow in Norfolk with a bunch of teeny-boppers from their church hardly qualified as "finding her own place near campus," but she was in no position to complain.

Her phone bleeped its text message alert. She ignored it and slid into the front seat, throwing her dance bag in back and cranking up her new *Flyleaf* CD. The pulsing rhythm seeped into her soul.

Most likely the text was from Andy. He hadn't let up since he arrived back in town from his summer mission trip to Africa. How'd he get her number anyway? She and Andy had their share of fun, she supposed, but as time passed, their personality differences became all too apparent.

Allie discovered alternative music about the same time Andy applied to seminary and started waking up at six a.m. for an hour of prayer and Bible study. He grew more and more judgmental of Allie's lifestyle until she couldn't take it anymore. When he informed her that a future pastor's wife should not be strutting around in a leotard...that had been the final blow. How could she ever have loved a guy like Andy?

A guy now serving as youth pastor at the church she detested?

She needed to put Andy out of her mind. Allie zipped through the streets of Chesapeake, letting the wind from the open car window whip through the loose strands of her hair. Breathing deep the fresh breeze. Enjoying the handling of her compact car. Being in control of her destiny. So much open pavement before her. So many choices.

Andy would never get it.

While Allie wanted nothing to do with him, the fact did not mitigate her loneliness. She missed the friends from her dance company and felt disconnected from old acquaintances in Virginia Beach. If Mr. Right didn't show up soon, she may end up dating Andy out of desperation.

Allie Vargas, the pastor's wife. Pastor's wife of The First Church of the Goody-Two-Shoes.

Like that was going to happen.

Why not strangle her now and be done with it?

She shot a dirty look toward her cell phone in the backseat. The guy needed to give up. Heaven help her if that phone rang one more time, Allie just might hunt him down and wrap it around his neck.

FIVE

Rain arrived to their scheduled meeting, late as usual, on Friday evening after dark. She dodged through book carousels and found the coffee shop in the back of the store. Despite her tardiness, the other girls welcomed her.

"Here she is." Allie stood to offer a hug.

Layla gripped Rain's elbows and kissed her cheek, switching from side to side three times.

Rain followed her lead. Must be a Middle Eastern thing.

"Go ahead and get something to drink." Layla sat back down. "We're just chatting."

"Don't talk about anything good without me." Rain walked to the register and perused the menu. As she assumed, all she could afford was a plain cup of coffee or tea. She decided on spicy chai and doctored it with cream and raw sugar, turning it into something akin to a latte. She took a sip. Better than expected. Tea and good company. Two things to be thankful for. Rain returned to the table and sank into a tattered chair.

Layla wasted no time. She had already devoured her panini while Rain stood at the counter. Putting down her coffee and pulling out her laptop, Layla began. "Okay, so this week's assignment says, 'Discuss one way in which you are a typical representation of your culture, and one way in which you are not. Each member will write their own separate essay on this subject to form a unified collection.' Who wants to go first?"

"Hmm." Allie held tight to a cup that smelled of mocha cappuccino with both hands. "That's a good question. Most Christians are into rules, but the Bible talks about freedom in Christ. I think what matters is who we are on the inside. Having a true relationship with God. Being kind and loving and compassionate. Helping others..."

"Can I stop you, Allie?" Layla said. "I'm confused. I thought most Americans were Christians, and I hope you will forgive me for saying so, but that doesn't sound like most Americans."

Rain couldn't agree more. She had researched religion extensively for her book. "Studies say over fifty percent. Most are only Christian in name, though. The word is supposed to mean *follower of Christ*. Usually they seem nothing like him, but Allie does."

Surprising moisture sparkled in Allie's eyes. Had Rain said something wrong? Surely her comments were objective enough.

"Thank you, Rain. That's one of the nicest things anyone's ever said to me."

Rain swallowed. Maybe Allie wasn't accustomed to being considered a shining example of Christianity. "Well, that little speech you gave reminds me of Jesus's Sermon on the Mount. I've studied the life of Christ along with Buddha, Mohammed, a few others. He was an incredible humanitarian."

"Me too." Layla looked up from typing notes into her laptop. "Most people assume Muslims know nothing about Jesus, but he was a great prophet."

"Huh." Allie took a moment to compose herself, pressing a finger to each of her eyes. "What I'm trying to say is that I interpret things differently than a lot of Christians. I don't really feel comfortable in church settings... And while a part of me knows better, sometimes I worry that Jesus might not be enough to solve all my problems." She paused and frowned. "No, that's not right. I think he *can*. What I doubt is my ability to hear his voice and let him do it." Shaking her head she said, "So, I guess we can add not being skilled at spreading the good news of the gospel to the list."

Odd. Allie was laying all her cards right on the table. What was up with that?

Something unreadable flashed through Layla's eyes. "But your honesty's refreshing. I have doubts and struggles too."

She typed down Allie's responses.

"Good. My faith is important to me." Allie took a few moments to explain her years spent touring with the Christian dance company and her plans to open a studio someday. Rain hadn't realized Christians were even allowed to dance. Who knew? She recalled some "born-again" friends from her teen years skipping the prom.

Rain was impressed despite herself. "See. That's cool. I love artsy, creative stuff. What about you, Layla?"

"I hope to be an engineer like my father." A sad wistfulness filled Layla's voice.

Since they had strayed off topic, Rain didn't push her. "I'll give a try to the question. It's hard since I'm not so easily defined, but like we've discussed, I will eat meat. That wouldn't go over well in the hippie commune where I spent my preschool years."

"For the purpose of this paper, let's define you as a hippie," Layla said. "What else is different?"

"Well, the older I get, the more I value structure and organization. But I'm not very good at them yet." Rain tapped Layla's hand. "Maybe you could give me some pointers."

"I'd be happy to."

"So, in what ways are you like them?" Allie asked. "Clearly in the way you dress."

Rain looked down at her gypsy skirt and laughed. "Yeah, and I love nature, keeping things simple, you know. Healthy food, healthy lifestyle."

"Does your home look like a place a hippie would live?" Layla focused on her screen.

"Right now all we have is some Salvation Army furniture, and the place is a mess, but I want it to look like a real house. Nothing groovy. No lava lamps or love beads. Just warm and cozy." If only James would cooperate.

"Who's we?" Allie took another sip of her chocolate scented drink.

"Me and James. The boyfriend with the dreadlocks."

Layla stopped clicking the keys. Her eyes registered shock,

but she didn't say a word.

"It's okay, Layla." Rain blew on her tea, not at all offended. "I know it's different than what you're used to."

"Do you...love him?" Layla ducked her head and glanced down in her own special shy and modest manner.

Rain took a turn at sounding inexplicably wistful. "Yeah. I do. We've been together since high school." Things got quiet after that.

"Okay, me." Layla piped up, but then stopped short. "Well... do you know much about Islam?"

"Some," Rain said. Mostly the terrorist stuff she saw on the news, but she wanted to learn more.

"I picked up a little in Europe, but not much," Allie admitted.

"There are many types of Muslims. Sunni, Shiite, and Sufi are the main groups. My family is Sunni, and we're fairly moderate, meaning we believe in the *Qur'an* as a holy book, but we also try to understand it from a contemporary perspective. We follow the five basic pillars of Islam: profession of faith, fasting, prayer, pilgrimage, and alms-giving. I guess the main way I'm different than other Muslims is..." She stopped again. This time she did not seem inclined to continue.

"It's okay," Allie said. "We don't have to put it in our paper."

"This is a safe place to share our truths." At least she hoped so. Rain eyed Allie warily.

"It's just that...Muslims aren't supposed to question the *Qur'an*. Ever. It's not that I don't believe. But I think if something is true, we shouldn't be afraid to challenge it. What are we trying to protect?"

"Wow," Rain said. "That's heavy. Americans question everything. Did you grow up in the states?"

"Yes, other than the summers, I grew up here. We kind of stayed in our own little community, though."

"What types of things would you question?" Allie prompted.

Layla paused and thought a moment. "For example, in much of the Middle East it's so easy for a man to divorce his wife, and she loses everything." She snapped her fingers. "Like that. Even her kids if he's inclined to keep them."

47

"No wonder so many of them put up with abuse. I had no idea." Rain stared at Layla, stunned that such injustice still existed in the world. Could the Middle Eastern mindset be any further from the higher consciousness she longed to attain?

"Exactly, and then there's the issue of multiple wives. Not only does the *Qur'an* permit it, it gives detailed instructions. Of course modern educated Muslims only marry one wife, but still, things like that bother me."

"Totally twisted." Rain shook her head. "Unless it lets women have multiple husbands. That might be fun. One to make the money. One to raise the children. One really hot guy for the..."

"Whoa, whoa." Allie cut her off. "One guy is more than enough trouble for anyone. You're right, though. It seems unfair."

Layla took her coffee in her hands and stared at it a moment. "And I don't want to blame Islam, but I don't feel women get equal treatment in our culture. Many Middle Eastern women still find their identity through men. We call my aunt *Um-Wassim*. That means mother of Wassim, her oldest son. And the old timers view women as sinful."

"That's so wrong," Rain shouted. Then she caught herself, embarrassed. James would not approve. "I mean, not that I'm judging or anything." According to James, right and wrong did not exist. They were merely social constructs. Although faced with such bigotry, she found the concept hard to swallow.

"It's okay," Layla said. "Even with the veil, it's rarely the woman who decides how conservative she will be. That's up to her husband or father, unless of course she wants to be more modest than they demand. That's how it is in my family. My mother is actually more religious than my father, and she makes sure we all keep in line."

No one cared how Rain dressed. Modesty existed as a foreign concept. She would never mention to these girls the family vacation at the nudist colony. The place gave Rain the creeps.

"Do you mind wearing the veil?" Allie said.

"This silly little thing?" Layla patted the yellow silk that fell over a matching embroidered tunic and jeans. "It hardly counts.

I'm honored to wear it."

"It looks pretty on you," Rain said. "All of the Muslim girls at ODU dress cute. I would have expected some to wear those long black thingamabobs." Mobile prison was the name that came to Rain's mind.

Layla laughed. "It's called a *niqab*. But the girls who wear those sorts of veils would never be allowed to attend a co-ed university. Probably wouldn't be permitted to pursue a higher education at all. Of course, that's more cultural than religious anyway. The *Qur'an* only mentions modesty in a general sort of way, and the *Hadiths*, our traditions, refer to a simple veil like I wear. Much of the Middle Eastern worldview predates Islam. They're stuck in a time warp. I'm so thankful my family isn't like that."

"Doesn't it bother you that the women need to identify themselves and not the men?" Rain eyed Layla warily now. How could she be thankful for such scraps of freedom?

"Not much. It's more about modesty than labeling. And Allie wears clothing that identifies her faith."

Today's T-shirt was gray with an eagle in shades of pink, blue, and violet. *They that wait upon the Lord shall mount up with wings*, it said. Layla's eyes remained glued to the words for a long time. Rain wondered what went through her mind when she read them.

"Don't you get hot in the summer with your pants and long sleeves?" Allie asked.

"It's a small price to pay to honor God." Layla's voice held a quiet conviction.

Rain wished she had convictions like that.

"Sounds like you and I have a lot in common." Allie leaned in toward Layla. "We both believe what we've been taught, but we're free thinkers too."

"Yes, I noticed that." Layla added the correlation to her word document.

"I think it's great," Rain said. "If you don't think for yourself, then you're just going through the motions."

"I get tired of going through the motions," Layla said.

"I know what you mean." Allie tucked a loose strand of hair into her bun.

"I wish I had some motions to go through other than this." Rain crossed her legs on the bench, pinched her fingers together, and chanted, "Ohm."

Several patrons swiveled to watch her, but Rain didn't mind.

Layla and Allie laughed. Then everyone sat still for a moment, digesting the enormity of Rain's statement.

"This is so weird," Allie said.

"I haven't talked to anyone like this in years." Not even James. These girls didn't brush off her questions with glib, pseudo-intellectual drivel. "Must be this crazy assignment."

"I haven't talked to anyone like this in...ever." Layla snapped shut her laptop and picked up her coffee.

Poor thing. It must be hard to live as a foreigner in her own land. The Middle Eastern culture seemed so oppressive, especially for women. And so violent.

She may not have a religion, per se, but she did believe in freedom and truth and self-expression. And she believed in some sort of benevolent divine being. She hoped Layla would continue to open up. Maybe she and Allie could help her somehow. A small way to continue her pursuit of social justice. "Hey, what do you ladies think about heading over to the Norfolk Waterside? I saw a festival going on there."

"What kind?" Layla asked.

Allie stood. She shot Rain a significant glance and nodded over Layla's head. "There's always something cool over there. I think this one might be music or jazz. It really doesn't matter. Let's go check it out."

"Sure, why not." Layla picked up her tray.

Rain thought back through the conversation as she headed out the door. Sometimes she wished she had something specific to believe in, or rail against. She was raised to see god in everything, which ended up feeling like a lot of ooey gooey nothing. James was right. These girls were getting to her head.

SIX

A *burqini!* Who would have dreamt it? Layla couldn't keep from staring at the close fitting Islamic bathing garb made of swimsuit fabric, complete with a slim attached veil. The costume named after the Afghani *burqa* resembled a scuba suit, only much looser. Who in the world thought up this revolutionary concept? She intended to jump online and order one the moment she got home.

In hot pink!

Layla reclined in a beach chair, hardly believing it was already the second week of school. She couldn't wait to munch on the grilled beef kabobs, chips, and sodas that filled the coolers. After a month of fasting, she would relish the food. The warm water rolled with waves, the sun shone golden, the breeze whispered and tasted of salt. What more could she ask for?

And an attractive, dark-haired guy gazed at her from the volleyball court. She didn't think he belonged to the MSU. Still, Layla felt she knew him from somewhere.

The Muslim boys wore their typical shorts and T-shirts. The girls varied in their dress, a few even sporting modest swimsuits with cover-ups. She really didn't mind her drenched capris pants and cotton oxford too much. *But the burqini!* Layla couldn't get over it.

The new guy glanced at her again. His toned body in his all-American Quicksilver board shorts and wife beater undershirt stood out from the other males.

A Muslim in a wife beater. *How ironic.*

Stop it. Layla chided herself. No more Brother Rasheed for her. She asked quite enough *Daring Questions* lately.

Besides, she wasn't even sure the cute guy was a Muslim. Hopefully he shared her faith, because unless she was mistaken, those glances and smiles indicated he was flat out flirting with her now. Layla guessed him to be a few years older than most of the students.

A good age for her. Hmm.

He bounced the volleyball from knee to knee and then to foot as if playing soccer, clearly showing off. He smiled right at her. Gathering her courage, she winked and waved back as the American girls did. She thought he would like that. He fumbled the ball and two appealing spots of pink formed on his cheeks as he ran to retrieve it. It rolled right up to Layla's bright coral toenails. That niggling sense of familiarity struck her again.

He scooped up the ball. "Hi, I'm Mo."

Mo for Mohammed? Did she detect a trace of Lebanese accent? Promising. "I'm Layla. Be careful with that thing." She shot a look at the ball, still trying her new Westernized flirtation.

He mopped the sweat off his face with his shirt, revealing a fine set of six-pack abs. "Yeah, I'll do that."

Layla squinted against the sun and shaded her eyes for a better look at his face. And quite a face it was. As he pushed his rumpled brown curls from his sun-tanned forehead, she muted a sigh. The scruff of a beard graced the underside of his strong cheekbones. He maintained a boyish air despite his maturity.

Why did he seem so familiar? "Do I know you?"

Mo scrutinized the woman's lovely features. He longed to reach out and stroke the sand away from her slim nose but clutched the ball in his hands instead. "I was thinking the same thing."

"Where are you from?" Layla brushed her toes back and forth across the beach in an innocent yet sensual way. This girl had no idea what she was doing to him

"Lebanon originally. I lived in Detroit for a few years. My

family's in Ohio now," Mo said.

"No kidding? I'm Lebanese, and I grew up in Detroit. We must have crossed paths." Layla shifted as if to examine him from another angle.

She just got better and better. "Layla. Hmm." He bounced the ball off his head, attempting to jog his memory. "What's your last name?"

"Al-Rai."

"Layla Al-Rai. Layla Al-Rai." Layla. Could it be? The girl who haunted his dreams all these years?

He swallowed and struggled to maintain a light tone. "Hey, I think we were in kindergarten together. Do you remember a Mohammed Hamoudi? That's me."

"Yes...kind of...not quite." Layla giggled. "But I do remember your face."

He tossed the ball back and forth from hand to hand, debating his next move.

"Hey, Mo. We ain't got all day," hollered one of the guys from the court.

"Sorry." He threw the ball to them and squatted down beside Layla. A question popped into his head. Dare he ask? What did he have to lose? He could hardly leave her moments after finding her again. "So, do you want to take a walk or something?"

"Sure."

Mo offered her a hand and pulled her up, but let go quickly under the watchful eyes of so many Islamic students.

As they jogged over the hot sand to the shoreline, he thought of the castle along the beach near Sidon. Even Muslim teens weren't above hiding among its corners and passageways to sneak a few kisses. But he'd remain on his best behavior today.

They turned to head down the moist strand. Layla splashed water at him playfully with her foot. "It's warm."

He splashed her back. "Almost as nice as the Mediterranean, don't you think?"

"Mmm." She closed her eyes for a moment, as if recalling the gentle blue sea. "Nothing's as beautiful as the Mediterranean."

Except for Layla.

The prettiest girl in the class. They used to push each other on the swing set in the playground. He wanted to kiss her once, but of course he never did. His family moved away shortly after.

"Sounds like you miss it," he said.

"I do. It's strange. I love Lebanon. But it makes me sad too. You stand on a main street in Beirut lined by the shrines to suicide bombers and the rubble of decimated buildings. Then you look to the left and see majestic tree-covered cliffs sweeping the sky, to the right and find the expansive sea. It's crazy. So much ugliness and so much beauty side by side like that."

Wow, the girl had a brain too. He might have guessed as much from the mysterious depths of her eyes. "I know exactly what you mean. Quite a conundrum, our country is. Too many ideologies clashing on that small piece of earth."

His fingers itched to reach for hers, but he ignored them. Instead, he smiled to her. Layla's answering grin lit the sky before she swung her head away to gaze at the surf.

"Do you read Gibran?" she asked.

"Our most famous poet? Of course. 'Your Lebanon is a political knot, a national dilemma, a place of conflict and deception. My Lebanon, is a place of beauty and dreams of enchanting valleys and splendid mountains.'"

She picked up the poem. "'Your Lebanon is empty and fleeting, whereas my Lebanon will endure forever.' I took a whole class on him at the university in Beirut."

He nodded. "Nice. I'm jealous."

Layla.

Beside him floated the girl of his dreams in a cloud of mist, beaming from beneath her sandy white veil—but everything was different now. Should he tell her? Why had he invited her to walk with him anyway? He should have thought the decision through. Surely she assumed nothing had changed. Only his closest friends knew the truth. Discretion was of the utmost importance.

She giggled up at him and splashed him again with her foot. He had a feeling he could trust her, but still, his secret would ruin this relaxed camaraderie. Would the remainder of his life be like this? Fraught with challenges and confusion? Could he just erase his natural desires after twenty-two years? This was uncharted territory. He had so much to learn.

It was worth it, though. Incredibly, wonderfully worth it. He had discovered his mission, his purpose, his calling in life. He could never turn back. Somehow he'd figure it out.

He took in a deep breath of damp sea air and pressed his rebel hand into his pocket before he scared away this precious creature.

Mo. It didn't seem possible. After thirty minutes, Layla still strolled the beach beside him, her feet squishing deep into the moist sand as the sun hid behind a row of Cape-Cod style houses. He didn't seem to mind the silence, both of them lost in their own thoughts while pink and purple tinged the sky.

The sky brought to mind her whispered petition as she stood on the patio, watching the shadow of a bird rising to the heavens. And the petition brought to mind the T-shirt Allie wore on Friday. The colors of Allie's top matched the horizon behind the bird that night to perfection.

Oh, to soar.

Waves lapped over her toes like a caress, calling her back to earth and the handsome young man beside her. What was she doing with this guy? She had no time for men. But Mo...the memories had trickled back as they talked. The way he pushed her on the swings. The time he helped her to the nurse's office when she scraped her knee. Might a gentle and kind man like Mo allow her to soar?

"Mo, do you remember that day on the playground?"

"The buttercups?" He grinned.

The day he said he loved her.

"I can't believe I nearly forgot." Layla wiped some windblown strands escaped from her veil.

What would her father think if he knew she was walking

alone with Mo on the beach? Maybe Father wouldn't mind so much, but Uncle would be furious.

She stretched her fingers and found Mo's pressed to his pant leg. Something flashed between them. Something electric and unfamiliar. His strong hand wrapped around hers. Mo's eyes held no censure, only surprise and tenderness. He tugged on her and drew her further into the crashing, salt-scented waves until they tumbled about her knees, pulling her to and fro.

What on earth was she doing, holding hands with a boy, and so soon after Ramadan, the holiest month of all? All that hard work. Had she undone it in an instant? She attempted to drown out her mother's voice in her head telling her that Allah must be judging her right now. She wouldn't believe it. This was Mo, and she had found him. Her heart sent a very different message. It said there was something oddly sacred about this moment—in a way that transcended religion.

Mo gazed deep into her eyes, his own brown ones glinting with fire from the setting sun. He enclosed her other hand as well. "I can't believe I found you after all these years."

"Me either." Like a dream. Surely it was too good to be true.

SEVEN

James wandered through the front door to the sight of Rain typing frantically into the stone-aged computer. "What you working on, babe?"

"Shh, not now." Rain returned to her manic writing.

This was a mood he understood. Not wanting to disturb her, James tried to be invisible as he prepared a ham sandwich with mayo and sat down at the kitchen table. Rain's writing talent amazed him, but she needed her full concentration when working on a new idea.

After about ten minutes she spoke. "Okay, I can talk."

"The prolific artist hard at work. It does my soul good." His eyes caressed their way down her body, from her light, curling afro to the leather moccasins encasing her feet.

"Actually, I need to ask you a question. I was working on a scene about that night of the drive-by when you bowed out of the experiment and called your dad for money. What was going through your head? I never understood. You were so determined to live like the homeless. I would have been okay. We would have managed. What pushed you over the edge?"

James stared out the window and pinched his tear ducts with thumb and forefinger. That had been one of the scariest nights of his life. Rain didn't remember all of it. Couldn't remember all of it. He dashed through the murky garbage-ridden streets holding her lifeless form in his arms. The nearest hospital lay only two blocks away, but they refused to admit her without insurance. Thank goodness they had the compassion to stick her in an ambulance and rush her to the county facility across town.

He sat beside Rain in the haze of flashing lights, holding her pale hand, weeping and praying to a deity he didn't believe in.

When he learned she needed an operation the county hospital couldn't supply, he tossed the experiment to the wind in a heartbeat. Without proper medical treatment she might have suffered life-threatening complications. None of his memories or animosity mattered in that moment. He called his father and begged him without regret to transfer the funds.

Rain was all that mattered. Rain was all that ever mattered.

He should have never risked her life in the first place, but she bought into his speeches and persuasion. Unable to overcome that driving need to fill his life with purpose, James crusaded for the little man, for the down-and-outers. He stood on his bandwagon and shouted to all who would listen, but he barely believed it himself.

How could he ever tell Rain the truth? He was scared that night. He loved her. He couldn't live without her. She might lose all respect, and what would happen then? Their relationship held a certain edge of hero worship he craved.

James shook his head. He stood at the window with his back to Rain. "It was a rational decision. A good decision. I weighed the costs and the odds and decided that a human life was more important than an experiment. Besides, it proved our point. Not being able to survive without private insurance. The need for better public health care. Stuff like that."

"You hate asking your dad for anything."

"I made an exception. Remember that old Christian proverb, 'The wealth of the wicked is laid up for the just.'"

"I guess that's fair." Rain turned back to her computer to type in some missing details. Her fingers clicked rapidly against the keys.

At least he wasn't quoting Taoists today. Counted the cost. Hmm. Rain counted, and things still didn't add up. Something was missing. Something he didn't want to tell her.

James hated his father. Rain never quite understood that. The few times she met him, he seemed cool enough. More than cool. Not many people could boast a Rastafarian singing sensation for a dad. James should eat it up. He loved attention as much as he loved Bob Marley.

And yet, he hated his dad and every last lyric of his bouncy tunes. The only thing he hated more was weed: another part of the equation that didn't factor. Even in high school, James avoided the common recreational drug like the plague, although it fit his lifestyle and personality. He made Rain swear off it long before they got serious.

Yes, her boyfriend was quite a paradox. A puzzle, wrapped in an enigma, shrouded in mystery. That was her man. No wonder she adored him. "Well," she said over her shoulder. "Whatever the reason, thank you. You take such good care of me."

James blew a kiss. "You're my baby."

She winced at the computer screen. Baby. Why did he choose that word? Did he suspect? She could no longer ignore the signs. Her period was weeks overdue and her body displayed subtle indications of change. Had he noticed? Maybe she should buy that pregnancy test. But the sooner she did, the sooner she'd have to decide whether to tell him the truth or keep it a secret. Better not to know. They had just started this new life together. She wasn't ready to lose him.

EIGHT

Allie surveyed her newly assigned dance composition group as they wrapped up their discussion. They sat cross-legged on the wooden floor of the university's sweat-scented dance studio during the second week of classes. Jenna, the classic ballerina. Jaron, tall and strong with his handsome mahogany skin. Shondra, sassy and stylish. Allie double-checked her notes. What was it with college and group projects? At least her suggestion of worship as a theme had drawn other believers to the group.

"Okay, so that's it." Shondra, a junior, seemed at ease in her role as leader. "Jenna, you have the classical piece to Handel's *Messiah*, Jaron, you have the Negro spiritual, and Allie will take the contemporary portion. I'll direct and work on the unifying theme and the costumes."

"You know." Jaron shoved his notebook into his backpack. "If this turns out well, we could travel the dance around to our churches. I know mine would love it."

"Mine too." Shondra jotted down the suggestion.

"That's a wonderful idea." Jenna turned to Allie, waiting for her to chime in.

Great. She really didn't want to go into all this right now. How could she explain to them that she didn't belong to a church and had no real desire to change the situation anytime soon? "I don't know. I'll check."

"Good start, everyone," Shondra said.

Allie's team dispersed. Already she brimmed with plans for the piece. She knew right away which song she would use.

"I Fade Again" by her favorite alternative metal band was far from a predictable worship song, but the intense lyrics stunned her with their depth. The song would be perfect for mixing contemporary dance with echoed hints of African and ballet, creating a unified theme for the piece.

She hummed the song. Poetic lines floated through her head as she walked out the double doors of the building and into the bright sunshine.

Fading, I fade again.
Into that place where I'm lost in your eyes.
Angels sing in tune with my cries
My lips tingle, longing to press
into the palms of your nail pierced flesh.
Colors swirl in rainbows of flame
Igniting my heart with the touch of your name.

Segments of the choreography formed in Allie's mind. She pictured the passionate jumps, earthy stomps, organic spins, ethereal hand movements. Unable to resist, Allie tapped out a few steps and spun in a circle, even as she made her way across the grassy quad, not caring who might be watching. The kingdom of God welled inside of her, pressing to burst forth.

Let them enjoy the show.

This dance would minister to Allie's own spirit as much as to anyone else's. She hoped Rain and Layla would attend the performance. Allie longed to expose them to this side of Christianity.

In you I live, I move, I am
I dive in your presence
I dream of your plan
I swim through your grace
I long for the day
Set free from time
Set free from space
We'll stand face to face lost in love

Yes, that was exactly what Rain and Layla needed to hear. Exactly what Allie needed to experience again. She never imagined becoming such close friends with unbelievers. Normally, she didn't have enough in common to maintain true relationships, but something was different with these women. They shared something significant.

A little tingle washed over Allie.

She grew aware of her surroundings once again. Summer thrived in southern Virginia. Flowers blossomed next to the redbrick dining hall. A few loose tendrils, fallen from her bun, danced in the breeze like golden ribbons. Sun kissed her face as she turned it toward the sky and twirled once again in a circle.

In you I live, I move, I am.

Reaching the fountain at the center of the university complex, she pulled out her iPod to listen to the song and ponder her ideas. Yes, if she sat still for a moment to look and listen, she could indeed sense God around her, dive into his presence. Now, to bring that wonder and awe to the stage.

How different this performance would be than her last months touring with *Alight*. What was it about the new director's brown mustache and hulking figure that gave her the creeps? Was it merely the three-piece suits he wore, reminding her so much of her constricting childhood church? Resurrecting that awful snake image that so often accompanied her memories of that place?

None of it made sense. She could only keep hoping God had some reason for moving her home, and that she hadn't made a terrible, irrational mistake. One thing she knew for sure, she couldn't let her family, that restrictive church, or the likes of Andy Vargas snuff out the life of God inside of her. She needed him too desperately to take that risk.

In you I live, I move, I am!

Later that evening, Allie stood humming the song in her mind as Sarah held up a beige cardigan. "What do you think of this one?"

Allie had managed to drag her eighteen-year-old sister away from the department store with its elevator music and into a junior shop. She surveyed rack after rack of stylish tops and jeans in all the colors of the crayon box. Still, the girl managed to spot the one boring item in the entire establishment. Mom trained her well.

"I think you're missing the point, Sarah. I wanted to buy you something different. Something exciting." Allie picked up a similar sweater in a soft shade of melon. "This would look pretty with your skin tone."

"Ouch. Are you kidding me?" Sarah squinted. "That thing hurts my eyes."

Allie thrust the hanger back onto the metal pole with a clack. "Now you're being silly."

Sarah crossed her arms over her well camouflaged chest. "It's just not me, Allie."

Of course not. Allie surveyed Sarah's navy jumper and white oxford. Who on earth wore a jumper to the mall? "Come on. We haven't tried my favorite store."

They traveled side by side through the open hallway. Maybe this mall trip wasn't such a good idea after all. But Allie finished work early on Thursdays, and she needed to escape the ruckus of her teeny-bopper roommates. She had been meaning to spend more time with Sarah. Teach her that life was about more than rules and restrictions. It seemed she was too late. Sarah had already mutated into a clone of her mother.

"Here it is." Allie turned to enter.

Sarah stomped her foot and stood firm. "No way. I'm not going in there."

"What's wrong?" Allie tried to see the store through Sarah's eyes. Black walls. A blaring blue neon sign. Heavy metal music.

"I hate this place. I swear it's straight from the pit of hell."

Allie took Sarah's arm and pulled her inside. "Sarah, this is the only Christian store in the entire mall. You'll find something you like."

Sarah frowned. She stopped and held up a slim blue T-shirt

sporting a skeleton. "Very Christian."

Allie read the inscription. *It is no longer I that lives, but Christ that lives in me.*

"It's hideous." Sarah shoved the shirt into Allie's hand and turned up her nose.

A salesperson approached from behind Sarah. "Hi, ladies. Have you been in our store before?"

"I have." Allie picked at her own T-shirt. "But maybe you can tell my sister about your mission here." She suppressed a chuckle as the pale young man with ink black hair and a spike collar turned to Sarah.

He smiled and gestured to the store. "We try to offer a safe place for kids to hang out and hear about Jesus. They come for the music and the clothes, but we use it as an opportunity to spread the gospel. What are you looking for today?"

Sarah shifted and took a step back. "Oh, this isn't really my style."

"Maybe I can pray with you then."

"Sure." Allie said. "Sarah was telling me about a big test she has tomorrow. She's pretty worried about it."

"I'm fine, really." Sarah pasted on her fake church smile and waved her hands in front of her. "No prayer required." Her voice rang tight and brittle.

Allie frowned at Sarah. She didn't need to be rude.

The guy let it drop and spoke to Allie. "I have a huge test tomorrow too."

"Where do you go to school?"

"Community college right now. Next year I'll transfer to Old Dominion." He adjusted the piercing over his eyebrow.

Sarah moved behind the guy. She waved to Allie through the giant gauge hole in his ear and made a face.

Okay, that was funny. Allie smiled. "That's where I am. ODU."

"You like it?" He leaned against the rack with the skeleton T-shirts.

"So far."

Sarah stepped to his side, rocking on her heels like an

innocent little school girl.

"Cool." He turned to Sarah, only inches from his face.

She jumped back.

"I think I know what you'd like." He led her to a long, empire waist T-shirt in shades of cream and tan. Next to a butterfly, hovering over a flowering vine, spread a scripture declaring all things created in God and by God.

Sarah reached out and touched the brushed cotton. "Not bad."

The guy held it up to a pair of straight legged blue jeans.

"Fine. I guess I could try it on." Sarah snatched up the clothing, checking the sizes. Apparently the clerk got them right. "Where's the dressing room?"

He nodded to a door covered with graffiti.

Allie gave the salesman a high-five behind Sarah's back as she headed to the rear of the store. Despite the black walls, a lovely spirit permeated the air. Light and airy like cotton candy. Why couldn't church feel more like this? She swayed to a song by one of her favorite bands while Sarah tried on the outfit.

The clerk stood behind the counter now. There was the sort of Christian Allie could hang with. Hmm. She headed that direction. "So what church do you attend?"

"You looking?"

Just then Sarah emerged from the dressing room in her jumper. "Sorry. It's not me. Thanks for trying."

"Reality Church," he answered Allie with a knowing raise of his pierced brow.

Sarah looked back and forth between them, but neither offered an explanation.

At that moment, a rich tenor voice suitable for radio announcements split the silence. "Hey, Josh, here it is. This is the one I told you about."

Allie spun and saw him across the store. Neatly combed golden-brown hair. Athletic shoulders. His face angled toward the T-shirt as he held it up for inspection by the teenaged boy beside him, but she would know that man anywhere.

"Oh, Allie look. There's—"

"Shh!" Allie ducked behind Sarah, her heart racing. That pinching sensation clutched her chest. "Get me out of here, quick."

"It's just Andy and Josh." Sarah tried to turn, but Allie held her steady from behind.

The guy at the counter laughed at her antics. "You know Andy? He's great."

Allie propelled Sarah to the door. She had to get out of this place. "Keep your head down and stay quiet."

"Sarah? Allie?" Andy called.

Too late. Allie couldn't seem to find enough air. "Keep going. Keep going." She continued pushing Sarah forward and hid further behind her slight figure.

"But Allie?" Sarah shuffled her feet.

"Where are you—" Andy sounded pleasant but perplexed.

Run, Allie. Just run! The old refrain ran through her head. The same one that had driven her from home eight years ago.

"Run!" Allie took Sarah's hand. They dodged through the remaining racks and into the bright hallway. Not stopping to look back, Allie dragged her mystified sister until they rounded a corner. Allie leaned against the wall and closed her eyes.

"What in the world is wrong with you?" Annoyance filled Sarah's voice in an impressive imitation of Mom. "Where are your manners? That was ridiculous."

"I'm...I'm not ready to see him yet."

Sarah removed her hands from her hips and took a hard look at Allie. "Oh, I forgot. The ill-fated engagement. Goodness, Allie. It's been so long. What happened? Andy's like the sweetest guy in the world. You two would make a perfect couple."

Allie took deep, soothing breaths.

"Are you all right?"

"I will be." Allie ran her hands over her face. "Just give me a minute. He caught me off guard."

Here she was running from him again.

She couldn't explain it to Sarah. She barely understood it herself.

NINE

Layla knelt on her rug among the women to the rear of the large open room of the mosque. The place had been designed with the look and feel of the Middle East. Tan stone walls. Curved windows. She attempted to pay attention as the imam droned on, but her feet were falling asleep beneath her rear. Her own sheik in Detroit was never so long-winded. And this man's conservative rhetoric grated on her nerves. There had to be a better mosque in town somewhere. She'd ask the girls at the MSU.

Auntie, kneeling at her right, nudged Layla with her hip and batted her eyelashes toward a rotund young man ahead of them, beyond the short partition separating males and females. As he turned his head to the side, Layla noted a kind, if not terribly attractive, face and crew cut brown hair.

She mouthed the words, "Are you kidding?"

"Bahiya's boy," she mouthed back.

Well that made sense then. He must be the son of Auntie's best friend. The women had already conspired to get them together. What was he? A doctor? A lawyer? Something impressive. His family was from Lebanon, but he had grown up in the States. Not terrible. Still, Layla was not the least bit interested.

"Not my type," she whispered.

Auntie scowled and held a finger to her lip.

How could she ever consider a guy like that after spending all last night on the phone with Mo? They had so much in common. Heritage. Goals. Interests. They had talked and laughed until late in the night. Yet another little secret she was keeping from her aunt and uncle. But it was far too precious to share. It's not as if she would ever lie to them outright.

Soon enough Mo would speak with them, but she wanted more time to treasure him to herself first. Her mind wandered far from the mosque and into the future. A future with Mo. With children even. Mo agreed that a woman should be able to have both a family and a career. And he was studying engineering too! Suddenly, she realized that she wanted a family. Mo's family. She could hardly believe her good fortune. She had never before allowed herself to dream of such a progressive husband.

Such a perfect match.

Auntie elbowed her. "He's coming to dinner."

"No!"

"Too late," Auntie mouthed and turned back towards the imam with a smug smile.

She didn't know whether to laugh or pinch the determined older lady. Layla would get through the dinner with Bahiya's roly-poly son somehow, but she'd never fall for the guy. Never consider a match with him. Mo had gotten into her head, and already she doubted any man could ever take his place.

Rain stepped onto the sagging porch of Allie's rental house. Cheerful shrieks came through the rickety front door. Before she could raise her hand to knock, it flung open and a giggling redhead bopped from foot to foot. "You must be Rain. I'm Brittney." She grabbed her by the elbow and pulled her in the door, sucking Rain forward into the scene straight out of a junior high slumber party.

Teenaged girls draped about the living room, faces covered with green goopy masks. One lay spread eagle in the middle of the floor with cucumbers over her eyes in a dramatic state of relaxation with a giant bowl of popcorn dumped on the carpet beside her. A noisy chick flick played in the background, and shrill voices battled for supremacy.

"You do too."

"Call him right now. Here's my cell." A girl with a trendy blond razor cut waved a bright purple phone in the air.

"I do not."

"Rachel is in loooove! Call him."

A brunette, evidently name Rachel, dove for the phone. "Give me that thing."

"You know you love him."

"Do not."

"Do too."

At the same time two other girls on the couch painted their toenails and debated the fate of skinny jeans. "I mean, they've been in for like five years already."

"I know, right. I can't even imagine wearing straight legs again. What were we thinking?"

"Or flares. Oh, I hate flares."

"Me too."

They squealed over their equal disdain for flared pants.

"Flares are so five years ago."

"Tell me about it."

"There should be, like, a law against them."

"We should hold a protest."

How old were these girls? Eighteen, maybe nineteen? Rain spent her eighteenth year of life crusading for the environment and social reform.

"Hey, everyone," Brittney shouted over the din. "This is Allie's friend Rain."

"Hi, Rain." They all hollered and dissolved back into giggles and chaos.

While Rain thrived on people and excitement, her head spun after less than a minute in the place. She tried to imagine her bookish ballerina in this house. Allie must hate it.

"Do all of you live here?" Rain asked the redheaded girl, who kicked aside an empty soda can and led the way to the bedrooms.

"No, just four of us and Allie. We go to the same church. Not that I've seen Allie there much. Her Mom came up with the idea."

Ah, the plot thickened. Allie must hate something—or someone—even more than this bungalow.

"The rest of the girls live in the dorms, but they crash here a lot."

"Wow." Rain couldn't think of anything else to say, and didn't feel like yelling. She pushed aside dirty clothes with her sandal as they trekked through the hall. She would not be surprised if girls started bouncing from the paneled walls.

Brittney knocked on a door. "What now?" Allie called.

"Your friend's here."

"Send her in."

Rain opened the door and a flood of noise followed her into the room. She slammed it shut and leaned her back against it as a blockade. "Wow. They are something else."

The room looked like Allie. Soft and pastel. Neat but homey. Quite a contrast to the living area Rain just passed through.

"Tell me about it. Did you survive okay? I should have warned you." Allie picked up her purse.

"You've mentioned the teeny-boppers, but I didn't expect this." Rain secured her hands more firmly against the wooden defense.

"Come on, let's get away from this place." Allie pulled out her car keys and jingled them.

Rain shook her head hard from side to side, clenching her eyes together. "No. Don't make me go out there."

"We could try the window. We're on the first floor, but I warn you, there's a rosebush."

"Anything's better than that." Rain walked to the bed and plopped herself down. "Seriously, it's kind of funny."

"Not at one a.m."

"Poor Allie. Hey, but before we head over to Layla's house, I wanted to talk to you about something. Well...about her."

Allie sat on the mattress beside Rain. "Okay."

Rain scooched to lean on the wall. "I'm worried about her. Do you think there's anything we can do to help?"

Allie twisted to face her. "Help Layla? In what way?"

"I mean, the veil, the rules. How does she stand it? Do you think there's anything we can do to get her out of all that?"

"Seriously? I can't even get me out of all this." Allie held a hand toward the door. A fresh round of ear-piercing cackles assaulted the room in display. "Did I tell you this was my mother's idea?"

"I heard. Sorry."

"I can't believe I let her talk me into this. And they torture me every Sunday that I skip church. I guess I should just be grateful that my parents are helping me out."

"I imagine you're supposed to be some sort of chaperone."

"If there's a fire, I'll make sure they all giggle their way to the exit. Other than that, those kids are on their own. Of course, to talk to my mother you might wonder who's supposed to be chaperoning whom. I swear she thinks the fact that I don't dress in calf-length skirts and pantyhose translates to partying and sleeping around."

Rain scrunched her face into an expression of comic disbelief. "Has she met you?"

"I know, right?"

Allie might be hip on the outside, but Rain had never met a person more quietly committed to their faith. Except for Layla. Rain steered the conversation back toward her original intent. "It's rough. I get that, but do you really consider this a problem compared to Layla's?"

Allie crawled over the bed and rested on the wall, looking at the ceiling. "No. But I'm not sure what to do about her. It's hard. I mean...if you care about someone and you see them headed in a direction you feel will hurt them, you've got to say something. Right? But Layla can't simply walk away from her religion like most Americans."

Rain crinkled her nose. Maybe Allie wasn't the right one to ask for help. "I didn't mean the religious stuff. I meant the repressive parts of her culture."

"It's all tied together. And it could be dangerous for her to explore other faiths. Even other lifestyles. I want to help, but this is uncharted territory. I don't want to hurt her." Allie clasped her hands in her lap.

"Oh, it's not that bad, is it? Layla seems pretty moderate. I'm sure her family is too." Of course, there had been an honor killing over a Muslim girl sleeping with an American guy in California while Rain was living there. Maybe she shouldn't push too much.

"I don't know," Allie said. "And besides, I don't want to encourage Layla to rebel. That would go against my belief system. She has a heart for God, and I'd hate to diminish that. I'm not sure how to teach her about 'freedom' in Christ without having that translate to being wild according to her mindset. I do want to help, though. I guess we try to be there for her and listen." Allie sat quietly for a moment.

She certainly did have a different take on the Layla situation than Rain expected. Rain had a hard time wrapping her brain around such religious thought processes. What in the world did Allie think of her? Rain wasn't sure she wanted to know.

The girls in the living room turned on blaring music over the chick flick. Allie covered her ears. "And, that's our cue. Let's get out of here."

"I thought you said your parents' church didn't allow rock music." Somehow the giddy teenagers didn't fit the somber impression Rain had gotten of the congregation.

"They have a 'dreamy' new youth pastor who's been loosening things up over the last few years. Thanks a lot, Andy."

"Great timing for you, huh?" Rain jumped off the bed. "Hey." She held up a finger as a suspicion developed. "You aren't going to try to make me get 'saved' or anything, are you?"

Allie stood and laughed. "I don't think anyone could make you do anything, Rain."

"Promise?"

"Pinky swear. I will never *make* you do anything." Allie mimicked the teeny boppers with a high-pitched squeal and wiggled her smallest finger in the air.

Rain linked hers, and they shook on it.

The music cranked up another notch. Allie gave a wry grin. "Right now, I'm incredibly thankful for any friend who's past puberty. I won't do anything to chase you away."

That was a relief. Allie was starting to seem more fanatical than Rain had suspected. "Come on. Layla's waiting for us. I don't want to be late this time." Rain reached for the door knob and winced.

TEN

A half hour later Allie pulled up to a house in the suburbs. McMansions lined the sparkling inlet. "Whew," she said to Rain, glancing down again to check the address on the pink embossed paper. "This is not the Virginia Beach I grew up in."

"Good, I thought I was the only one." Rain stepped out of Allie's used Mini-Cooper, clearly the cheapest car on the block. "Yep, there's Layla's convertible. This must be the place."

Allie took a deep breath and led the way to the mammoth, modern, stone-front home. "What did she say her uncle did for a living?"

"I think he owns a chain of Middle Eastern restaurants or something."

"The food service industry has been good to the Al-Rai family."

Layla opened the door before they reached it. She wore a huge smile, and for once, no veil.

The girls walked through the double doors oohing and aahing over Layla's silky raven-colored hair. "You're so pretty," Rain said. "I mean, you always look pretty, but I like seeing you this way."

"So natural and relaxed." Allie spun around to examine the ornate entryway with its marble floor, spiral staircase, and wrought iron banister.

"Thanks. I don't have to veil at home, and since you're both women, I can go without tonight."

"Are your aunt and uncle here?" Allie ran her fingers across a round table, which sat in the center of the foyer for the sole purpose of holding a huge vase of fresh cut flowers.

"No. They're off playing cards with friends." Layla turned. "Come into the kitchen. My aunt left snacks."

"This is so much better than my place," Allie said.

"Oh, Layla, you would not believe Allie's roommates. I was just waiting for a pillow fight to break out."

Layla gestured to a graceful archway leading to the next room. "Don't they study?"

Allie rolled her eyes. The teeny-boppers? Study? "Not that I've noticed."

She and Rain followed Layla through a giant living room with overstuffed leather furniture and into a gourmet kitchen complete with copper cookware hanging from hooks on the ceiling. Off to one side sat a sunny breakfast nook with wicker furniture featuring flowery cushions and a glass-topped table. The whole place exuded a warm Mediterranean feel.

Across the center island in the kitchen spread trays of stuffed grape leaves, meat pies, pita, dips, and baklava filled with green pistachio nuts.

"Oh my," Allie said. "You've got to be kidding me." Was this Layla's idea of a little snack?

"Is this for us?" Rain's stomach growled loudly enough for everyone to hear. "Sorry. I missed dinner."

"Auntie knew I invited some girlfriends over. She probably assumed you were from the MSU."

Allie rubbed her hands together. "Right about now, I am so glad all I had to eat was a Lean Cuisine." She could get used to this Lebanese lifestyle.

The girls filled up plates and sat down at the table while Layla poured the Turkish—or as she called it, Lebanese—coffee into tiny demitasse cups. Allie gazed over the patio and the inlet beyond. Yachts and sailboats lined the stretch of deep-water access, flowing into the Chesapeake Bay.

"This is so beautiful," Rain said. "You really eat like this every day?"

"It's no big deal." Layla ducked her head. It was odd to see her do so without her veil.

"Is your family in Lebanon wealthy too?" Once they were out, Allie realized her words were a bit rude, but she wanted to understand this girl.

"Oh, about the same. Let's not talk about me." Layla brushed away the subject with a sweep of her hand.

"Please." Rain picked up her meat pie. "This is all so fascinating to us. Have you spent much time in Lebanon?"

"Pretty much every summer, and then most of the last four years," Layla said.

"So that's why you're getting a late start on college. What were you doing there?" Allie popped a lemony stuffed grape leaf in her mouth. "Mm."

"I stayed with my grandparents," Layla said. "They're getting old, and the family decided I would be the best one to keep an eye on them. My younger cousin is there now."

"Wow, so family's a big thing," Rain said.

"No, family's not a big thing. Family is everything." Layla joined her hands in front of her chest.

"Did you have any fun in Lebanon?" Allie asked.

"Of course. The servants help. My parents just wanted me to stay with *Jidu* and *Taeta* to keep them company. I took some classes in Islamic studies and Arabic literature. I enjoyed discovering my roots, but I went to plenty of parties too. I even helped at an after school program for poor Muslim street children. That was my favorite part."

"Wow. You never mentioned it," Rain said. "So we all spent our time off involved in some sort of outreach. That's cool."

"Do they offer many programs like that in Lebanon?" Allie thought Christians had the market on such things. She bit into a savory meat pie and moaned.

"No, not nearly enough. I worked with an American organization. They try to keep kids from getting caught up in terrorism. Give them something safe to do. Keep them busy. I taught craft classes and helped them with their homework. Children who roam the streets are prime targets for radical recruiters. The terrorists can seem so good-hearted, you wouldn't believe it. They really confuse the kids."

The room grew quiet. Allie didn't know how to respond to this unexpected reminder of the violent aspect of gentle Layla's religion.

"Let me grab my laptop," Layla said. "We should get started." This strong Muslim woman never ceased to impress Allie.

Layla sat back down at the table. "So today's topic is, 'How do those in your culture generally believe concerning some of today's tough issues? Do you agree or disagree? Write a contrast essay together as a group on three of the following issues.' Ouch. This is going to hurt. Rain, you want to pick one to start?"

"Sure, how about the war. I think it sucks. 'War...what is it good for?'" Rain sang the familiar words, and the other girls chimed in. "What do the insiders think, Layla?"

"Well, I'm hardly 'inside' Iraq, but Muslims don't like Westerners getting involved in their business. Most take offense to Christians ruling over our own people in our own countries. I do have an appreciation for democracy, but why do Americans feel like they have to swoop in and save the whole world?" Layla turned to study Allie.

Rain did too.

"Hey, why are you both looking at me? Do I have right-winged conservative tattooed across my forehead?" So much for pushing past their stereotypes.

"Pretty much." Rain shrugged.

"Whatever." Allie hated the way people assumed her religion came wrapped up in a neat political package. "I think the war in Iraq is complicated. I do believe the president had good intentions, but he underestimated the issues involved."

"Exactly." Layla's hands shook as she typed. "Americans don't understand our internal politics. They need to let the Middle Easterners police themselves. Or blow each other off the face of the map. I'm not saying it couldn't happen...but it's not America's business. Freedom is exactly that, freedom to make good choices or bad."

"Wow, Layla has some passion boiling under there," Rain said.

"Who knew?" Odd how these assignments had a way of

drawing them together despite their varying views. Allie tested the tan goop Layla called hummus with some bread. Not bad. They discussed the Middle Eastern politics for several minutes.

Allie had never considered Layla's point. Freedom meant the right to make good or bad choices. That accounted for the deterioration of democracy in Afghanistan. Americans could offer a free political system, but they couldn't change minds and hearts.

"Okay, I think we covered that one." Layla pointed at them one by one. "Sucks, complex, go home. I want to hear you two battle it out over homosexuality now." Layla giggled.

"Fine." Allie stood to refill her plate. "But first you need to give the Islamic view."

"On the record, it's a sin, an abomination. Behind the scenes... Now that's a whole different story."

"Juicy," Rain said. "Dish."

Allie returned to the table. "I heard from a missionary once that suicide bombers get seventy-two virgins and little boys as rewards in heaven."

"Oh sick!" Rain said. Layla and Allie both joined her as she added, "Not that I'm judging."

"I guess some Muslims might interpret it that way," Layla said. "Paradise, *Jannah*, is a place where pleasures forbidden on earth are allowed. But I agree with Rain, that's sick. I've always believed the reference implied young male virgins for the martyred women."

"That's better...I guess." Allie wasn't completely convinced. There were still seventy-two of them.

"It can even be translated as seventy-two grapes or raisins. Not that anyone really thinks that way," Layla added.

Oh, man would those suicide bombers be disappointed.

"Seriously," Rain said. "Let Layla off the hook. It's your turn to talk about homosexuality. You know where I stand, right? 'We're here. We're queer. Get used to it.'"

"Enough with your pithy quotes. You're like the liberal version of my mother." Allie took a deep breath. *God, I could use a little help.*

She sat for a moment, and then it came to her. "Well, I'm sure you know the Bible calls it a sin. That's what you're waiting to hear me admit, right? But I don't think you understand how Christians define 'sin.' When we say something is a sin, we mean it will pull you away from God, hinder you, not that it makes you a horrible, wicked person. The Hebrew word is 'het.' It means missing the mark."

"Okay," Rain said. "That's a little different than I expected. But why should it pull them away from God? Didn't God make them that way?"

"I'm not ready to insist there can't be a genetic component. I mean, alcoholism has a genetic component. But God does not offer us a sexual bill of rights in the Bible. He says that if your right hand offends you, to cut it off." Allie snipped the air like scissors.

"Ouch," Rain squealed.

Layla hid behind her hand and smiled. "Ouch indeed."

"I know it seems harsh, but the Bible isn't a set of rules to make us miserable. It's a sort of user's manual, like when you get a new appliance and the book says, 'To enjoy maximum efficiency and longevity, please follow these guidelines.'"

"Okay, enough Christian mumbo jumbo. Hate the sin. Love the sinner. I get it. You're not really a homophobe." Rain rolled her eyes.

Allie didn't take it personally. "No, I'm okay around homosexuals. According to the Bible anyone who has sex outside of marriage is a sinner, along with gluttons and gossips and worriers. We're all pretty much sinners. I certainly am."

"At least you have a nice attitude, Allie," Layla said. "You don't come across as judgmental."

Rain slapped the glass-topped table, sending quakes through it. "Not judgmental. She just called us all sinners."

"Yeah." Layla looked up from her laptop and stared Rain down. "Including herself. I'd say that's fair, and if you lived in a house where your uncle referred to ninety-nine percent of the population as evil infidel pigs, I think you'd agree."

Rain took a deep breath. "I guess so. I'm not used to such

strict standards. This whole idea of treating a book as absolute truth seems crazy to me." They hashed out the subject a little longer. Rain was right, both Christianity and Islam considered their holy books to be infallible. Sources of divine inspiration.

Of course, Allie believed that without a personal relationship with the author, the Bible could easily be turned into a set of brittle ordinances. Still, she couldn't imagine living without a standard for right and wrong. How did Rain do it?

The topic switched to abortion.

Allie volunteered to go first this time. Might as well get it over with. "I do believe all life is a gift from God, and I do believe abortion is taking a life. That makes it killing. That makes it a sin. Abortion victimizes women, and it ticks me off that pro-choice people sweep the gruesome details under the carpet."

Rain turned her head to consider that statement. "Now that you mention it, I have seen women traumatized after abortions. It's hard either way, I guess. I could never do it. But who is the government to control a woman's body and force her to carry a child she doesn't want? That's way too invasive."

Whew! Allie had expected a much stronger reaction. "Maybe you're right. The political side is complicated. Maybe it is invasive. But tearing a baby to pieces and sucking it out of the womb is invasive too." Allie hated to bring it up, but it was true.

Tears pooled in Layla's eyes. "Oh, that's horrible."

"What do you think about abortion, Layla?" Rain asked.

"It's not really an issue in the Middle East. People are pretty pragmatic about it. Children are so highly valued that if someone wants to get rid of one, we figure they must have a good reason. But what you said, Allie, that's awful. Can the babies feel it?"

"I don't know for sure, some people say they can." Allie bit her lip.

Layla took notes as Allie shared what she knew about abortion techniques and statistics. A part of Allie agreed with Rain, but when she considered the barbarity surrounding the issue, she simply couldn't justify killing the unborn. On the other hand, she also believed Christians would be wise to focus on the roots of the problem rather than try to mandate radical legal changes in a country unprepared to accept them.

"This is too sad. Do we have enough on this one yet?" Rain said. "I don't want to talk about it anymore."

Allie still couldn't believe her ears. She had expected Rain to be hardcore pro-choice. What was going on?

"None of these issues are very easy, are they?" Layla said.

"No." Allie couldn't agree more. Why did Christians pretend everything was simple? She understood black and white, hot and cold, but that didn't minimize the complexity of life. Wasn't this sort of honest dialogue much better?

"Life's a mess," Layla said.

"A beautiful mess," Rain whispered.

After hashing through the details one more time and finalizing plans for their paper, the girls wrapped up the official business. They moved outside to sit along the dock, swish their feet in the inlet, and watch the sunset. After her *wudu*, Layla slipped quietly to the side for prayers. She knelt low and pressed her face to her small rug. Allie admired such dedication. She could use more dedication in her prayer life.

"How lovely," Rain said.

She and Allie looked on as Layla dipped and bowed her neck, up and down, like a graceful swan silhouetted against the gold and orange remnants of the sun. Allie agreed. Life. A beautiful mess. This committed Muslim woman put Allie to shame.

Rain sighed. "I wonder if she really does need rescued?"

Allie's heart clutched to hear Rain say such a thing, and yet didn't a small piece of her wonder as well? Layla had such a dear, sweet heart for God. Allie could see how God could use her in the lives of these women. Use them in one another's lives.

This assignment truly was something special. She cared about Rain and Layla so much already. And no matter what anyone else might think, Allie had spent the last eight years spreading the news of Christ. She shouldn't let the opinions of her family define her. Rain thought she was a real Christian. The right sort of Christian.

Maybe Allie should go to church tomorrow. As much as

she hated the idea, it would be good for these girls to see her attending service with her parents. Especially Layla. Family was so very important to her. An upcoming assignment involved visiting functions typical of their cultures. Allie wanted to take them to church. A church where she knew people. Not a strange church.

Yes, she should definitely go tomorrow. Take a look at the service through Rain and Layla's eyes and make sure it was a reasonable plan. And getting Mom off her back in the process provided added incentive.

Oh, but could Allie handle sitting through the entire suffocating morning?

And what about Andy?

Might as well get it over with. She'd have to face him sooner or later. As much as this would kill Allie, somehow she felt it was the right plan. She would do it for Rain and Layla's sake. If this could bring them even one step closer to the God of love, it would be worth any sacrifice.

ELEVEN

Why must she always question? Layla leaned against a shady tree in the quad, working on her portion of the contrast essay. As she looked over her notes neatly organized on college-ruled paper, she revisited the conversation with Allie and Rain from the night before. Thoughts of Fatima, oppressed and dehumanized, floated through her mind. Thoughts of child terrorists, political strife, domestic violence, forced marriages of girls as young as nine. Where did these issues fit with her Islamic faith? Her life was pleasant enough, but should she be content with that?

She hadn't wanted to ask Allie too much, but she could read between the lines. Besides, she had heard it all from Brother Rasheed, live via satellite. The Christian faith was all about love and forgiveness—forgiveness from sin was a gift. The very Son of God gave his life on a cross. Suffered and died to set her free. *Free?* It was too simple, yet much too complex to grasp.

This God who was three in one, how could such a being exist? No, too much about the Christian faith struck her as far-fetched. Layla grew up with a good, solid, practical religion. A religion based on rules and works.

That, she understood.

But what if the God of the universe really did love her, want a relationship with her? What if she really could have assurance of eternity in paradise? Might that be worth the risk?

What if it meant she could be free, throw her veil to the wind? Stand before her God without shame?

Although she had sworn off Brother Rasheed, she couldn't

escape his voice. It followed her everywhere. Echoed in her heart. On the wind. His stories of Mohammed and Jesus. How Jesus stood up for women. How his apostle Paul taught there was no male or female in Christ.

What if?

Two girls from the MSU walked her way and waved. You couldn't miss them in their bright veils.

"*As-Salaam-Alaikum.*" Iman nodded to her.

"*Wa-Alaikum-Salaam,*" Layla offered the requisite response to the traditional Muslim greeting.

"Join us at prayers later?"

"Sure. I'll be there."

"Hey," Aisha said, stopping in front of her. "I heard through the Middle Eastern gossip chain that you had a date with Fadi Abdallah."

Layla threw up her hands. "Sheesh. It's as quick here as in Lebanon."

"Yeah, there aren't that many of us. News travels fast." Iman laughed.

"Don't believe everything you hear," Layla said. "It was far from a date. My aunt invited his family to dinner. I could hardly get out of it."

"Yeah." Aisha's brown eyes gleamed mischievously. "Like I said, a date. What's your point?"

"Funny." Layla grimaced. That pretty much was the Middle Eastern version of a date.

"So, did you like him?" Iman fiddled with her purple silken veil. The girl was so beautiful with her golden skin and hazel eyes. No doubt she could catch any man she wanted. Suddenly, Layla wondered if any of her MSU buddies might have boyfriends on the sly.

"Totally not my type." Layla slapped her book closed to drive home the point.

"Yeah, you could do better," Iman said. "What was your aunt thinking?"

"I have no idea." Layla tilted her head. "Are either of you committed to anyone?"

84

"My parents hope I'll marry this nerdy distant cousin when I'm done here. Boy will they be surprised." Aisha might not be as stunning as Iman, but she made up for it with that glimmer of spirit.

Yes, if anyone had a secret boyfriend, it would be Aisha. Layla didn't want to know, though. She wouldn't want to be responsible for that sort of information.

Iman looked at the sidewalk. "I'm engaged. He's a businessman." Her lack of excitement spoke volumes.

"Have you met anyone that interested you?" Aisha hoisted her books on her hip. She wore a slim long-sleeved T-shirt over jeans. Only the veil gave away her heritage. "I saw you walking with Mo at the beach. Now there's a catch."

Layla bit her lip. "He's an old friend."

"Yeah, right." Iman raised her eyebrows. "You looked really friendly."

"I just want to focus on my education right now. I'll worry about men later." Layla wasn't ready to admit her secret, even to these girls who would surely understand.

"Try telling that to your aunt," Iman said.

"I wonder who she'll find next. Be sure to keep us posted," Aisha added.

"Oh, I'm sure you'll know long before I do." Layla shook her head.

"Anyway, we'll see you at noon." Aisha and Iman leaned down to give Layla the requisite kisses and good-byes.

A few handsome young guys walked toward them from the opposite direction on the sidewalk. Aisha smiled and waved. But Iman kept her eyes on the ground and scurried past, as if the fabric draping her head was made of lead.

Fatima jumped to Layla's mind again. She should write Fatima another letter. She'd be tickled to hear about the *burqini*. And Mo, of course. She had to tell Fatima about Mo. Layla couldn't fathom living life locked faceless behind the *niqab* like Fatima. Perhaps she should try truly praying for Fatima, as she had seen that Christian named Sister Amani pray for the oppressed females of the Middle East on *The Muslim*

Woman show. But would the God of the universe listen? Did he care?

Something deep inside of Layla screamed, *Yes. Yes, he does.*

Mo peered from around the corner of a brick building across the quad at the beautiful lady full of grace and light sitting under the tree hard at work. A breeze trailed over his skin, as soft as her caress. He made a huge mistake with Layla. For the first few days he called and texted her. Talked of meeting her family. How foolish of him. Already she stole a piece of his heart. Somehow he needed to get it back.

"Is that her?"

Mo blinked and turned to his buddy. He had almost forgotten he was meeting someone. This guy had become a spiritual advisor of sorts over the past months. Mo wished the friend hadn't caught him in such a trance. "Yeah. That's her."

A.J. put a firm hand on Mo's shoulder. "She's pretty enough, but so are most of the girls around here. Spying on her isn't going to make you feel any better. She can only bring heartache."

Mo let out a sigh. "I know. It's hard, though."

"Think of how hard it would be on her if you got together. Better to stay away from women for a while."

"You're right, of course." He swallowed down a lump in his throat. A.J. made it sound so simple. It wasn't simple at all.

"Focus on what matters."

Mo's future was far too uncertain. He couldn't guarantee that he'd even be alive next year. Yet his hand trembled with the memory of her silken touch.

His friend gave his shoulder a wake up shake. "You can make a real difference in this world."

Glancing at her, sitting still and peaceful, Mo considered how much his parents would love Layla. A Sunni Muslim girl straight from Lebanon. What were the odds? The perfect female resurrected from his past, as if God designed her just for him.

But it was impossible.

"Let her go, man. You'll be glad you did." A.J. turned and led the way to the library.

Layla would never understand. They could never make a marriage, a family together—and to a girl like Layla, he could never offer anything less. "You're right. I need to put her out of my mind." Mo shifted his feet to walk away. With monumental effort, he followed A.J. in the opposite direction.

But his heart remained under the shady tree with Layla.

No amount of coaxing could ever change that.

Allie sat in the hard-backed pew beside her family with fake smile glued firmly in place. The tan and brown sanctuary of the First Church of the Stick in the Mud loomed around her. She endured the two fast songs followed by the two slow, the three minutes and twenty seconds of announcements, the horrific meet and greet, the antiquated organ special, and now suffered through the hour-long sermon, full of the Word but lacking spirit, as usual. The service would conclude with the obligatory altar call, to which, of course, no one would respond.

Seriously. Seriously? How much more could Allie take? Her pantyhose suffocated her legs. Her shiny heels pinched worse than her satin *pointe* shoes. Pinched clear to her soul. Allie fought to keep her breathing steady. She just wanted to throw off her ugly church dress and hit the beach.

Unable to take it anymore, Allie slipped out of the pew and headed for the ladies room, but once in the foyer, the sensations grew worse. A vague recollection of some nasty suit-clad usher hollering at her for spinning in the hallway on the way back from the bathroom flashed through her head. This morning was going from bad to worse.

Who was that awful usher anyway?

Allie sagged against the wall, pressing the back of her head to it and closing her eyes. She almost captured his face in her memory. Then it flitted away. Instead the familiar image of a spotted snake with a wide open mouth flashed in her mind.

The scary python from the old *Jungle Book* movie with his hypnotizing eyes. She felt it wrap about her neck, choking her, and circle around to squeeze her chest, constricting her airway. Continue downward to press against her stomach.

Opening her eyes and shaking her head clear, she pushed aside her fright along with the troubling responses. What was wrong with her? Could the sensations simply be a reaction to feeling bound in this church atmosphere? The gaping-mouthed snake seemed a bit extreme.

What on earth could it mean?

On second thought, the sanctuary had been much better than the foyer. She didn't need to use the bathroom that badly after all. She scrambled back down the aisle and into the safety of her family's pew.

She picked up her bulletin and waved herself with it for a moment. Once she settled back in and relaxed a bit, Allie pulled a pen out of her purse to doodle pictures on her bulletin with its fill-in-the-blank platitudes. Hopefully that would distract her from her ever-increasing discomfort with this place.

Sarah shot a reprimanding glare her way, but Allie ignored her little sister. Glancing over, she noticed every line on Sarah's paper completed to perfection. Sarah would probably hide the answers if she tried to copy them.

Allie choked back a laugh. At least she still had her sense of humor. Hmm, maybe she could use this time to brainstorm about other churches to visit.

There was Extreme Church. No, too intense.

Vineyard seemed too...grapey.

New Horizons might be okay, maybe a little boring.

Reality Church sounded about right, but who on earth wanted to wander into a strange congregation?

Maybe she needed to bring Rain and Layla here after all, no matter how hard it might be for her. Pausing to look at the place around her through her friends' eyes, it wasn't so terrible. Some of the teens wore casual clothes. The sermon wasn't a complete disaster. The plain sanctuary had a warm feel. And the members of the congregation had tripped all over themselves to welcome Allie home.

Sarah bumped Allie's shoulder and pointed across the pews.

Andy caught her eye and waved.

Certainly not on the positive list.

Ugh! She resisted the temptation to stick out her tongue. He might assume she was flirting. She shot daggers at him with her eyes instead.

"Be nice." Sarah scribbled beside her copious sermon notes.

"He's sweet."

Leave it to Sarah to consider sweet a good thing. Her sister's support of Andy chased away any last doubts. She had to get rid of that guy. To what ridiculous lengths would she be forced to go? Who cared if he looked cute with his waving hair and amber eyes? He also looked far too at home in this place. He worked here, for crying out loud! No amount of attraction could make up for that. Andy was her past, not her future.

How could he ignore what had happened between them? She would never forget prom night senior year. While the rest of the football team snuck off with their girlfriends, hoping to get lucky, Andy had given her an engagement ring. He claimed God told him they would be man and wife. Oh, how that ring squeezed about her finger.

At the time, Allie accepted. She didn't know what else to do. He seemed so sincere. She felt so trapped. On graduation day, she silently slipped the ring back into his hand with tears in her eyes and ran away.

And now? Now she realized he had some nerve deciding he could hear from God on her behalf. What a jerk. If God wanted her to marry someone, God would tell her himself. Allie just wished he'd hurry.

Because Andy still stared at her from across the sanctuary. And the glint in his eyes told her he was about to do something drastic.

TWELVE

Andy could hardly believe his eyes. Allie was home and sitting across from him in the curved sanctuary beside a row of perfectly bedecked Carmichaels. How many years had he hoped and prayed to see this very picture? He gripped his worn leather Bible to keep from waving a second time and making an utter buffoon of himself. God had done a mighty work, and yet the few pews between them may as well be a continent. He could see it on her face.

Andy had hurt this girl. He failed to understand her, failed to see her as God viewed her, as a beautiful free bird created to reflect a unique aspect of his vast and paradoxical personality. In those days Andy's God was much smaller. His own construct. His own idol. Instead, Andy had tried to conform Allie to his own image. He tried to shove her into a little Christian box.

She was right to run away.

The senior pastor dismissed in prayer, and Andy headed in Allie's direction. Now he served as youth pastor for the church she left behind long ago. No wonder she didn't trust him. What could he do to change her mind? If only she would give him a chance. He needed to convince her he was different.

"Morning, Andy, fine service."

"Yes, it was." He smiled without registering the face of the commenter. He had to get to Allie.

If only he could return to that night so long ago. When she pressed the ring into his palm, it cut like a knife straight to his heart. If only he had run after her, crushed her to his chest and kissed her until she melted in his arms. If only he had seen her true beauty. If only...

Another parishioner caught him and shook his hand. Allie faded into the crowd. Andy spent the last eight years counting the "if onlys." If only he could reach her. If only he could talk to her, he just might stand a chance.

"Andy." Someone pulled at his shoulder. "I've been meaning to speak with you."

"Uh, sorry, Bill. I've got to run. Can we talk later?"

Allie was nowhere in sight. Andy shoved past Bill as politely as possible and made a dash for the exit.

Once outside he spotted her in her conservative, pink-flowered skirt and sweater set. "Allie. Allie, wait up." He sprinted through the parking lot toward her retreating back. "Please!"

She turned and spotted him. Her eyes darted about, as if looking to make a break. He thought she might try to run and hide like she had at the mall, but instead, she pasted on a stiff smile and waited for him.

Andy stopped short. Winded from his sprint, he placed his hands on his bent knees and took a few deep breaths. "Well, I guess my football days are far behind me."

Allie tapped her toe in annoyance.

"I've been trying to catch you for weeks."

"Nooo! Really?" She shot him a dirty look.

"Seems like you don't particularly want to be caught."

"You think?"

"Come on, Allie. It was a long time ago. If nothing else, at least forgive me, and let's be friends."

"Fine. Friends. Happy?" She crossed her arms.

"Friends who have lunch?"

Allie stormed at him, poking her finger into his chest. "See, I knew it. I knew you wanted to go out. Well, let me tell you, Andrew Simon Vargas. I will never, ever, as long as I live, go out with you again. Do I make myself clear?"

"Very." He wished she had punched him in the gut instead. It would have hurt less.

Allie turned on her heel and sashayed away across the steaming gray asphalt with her head held high. Ha! How do you like that Andy Vargas?

"And I will never...ever...as long as I live...stop loving you, Allie Carmichael."

That halted her dead in her tracks. She didn't turn. She didn't look at him. She just dropped her head as tears filled her eyes.

"'Love is not love which alters when it alteration finds, or bends with the remover to remove.'" He quoted her favorite Shakespearean sonnet. Always the romantic. Andy knew her too well. His smooth voice turned the verse to music in her ears.

A four-letter word slipped from her mouth, clanging against the poetry. Allie spun around and clasped her hands over her lips. To her great surprise, Andy started to laugh.

"That was dramatic. I guess I always did bring out the worst in you." He crossed to her and tucked a flyaway strand of hair behind her ear, caressing her cheek as he did. "And the best."

Allie was not at all pleased by the warm flush in her cheeks or the pleasant shivers running down her spine. Darn her traitorous body! What was this man doing to her?

"Stop it." The words escaped as a whisper.

Her stomach tied to knots. This was not what she wanted. How dare he? She pushed away his hand and dashed for her car. Lord help Andy Vargas if he tried to stand in her way. She might run him over in the parking lot and be done with this here and now.

Rain worked a comfortable indentation into the soft sand for her bottom. She sat cuddled between James's knees on the beach on the quiet Sunday afternoon. A hurricane heading up the coast toward Virginia Beach had turned the day overcast and blustery. She took a deep breath of the salty air. "I love this weather."

"Yeah, there's something raw and elemental about it." He kissed the top of her head.

The refreshing wind brushed cool against the skin exposed by her ankle length sundress and sandals. She turned her face to better catch the breeze and ran her hands over her boyfriend's forearms where they wrapped about her chest.

High-pitched laughter met her ear as a little girl in a flowered bathing suit chased a beach ball caught by the wind. Curling mahogany ponytails tied up with ribbons bounced about her cherubic face.

"Oh." She tapped James's arm. "Look how pretty."

Such innocence and merriment proved contagious. Rain smiled and waved to the fairy-like child. She wished she could reach out and pull the girl into her arms. Maybe plant a little kiss on her silky head. She longed for her own. Without meaning to, Rain clutched a hand protectively over her womb.

James flinched as the little girl's mother scolded her for running too close to the crashing surf.

"What a..." He caught himself in time. Rain didn't like for him to use that derogatory term for women. He clung tight to her as she sat between his legs. Pressed his feet harder into the sand.

"James." Rain swatted him. "Look at those waves. They're huge. Her mom's worried."

He hated to see any child berated. Even if the parent did care. The tears running over the small girl's cheeks and toward her down-turned lips broke his heart. "She was playing. She only wanted to catch her ball."

The mom drew the girl into a hug and wiped away her tears.

No one ever wiped away his tears. Marijuana was supposed to give a high, make people happy. All James ever witnessed in his father were the devastating after-effects: depression, anxiety, panic. His paranoid dad needed to control everyone and everything, most of all James. He was just a little boy. People thought he had it so great. If only they knew.

He recalled that afternoon when he lay tossing his baseball on the couch.

A dark murkiness enveloped the house, even in the middle of the day.

Dad always kept the curtains closed. The man detested the blaring racket of the television, and a driving rain kept James from playing outside that afternoon. So James tossed his ball, innocently from hand to hand, daydreaming and staring at the smoke-stained ceiling.

His mind must have strayed too far. The ball careened into his father's favorite bong, a handmade piece of drug paraphernalia from Mexico, red and yellow shards shattering in all directions. Dad, who had no use for him any other time, came storming from his bedroom, strewing a vile string of curses, with murder in his eyes....

The memory cut off there. They always cut off there. James had no need, no desire to recall the rest.

Where had his mother been? High on the streets somewhere? Childhood was not a magical time. It was a nightmare. He would never bring a child into this horrible world, no matter how cute the little girl now held safe in her mother's arms.

Rain felt tension seep through James's body and into her own as he watched mother and daughter. Wind whipped her curls into her eyes. As she brushed them away, the girl returned to her merry frolicking as though nothing ever happened. "Look, she's fine. Everything's fine, James. Do you want to talk about it?"

"There's nothing to talk about." His gruff reply put a quick end to the conversation.

She wished she knew what happened to James. She felt for him, really she did. Something terrible occurred in his childhood, that much she understood. Having grown up with a psychologist for a mother, she knew he'd never get past it until he was willing to talk. She wished she could go back and ease his pain. She wished they could move beyond his fears and start a family of their own. She could hardly imagine life without a child.

Their child.

She had found Mr. Right.

So why was everything so wrong?

THIRTEEN

Layla took a hearty bite of her sandwich and watched as Rain hurried through the dining hall on Thursday afternoon. Rain was so predictable. Allie grinned at Layla and rolled her eyes.

The hippie member of their trio crashed into their cafeteria table, wearing a loud patchwork skirt. "Hey, guess what."

Only five minutes late. She was improving.

"I made another Jesus friend today in government class."

"*Another* Jesus friend." Allie made a face. "Is that what you call me?"

"Sure." Rain tossed her sack onto the adjoining seat.

Glancing from Rain to Allie and back again, Layla smirked into her turkey sandwich on thick grain bread. The spicy mustard made her eyes water.

She always called Allie her ballerina friend. That was scary enough in her circles.

Allie put a hand to her chest. "Should I be offended or something?"

"No, it's a good thing. Her name's Venessa, and she goes to some cool college church on Sunday nights close to campus. Sounded all ooey gooey and spiritual. Maybe we should try it. It might be what you're looking for, Allie."

Layla wished she could be supportive, but it sounded like a bad idea for her. Auntie and Uncle would freak if they found out she attended a church. She could almost hear her mother in her head saying that Allah and his angels would curse her if she did. Although she had to admit, she was a bit curious.

Allie took a deep breath and a sip of her diet soda. "Why

don't we start by checking out my parents' church first? That can be a field trip for our next assignment. I almost hate to subject you to it, but then if we visit somewhere else, you'll know what I'm comparing it to. It will explain a lot about my background."

Had Allie been reading her mind? Longing and terror filled Layla at once. Her mother's opinions aside, she so wanted to try this new experience. "I guess it would be okay." She tugged at her veil. "Just this once—for research."

Her family was all for good grades. This might be the perfect opportunity. They would want her to work diligently on her English paper. No need to bring up the details. She could almost hug that professor for assigning them to visit a typical cultural event with their group members.

"Yeah, for research." Rain dug into her salad.

"I was thinking about taking you all to a Middle Eastern party," Layla said. "I think you'd learn more about our culture that way."

"Sounds fun." A look of relief washed over Allie's face.

Layla understood. What American girl would willingly attend a mosque and sit veiled in the women's section? "Friends of ours are throwing one this Friday night. It's an engagement party. Wait until you see the food. Oh, and I can introduce you to the ridiculous guy my aunt is trying to fix me up with."

"Cool. I can't wait." Rain devoured her food like the starving homeless person Layla had once imagined her to be.

"How about you, Rain?" Layla said. "Have you thought where you might take us?"

"Hmm, well there's a Friends of Lesbians and Gays protest rally coming up."

Allie blanched.

Layla giggled.

"Kidding. I wouldn't do that to you." Rain took a few more bites. "No, seriously, there's a multi-faith fall equinox ceremony coming up: very hippie and New Age. I thought that would work. My parents never missed a good equinox celebration."

"Hmm, I'm not sure that's much better," Allie said.

"The whole point is to learn more about one another."

Perplexed, Layla twisted her face at Allie's response.

"Don't worry, Allie." Rain smiled. "They aren't hardcore pagans. There's some Druid influence mixed in with some Native American and a dash of Christianity thrown on top for good measure. It's like a harvest fair. Crafts and entertainment and stuff."

Allie took another deep breath. "Okay, if Layla can brave a church service, I guess I can handle an equinox festival."

"Don't you want to expand your horizons?" Layla asked, disappointed in Allie. Up until now, she seemed interested and open to new ideas.

"I do. I...just...it's hard to explain this without sounding offensive." She wiggled on her seat.

"I think we're past all that now. Spit it out. We'll deal," Rain said.

"Christians, at least most Christians, believe there is an active evil force in the world. I'm not sure what kind of spiritual atmosphere I'll be walking into at the festival."

It seemed Allie did not fully understand that Layla felt the exact same trepidation about walking into a church. But she had picked up a few tidbits about Christianity from Brother Rasheed. "Well, if you believe this is true, then don't you believe your God is stronger?"

Last night's show had focused on the miracles of the Bible compared to the miracles of the *Qur'an*. Islam had not fared well in the analysis. She should look into it more.

Allie squinted one eye. "Yeah, I guess we do believe our God can overcome evil. I'm just not always so sure about myself. How did you know that, anyway?"

Layla shrugged. Oops. "I hear things."

Mo entered the cafeteria at that precise moment. Layla turned her head away from the door. She dropped her sandwich to her plate. Appetite gone. He had ignored her ever since that first week after the beach. She certainly didn't want a confrontation with him in the middle of the dining hall.

"Well, she got you good," Rain said. "You have no excuses left."

"No. I'm sure it will be...enlightening," Allie answered, but Layla hardly heard.

Rain's eyes darted back and forth as Allie spoke. "Hey, Layla, who's the total hottie checking you out over there? Talk about major eye candy. Yum!"

Layla's chest constricted. She grabbed Rain's hands before she could point. "Stop it. You're embarrassing me."

Allie rolled her head from Mo back to Layla. "She's right. That man has his eye on you."

There was no avoiding him now. Layla waved to Mo, glad her veil hid the warm flush rising up her chest. He waved back with a sad smile and, dipping his head toward his lunch tray, walked to the other side of the cafeteria.

"That was weird," Allie said. "I would have sworn he wanted to talk to you. Do you know him?"

"I met him at a beach party. We went to kindergarten together."

"He's probably shy," Rain offered.

"Yeah, probably," Layla said, although Mo seemed anything but shy that Saturday. Or the following days in his calls and texts. Something was wrong. All communication just ceased. She had wanted to introduce him to her uncle.

"So Layla Al-Rai has herself a man," Rain said.

Layla shook her head. "Not even close."

"Oh, I saw the look in his eye." Rain leaned in toward Layla. "That guy is c-a-u-g-h-t, caught."

Layla felt the flush reach her cheeks. She turned her attention to her bowl of soup.

"Nothing. You've got nothing to say?" Rain took Layla by the shoulder and shook her. "You got nothing for an old committed lady dying for some romance?" Rain sat back down and pouted her lower lip. She turned to Allie. "What about you? Any juicy guy gossip?"

"Gossip's a sin." Allie focused on her soda can, noticeably avoiding eye contact. What was the girl up to now?

"Oh no, she's hiding something. Dish!" Rain looked ready to shake Allie too.

Layla was glad to see her attention diverted.

Allie held up her hands to fend off Rain. "Just an old boyfriend who's determined to get me back. He's driving me nuts."

Boyfriend. Such creatures didn't exist in Layla's culture. Only forbidden men, family members, and fiancés.

"Hmm, is he cute?" Rain asked.

"Is that all you care about?" Allie shook her head in disgust.

"Come on, throw me some scraps. I'm starving here." Rain settled back down to her lunch.

"Fine, he's cute and athletic and smart. Oh, and did I mention he's a total stick in the mud? There. Are you happy?" Allie said.

"Not really, I was hoping to hook you back up." Rain frowned.

Hook up, yet another term never used in Layla's culture. "Where do you know him from?" Layla said.

"We went to school together, but he works at my parents' church."

"So your family approves?" Layla smiled. This man might have potential. Her parents would adore Mo. If only she could figure out what was going on with him.

"They loooove Andy." Allie frowned. "More than me probably."

That piqued Layla's interest. "Maybe we'll see him Sunday."

Rain clapped. "I can't wait."

"You two better behave." Allie pointed an emphatic finger at each of them.

"Maybe," Rain said.

"Maybe not." Layla had so much fun with these girls. Rain definitely brought out her impish side. She glanced down at her watch. "Hey, ladies, I have to go. I only have five minutes to make it across campus for noon prayers."

"Will Mo be there?" Rain wiggled her eyebrows.

Layla gathered up her things. "Doubtful. He's never been before."

Which, now that she thought about it, made no sense at all. Mo had gone to a Muslim school with her. His parents wouldn't have sent him there if they were nonreligious. Why was he skipping prayers? Of course the subject of faith hadn't really come up between them. She just sort of assumed he still believed the way he was raised.

Something was wrong, she thought again. Something was definitely wrong.

FOURTEEN

Come Sunday morning, Rain was hardly ready to stand up on the pew, wave her Bible in the air, and shout, "Praise be to Jesus. I need to be saved." Still, letting the altar call slip by without response left her with a quiet sense of dissatisfaction. She understood why this church didn't meet Allie's needs. The mud-colored monstrosity didn't fit her personality at all, but something in the place spoke to Rain.

She eyed the carpeted steps leading to the prayer rail and the cross hanging over the center of the stage.

The lesson about Jesus as your best friend touched her heart. Rain's deities were nothing but disembodied spirits. This God had a face to seek. He extended his right hand. You could actually sit down with this personal God and have a conversation. Allie never mentioned that.

As the portly gray-haired Pastor Jenkins in his three-piece suit dismissed the sermon, a group of ladies, led by Allie's sticky sweet Southern mother, descended upon Layla, desperate to make her feel at home in a place she clearly was not. Rain in her long, loose skirt flew under the radar for now. She took a moment to check out the crowd.

Who was that fine looking young man with the endearing smatter of freckles staring at Allie from the back of the sanctuary?

Could it be the high school boyfriend? He didn't look wound too awfully tight. Unlike most of the males, his amber-colored hair fell in gentle waves over his ears and open collar. He wore his untucked dressy-casual shirt with a nice pair of jeans. In fact, he looked more relaxed than Allie this morning.

Rain coughed into her fist. She spoke into the back of her hand. "Allie, massive cutie at ten o'clock."

Allie pulled herself away from the gaggle of well-meaning ladies. "Don't look. Don't look at him. That's Andy. Stop it. Please." She hid her face behind her bulletin, as if he wouldn't see her.

"Don't be silly. He's hot."

Allie peeked from behind the folded paper. "Seriously. Is that all you care about?" She twisted again toward Layla, a look of concern on her face.

While Allie's back was turned, Rain waved to Andy and beckoned him over.

He pointed to his chest and mouthed, "Me?"

Rain winked. "Yeah, you."

Layla wanted to sink into the brown carpet as the ladies crowded in on her. What had she gotten herself into? This was no simple Catholic mass; this was a hell-fire-and-brimstone church extraordinaire.

Although she had whispered *Astaghfar Allah Al Azeem* several times, begging forgiveness during the blasphemies spoken in the sermon, she wondered if Allah might be judging her nonetheless. Despite her father's more liberal views, her mother's voice reverberated in her head, yelling that Allah and his angels cursed her for even entering this evil place. Layla should probably slip off to the bathroom for a ritual cleansing after all she had been exposed to this morning.

And now on top of everything else, she feared the swarm of ladies surrounding her would like nothing better than to rip the veil off her head and hand her over, kicking and screaming, to Jesus.

The ridiculous image brought a smile to Layla's lips. Actually, the pastor's sermon made coming to Jesus sound quite appealing. And the lovely music about the friend we have in him had stirred that place deep in her heart that insisted on questioning her religion again and again. Still, under the onslaught of the overzealous church women, she turned to Allie and shot her a look of desperation.

Allie wove her way into the center of the circle. "Ladies, ladies, don't overwhelm the poor girl." She put an arm around Layla. "They just love Jesus so much, they can't help themselves." Allie pasted on a false smile. It took a few minutes before she managed to maneuver Layla out of the group.

Allie's mom called after her, waving and raising her voice as Allie dragged Layla away. "Do come back. And remember, this is the day that the Lord has made. Rejoice and be glad in it. Jesus is knocking at the door of your heart. All you have to do is let him in."

Allie rolled her eyes apologetically and whispered, "Sorry. She tends to overdo it with the Christian clichés. And that Southern accent certainly doesn't help."

Layla pressed her lips together to hide her shock.

Jesus is knocking at the door of your heart.

The same words Brother Rasheed had spoken.

"It's okay," Layla managed to choke out, but she couldn't shake the echoing words. The world tilted and grew swishy. She took a few slow breaths to steady herself.

By the time they reached Rain, she was chatting up a tall, handsome guy with light brown hair and warm hazel eyes. Thank goodness, something other than religion to focus her mind on. Although smitten by Mo these days, Layla thought this attractive man would catch any girl's notice.

"Allie, look what I found." Rain sounded naughty as she said it.

Oh, this must be Allie's old boyfriend.

Allie looked ready to slug Rain.

The perfect distraction from Layla's disturbing thoughts of Brother Rasheed. Praise be to Allah.

"We were discussing how Andy taught you to surf. Isn't that romantic, Layla? Don't you wish you could surf? I sure do." Rain laughed and placed a familiar hand on Andy's arm.

"Yes, surfing sounds nice." Layla didn't know what else to say. No one had given her the script for this impromptu theatrical.

"Andy, I know," Rain said, leaning toward him. "You should take Allie surfing again. Don't you think that's a great idea, Allie? Why, Allie was telling us how she missed surfing."

Layla recalled no such conversation, but oddly Allie gave a wry half-grin and turned her gaze to the wall. Did she miss surfing, or did she miss this nice-looking young man?

"Uh," Andy said, raking his fingers through his hair. "I think we're making Allie uncomfortable. I mean, I'd love to take her surfing anytime, but..."

Allie just stood there staring at the wall.

"Come on, Allie, cut the poor guy some slack." Rain shoved Allie closer to Andy.

Allie blinked a few times.

Layla saw something surprising flash through Allie's eyes.

"Come on, Allie. Give him a chance."

Even her friends wanted her to give Andy another try. Guilt had wracked Allie all week, and there it was again. Clanging in her chest. She winced at the memory of how terribly she treated him during their last encounter. Maybe she wasn't being fair. Maybe Andy had changed. He certainly didn't look like the same old straight-laced Andy, as he waited for an answer in his casual attire. Were those seriously tennis shoes on his feet?

He gazed deep into her eyes. "Come on, Allie. Give me a chance. It's been a long time." He reached out and took her hand in his.

She stared down at their joined fingers. Zaps of electricity flowed between them. Her head grew light and tingly. On top of everything else, she did love to surf and hadn't had a chance since returning home. What if by running from Andy, she was running from the very future she desired?

Could she try again?

"I guess so." Allie gave Andy a timid glance. Oh boy, she was going to regret this.

FIFTEEN

Tonight should be fun. The week had sped by, and here Rain was car-pooling with Allie to the far side of Virginia Beach once again, this time for their first official Lebanese party. She dug a compact from her sack, sat up straight in the black leather seat of the tiny car, and flipped open the passenger side mirror.

"So I didn't get a chance to tell you." Rain applied a hint of earth-toned blush to her cheeks. "Even though it doesn't fit you, I kind of liked your church. Some of the stuff your pastor said stuck with me. You know, about seeking God's face. I never thought of God having a face. I've been doing that, imagining his face and spending time with him."

What an amazing week it had been.

Life-changing.

An actual, personal deity.

Allie pulled the steering wheel to make a right hand turn. "Um...I hate to tell you this, but I'm not sure he meant it that way. I've never heard of anyone *imagining* God."

"What else could he mean? Open the eyes of my heart. Show me your face. That's exactly what I did." Was Allie going to try to tell her that the one good thing she got out of church was wrong?

"I don't know. Maybe you got it, and I didn't."

"You should try. Seriously, it's amazing." Rain added some apricot tinted beeswax to her lips.

Allie tapped the steering wheel with her forefinger. "I wonder if that's what people mean when they say God gives them pictures?"

"Probably. That sounds about right." Rain put the tube back

in her sack and fiddled with her curls.

"I always wished he would give me pictures, but I thought it would be supernatural and dramatic." Allie waved her hand around. "Like a flash that blocked out my normal eyesight. I never thought it might be something as simple as imagination."

"The best things usually are simple. Venessa, my other Jesus friend, gave me a copy of The Message. It's simple. I like it. Have you read it?" Rain was enjoying her new contemporary version of the scriptures. It was straightforward. Blunt even. Although the translator possessed a serious poetic streak.

"Not yet." Things went silent again.

"Anyway, I just wanted to let you know I got something out of the sermon," Rain said. Allie was so weird sometimes. "And I enjoyed meeting your family. Your mom was a bit much, but your sister seemed sweet and your brother was cute. I wonder if Layla would be interested."

Allie shot a look sideways. "In my brother? I think Layla's interested in Mo."

"And your dad was really funny."

Allie shook her head. "Oh, he's hysterical when he stands on Atlantic Avenue yelling at everyone that they're going to hell."

Rain could picture it. She'd argued with those guys on the street corner before. She snickered. "That would be pretty funny."

"As funny as your little stunt with Andy?"

"Admit it. That was awesome."

"I'm not admitting anything."

Rain poked Allie in the rib with her elbow. Someone needed to snatch up that adorable man, and quick. Might as well be Allie. "Come on. Admit it. He's hot. You want him."

Allie batted away Rain's elbow. "So what if he's hot? We have nothing in common. He's like everyone else at that ridiculous church, all about the outside. I'm sick of the outside."

Rain could hardly argue with that. "Yeah, even though I learned something at your church, I understand how you feel. Let's make it a project to visit churches and find one that fits you." Who knows, maybe Rain would find one that fit her too.

"It's time for us to stop worrying about who we're supposed to be and start figuring out who we're going to become. Do you think Layla would join us?"

"I don't know," Allie said. "We talked about this. It's harder for her. Anyway, tomorrow I have to go to my old church. Someone, who shall remain nameless, set me up on a date, and we're leaving straight from the potluck after service."

Allie swung by Layla's house to pick her up before heading to the party, still thinking about Rain's offer to visit churches with her. This could be the perfect opportunity for both of them, and maybe visiting new churches wouldn't be such a nightmare with a friend along.

Layla guided her along the route and then instructed her to pull over. Middle Eastern music, twangy and nasal, met them at the street corner of the host home. Allie slid the car into a small opening, and they all hopped out.

"Look at you two. You match." Allie pointed to their gypsy skirts and tunic tops. Rain's appeared rumpled, comfy, and functional. Layla's evoked style and flair.

Rain held up her skirt, as she and Layla struck a pose. "What do you think?"

"I'm wishing I hadn't left mine at home." Allie sported her dressiest black jeans with a long, sparkly T-shirt and jeweled flip flops. Her amusement turned to trepidation as they approached the house. The basic brick ranch wasn't nearly as large as Layla's home, and people spilled from the doorways. "Oh my."

To Allie's surprise, she noted girls in tight, skimpy outfits worthy of a nightclub conversing casually with those in long skirts and veils. It seemed this culture would prove more diverse than she expected.

Once inside, they were welcomed into the throng. Layla's aunt and uncle looked startled by her new friends, but Lebanese hospitality reigned supreme. The girls filled their plates with hummus, tabouli, stuffed zucchinis, olives, spinach pies, and kefta meatballs on a stick. They sat down to enjoy the dinner.

"Check it out," Allie shouted, pointing to a group of veiled girls with smiling faces, belly dancing in one corner, like a garden of flowers bobbing merrily in the breeze. "Aren't they going to get in trouble?" Although they were dressed modestly, the girls gyrated and shimmied in ways that would have shocked Allie's conservative church friends.

"No, silly." Layla laughed. "That's the way everyone dances. It's part of our culture. No one thinks anything of it."

Sure enough, a group of young men joined the girls and began to shake and shimmy as well. The movements did not appear suggestive on them. More toward comical.

"Hey." Rain pointed to Allie. "Let's see you strut your stuff, dancer girl."

"Let's see you." Allie stuck out her tongue.

"Fine." Rain put all three plates on a side table and took Allie and Layla's fingers in her own, holding them high over her head and leading the way to the dance floor. She let out her own version of a rhythmic Lebanese trill, that sounded more like a pathetic, "A, la, la, la, la," when she did it.

Not shy in this setting, Layla demonstrated some basic moves.

Allie gave them a try, her spine swinging freely from side to side in a manner ballet did not require. "I didn't know I could move this way. Look, I have hips," she shouted and giggled over the music.

Once the girls resumed eating, Layla's aunt and uncle came and sat with them on the spice colored oversized couches. Rain observed the fierce protectiveness in their eyes as they questioned the girls, ascertaining their suitability. How their accented voices filled with warmth as they relaxed and shared stories about Layla's childhood. Her auntie reached over and patted Layla's knee when Allie mentioned how much Layla had been teaching them about Islam and the Middle East.

"We're so proud of our Layla." *Um-Wassim* gave Layla's leg a possessive squeeze. "She brings honor to our family."

"Yes." The uncle appraised Layla with joy shining in his eyes. "That's our girl. We've raised her well in the paths of Allah."

"It's nothing." Layla ducked her head. "It's part of the assignment. I've learned so much from them too. I didn't even know the term postmodern until Rain taught me."

Rain appreciated that Layla didn't mention some of the other terms she'd taught her. Like misogynist. She chuckled to herself. As much fun as Rain was having, she felt melancholy at the same time. Layla's closeness with her aunt and uncle far surpassed Rain's with her own parents. They treated Rain more like a houseguest than a child. Insisting she call them George and Mary. Refusing to make rules or give advice. Demanding she follow her own paths, even if she had no idea what those should be.

Layla had traditions. These parties probably hadn't changed in a thousand years, except microwaves warmed the food and the music came from a CD player. Middle Eastern Christians and Muslims mingled freely in this setting, sharing more values and heritage than any set of next-door neighbors in America.

These people cared about Layla, even if they spent too much time in her business. When Rain had a child, she hoped to be more like this family. But would James ever agree?

SIXTEEN

"Oh, no." Layla pressed herself deeper into the couch cushions, turning her head away from the door and the unwelcome face entering the Lebanese engagement party. Her neck tensed. At least Auntie and Uncle had gone to mingle with friends. Maybe she could manage to avoid him. She had really been enjoying this evening.

"Uh oh, what now? Are we hiding from another guy?" Rain bent out past her on the couch and craned her neck right and left.

"Cut it out!" Layla swatted her shoulder. "He's going to notice."

"Who is *he*?" Allie faced the doorway from the loveseat. "The guy who just came in? Looks harmless."

"That's Fadi Abdallah. The man my aunt is trying to fix me up with." He had been nice enough, but that made it even worse. She'd hate to reject him outright. Better to evade the issue.

"It's like Andy Vargas all over again. Maybe we need some sort of hand signals." Rain touched a finger to her nose and then pulled on her ear.

Layla burst into giggles and was still laughing when she felt a tap on her shoulder. The giggles died on her lips. She turned with jaw clenched. There stood Fadi, as rotund and mediocre as she remembered. But, that pleading look in his eye was new.

And the red flush in his cheeks.

Good grief. The guy must have a crush on her.

She stood to greet him as custom demanded. "Fadi, I didn't know you would be here. What a nice surprise." She hoped she managed a pleasant expression to match the words.

"Hi, Layla. You sure look pretty tonight." He shoved his hands into the pockets of his dress pants.

Layla almost choked. "Why...thank you, Fadi." Quickly breaking eye contact she gestured to the girls. "Let me introduce you to some friends from ODU. This is Rain Butler-Briggs."

Rain offered a small wave and mischievous smile.

Layla nudged her with a foot, hoping she'd get the message and behave. "She's a writer. And this is Allie Carmichael, ballerina and businesswoman."

"Hi, Fadi." Allie nodded. "Nice to meet you."

"Fadi's a doctor." Layla sat back down next to Rain.

"Well," he said, glancing at his toes in what appeared to be an attempt at humility, "medical resident at the moment." However, the way he rocked back and forth on his heels with his chest swelling indicated he was proud of his accomplishments.

"Where do you know Layla from?" Allie bit her lip, no doubt hiding her own ornery grin.

"My mother and her aunt are best friends. I think they might be up to some scheming where we're concerned. Not that I mind." He glanced at Layla, the flush in his cheeks extending to meet the one rising up his neck. "It's not often such a lovely young lady comes to town."

"And you get first dibs. Aren't you the lucky guy?" Rain wiggled her eyebrows.

Ugh! Rain and her big mouth. Layla twisted toward Fadi, purposely elbowing Rain in the process. Two could play at this game. "Fadi, why don't you tell Rain and Allie about that fascinating new laser procedure you explained to me?" The story took a good ten minutes and had nearly put Layla to sleep right over her dinner plate last week. She squelched her own chuckle.

A month ago, she might have found Fadi a decent match. He was a gentle man, intelligent, with a good career. If he had been willing to wait a few years, she might have considered him. But how could any guy compare to Mo?

She focused on his gang of ODU buddies over in a corner. Might Mo show up tonight? Layla pictured his rumpled silken curls and muscular physique. How could roly-poly Fadi with his prickly crew cut ever live up to that? While Fadi droned on with his dry lecture about subcutaneous something or another, she recalled Mo's wit, the way he had her crying with laughter over the phone.

Rain poked her and raised her eyebrows. For once Layla felt no compassion. Rain had brought this on herself.

Mid-lecture she cut him off. "Fadi, this is so fascinating. I know Rain and Allie want to hear more, but if you'll excuse me, I need to use the ladies room."

She ignored Rain's little high pitched, "Uh!"

"Sure, Layla. I'll be right here when you get back." Fadi patted the arm of the couch where he had settled next to Rain at some point during his medical tirade.

Layla snickered as she headed towards the bathroom. When she dreamed of entering normal American society, she never imagined she would turn so feisty. Her impish friend Aisha would approve. Too bad the girl wasn't here to witness Layla's antics. She went to the rest room and managed to waste several minutes brushing her hair and freshening her makeup. Makeup was a must at Lebanese parties. Plenty of it.

She thickened the black lines around her eyes and smoothed on bright red lipstick. Holding the tube beside her mouth she examined her reflection more closely. So much artifice in her life. The scripted conversations. The false smiles. No wonder Allie tired of her church. They could both learn a lesson from Rain with her clean, natural face and blunt speech. Maybe if she just told Fadi she wasn't interested, she wouldn't be hiding in the bathroom right now.

When she finally returned to the sitting area, she had a plan in place.

"Oh!" Layla feigned excitement. "Will you listen to that music?" Layla pointed to the air and bobbed her head in time. "Fadi, let's teach these girls the *Dabke*."

That would shut him up for a while.

"The *Dabke*?" Allie sounded frightened. No doubt slightly scarred from the graphic details of the laser surgery.

"Don't worry." Fadi stood and stretched. Looked like he nearly put himself to sleep as well. "You'll love it. *Dabke* literally means stamping of the feet. It is the most popular folkdance in a number of Arabic countries including Lebanon, Iraq, Jordan, Palestine, and Syria. It's performed in a line or circle, generally at weddings and other celebratory gatherings. The leader should be like a tree. He holds his arms proud and upright like the trunk."

Goodness, the man could make anything boring.

Layla steered Allie towards the dance floor. "Why don't we just demonstrate?"

Rain trailed after them at a jog with eyes wide and desperate. The girls joined arms and shared a private giggle when Fadi raised his hands proud and strong like a tree.

"Okay," Rain whispered. "Enough. You win. No matchmaking with this guy. We'll find you someone else."

They all followed Fadi through the rhythmic kicks and stomps of the repetitive dance. After a few rounds Layla slipped away again, but Rain and Allie seemed to be having too much fun to stop.

Layla thrilled to see her friends enjoying the party. She leaned against the textured stucco wall and surveyed the room filled with a rainbow of colorful, glimmering Middle Easterners. Even if she nursed her own doubts, she wished to share the beauty that existed in her culture.

A familiar chuckle met Layla's ears. She turned and saw Mo with the group of ODU students in the far corner.

"Layla," one of the other guys shouted.

She smiled and waved, attempting to include Mo, but his face tightened into a steely expression, and he turned away without acknowledging her.

Tears stung Layla's eyes. She gasped as pain sliced through her like a knife to the gut. Grabbing Rain and Allie out of the bouncing throng, she dragged them, still laughing and dancing, toward the backdoor. For just one moment she wished that she wore her emotions on the surface as these American girls did.

Outside, Allie stopped and focused on Layla's face. "What's

wrong, sweetie?"

Where should Layla start? She'd barely mentioned Mo to anyone. "Remember that guy who was staring at me last week?"

"Mo? The hottie from the cafeteria? Yum! Is he here? That's more like it. Let's go find him." Rain grabbed at Layla's arm.

Layla jerked away. "Settle down. It's not that simple."

She explained the situation the best she could, attempting to give a sense of how much she liked Mo without being melodramatic. After all, they only spent one evening together, and that in a group. But she recounted how after giving her every expectation they would start a relationship, Mo now refused to speak to her.

"Something's wrong." Rain repeated her remark from the cafeteria. "Something's definitely wrong. That guy likes you. I know it."

"Maybe I did something to offend him." Maybe her forward behavior pushed him away.

"You'll never know until you talk to him," Allie said.

Rain shrugged, wiggling to the music again. "Do you want me to say something?"

Layla gaped, horrified. "No. Of course not!"

"Then just talk to him. Open communication is always the best route. Explain how you're feeling. Don't just guess at why he's ignoring you." Rain gave Layla a hug. "You can do this. I have faith in you. Allie and I will be occupied with our new favorite pastime." Rain let the trill fly again.

Layla shook her head as her friends shimmied away. Rain and Allie had no idea how important this guy was to her, but she couldn't blame them. Layla had done her best to keep it a secret, to hide her feelings even from herself. She should talk to Mo.

She should.

He had no right to treat her this way. Who did he think he was, to trample all over her emotions and try to get away with it?

Indignation rose hot within her, and she marched over to Mo and his buddies. She grabbed him by the elbow and swung him around to face her. "I need to speak with you."

"Ohh," their mutual friend Salaam said. "Mo's in trou-ble."

"Shut up, Salaam," Layla snapped, surprising even herself. Rain and Allie were rubbing off on her. She pulled Mo outside and behind a secluded grove of trees in the backyard. Leaves fluttered overhead. "So what's going on? You've been avoiding me."

Mo looked at the leaves. "Nothing. I don't know what you're making such a fuss about."

"Call me stupid, but I thought something happened between us. Walking alone with a man is not 'nothing' to me. You know that. It was a very special evening. We talked until midnight. And what about the calls? The texts? That was nothing to you?"

"We took a stroll, Layla. Everyone could see us. It was no big deal." Mo directed his words to the tree trunk behind her.

Layla took his face in her hands, shocked by the sparks that flew between them. "Look at me. Look me in the eye and tell me it's nothing."

Mo didn't utter a word, but Layla saw the truth displayed across his face. Mo didn't just like her. If he weren't acting so strangely Layla would swear that...he was in love with her.

Pain flashed through his eyes, and he tore his face from her hands. "You don't understand, Layla. I care about you, I do, but I can't do this. My life is complicated."

She struggled to find her breath. He cared about her. He admitted it. So why did a wave of hopelessness wash over her? "What's so complicated? Explain it to me. We can work it out."

Mo took her hand in his and kissed her palm, sending warm shivers up her arm. He closed it and held on for a moment. "No. No we can't."

Layla felt as if her heart reached out and wrapped around Mo's. They were linked. For better or worse, she and Mo shared something special. Nonetheless, he dropped her hand and walked away. She felt the tenuous thread between them stretch. It hurt, but it didn't break.

"Is there someone else?" she called after him.

"Not exactly," he whispered over his shoulder.

What on earth was wrong with Mo? He was perfect for her. Tailor made. She couldn't ask for better.

He strode with determination back to his buddies, then it hit her.

Wait. Not exactly someone else? His life was complicated? *Is Mo a terrorist?*

The warm tingles of a moment earlier turned to icy fear.

Uncle's voice broke into her thoughts. "Who was that boy you were talking to?"

She flinched. "An old friend from Detroit."

"I don't like him. If he touches you again, I'll shoot him." Uncle frowned in Mo's direction.

Layla attempted a laugh, thankful for her uncle's support, but she felt no joy. "You would never." She looped her arm through his.

He grunted. "I might."

"You're all talk."

"Yes, but I do love you, and I will protect you. I've heard rumors about this boy. Mo, isn't it? He's not the good Muslim he appears to be." Uncle led her across the crackling grass of the backyard and toward the house.

Did he suspect as well? Better change the subject. "Don't worry, Uncle. He doesn't like me that way."

"I hope not."

Layla couldn't disagree more. She kept her mouth closed despite her weeping heart. Nothing else mattered in that moment. Not school. Not family. Not anything. All that mattered was Mo, and he had walked away.

SEVENTEEN

Allie rested cross-legged on her bed Saturday evening recalling the bizarre day. Her laptop sat in front of her on the quilted pastel comforter with several windows open to websites she had been studying. She reflected over the long list of things that made her uncomfortable at Rain's equinox festival. The telltale sweet-smelling smoke wafting through the place. Pagan symbols. Same-sex couples draped across one another. The strange groans emanating from the tents Rain hurried them past. Allie didn't even want to picture what went on in those.

Pagan religions took great stock in sex as worship. Allie's new Message version of the Bible replaced the word pagan with the phrase "sex and religion." Their "sex and religion" shrine it would say, or gods, or poles. Orgies and murder as worship? No wonder God judged the pagans in the Old Testament so severely. Something about the blunt phrasing kept her turning pages. She read more scriptures since purchasing her Message that afternoon than she had in years.

And to think that this morning, Allie strolled through a festival not completely unlike those pagan rituals mentioned in the Bible. Okay, to be fair, she spied nothing resembling child sacrifice. Thank goodness.

Despite all that, Allie had to admit she also saw something at the festival that touched her. The whole place exuded such an earthy, organic feel—girls in soft, loose clothing and bare feet, in touch with the nature around them—all the wonders of creation. Hair flowed free, faces glowed with wholesome beauty as God intended. No heels, no awful pantyhose.

And the dance.

The dance at that place ministered to something deep in her spirit. The way the Native Americans stomped and spun their feet into the dirt called out to her. When she spoke to the principal performer afterward, she discovered many members in their troupe were Christian believers, followers of the Great Spirit, who used their gifts to minister light into dark places like the multi-faith equinox festival.

At least she had gone to the festival prayed up, and she did indeed sense a shield of protection around her. Layla's devotion to prayer challenged Allie to strengthen her own faith. She couldn't stop thinking about what Rain said last week either.

Imagining God.

Meeting with him face to face. Oh, how Allie longed to do such a thing. Coming home had been so hard. Facing so many issues from her past. Now Andy. Maybe she did need to deal with him once and for all. She felt out of balance deep inside. More than anything she wanted to get back into sync so that she could move on with her life. Understand God's plan for her future.

Maybe this was exactly what she needed. A meeting with God as Rain suggested. Allie didn't want to randomly grab concepts from other cultures and religions and water down her own beliefs. Yet she wondered if others might sometimes stumble upon truths in their searching that could illuminate concepts found in God's Word. Rain's child-like faith led her to this place.

Allie picked up the laptop. She had just finished searching the term "imagine" combined with words like Bible and Christianity on Google. Again, she read over the page from the ministry that specialized in communing with God. A bright blue logo with a wispy white dove ran across the top. It said the Hebrew word *hagah*, translated in most English versions of the Bible as meditate, could also mean imagine. The website didn't seem New Age at all. In fact, the principles were grounded systematically in scripture after scripture.

It made sense, meditating on his word day and night, meditating on God's works and ways, his wonders. Seeking

God's face. Where else might one seek God, but in his kingdom that dwelled deep within? Allie always struggled with her unruly thoughts and imagination. Maybe the point wasn't to shut them off, but rather to engage them in encountering God.

Why had Allie never known?

All these years she longed to grow closer to God. All these years something held her back. Something in her left-brained, word oriented church hadn't computed. Only when she danced did she sense his presence. She desired truth in the inmost parts as the Psalms described. David was a worshipper, a musician, a writer. He understood. She needed a deep, personal, and experiential encounter with God.

Show me your face. Open the eyes of my heart. The words of scripture and song took on new meaning.

Allie decided not to wait one moment longer. Pressing her knees to the carpet beside her bed, she rested her bottom on the floor next to her feet. She folded her hands against the mattress and laid her face upon them. She hummed through a few worship melodies, picturing the words in her mind. Exhaling all her worries and doubts. Inhaling the very presence of God. She imagined meeting with Jesus on a mountaintop at sunset. He held out his hand as she approached. In her mind's eye he wore jeans and a white T-shirt with brown leather flip-flops.

"I've been waiting for you," he said. "What took you so long?"

She ran into his arms and, as he crushed her to his chest, began to weep. "I didn't know."

He wiped the tears from her eyes with his fingers, rough from his carpentry work. They smelled of wood and fresh air. She pictured her hair flowing free in the wind. Not held tight in its normal bun. He pushed it from her face. "You're here now."

She sat with Jesus. Talked with him. Danced with him. She chose not to analyze, but to let the thoughts, images, and impressions flow free, flow like rivers of water from her spirit. God had been there speaking all along. She simply never stopped to listen.

Afterward she wondered if it had just been her own fanciful daydreaming, but she knew that wasn't possible. Daydreaming never left her soothed to the core of her being, as if an oil of anointing poured over her heart. Jesus said much that sounded familiar, yet much that surprised her and could not have come from her own mind, including a simple yet significant statement as she fussed at him about her need for a spouse.

Take another look at Andy.

Boy, did that hush her up quick.

Layla awoke to bright golden sunshine streaming in her window from high in the sky. She rolled over and picked up her clock. Eleven o'clock. Auntie rarely let her sleep this late. She must have been grumpier than she realized last night. Around this time a week ago she had been listening to the sermon at Allie's church. Could it be possible that only seven days had passed? So much had happened.

Doubts had flown through her head at a frenzied pace ever since that morning at church.

Then the party.

The suspicions about Mo.

It was all too much.

She pulled on jeans with a long sleeved T-shirt and headed for the living room, her mind still muddled with sleep.

Auntie rushed toward her in the hallway, waving her hands as she came. "Layla, we have guests. Go fix up."

Too sleepy to question, Layla turned back to her room. Unexpected guests popping in night and day was one of the hazards of living in a Middle Eastern home. Layla always swore she'd make calling cards clearly displaying visiting hours once she had a house of her own. Not amused, her mother threatened to disown her over the idea.

She added her thin denim veil and a few strokes of eyeliner and lipstick before heading back out. Why hadn't she thought to ask who had come? What if it was Fadi again? The man had a medical degree. Surely he was intelligent enough to take a hint.

As she rounded the corner and passed through the archway,

she suddenly longed for Fadi's roly-poly face. In front of her, leaning against the fireplace and feigning a nonchalant post, stood a long-haired contender for an Antonio Banderas look-alike contest. Only his broad nose gave the man away as Middle Eastern. He angled his head toward her with a seductive grin. *Ya'allah!* This was not how she intended to start her day.

"This must be Layla." He sauntered across the modern art throw rug in her direction, gushing in Arabic. "My love, you are every bit as beautiful as your charming aunt described."

Seriously? Layla switched to English. "And you are? Don't tell me...Zorro."

Uncle snorted in a laugh.

Layla bit her lip. Where did that come from? Some combination of her sleep-clouded brain and Rain's influence no doubt.

Her comment threw the preening player off his game. He tilted his head in confusion, stroking his waving hair, heavy with gel.

Two elderly guests fidgeted on the couch, as perplexed as the young man.

"*Afwan?*" *I'm sorry,* he said, shifting the conversation back to Arabic with a broad, toothy smile.

Uncle translated the joke, and they all laughed.

"Ah," the young man said, charm still spewing. "Zorro, funny. I get that a lot." He struck a debonair stance and slashed an imaginary sword.

Auntie straightened a doily on the sofa arm with a touch of violence. No doubt she'd prefer to straighten Layla's attitude. "Layla, this is Bassam. Nephew of our dear friends Ali and Samia. He's visiting the states from Lebanon."

Just as Layla suspected. Fatima had a name for such men. F.O.B.

Fresh off the boat, and no doubt in search of a green card. Like most of them, he hadn't even bothered to learn English. Well, he could look elsewhere for his ticket to America.

He crossed the remaining steps to her and took her hand. Leaning over it, he kissed her fingers. "*Enchanté, mon amour.*"

Auntie drew in a breath but didn't say a word. She must be growing desperate after hearing about Layla with Mo at the party.

Touches were rarely allowed between unrelated men and women in the Muslim culture. But this guy was pulling out all the stops. Maybe he thought if he couldn't speak English, he'd wow her with his impression of a European dandy and prove himself progressive. No doubt the man was a hot commodity in some hillside village. Perhaps he could have his goats and chickens shipped to America and impress her further.

Layla turned to Auntie and frowned.

What was the woman thinking? Even if Layla could be swayed by the man's good looks and slick manners, she was years away from settling for a green card marriage to some guy who couldn't even speak the language. Yes, she wanted a career, but that didn't mean she wanted to support a freeloader to ensure her place in the work force. She had barely escaped a barrage of such proposals in Lebanon, but in the end, her grandfather respected her desire to find a husband reared in America.

"Come join us for brunch, Layla. I was just about to get you from your studying," her aunt said.

Studying? Nice one. Now it all made sense. Auntie let her sleep late to keep her from slipping out of the house before Antonio arrived. Only Auntie had miscalculated.

"Oh, I can't. I'm meeting friends at the university. Remember?" If Auntie could be flexible with her treatment of the truth, why couldn't Layla? She was not about to subject herself to another fix-up meal.

The old lady on the couch adjusted her pantyhose and coughed into the air. The man fidgeted and scratched his rear. Layla surmised the relatives were barely off the boat themselves.

Bassam did a little step, shifting from foot to foot in front of her and holding out his palms. Dance move? Soccer block? Layla wasn't quite sure.

"Please, *jolie*, stay and do me the honor. I was so looking forward to spending time with you." He floated between French and Arabic now, as so many cultured Lebanese people did. Yet something about his clothes shouted the manners were an affectation. Perhaps it was the misspelling on his embellished T-shirt.

Adidias.

"You know how it is with these busy American lives. I'm sure you'll understand once you've been here awhile. Commitments, commitments, commitments. Maybe we can schedule something for another time. Good-bye everyone. Peace be upon you. Such a pleasure to meet you all." Layla waved, grabbing up her purse from the armoire and dashing out the door before they could catch her.

That may have been a little rude by Middle Eastern standards, but surprising a young woman at 11 a.m. on a Sunday morning with an Antonio Banderas wannabe was more than a little rude by American standards.

Layla breathed a sigh of relief as she slammed the car door and started the engine.

EIGHTEEN

The silence was deafening.

Andy made several attempts at small talk only to be met by Allie's monosyllabic answers as they drove in his windy, open Jeep toward the beach. She sat beside him in her black bathing suit cover-up with her arms crossed tight over her chest. There was no turning back now. He had finally won his long-awaited date, but Allie didn't intend to allow him any pleasure from the victory.

He turned on the radio and grimaced at the slow worship music. That wouldn't help his cause. He needed to convince Allie the old Andy no longer existed. Today he wore trendy board shorts with his white shirt unbuttoned over top. Not only did the outfit show off his hard-earned physique, he never would have been caught dead in it during high school. If only his hair would grow out a little quicker. All these years of wearing it to Navy regulation length, he never realized it would wave into such a roguish style.

He glanced around the front seat and let out a sigh of relief. One of his youth group kids had left a heavy metal *Red* CD in the console. He didn't love it, but he could tolerate it, especially for Allie.

He popped the disc in the player. Her eyebrows rose in surprise, but she continued staring straight ahead.

"So I guess you've heard how well the youth are doing." Andy figured that should be safe territory. Allie's youngest sister, Sarah, still attended the group.

"No."

"We're growing really fast." He shouted over the music and the wind. "The kids have been doing a great job reaching out to their friends."

She tilted her head. At least it was something. "Oh...ah... good."

Hadn't the girl spent the last eight years touring the globe as a missionary? He expected more than *ah...good.* "We've been having Christian rock bands in once a month, and we're thinking about building a skate park out back. There's plenty of room."

"Hmm..." She shook herself out of her funk. "Actually, that's really good, Andy. The teens need that. I think a skate park would be a huge hit."

"At least with the boys, and we figure the girls will come to watch."

"Yeah."

No! Not another one syllable answer. Andy made a lame attempt at a joke. "It should be good job security for me." What a dumb thing to say.

Allie's hands tightened into annoyed fists. "I wouldn't worry about that. The church seems to be doing just fine."

"Sure, with our parents' generation. The youth group had all but dried up before I got there, though."

"No wonder."

Three whole syllables. Did that count as an improvement? "Well, do you want it to change or not? You're not making much sense, Allie."

"Then I'll shut up."

And she did.

Andy cranked up the *Red* CD and gripped the steering wheel till his knuckles turned white. The music wasn't as bad as he remembered. The band incorporated some classical string sections, and they mixed in a wonderful worship song about being lost in God with their heavier pieces.

God. Yeah, he should focus on God and get his mind off the grumpy, enticing woman beside him.

Leading the youth group gave him a new perspective on

God. He had spent his whole life trying to please his elders and authorities, trying to live up to their standards while most of his friends fell away from the Lord. Now that he held the position of authority, he realized those standards never did make sense or accomplish a single thing in the first place. He wanted to reach kids, to bring them to Christ. He could never force them to live up to a bunch of phony rules and risk turning them away. The only standards he would present to them would be God's standards, never the archaic expectations others had thrust on him.

Andy drove the rest of the way to the beach, parked, and pulled the surfboards from the back of his Jeep. Allie slammed her door and fell into step beside him. He wanted to shake the girl.

The sun broiled overhead. Things would be better once they got in the water. They laid their stuff down on the beach and stripped off their outerwear. Allie wore little black swim shorts with a powder pink surfer's rash guard T-shirt. It showed off the subtle curves of her dancer's body, sleek like a racehorse. Glistening blond hair tumbled from that perfectly messy up-do of hers, whipped to a frenzy by the wind in the Jeep. If it hadn't been for the scowl on her face, Andy would have sworn she was an angel.

They scooped the boards under their arms and jogged past the breakers.

"Do you remember much?" He left his own board bobbing on the waves.

"It's like riding a bike, right?"

"Not exactly. You need to get a feel for the rhythm and flow. Remember how I taught you to be one with the surf. Here, I'll help you on."

Andy reached around both sides of her from behind to steady her board. For a moment, there she stood, in his arms, just like he dreamed all these years. His breathing grew raspy as he took in the watermelon scent of her shiny hair. He wanted so badly to sneak a kiss, right on the shadowy hollow of her neck.

The next thing he knew, Allie slipped underwater and

emerged like a sea nymph on the other side of the board. Far outside his grasp.

"I can get on by myself. Thanks."

Take another look at Andy. Well, here she was, chest deep in the rolling ocean, up close and personal as Andy recounted the basics of surfing. At least she hadn't run away, no matter how tempting it had been. She would face this thing. Allie wiped the salty water from her eyes and took another hard look at him, precisely as instructed.

She observed Andy's boy-next-door features, covered with a scruff of beard from lack of shaving. Since when did Andy neglect to shave? On a Sunday of all days? Wasn't there some eleventh commandment about that? Her body's shivering reaction to his nearness left her outraged. For a moment, she had wondered if he would sweep her around and kiss her, but she ducked away before she could find out. Dipping beneath the cool water had straightened her thinking.

She slid onto the board, sat up, and paddled lazily in the water, waiting for the perfect swell. Andy climbed on his board beside her.

Behind him stretched the rock pier where they once climbed late at night so many years ago. Their relationship was strewn with rocky boulders, but might it be worth the effort? Here in the open expanse, she experienced none of the sensations that tangled him to that awful church. She almost wished she could. They were more comforting than these confusing tingles and shivers.

The first good wave of the day rolled in, and they both caught it. Allie had forgotten the elemental force of the ocean, the pure bliss of being swept away in its majestic flow. Sort of like God. She could get lost in the swells of the sea.

They both rode to shore. Allie laughed and squealed as her board burrowed into the sand and she skipped off. Andy caught her around the waist and swooped her in a circle, setting her down safe on the ground.

"That was awesome!" He gave her a high five.

"See, I told you. Like riding a bike. I never forgot." Allie tugged her shirt back over her belly and pushed some flyaway strands of hair from her face.

Andy caught the strands on the other side, his hand lingering against her cheek. "Neither did I," he said with so much meaning.

"Come on. I'll race you." Allie dashed back out into the surf. She wasn't ready to deal with Andy's romantic advances, but she did miss him. She had forgotten how much fun he could be.

Floating on her surfboard once again she couldn't resist teasing. "So what was that awful racket in your car?"

"The music? I thought you'd like it." Andy's smile faded.

"I would have liked the worship music just fine, if anyone but *you* had turned it on," Allie said with a sassy snap of her head.

"So, it was a good move then."

"What, cranking up a few tunes by a cross-over grunge band hailing from Nashville Tennessee whose fusion of alternative metal and classical styling took the music world by storm in 2006, earning them a Grammy Gospel nomination for their debut album *End of Silence?*" Allie batted her eyelashes in feigned innocence.

Andy splashed her. "You brat. You knew who they were."

Allie cracked a smile.

"So I did good?" Andy looked like a puppy begging for attention.

"You did good." She splashed him back.

The tension between them gone, Allie and Andy surfed, played, and joked the afternoon away, just like the old days.

Finally exhausted, they laid their boards side by side in the gritty sand. Allie watched as Andy took a few deep breaths and stretched his arms overhead, working the tension out of his back.

Why did he have to look so darn good?

Allie pulled off her rash guard and wrung out the excess water. As she went to slip it back over her top, Andy snatched it from her hand and tossed it on her board. His arms threaded through hers and eased her toward him.

Allie's limbs turned to warm syrup at his touch. Her knees went limp and fluid, but Andy caught her and crushed her body to his, tangling his fingers through her hair and tipping back her head in the process. His mouth captured hers, searching and probing in a searing, heart-stopping kiss.

This is not the same old Andy was the last thing to pass through Allie's mind before all thoughts melted to a haze. Time stopped. The ocean faded. Nothing existed except his mouth on hers, his body pressed against her, harsh ridges to soft curves.

He pulled back to gaze at her. "Will you give me another chance? Please?"

"How can I resist?" Breathiness filled Allie's voice. She gave him a little peck on the lips, and settled her head against his strong shoulder.

How on earth could something she had steeled her heart against feel so incredibly right? Here she stood in the arms of the one man she vowed never to return to. Yet she couldn't bear to leave.

Oh, she was really going to regret this.

NINETEEN

Rain sat quietly at the lunch table on Tuesday, alone, waiting for Layla and Allie to arrive. The din of the dining hall scratched against her nerves. Students clattered trays on the metal rails, dropped dishes, squealed, hollered. Too many noises. Too many smells. Sauces, roasting meats, fried breading, sugary cakes all competed for dominance in her nostrils. None of them appealing.

At least she was getting the hang of this on-time thing, except the one instance that mattered most. No, being prompt to the cafeteria would do nothing to solve the life-shattering problem Rain faced this day. Should she tell Allie and Layla? She didn't have much choice. She had to tell someone. Her parents were deep in the recesses of the African rainforests. She shouldn't try to deal with this alone, but she couldn't tell James. At least not yet.

"OMG, will you look at this." Allie sat across from her.

"Rain, on time? Has the apocalypse come?" Layla slid in beside Allie.

"Maybe we should call a doctor." Allie took a closer look at Rain. "Hey, what's up? Is something wrong for real?"

Rain felt the tears puddle in her eyes. Doctors. Apocalypse. No use holding back. She knew they would get the truth out of her soon enough. "I'm pregnant."

Layla and Allie stared at her for a moment, managing to keep their mouths from gaping, then at each other and back to her again.

"I'm sorry," Layla said.

What else could she say? Rain could only imagine what went

through Layla's mind. In her culture an unwed pregnancy could lead to tragedy. But was Rain's situation any less tragic?

"So, I take it you don't want the baby," Allie said. "I would have thought since you and James were such a steady couple..."

"That's just it," Rain shouted, tears streaming now. "I do want this baby. I love it already. It's James. James doesn't want children. Ever."

"I'm sorry," Layla said again, skipping like a scratched CD.

"Are you sure?" Allie reached across the table and laid her hand on Rain's arm.

"Very. The whole subject drives him to a fury. I'm afraid he'll think I did this on purpose. I'm afraid he'll leave me."

"He sounds like a great guy from everything you've told us. I don't think he'd do that," Allie said.

"Over anything else, no. Over this...he might." Rain folded her arms atop the table and buried her head.

"Were you careful?" Layla asked.

"I've been on the pill since we started dating." Rain's words filtered through her shielding arms. "I didn't miss any. I swear it. He's going to be so mad. What are the odds, like one percent?"

"One percent too many." Allie sat her hand on Rain's folded arms. Rain's fingers emerged from her protective cocoon and latched hold of Allie's.

"So, are you going to..." Layla trailed off.

Rain picked up her head and sniffled. "A few months ago I might have let him convince me to get an abortion, but not now. Not after all of our conversations. I talked to God about it too."

"What did...he say?" Allie asked.

"Well, he was kind of quiet, but I saw such sadness in his eyes. I could never do it. Boy, am I glad I read about all those cattle he owns. If James runs out on me, I might need him to sell a few for rent."

Confused, Layla said, "Cattle...rent...huh?"

"Never mind. Off topic." Rain shook away her random thoughts. She had been reading too much of the Bible for her own good lately. "The point is...what am I going to do?"

"We'll help you." Layla placed her hand atop Rain and Allie's joined ones. They looked oddly poignant with their varying shades: Allie's in a light golden-tan, Layla's with its medium olive tint, and Rain's café au lait tone.

"And there are churches and organizations who offer assistance," Allie said. "Especially if you decide to go the adoption route."

"I hadn't thought that far. But I'm twenty-five, and I want children. I want James's child."

"Oh, Rain, this is so hard." Allie bit her lip.

"I can't even imagine," Layla said.

"I know." Rain wiped her eyes and sought to compose herself. "Be thankful you'll never have to deal with anything like this, Layla. With freedom comes responsibility. Our liberated Western lives aren't all they're cracked up to be."

"Way too much drama." Allie nodded. "When are you going to tell him?"

"I don't know. I keep going back and forth. The sooner I tell him, the sooner I could lose him, but the longer I wait, the angrier he'll be." Rain pushed her spaghetti around on the plate. She picked up a forkful but then laid it back down as her stomach churned.

"There must be some way you can tell him without sending him off the deep end," Layla said.

"If so, I have no idea what it is. I suppose I should try to find something to be thankful for." Rain thought hard. "At least I have you guys. Right? I think James is hiding some old wounds that will need to heal before he's ready to deal with this."

"More drama." Allie smiled her reassurance.

"Drama! Allie, your date. We didn't even ask how it went." Rain happily deflected to a new subject. "How is the oh-so-cute Andy?"

Allie turned an endearing shade of pink. "He's fine, I guess."

"Did he kiss you?" Rain said.

"You really want to hear about kissing right now? Isn't that what got you into this trouble?"

Allie hadn't meant to say that. Her emotions remained a tumbled mess. She glanced at Rain, hoping her regret was apparent in the twist of her lips, but not daring to say another word. She shoved her grilled chicken into her mouth, praying no one would push the issue. The last thing she wanted to talk about was Andy.

"Ouch, Allie." Rain clutched her heart. "That kind of hurt... which is not like you at all...which means..."

Layla picked up the train of thought with a big grin. "She did kiss him. Oh, Allie, what was it like? Was it nice?"

"Way too nice." Allie covered her face with her palms. If only they knew. Her lips tingled at the memory.

"Allie Vargas, the pastor's wife. How adorable is that?" Rain wiggled her brows over watery red eyes.

Now that comment hurt. Rain had no idea. "Ugh. Stop it. Don't remind me. What in the world was I thinking? I let myself get caught up in the moment, but being a pastor's wife at the First Church of the Fuddy Duddy is not what I have planned for my life."

"So why did you go out with him?" Layla asked.

"I don't know. Some people, who shall remain nameless, pressured me into it. But I guess I did miss him."

"How many boyfriends have you had?" Rain observed her pointedly.

"Really...only one. I went on some casual dates, but nothing else ever stuck. For me, dating is a prelude to marriage. If it doesn't look like it's heading that way, I break it off."

Layla sat down her fork and gave Allie her full attention. "Then why did you date Andy so long in high school?"

"I was young and stupid. Everyone else had boyfriends. It kept the other guys away. I guess it was easy." Allie studied her hands. Would they buy that? Did she?

"And do you expect us to believe that the subject of marriage never came up?" Rain asked.

Allie sat for a moment attempting to untangle her thoughts. Tangled. Like Andy's arms tangled through hers, like his fingers tangled in her hair. Tangled, like her feelings for him and her feelings for his horrible church. "He wanted to marry me," Allie whispered. "He proposed at prom. I didn't know what to do. I just took the ring."

She stopped and swallowed down the pain. "We were supposed to go to college together. But I felt so trapped, so strangled. The band constricted around my finger like a tiny snake. On the night of graduation, I gave it back. I made a few phone calls and took a bus to Dallas to audition the very next day."

"Oh, Allie." Layla pressed her hand to her lips. "You do love him."

"I do not," Allie whispered.

"Are you sure?" Rain asked.

Was she? It didn't matter. This thing with Andy was a mistake. God told her to take another look. That's all he said. Allie let go of her pride, and she did it. She looked, hard, and she did not like what she saw.

As if a switch flipped, her hollow sadness turned to hot anger. "He's such a phony. He hasn't changed. Sure, he's playing the role of the too-cool youth leader right now, but that's just job insurance. He wants me to think he's different so that I'll take him back. Why would I love a guy like that?"

Yeah, Allie, why do you?

Rain and Layla said nothing.

"So what if his kisses melt me. So what if my mind gets all fuzzy. What's that? It's hormones. I'm not going to let some stupid physical reaction to a guy run my life. I've wasted too much time on Andy Vargas. I need to get serious and start looking for the right kind of guy."

If only Allie could convince herself. But what if those reactions pointed to something more? To something going on deep in her heart that she hadn't yet addressed? It was her turn to deflect. "Anything new with Mo?"

Mo. So unfair. Layla's eyes dropped to her half-eaten lunch. Why did Allie have to bring up Mo? Wasn't it bad enough he had torn Layla's heart to pieces and left it bleeding in her chest? She scanned the dining hall, full to the brim with college kids at rectangular tables. A deep voice shouted across the room. But it was not the voice she longed to hear. Mo was nowhere to be found. "It's not going to work out."

"Are you sure?" Rain said.

"I didn't want to bring it up at the party, but I'm worried about him." Layla wrung her hands upon the table.

"Why?" Allie said.

"I've been thinking about this for days...and it's the only thing that makes sense." Layla leaned into the center of the table. Her eyes darted about before she spoke. She wouldn't want the wrong ears to overhear, but she couldn't bear this burden alone. "I'm afraid he's involved in terrorist activities."

Rain and Allie both gaped, and their eyes grew huge. Layla could hardly blame them.

Allie reached for Layla's hand. "That's awful."

"He looks so normal."

"Maybe you misunderstood."

"How could he?"

Their comments swirled around Layla, the same thoughts that spun through her mind all week. "I don't know. Maybe I'm wrong. Maybe I just don't want to accept that he's rejecting me. I've never felt this way about a guy before. I thought I'd never get a chance to choose a man for myself. Then Mo came along."

Her voice caught in her throat, but she pushed past. "He made my heart sing. I felt like myself with him. I felt almost... free. And he's gone already. I don't know what to do. I'm not sure how to keep living."

A deep guttural moan escaped her lips, but Layla managed to hold back the tears. No point in crying. It wouldn't solve a thing. "It's so ridiculous. There's no logic, no fact behind it, but

I can't shake this sense of hopelessness."

Allie wrapped an arm around Layla's shoulders. "You poor baby. I had no idea how important this was to you. And here we danced off that night. I'm so sorry. If Mo's the kind of guy who can make you feel this way, then you must be wrong. It must be something else, Layla. You can't give up. You have to talk to him."

"I tried to talk to him. At first he turned hard and cold. Then I saw it. I saw it with my own eyes. He loves me. I know he does, but he's confused. Something powerful is holding him back. It has to be the radicals. You don't understand how they get in your head. They convince you violence is Allah's will. They make it seem so noble, so worthy. They promise paradise for you and your whole family."

Dishes clanked in the background, as if life went on as usual. Layla stopped to catch her breath. "We don't have eternal guarantees in Islam—other than the martyrs. Think about it. If someone really buys into their propaganda, how could they say no? How could any decent guy turn his back on God and family? I know they're lying. You know they're lying. But what if Mo believes it? They take the *Qur'an* and twist it for their own purposes."

At least that's what Layla had been taught. She didn't want to blame the atrocities of terrorism on her religion, yet the *Qur'an* contained much about Holy War and killing infidels. It all depended on your interpretation. A good guy like Mo could be led astray.

"Wow, that's way out of my league," Rain said. "I have no idea what to tell you."

"Maybe we should pray about this." Allie gave Layla's shoulder a squeeze.

Pray to Allah that Mo would lose his desire to spread Islam through violence? That would never work. Allah's will had been set long ago. Their idea of prayer was obviously very different from hers. "You guys pray for me. I'm too confused," was all she said.

"So, are we going to try this new church together this week

or what?" Allie asked.

No matter where this conversation led, somebody got hurt.

"I can't," Layla said. She was done talking. She didn't even want to explain.

Rain grimaced. "I don't want to do anything else to make James mad right now, Allie. I really shouldn't."

"Gee, thanks guys," Allie said. "I guess it's Fuddy Duddy Chapel for me."

Layla understood Allie's frustration. More than ever before, going through the motions of religion exhausted her. Life exhausted her. Where could she go from here?

TWENTY

Rain rehearsed her speech in the bathroom mirror for the tenth time. She splashed cool water on her face before trudging into the living area of their studio apartment. Taking a moment, she straightened a stack of newspapers on the coffee table. She had prayed the entire week, but all she sensed God saying was, *I'm here*. What was that supposed to mean? It didn't bode well.

James sat on the couch watching the evening news. Now that Rain had gathered her resolve, she didn't want to wait any longer. "Sweetie, can you turn that off? I need to talk to you about something important."

James clicked the remote and scanned her head to toe. A hard gleam entered his eye, and his lips tightened into a scowl. "I'm not going to like this, am I?"

His perceptiveness unnerved her. James had an uncanny way of sizing people up. He used it for his benefit, always able to persuade, always able to get his way. Rain steeled her heart against his tactics. Too much was at stake. This time, she couldn't let him win.

Her mind scrambled to recall her speech, but instead she blurted out the words. "I'm pregnant."

"You're...pregnant. Like with a...baby."

He stood up, pulled at his dreadlocks, and stormed across the room. Then he turned and smiled with murder in his eyes. "See, I know that isn't what you just said. I know you wouldn't go and do the one thing I made you promise never to do. My girl wouldn't do that..." He turned and swiped the clutter from the counter, sending it to the floor with a crash, "...to me!" James shouted the last words.

Rain froze. In all these years, she had never seen James turn violent. He was chill as ice. Too laid back for emotional displays. She expected mocking, coercion, frustration, never this. "I didn't mean...I was taking the pill. What can I...it was a..." Mistake? No, Rain couldn't say that. "It was an accident. It was an accident, James."

"Well, thank that new God of yours that these accidents are easily remedied." He stomped toward her.

Rain feared he would attempt to remedy the situation right here, right now. "No, James. I won't kill our baby. I can't do it." "You can, and you will." James hurled an ugly insulting curse at Rain.

Who was this man?

"You are my woman, this is our problem, and you will do as I say. I will not be a father. I'm sick of you calling the shots. I'm sick of you controlling me. You can't control me. You can't make me be something I won't." The next stream of curses cut even deeper.

Rain began to shiver. She backed up to the couch and fell onto it as her knees buckled. What was he talking about? Rain didn't have a controlling bone in her body. James called all the shots around here. He always had, with his oozing charisma. Rain could never tell him no. But this fiend, this angry monster, she could turn down in a heartbeat.

"You did this on purpose." He kicked a hole in the rickety wall. "I knew it. I knew you would try something like this. You scheming, conniving..." He let out a roar.

Despite the furor on his face, Rain spied tears in his eyes. *Oh, James, what did he do to you?*

She took a deep bracing breath. "I know this is hard for you, James. I don't understand what happened to you as a child, but maybe if you'd tell me, maybe if we'd talk about it you could move—"

"This is not about my childhood. This is about our future, our relationship. You betrayed me. How can we follow our dreams with a kid to weigh us down?"

"We'll figure something..."

"No! We will not figure something out because this is not happening. You will go to a clinic, and you will take care of this." James crossed the room and jerked up her chin. "You hear me?"

The muscles in her neck strained against his touch. "James, you're hurting me."

When he looked into her eyes, something snapped. He clasped his head in his hands. "No! I'm just like him. I won't be like him. Don't you see? This is why. This is why I can't do it." James stumbled to the door weeping. "I can't do it, Rain. Please don't make me do it."

James stumbled to his car. He felt in his pocket. No keys. But he wouldn't go crawling back so soon. He couldn't. Rain would give in, she always did. Ever since they met, he could twist her like putty. He pulled himself together and headed toward the park through the twilight.

But what if this time was different? He glimpsed such quiet determination in her eyes. Deep down he always knew she wanted to be a mother. He knew she offered only lip service on this subject. He could convince his woman to give away her last shred of clothing, to stroll through disease-ridden hellholes, but could he convince her to get rid of a child?

What if he couldn't? How dare Rain force fatherhood on him? Even if he left her, which he most certainly planned to do if she dared defy him, would that make him any less of a father? He felt so robbed. How could she take this decision out of his hands? So what if he made love to her? That liar was supposed to be on the pill. Had she been flushing it down the toilet? Rinsing it down the sink? She may as well have ripped his sperm right out of him. She stole a part of him that he could never take back. That was not love. They should make this decision together.

Shaking, James made his way across the grassy field. He

situated himself in a rusty, creaking old swing. His head hung low as he rocked back and forth. Playgrounds had always been a refuge from his father. Now here he was running from Rain.

Someway, somehow, he would make her do this thing. Control. He couldn't live without it.

He was just like him after all.

No, James could never be a father.

He'd wait a few hours and then go pack his bags. He'd stay at one of the frat houses with his pre-med buddies. That would strike fear in Rain's heart for sure. Before long things would be back under control again.

Rain watched the love of her life walk out the door for the second time that evening with a slam, this time with suitcase in hand. She had stood her ground. She should feel proud of herself, but all she felt was numb.

"Oh, God, help me please."

She turned and spied her cell phone sitting on the end table. She picked it up and dialed Allie's number.

"Hello," came the soothing voice.

"Allie, get over here, please. I need you."

"I'll call Layla and head that way."

"Thanks."

A deep peace settled over Rain. She heard the words again. *I'm here.*

Allie supplied ice cream for the three of them to curl into the couch with their matching tubs and oversized spoons like junkies in need of a fix. After a long night of talking, crying, and hugging, Allie packed up to head back to her bungalow.

She took Rain's hands in her own. "Are you sure you'll be okay?"

"For now." Tears still trickled down Rain's cheeks.

Allie wiped them off with her thumb. It was a wonder Rain had any left. But she looked better than when they arrived.

"Don't worry." Layla came up from behind and kissed Rain on the cheek. "We're here for you."

Rain's troubles certainly put Allie's into perspective. She had sat at home in a funk all day. Skipped church again. She didn't want to deal with Andy after ignoring his calls since Tuesday.

Oh sure, a part of her felt incredibly pleased that Rain had chosen life, had chosen to save her baby. Yet another part feared this break-up was all her fault. Rain had been happy enough before she met Allie. Being a Christian was not as easy as it seemed.

All these absolutes.

"Just let us know if you need anything." Maybe she could take up an offering at church. They were supposed to be pro-life. Would they prefer the unwed mother suffer as an example of what not to do, pay for her sin, or had they changed in this area?

"I'll be fine. We'll be fine. You two go get some sleep. It's late."

After another round of hugs, Allie pulled herself away and headed toward her car. She waved to Layla as she drove off.

Was this really the best thing for Rain? Raising a child with no husband. With no income. Would she become another welfare statistic? A future pastor's wife would never ask these questions. At least not the pastor's wife of a church that clung to clichés and easy answers like life-preservers. Allie sighed. Somehow she needed to find the strength and the peace of mind to face another day.

Tomorrow Andy would call again.

Tomorrow Mo would ignore Layla.

Tomorrow Rain would wake up pregnant and alone.

She should stop and pray. Not toss her petitions to the sky, really listen and ask God to lead her. How else could she get to the bottom of these issues still brewing somewhere deep inside of her and move forward with her life? Then Allie thought back to the last time she talked to God. She hadn't been at all pleased with the results.

"Run, Allie. Just run," she said to herself with a smirk. Run

from whom? Andy? Herself?
Or was she running from God?

TWENTY-ONE

Layla waited outside Mo's classroom, leaning against the wall in the dim hallway. She had tossed it over in her mind all week. By Wednesday she had to talk to him—at least she needed to try. So what if she'd been watching him? So what if she'd memorized his schedule? So sue her. She cared about this guy, and more than that she needed him. Layla prided herself on being rational and logical, yet somehow she couldn't shake this sixth sense. Mo represented her last chance at happiness.

His face registered no surprise when he spotted her. "Layla," he said, his voice full of resignation.

"Please, Mo. Please can we talk? I promise not to give you a hard time, but there's something very important I need to speak with you about."

"So talk."

"Not here. Can we go somewhere private?"

Mo quirked an eyebrow at her.

She shouldn't be alone with him. He was right. But this was too important. "Please, Mo. Anywhere. Let's take a walk or a drive or something. I can't let this go."

He blew out a breath. "Okay, Layla. If you insist."

"I do."

They exited the polytechnic building and strolled through campus in uncomfortable silence. Mo led the way past the football field and turned toward the dormitories. He glanced down at her hand several times. She could tell he wished to hold it as he had that day on the beach. They passed Crenshaw Hall and continued through the surrounding neighborhood.

Mo clutched tight to his advanced calculus book.

"How are your classes going?" Layla turned to watch his response, wishing she could somehow slip inside his head and comprehend its inner workings.

"Classes?" he muttered. "Is that why you dragged me out here? To ask about my classes?"

"No." Layla glued her eyes to her toes.

"I'm thinking about switching majors," he added with no preamble.

"Oh." Why did he bring it up? She certainly had no right to weigh in on his life decisions right now. Did he want to prove they had nothing in common? Engineering had been a strong area of commonality for them. Not many people could bond discussing physics and diagrams.

Must he reject even that connection?

Wasn't it enough that he rejected her?

"For a girl who wants to talk, you sure don't have much to say."

Layla's eyes burned with unshed tears. "Mo, why are you being mean to me? I don't believe this is you."

They reached the Elizabeth River with its dock and benches. The area was deserted. Leaves rustled in the breeze, a fluttering canopy that filtered sunshine into a waltz of light and shadow. The river floated by, serene and gentle. If only their relationship could flow so smoothly.

Mo laid his book down on the bench and sat with his head in his hands. "The last thing on earth I wish is to be mean to you, Layla."

"Then why are you?"

"Because I want you, and I can't have you." He shoved back the curls from his brow. "There, I said it. It's killing me. I'm trying to push you away. Don't you get it? Why can't you let this go?"

Layla choked down the pain, sat, and swiveled one blue-jean clad knee onto the bench to face him. "That's not the reason I brought you here."

Mo kept his head down. "Then what is it?"

"I'm worried about these 'complications' in your life. I care about you whether or not we're together. I realize there are people who are very persuasive. People who might confuse you, rally you to a cause you don't quite believe in. Mo, it's not too late to turn back. Others might suspect, but I don't think anyone knows for sure."

Mo's head snapped up. Fear knotted in the pit of his stomach. He looked over the shining water, hoping it might supply some answers. Then back to Layla's mesmerizing features and liquid brown eyes. How did she know? Did she, or was she guessing? "What do you know? Who told you?"

"No one told me. We might not have seen each other in decades, but that was you, the real you on the beach. Your behavior since doesn't add up. This is the only thing that makes sense."

"I don't know what you think, Layla, but I'm not doing anything wrong."

"I understand you believe it's right and honorable. I know how convincing they are. Maybe you have some sin you wish to atone for, but Mo, this is not the way. Violence is never the answer."

Violence?

His mind spun. What in the world was she talking about? He replayed her comments and the answer hit him. Layla thought he was a terrorist. He laughed. He actually laughed. That was pretty funny. Sure he had a brief moment of fanaticism in his late teens, but he would never resort to violence.

"It's not a joke, Mo. This is serious. These people are evil. The *Qur'an* talks about holy war, yes, but not suicide bombs stealing innocent lives, destroying families. There's a difference. A huge difference. There has to be."

"Layla." He wasn't sure how to tell her, but anything was better than being pegged a murderer. "I'm not a terrorist. I'm a...." Mo's eyes darted around the area. They were still alone, only the rustling trees and some random squirrels kept them company. He took Layla's hands in his. "Can I trust you?"

"Of course." Her huge doe eyes pleaded with him beneath her yellow silken veil. She looked like sunshine. A ray of light in his dark world, even as the shadows flitted across her face from the leaves in the wind.

"Layla, I'm not a terrorist. I'm a Christian."

Layla pulled her hands to cover her mouth. She let them slide down as she spoke. "No. Tell me it isn't true. How could you?"

"Don't you ever wonder? Don't you ever doubt? Don't you wish there was more? There is more. So much more."

"A Christian? A Muslim Background Believer? Like Brother Rasheed?"

Hope and wonder filled Mo like a warm river rushing through his veins. Maybe this relationship wasn't as doomed as he feared. "You watch. You know. You get it, don't you?"

Layla stood and walked several paces away, leaning against a tree. "I do and I don't. Mo, how could you turn your back on your family? Your heritage? Do your parents even know?"

"Only my parents and my Christian friends. This is all new to me. My parents were furious. They pretty much stopped practicing Islam when we moved away from my grandparents, but it's still a huge embarrassment. They swore me to secrecy. They think it's a phase that will pass, but Layla, this is no phase. It's the most wonderful thing that's ever happened to me. I don't know where to begin." Warmth filled him again as his mind scanned through the amazing changes in his life and heart.

"Spare me the sermon." She bent down and picked up a rock, tossing it deep into the water.

Layla took out her anger on several more stones, sending them to drown with a plop in the depths along with all her dreams. *A Christian?* A terrorist she could conceivably bring home to her parents, but a Christian? Never. Their last chance flew out of her fingers like the pebbles from her hand.

Mo came up behind her and encircled her waist. He buried his head into her bright yellow veil as if he wanted to pull her in and never let go. Layla settled against his strong length in spite of herself. Anger turned to tears. She swiveled in his arms and whimpered against his chest.

"This is my life now, my dream, my passion," Mo said. "I want to tell people about Jesus. I want to loose Muslims from their chains. Let them fly free, Layla. Let me start with you."

She sniffled against his soft knit polo shirt, clutching it in her hands. He offered everything she ever dreamed of. "I can't," she said in a breathy whisper.

"Maybe someday?"

"Maybe." She wanted to fly free. Oh, she wanted to. How did he know? Of course, he had been here too.

Mo tipped up her head and caught her mouth in a brief kiss sweeter than honey.

She pulled back and pressed her hands against his chest. "No. You were right. This will never work." She picked up his calculus book and handed it to him. Logic and reason prevailed. No hope remained. "Let's go."

At least she'd have one priceless kiss to savor for the rest of her long, tedious life.

She trudged a few steps back towards campus, her feet as heavy as lead. But she stopped when she realized Mo remained behind. He sank onto the bench dejected with his head between his hands. At least this was as hard for him as it was for her. He looked up and saw her waiting.

"Never mind." Layla turned and walked away. How could she possibly wake up tomorrow and go through the motions as though everything was fine? Nothing was fine. Life would never be the same.

Could she possibly look forward and dream of her degree?

Meet a nice young man at the mosque and settle down?

What choice did she have?

If she had learned one thing living through a war in Lebanon, it was that life went on, no matter how much pain churned beneath the surface.

Rain meandered aimlessly around her apartment on Saturday evening, straightening and organizing as she went. She was finally getting the hang of this cleaning thing, and the house smelled of organic peppermint soap. She had even painted an abstract design on a huge canvas from a secondhand store and hung it over their bed. James would be in for a huge surprise when he came home.

When.

Not if.

She refused to even think in terms of if.

James held down the full-time employment in their makeshift family. Rain had no job, no money, no plans without James. Her role was to write. That was their agreement. She rubbed her hand over her womb, still flat and tight. How on earth would she care for this precious creature without James? Would he come through with rent next month? At the moment it seemed unlikely. And her parents were still off roaming Africa with no way to reach them.

She took a damp cloth and ran it over the furniture, remembering the special origin of each piece. The slick polished surface of the rocking chair from her parents. The rough grain of a footstool from James's childhood bedroom. The dining table they found together on the side of the road. She recalled hauling it home tied to the roof of their VW by a wool scarf. Chairs littered the car, leaving room for nothing but her legs. Rain sat out the window to steady the table. The wind whipped her hair and the sun warmed her skin as the table thumped overhead. She and James had laughed the whole way home.

Their lives wove together like the furniture in their apartment. She dusted the frame of the new picture over the sofa, although it looked clean enough. The dusting gave her a chance to examine the postcard collection she lovingly glued overtop the cheap piece of Motel 6 artwork: a sweeping panorama of Los Angeles, the Statue of Liberty, an Indian reservation in New Mexico, the beach at Miami, the Golden Gate bridge. Each one held dear memories, memories of her and James happy together. She laid down the cloth and pressed her fingers against the cards.

Her mind wandered back to the day they decided to race across the mammoth, fog-shrouded bridge in San Francisco. She almost kept up until she twisted her ankle and let out a shriek. James hoisted her horsey-style onto his back and continued merrily across the bridge as she cracked her imaginary whip and called, "Giddy up." At the end they snuggled together against the backdrop of the churning bay. James hummed "Red Red Wine" in her ear as she gazed over the water.

"You're my baby, right," he whispered in her ear, causing tingles to travel down her neck.

"Always." She snuggled against his gruff chin.

"Just you and me against the world." James turned her in his arms and kissed her. They had melted into one being. Never to be parted. Or so she thought.

Had she ruined everything? Could they be happy again?

Maybe she should give Venessa's church a try. The thought had niggled in the back of her mind for weeks. Maybe she could find some answers there. She didn't have much to lose at this point.

But what if James came back? She didn't want to cause any more ripples between them. James made it very clear that he would never accept the possibility of a benevolent creator. As far as he was concerned, humans were nothing but victims of biology and random chance. It comforted him somehow. If God did exist, that meant there must be some grand injustice in the world, and James could never tolerate injustice on such a cosmic scale. No, chalking it up to mindless fate made James much happier.

And living with James made Rain much happier.

He would never understand her desire to attend a church. An actual organized religious construct. It would only drive another wedge between them. "'In our teen years we replaced

God with drugs. Today we prefer a good stiff gin.'" Rain imitated one of James's favorite quotes complete with his low, suave intonations and broken down stance.

But she could pray. At least she could pray. She dropped to her knees right there before the sofa and poured out her fears. *Be patient.* The words welled up from her heart. *I'm working on him.*

James checked the locks at the storage facility one last time. He rattled the chain. A similar ugly, rusting enclosure surrounded his childhood home. He smacked it with his hand for the feel of the rough metal biting into his flesh. Returning to his station, he tried to read his anatomy text, but he couldn't focus. He kept thinking about Rain. The problem growing in her womb.

He slammed the book shut and pulled out his cell phone. He jammed in the numbers.

Rain picked up on the other end. "Hello?" She sounded scared. She should be scared.

"Have you done it yet?" A week had passed, more than enough time.

"James. Please. Come home. Let's talk."

"We're talking now. Did you do it? Did you do what I asked?" His hands shook.

"Ordered is more like it. Since when do we order each other?"

"That's not the point. Did you? I'm not coming home until that thing is gone."

"It's not a thing, James. It's a baby. Our baby."

"So should I take that as a no?" His whole body began to quiver. Molten steel filled his veins.

"No. I mean yes. I mean...I didn't do it. I won't do it." Rain sighed. "Please just come home."

James remained silent.

Sobs choked her voice as she said, "It's our child. I love it. I can't destroy it."

James's heart twisted in his chest. He hit the end button and hung up.

TWENTY-TWO

Allie led a reluctant Rain and Layla several blocks from the free parking on the side streets toward the boardwalk of Virginia Beach. She plucked a purple flower from a bush extending into the sidewalk and twirled it in her fingers, taking a deep breath of its sweet scent. Although in truth, the prickly cactus up ahead better reflected her mood.

Since Allie was the jilter rather than the jiltee in their tragic love sagas, she decided to organize a distracting Sunday evening outing for her friends. They had all three moped their way through another school week. Enough was enough, and the yearly Neptune Festival was just the thing to pull them out of their doldrums.

"This is the worst idea ever. I met Mo at the beach." Layla dragged her feet as she walked.

"I've only been here with James," Rain whispered.

"Yeah, yeah, and I had my tragic surfing date at the beach. Come on, you two. There's miles of oceanfront. It's time to make some new memories. This festival is iconic. You have to at least give it a try."

They waited in silence at the busy intersection for the green light and moved onward like women being led to an execution.

But once they reached the boardwalk, Rain and Layla couldn't keep their faces from lighting up. Past the railing upon the beach sat the mystical wonder of a ten foot sand castle complete with pointed windows, spiraling stairways, turreted towers, and an inviting drawbridge. Flags along the top seemed to magically sway in the breeze. To the right of the

155

castle sat a soaring abstract statue made of the same soft beige sand crystals.

"Oh, they're beautiful." Layla clasped her hands to her chest.

"The sand sculpture contest. I told you. Iconic. Come on." Allie tugged their arms. "This goes on for blocks."

"Wait," Rain said, still transfixed. "Give me time to take in each one."

So they stood gaping along the railing and slowly slid past the sand sculptures, marvel after marvel. The curves and arches of the modern art masterpiece. An old scraggly sailor, nets in hand, in a fishing boat with a pelican resting on the bow. A mythical collection of mermaids alongside King Neptune with his trident. Dolphins at play leaping out of sandy waves. Their favorite was a spherical earth surrounded by children of varying ethnicities, all reaching to clasp hands atop the North Pole.

"So much time. So much love and effort and artistry for something that will be wiped away by the next storm." Rain's voice reflected her awe.

"It's inspiring." Layla shook her head. "Do you have any idea the geometry that goes into building these structures?"

Allie turned and hopped to sit on the railing facing her friends. "It makes you want to build a better life, doesn't it?"

"Yes." Rain leaned over the rail. "But a life full of things that will last."

"Watch it." Layla turned Rain away from the sand sculptures. "We're sliding into dangerous territory. Today is supposed to be fun, remember."

"Yes." Rain pulled Allie down and they waded their way into the crowd along the boardwalk. "Fun and excitement. Woo hoo!"

"Yeah, who hoo," Layla echoed with no inflection.

"No," Allie said. "That's who hoo!" She punctuated the words with a little jump.

Andy held the hymnal with two hands and tried to sing the

tune with the joy it deserved as the organist pounded out the notes for the evening service, but he couldn't find the strength. Allie had avoided church yet again. She wouldn't answer his calls. He was about to do something drastic he might regret.

Scanning the congregation, Andy spied Allie's mother with her perfectly curled and sprayed hairdo. The two women were nothing alike. Mrs. Carmichael was as short, curvy, and bubbly as Allie was tall, lean, and introspective. Perhaps the towering man standing beside her held the key to unlocking the mystery.

Andy always looked up to Deacon Carmichael. The bold believer never missed an opportunity to share his faith. Yet Andy had to admit he no longer admired his tactics. Did standing on Atlantic Avenue shouting to masses of strangers about hell and damnation really change anyone for eternity? At least Allie's father meant well. The man was fearless.

He continued gazing down the line of perfectly attired Carmichaels. Richard was off at a Christian university, but Robert attended the local community college and remained active in the church's singles group. With his tie, collared shirt, and perfect crew cut, he reminded Andy of himself a few years back. Sarah appeared sweet and demure in her long skirt and matching blouse. Andy knew Sarah's conservative nature went to her very core. She single-handedly kept half the kids in his youth group on the narrow road.

Poor Allie. She never did fit with that family. She must have inherited some recessive genes. Which made Andy feel even worse about what he planned to do.

The lead singer finished up the song with a swoop of his arms. "Everyone, please take a moment to greet one another."

Andy pasted on a stiff smile and turned to clasp the hand of one of the youth group parents.

"Andy! Jason had so much fun last week. Thanks for stopping by to pick him up."

"You're welcome. Anytime." He was in no mood to be cheerful. This must be how Allie felt every time she came to church. Andy didn't like playing games. Instead he swiped his hand over his face and allowed a sincere frown to settle on it.

"Something wrong, son?" the older man asked. Concern etched in the lines of his face.

"Sorry. If you don't mind, I need to speak with the Carmichaels."

The man's eyes widened "Ah, of course." He slapped Andy on the back. "Go."

After gorging on overpriced festival food and braving the crowds for nearly an hour, Layla tugged the girls toward the open shoreline. Rain seemed to thrive on the energy and excitement of the mob, but Allie was wilting, much like Layla. They took off their shoes. Layla regretted that last round of blooming onion that settled like a lump in her stomach. She stepped into the surf and allowed the waves to wash her feet deep into the cool sand.

"What are those bubbles?" Rain stood at the shoreline pointing at the ground.

"Little creatures, clams I think, digging their way under the sand." Allie bent down to try to scoop some in her hand, but she was too slow.

Layla bent over as well, as another tumbling breaker deposited more creatures at her feet. "Can I join you, little clams?"

"Come on," Allie said. "I have an idea."

She headed toward a deserted lifeguard tower and climbed up the ladder.

"I don't think that's a good plan, Allie." Layla stared, horrified.

Rain scurried up the rungs behind Allie. "Come on, Layla. Live a little. The whole point of this festival is that the tourists have gone home. The lifeguards are off duty. No one cares."

"Seriously." Allie waved her up. "It's fine."

"Are you sure?" Layla wavered, reluctant to pull her feet out of their chilly hiding place.

"Shut up and climb the ladder, you big chicken," Rain said.

"We're supposed to be having fun."

"Fun, fun, fun," Layla muttered as she climbed the broad wooden rungs that scratched against her palms. Once on top, she relaxed. The lifeguard tower was huge, and they all fit comfortably upon the bench. It seemed designed for such a purpose, offering an exquisite view of the horizon.

Navy planes flew overhead in formation, celebrating the end of tourist season and drowning out any further conversation. The roaring jets faded into the distance as a young African-American couple strolled past snuggling a baby with skin the color of coffee and cream. In the twilight Layla watched tears fill Rain's eyes.

"Fun." Layla clapped her hands together.

"Hey," Allie said. "Let's work on our drama."

"That's your idea of fun?" Rain swiped her tears away.

"For class. The script we have to write for class. I'm a performer. What can I say?" Allie shrugged.

"We don't have much space up here," Layla said.

"Well, I was thinking." Allie stood. "What if a member from each of our cultures got stuck in an elevator together? What better place to force them to interact?"

"That's kind of cute," Rain said.

Layla's pink veil flapped in the wind, and she pushed it out of her face. "It might work."

They sat and brainstormed for a few minutes and decided to adlib to see what they could come up with. The approach did not strike Layla as very efficient, but since this wasn't her field of expertise, she decided to give it a try. This might prove an unexpected opportunity to share the powerful words of the *Qur'an* with her friends. Perhaps they would be moved by them. She was curious to find out.

Mo sat in a Sunday evening worship service with his head drooping and hands gripping the denim fabric at his knees. His friend A.J. stood beside him, clapping and stamping his feet to the upbeat tune that surrounded them. "God please," Mo whispered, "bring her back to me. Bring her to you. She needs you so badly. She just doesn't understand. I need her so badly. God, I don't know how much more I can bear."

Maybe there was still hope. On rare occasions Muslim families in Lebanon allowed their daughters to marry moderate Christians. Christian men had a reputation for treating their wives and children well. Maybe if he allowed Layla to remain Muslim?

Instead of focusing on the music, he turned his thoughts to the timeless words of the Lebanese poet Gibran. He had memorized them as a teen and been rereading them all week. *When love beckons to you, follow him, though his ways are hard and steep. And when his wings enfold you, yield to him, though the sword hidden among his pinions may wound you... For even as love crowns you so shall he crucify you.*

Mo stared at the pastor on the platform. He stood smiling next to his beautiful wife, who held their smallest child snug in her arms. She wore jeans with a tank top and swayed in time with the music, her dark hair falling in beaded braids down her cheek. As much as Mo admired the man and strove to emulate his spirituality, Pastor Mike didn't understand the issues he and Layla faced.

He wanted nothing more than to remove Layla's precious soul from that dark and oppressive lifestyle. Wanted her to live free and light like the woman on the stage. Maybe if he could let Layla see a different sort of existence, there might be a chance.

The shrill pang of an electric guitar pierced through his haze and scraped across his eardrums.

He returned his soul to the soothing words from "The Prophet." *And then he assigns you to his sacred fire, that you may become sacred bread for God's sacred feast. All these things shall love do unto you that you may know the secrets of your heart, and in that knowledge become a fragment of Life's heart.*

He had stumbled on to some scriptures about the believing spouse changing the unbelieving spouse. If only he had found and married Layla before he converted. Yet, he couldn't quite bring himself to think of her as an unbeliever. She simply needed time. She needed space and the right sort of influence. He could be a friend to her. Keep things platonic. Couldn't he?

How could he turn his back on Layla? He had adored her since childhood. Tasted the sweet nectar of her lips. The only woman he ever loved. The only woman he ever dared kiss. Turning his back on Layla was like turning his back to life itself.

Love has no other desire but to fulfill itself. But if you love and must needs have desires, let these be your desires: to melt and be like a running brook that sings its melody to the night. To know the pain of too much tenderness.

His heart ran like a brook straight to Layla. And, oh, did he know the pain.

Mo refused to accept there was no hope for them.

Rain giggled, actually having fun as they rehearsed the skit for the second time. She pretended to poke the elevator button atop the lifeguard stand, and all three girls stared at the imaginary metallic sliding doors until they opened. Without looking at one another, they stepped into the nonexistent machine and turned on cue to face back toward the closing doors. Each pressed the button for their floor. They gazed at the fictional numbers overhead as the elevator ascended.

"Hey, what gives?" Layla said, feigning agitation. "It skipped my floor."

"Me too," Allie said.

Rain jerked from side to side. Layla fell to the floor and grabbed hold of Rain's legs. Allie pressed both hands against the corner walls to steady herself.

"No," Rain cried.

"You've got to be kidding me," Allie said.

"Oh, this is not good." Layla stood and brushed herself off.

The women finally took a hard look at one another. Allie turned to better examine the elevator. "Great," she said.

Layla tapped her toe and took a deep breath.

Rain straightened her bag on her shoulder. "Any ideas?"

"Scream," Allie said.

"Stand and wait," Layla leaned against the imaginary wall.

"That's no good," Rain said. "We must be stuck here for some cosmic purpose. We need to discover the meaning. Once we do, I'm sure the universe will set us free."

"Seriously?" Allie rolled her eyes. "I'm stuck in an elevator with one of those."

"We've got nothing better to do," Layla said.

"See." Rain brightened. "What do we have to lose?"

"Fine." Allie shot her a sassy grin. "Maybe we're stuck here so I can tell you to repent and turn from your sins. How's that? Hmm, not enough." She waved her hands through the air. "Repent! Repent! I tell you, surely a hot and fiery place awaits all those who sin against the Lord. There will be wailing and gnashing of teeth. Repent while you still can. *Et voilà!*" She snapped toward the doors. "Open sesame."

"You don't have to be a smart aleck." Rain crossed her arms over her chest in mock frustration. "I was thinking that maybe I should set up some sort of relief fund for elevator victims or something. Sheesh. Some people can ruin anything."

"Well, this devil elevator is ruining my day." Layla kicked the imaginary door. "My parents are expecting me home soon. I was just running back upstairs for some papers. And how am I supposed to know when it's time for sunset prayers?"

"Devil elevator." Allie laughed. "I like that."

"If it does not know to honor a follower of the great Allah, this elevator must be evil." Layla kicked it again.

"Settle down." Allie sat cross-legged on the floor. "Why don't we all relax? Violence won't solve anything. Come on. Join me."

The others sat and Allie took their hands. She began singing "Kumbaya." Rain joined in with gusto, but Layla sighed loudly.

She turned to the corner and knelt. "You know what, I'll just pray until we get out of here. Then I'll be on the safe side." She bellowed her Islamic chants, drowning out the singing. Then she switched to English. "Oh great Allah, please return us to the first floor from which we came."

"Okay, okay," Rain said. "Maybe 'Kumbaya' is overkill, but I need to go to the roof. Watch what you're asking for over there." She pinched her fingers into a meditation pose. "I wonder if I could levitate this thing to the top floor." Rain oohmed.

Layla continued hollering Arabic prayers.

"Okay." Allie stood. "Okay, so that's how you want to play it. I command this elevator to repent and return me to the fifth floor. Repent. Turn back before it's too late...I command you. I...command this elevator..."

Layla peeked her eyes open. "Ah, guys. Nothing's working."

Rain blew out a frustrated breath and looked up. "What's that button?"

Allie turned to look. "You mean the 'open' button?"

Layla said, "Didn't we try that?"

"Nope," Rain answered.

Allie reached over and tentatively pushed it.

Their eyes followed the imaginary doors as they swung open. They gathered their belongings. "Well, that was too easy," Allie said.

"Looks like we're stuck between floors." Rain ducked her head and then hopped down. "There, that wasn't so bad."

Layla and Allie followed suit. Layla spun in a circle. "Where are we?"

Allie pointed to a number on the wall. "I guess it's the eighth floor."

"The eighth floor," Rain said. "No one wanted to go there."

"But it sure is pretty." Layla took a few steps forward.

"Check out the buffet," Allie said. "Do you think it's free?"

"And the view is gorgeous." Rain ran toward an imaginary window.

"Maybe we should have been heading here the entire time." Layla delivered the agreed upon final line of the skit right on cue.

"That was great," Allie said, holding up her hand for a high five. "You guys are born actresses."

"As long as the play earns an A, I don't need an Oscar." Layla slapped Allie's palm.

"I think we created a hit." Rain high-fived as well. She loved the conclusion of the play. That part was her idea.

Layla took a deep breath. "And for a whole ten minutes, I almost forgot about *him*." She slumped back down onto the bench.

"Yep." Rain sank beside her on the cool bench as thoughts of James filled her mind. The turkey leg she had eaten earlier warred in her stomach with the funnel cake. "Ten whole minutes."

"You guys stink at having fun." Allie sat as well.

At that moment, fireworks split the sky in a shower of red and green sparkles that reflected against the murky water. Sunset had come and gone without anyone noticing. Good thing Layla had prayed in the elevator. Rain smiled, watching another round of bright color burst against the dark sky. She wondered what James was doing tonight.

James sat on a swing in the playground after sunset, clutching the cool, metal links. He watched as a young father played football with his two small sons in the grass patch to his right beneath the streetlights. The dad tackled one of the tykes, tumbling him to the ground and rolling over top, taking the weight upon his own strong biceps, and the child squealed and giggled beneath him. The second preschool-aged boy dove atop the fray, and the dad hugged him into the embrace as well.

The youngest scurried back to his feet. "Daddy, Daddy, look how fast I am."

"Not faster than the kissing monster." The father hopped up and held his arms in front of him like a zombie. "Grr. Grr." He chased after the little boys in the twinkle of the overhead lamp.

"No. Me, me, Daddy," the older child cried, zigzagging in the opposite direction.

"I'll get both of you. Grr. No one shall escape my kisses tonight."

Unable to take it any longer, James stood and trudged down the street, his feet scratching against the dirty pavement. He headed toward the convenience store to grab a beer, or maybe a six-pack. Along the way, he saw the shadow of a dusty old man sitting on a rusting electrical box. The man stared into space with an empty whiskey bottle drooping from his hand. He looked so pitiful. So alone. How could a man live so many long years and have nothing to show for them?

James turned and headed back to the frat house. The thought of beer no longer appealed to him. The striking dichotomy between the joyful young father and the lonely old man slammed into him like a freight train. He couldn't go on this way much longer.

TWENTY-THREE

Allie checked the time on her cell phone as she dashed toward the front door of the dance studio. The mocking numbers *6:14* glowed back at her. She groaned. Mom knew her classes ended at 6:00. What she didn't know was how many students and parents stopped her to talk on the way out of the building. Why must she insist on dinner at precisely 6:30?

There was no chance Allie would make it to Virginia Beach through the evening traffic in time. She didn't even have an opportunity to change her clothes. She still wore dance shorts and a leotard with convertible tights pulled up to her knees and flip flops shoved on her feet in place of ballet slippers.

As she dug the keys from her bag, Allie stopped short ten feet in front of her car. There, leaning against the hood and grinning, stood an unfortunately handsome Andy Vargas.

He walked to her and snatched the keys from her hand. "You won't be needing those." He scooped her elbow into his hand and led her to his Jeep.

"But...wait...I..."

"No time to argue. We're late already. Your mom won't be happy with us at all." He opened the passenger door. "Jump in. We need to hurry."

"But..." Allie couldn't think straight. Was the whole world conspiring against her? "You've got a lot of nerve."

"Well, you didn't leave me much choice." While he walked around the Jeep, she heard pieces of his mumbled rant. "Stupid girl thinks she can kiss a guy...hopes up...mind all fuzzy...ignore his texts." He pressed his lips together as he sat down beside her.

Andy raised his volume back to a normal level. "I'd say you're the one who has some nerve."

"Andy, what are you trying to prove? You keep pushing. Just like high school. I knew what I wanted all along, and it's not you. I don't want to be a pastor's wife. I don't even want to attend that awful church. I'm not the right one for you. Why won't you accept that?" She slammed her bag against her knees.

"I think you know the answer."

Allie stripped the ponytail holder from her hair and raked her fingers through its length, attempting to straighten it even as she straightened her thoughts. Somehow, the weight against her neck made her angrier than ever, reminded her of that python wrapping around the back.

She wrangled the hair into the safety of her messy bun. "Love. Is that what you're going to say? What's love anyway? Feelings. Hormones. You need to find someone else to *love*, Andy. Marriage requires a lot more than googly eyes and fuzzy thinking. It requires common goals, common interests, unified vision. We don't have any of those."

"I think we do." He clenched the steering wheel. His knuckles turned white.

"I say we don't." Allie snapped the visor mirror closed.

"You don't want to love and honor and serve God?" Andy swiveled to look into her eyes.

Allie turned away. "Of course I do, but not as a pastor's wife. Not in that church."

"I don't care about any of that as much as I care about you, Allie. I've struggled through life for eight years without you, and I don't want to live like this for one more day."

"Andy, you don't mean that. If you gave up everything that's important to you, you'd resent me. It would never work." Allie laid her hand on top of his along the center console. "I can't lie. This is hard on me. You have brought back some old feelings, but I've given this a lot of thought. It won't work."

Andy flipped his hand and captured Allie's. He lifted it to his lips and kissed her fingers as if he wanted to drink her into his very being.

Allie shuddered, terror and desire streaking through her at once.

"We have to try. Please, Allie. Give it a try. For me."

Allie stared out the windshield. Tears blurred her eyes. *Oh, Andy Vargas, what are you doing to me?*

Oh, Allie Carmichael, what have you done to me? The scent of her lavender perfume drifted across the Jeep. Andy hated being reduced to begging and underhanded tactics. He schemed with Allie's mother, for crying out loud. It's a wonder Allie hadn't jumped into her tiny car and run him over in the parking lot.

But what else could he do? He couldn't eat. He couldn't sleep. He could barely think straight. He simply lived and breathed Allie Carmichael these days. Ever since that kiss on the beach, he was doomed. No matter how much he prayed, immersed himself in his Bible, in his work, nothing helped. This beautiful woman sitting beside him had turned him inside out and left his shredded heart exposed.

"Did I mention how beautiful you look tonight?"

Allie shot him a teary-eyed glare. "Shut up."

Allie entered her parents' home with Andy at her elbow, ten minutes late and still in a daze. Mom rescued her and spirited her into the kitchen where she was flooded with the smell of roast beef and vegetables.

"What are you thinking? Look at you." Mom huffed and waved her hand up and down Allie's body. "Don't you even have the decency to pull on a pair of jeans?"

"I was late. I didn't want a lecture." So much for that. "I had no idea Andy would be waiting to ambush me."

Mom surveyed her with confusion and angst in her eyes. As always. "What that boy must think. You look like a brazen hussy in those... What do kids call those things? Booty shorts?"

"Hussy? Mom, give it a rest. Andy doesn't care. He happens to like what I'm wearing. He said I looked beautiful."

Mom huffed over to the counter and doused the salad with dressing. "Of course he did. You probably got him all riled up in that ridiculous get up. We should never cause our Christian brothers to stumble."

Why didn't Mom just say what she was really thinking: *Where did I go wrong with you, Allie?* She surveyed her June Cleaver-esque perfect mother again. Hair perfect, makeup perfect, perfect Southern charm.

A funny thought popped into her head. "Well, look at you showing off your elbows. Layla would be appalled."

"Layla? Your Muslim friend? What does she have to do with anything?" Mom washed off her hands and dried them in the sink. She whacked the salad bowl into Allie's stomach, nearly knocking her over, grabbed up the casserole dish, and headed to the dining room.

Allie followed, not ready to back down. "I'm just saying, you could be a little more modest yourself, Mother. Maybe you're more of a hussy than you think."

Mom's face turned red. "That's just mean, Allie. I'm not part of that culture, and I have no desire to be." She put the dish down on the table and swiped the salad bowl from Allie's hands.

"Oh." Allie placed her hands on her hips. "So you admit modesty has to do with culture and isn't so absolute after all."

"I admit nothing of the sort, and I'm quite finished with this conversation." She huffed to the dining room door and hollered, "Dinner's ready."

Allie smiled to herself in victory. She would relish every bite of the lovely home cooked meal while wearing her leotard and dancer's "booty" shorts.

Allie pushed the cheerful orange carrots back and forth on her plate. Squashed one under her fork. Andy sat to her right.

Dad at the head of the table as always. Mom across from him with Rob and Sarah filling the seats in between. Could they be any more predictable?

"That was quite a storm." Andy smiled as he passed the gravy.

"Indeed it was." Dad swooped up the boat and doused his potatoes.

"Ten inches in two days. Can you believe it?" Sarah pulled the linen napkin from her lap and wiped a microscopic spec from her lips.

"Ten inches isn't so much." Rob took another bite of roast.

"Just look..." Andy started the phrase.

"At Noah!" They all joined in on the private joke and laughed hysterically.

Allie frowned. Sarah shot her a questioning glare.

They should adopt Andy, form one happy family, and be rid of me. The dinner conversation flowed freely, although Allie took little part in it. Her family thrived at the fine art of small talk. Andy fit right in. They discussed upcoming church events, Sunday's sermon, even the weather with great relish. Why couldn't Allie bring herself to care about any of their enthusiastic topics?

"So the bake sale is coming up on Sunday." Mom stood to fetch the water pitcher and refill Andy's glass.

"I can't wait, Mrs. Carmichael. Will you be gracing us with your award-winning sweet potato pie?"

"God willing, you know I will, sugar." Mom winked at Andy. Sugar? Gag.

Allie glanced around the brown and beige dining room. Sarah matched it perfectly, but Allie's leotard stood out like a hot pink sore thumb. Like the rest of the home, the room looked cozy in a plain vanilla sort of way. She hated vanilla. It went in sweet potato pie.

On the other hand, although she would never admit it, she liked having Andy by her side. His thigh brushing against hers, shooting little tingles of electricity, his toes finding her bare ones beneath the table. He had deflected several of Mom's strategic attacks. Somehow, she felt more a part of the family just because he was there being a part on her behalf.

"Family game time!" Mr. Carmichael hollered from the living room, clapping his hands and rallying everyone to join. Andy tossed his linen napkin onto the table. Allie's dad was a hoot. Andy couldn't wait to take him on.

He stood from the table and scooted out Allie's chair.

Allie pushed up from the seat. "Oh, I really should—"

Her mom cut her off with a warning look. "You really should spend more time with your family. God first. Family second. We taught you better, Allie."

Andy placed his hand on the small of Allie's back. "Come on. It will be fun." Poor Allie. He could see how hard this was for her. Sure, her parents were a little controlling. But weren't all parents? They simply wanted what was best for her.

Allie needed to stop focusing on the silly external differences between herself and her family and enjoy them for the fun people they were. She probably felt guilty around her mom. Allie seemed happy enough with her life, but her mother was a walking reminder of the expectations she failed to live up to. If she could stop concerning herself with her mother's judgment, maybe that would free her to love her family the way she needed to. No doubt wanted to.

Allie needed to let go of her offenses and see her mother as a sister in the Lord with her own weaknesses. A sister who, for some reason, needed to cling to rules and conventions. Allie was just confused. He could see it in her eyes. He wanted to help her, if only she'd trust him.

Andy sat beside her on the carpet next to the coffee table and took her hand in his. Allie's mom smiled like the cat who had eaten the proverbial canary. He hated being on her side in all of this. But he loved that Allie was seated at his side, looking up at him with glowing blue eyes for strength and support. She'd survive game night. He'd make sure of it. More than that, he'd see that she had a good time.

Allie didn't know whether to be angry or thankful as Andy shared his thoughts about her mom along the ride home. She sat in silence next to him in his dark Jeep taking it all in. Glad he understood, appreciating that he thought her a strong believer, yet feeling judged nonetheless.

"I don't really see how my relationship with my mother is any of your business, Andy."

"It's not. I just thought an outside perspective might help."

She gazed at the stars for a few moments and considered his words. "I guess I have held on to some offense. I felt justified for wanting my freedom and never stopped to realize I was nursing a grudge."

"You want to be free, but you've let yourself be caught in a different sort of prison. God's the only one you need to please. Believe it or not, that's sort of how I felt about church for a while. When I realized that I could stop worrying about their expectations and reach out to make a positive change, it was like a whole new ministry field for me."

The church of the stick in the mud? A ministry field? Allie couldn't begin to fathom it. How did one minister to people who thought they were perfect already? She shook her head and tried to unravel her thoughts.

"Well," Allie said as they pulled into the deserted studio parking lot, "I have to admit that you made the evening more bearable. Who knew?"

Andy stopped the car and took her hand into his again. "I don't want to hurt you, Allie. I want to make your life better. I wish you would believe me."

Allie wrapped her other hand around his and looked deep into his eyes. "I know that's what you want, Andy. I know that's what you mean. I'm just not sure it would work out that way."

"You said you would give me a chance. I'm holding you to your word."

She turned her gaze down to their entwined hands. "I need time to think and to pray."

"You haven't done that yet?" Disappointment tinged Andy's voice.

Allie didn't dare look up. "Not really. I made up my mind years ago. You don't understand how suffocated, how trapped I felt when I accepted that ring. It was awful."

"I shouldn't have let you go so easily. I should have loved and cherished the real Allie Carmichael. I'm sorry. You have no idea how sorry I am. How many sleepless nights I've spent regretting everything."

Allie let go of his hands and sat back against the seat. "Oh, Andy. I don't want you to beat yourself up. Either this is God's plan or it isn't. We need to come to the same conclusion. But at least I'm open to the possibility. That's something. Right?"

More than she ever expected to offer.

"It's all I could ever ask for." Andy stepped out of the car and walked around to open her door. Good old Andy. Always the gentleman.

Allie took his hand and stood to meet him. "Give me a week. Okay? I promise I won't ignore you, but I need time."

Andy shut the door. "Well, while you're thinking, keep this in mind."

He swept Allie into a crushing embrace, and his mouth seared hers. She met his frantic kiss with her own longing, and they were a tangle of arms and lips once again. Nothing had ever felt so good in Allie's whole life as Andy's soft mouth pressed against hers. His warm arms wrapped around her. She wanted to melt into that moment and never leave.

His lips slid like silk along her neck, her ear, her temple. He shifted her toward the hood of the car, sat her upon it, and deepened the kiss. Fire shot through Allie in response. Fire and shivers and that warm syrupy feeling that left her in a swoon.

She sensed he was caught in the moment, in the passion as well, to a degree that shouldn't happen to an uptight, goody-goody like Andy. Allie didn't know whether to giggle, panic, or draw him closer.

But before she could decide, Andy wrenched himself away from her. He turned his back and took several paces, raking his fingers through his hair. "Ugh!" He swiveled to Allie and threw his hands over his head. "Look what you do to me."

"Me?"

"Yes, you. I want to make you my wife. I have for years. I'd marry you tomorrow. Tonight! How many times have I thrown that verse at the kids about not awaking love before it pleases? Yet here I am, tumbling into temptation. For crying out loud, Allie. I don't know how much more I can take."

His words cut through the fuzzy champagne cloud in her brain. Spouting scriptures again. Judging her just like she expected. Great. "We got a little carried away. It's not the end of the world."

He kicked the tire. "It is to me. I'm responsible to those kids. My example matters."

Allie struggled to slow her pulse. "Hey, I'm willing to pray... I'm willing to give this a try. But not if you're going to pressure me and blame me for something as natural as responding to our kisses. Kisses that you initiated."

He stomped his foot and shook his hands in frustration. "I love you, and I want to be with you. You're killing me."

"This little tantrum isn't doing you any favors, Andrew Vargas." She could hardly believe her eyes.

"I'm sorry." He took a few deep breaths and clenched his hands on his head. "It's all my fault. But please, call me soon. Don't ignore me this time. I can't take it." He turned his back again and stared into the sky.

She let out a sigh. "It's no one's fault. It's something we need to figure out. This is difficult for me too. You have no idea how difficult." Allie, cold all of a sudden, curled into a ball and rubbed her hands over her bare arms.

Andy took a moment to compose himself. He came to sit beside Allie on the hood of the Jeep and took her fingers in his again. "Allie, I want to make sure you understand. I treated you wrong, and I know that. I was young and stupid. I tried to change you when you were beautiful just the way God made you.

I don't want to change you anymore. I want you to change me. If you really can't go back to our church, then I will seriously consider leaving. I mean it, Allie. You are the most important thing to me."

"Oh, Andy. One week. Okay?"

Allie gave him a parting kiss on the cheek and headed to her car. *Take another look at Andy.* She already knew the answer. Somehow, she had to find a way to let Andy back into her life. She had a lot of praying to do between now and next week. Maybe she had let unforgiveness and offense build up against him as well. Maybe she had let her feelings for the church tangle with her feelings for Andy far too long.

TWENTY-FOUR

On Thursday morning Layla suffered through a physics lecture. She leaned her chin to her hand as the teacher's voice droned, but she couldn't bring herself to pay attention. Mo had class merely a few rooms away. Logic and reason failed her this time. Science and deduction did not work in her favor. Her resolve proved worthless. Apparently she had a passionate, emotional Middle Eastern streak after all. Unfortunately, hers went against the cultural script instead of conforming to it.

She longed for Mo as much as she did weeks ago when she first walked away from him. Longed for him in a tangible and factual sort of way she could not deny. She barely ate, barely slept. She had difficulty focusing on her schoolwork. Her heart beat rapidly when she thought of him, which was more often than not. She surfed the web just to spot a glimpse of him. Followed him on Facebook like a bona fide cyberstalker.

Layla tried to listen to the professor. "So even at this level of physics, it all goes back to the basic laws of thermodynamics. Objects in motion stay in motion, and objects at rest stay at rest."

Inertia. That described her life perfectly. She had started down this path away from Mo and didn't know how to turn around. How could she walk away from the one man who could give her the life she desired? Mo planned to be an engineer, for crying out loud. How much more perfect could he be? Except for that one little flaw that ruined everything.

Couldn't there be some way to work around it? Layla met a Lebanese Muslim girl married to a Catholic once. It happened on rare occasion.

But never here.

Never in the states where the cultures were so disparate. But Mo shared her background. Couldn't there be a chance? Did it even matter? He didn't want her anyway. Not unless she converted. He made that clear.

"So what we need,"—the teacher's voice broke into her thoughts—"is for an outside force to come in and shake things up."

No. She would never, ever convert. Of that she was certain. Not Allie, not Brother Rasheed, not even Mo could convince her to do so. She would never. Would she?

Didn't some part of her still wonder? Didn't some part still question? Still long to stand before her God without shame?

She had been so pleased when they did the elevator skit for class. Honored to declare the holy words of the *Qur'an* freely as she acted out her part. She had hoped that their power would be evident to all the students. *I seek refuge with Allah from the accursed Shaytaan.* Even at the beach she had watched for Rain's face to light up in interest and wonder as it had at Allie's church.

But nothing.

Not even in her own heart.

Despite her disappointment, Layla was still a good Muslim woman. No. She could never consider converting. The price was far too high. She'd have to settle for roly-poly Fadi, or worse yet, Antonio Banderas and his herd of goats.

Back to physics. Layla forced herself to focus.

"Again." The professor tapped on the chalkboard. "It's a basic issue of e equals mc squared."

Yes, a world where phenomena were predictable and rational and worked by formulas. Where energy flowed in prescribed patterns and ratios. That's exactly what she needed. Not the insane electricity that jumped at random between her skin and Mo's. Not the tingles dancing unbidden across her lips.

Physics. Focus.

As she exited the classroom, Layla gasped to see Mo leaning against the wall outside. She approached tentatively.

A warm smile spread across his face. "What? You didn't think you were the only one keeping track of schedules did you?"

Her heart skipped a few beats. "Mo, what are you doing here?" She wanted to dive into his arms, sink into his skin, but what good could possibly come of it?

"I made a mistake. I shouldn't have pushed you away. I want to spend time with you. Let's forget about all the complications for now and just be Layla and Mo running together on the playground again. What do you say? Friends?" He pulled a bouquet of buttercups from behind his back.

Layla's heart did a complete flip-flop. Two-dozen long stemmed roses—even diamonds—could not have meant more to her than the thoughtful gift Mo held in his hand. After all these years. Buttercups. Like in the schoolyard. He must have ditched class early to pick them fresh. She stretched out her hand and allowed it to linger against Mo's as she received the priceless blossoms. She hugged them to her chest and breathed in their delicate scent.

"Is that a yes?" Mo's eyes held such hope.

Layla blinked, not sure she understood correctly. "You want to spend time together?"

Mo took the hand with the flowers into his own and nodded.

"Just Layla and Mo. No complications." She echoed his words in awe.

"Yes."

Her fingers trembled. Then reason dawned, and she jerked away her hand. Her eyes darted around the hallway for members of the Muslim Student Union. Seeing all was clear, she asked, "When?"

"Now."

Layla knew she should run away as fast as her legs could carry her, but her heart cried out to stay with him. She whispered, "Okay."

"I parked near your car. Follow me out in a minute. I'll be in a black SUV."

She stared into his eyes for one more moment before he walked away. Layla felt her heart tightening around his. Oh, she would regret this later, but for one bright fall afternoon she would cling to Mo's hand and pretend a future might be possible.

Layla pulled her red veil farther over her face and inspected the parking lot before dashing to Mo's car. She dare not let anyone see her driving off alone with a man, even if he was only a friend. Gossip traveled as quickly through the local Muslim community here as it did back in Lebanon. She would say even quicker, but science had proven nothing could move faster than the speed of light.

Mo helped her in. The sunroof was open, but the windows were tinted. A lively Arabic tune sprang to life with a turn of the key, and Mo sped out of the parking lot. Layla hunched and hid behind her red veil for the first few stoplights, but once safely past the school, she began to relax.

"Nice music." She was sitting beside Mo. Wasn't this what she dreamed of?

"Thanks."

"Are you sure about this?" She examined the sidewalk once again for Middle Eastern faces.

"Positive."

She should live in the moment. Forget about prying eyes. Surely they had left them far behind.

She laid her books and flowers on the backseat. The music seeped into her. The energetic drumbeats filled her soul. Layla longed to dance with joy. She took in the lines of Mo's chiseled profile, his strong hands gripping the steering wheel.

As they sped along Hampton Boulevard toward the highway, Layla had no idea where he was taking her, and for once in her life she didn't care. Her own hands began to flow in rhythmic motions through the air to the wail of strings and pipes.

She only needed Mo.

He turned and smiled at her. "That's more like it."

A light sense of freedom overtook her. Layla's veil thrashed in the wind blowing through the sunroof, the ends of the fabric pulling free from her collar. She tried several times to tuck it back in, but could resist no longer. In an impetuous burst of spirit, Layla ripped the veil from her head and let her hair flow wild in the breeze as the fabric whipped in her hand.

Any fear of consequences flew out the sunroof with the swift current of air. Mo looked at her with surprise and tenderness. He picked up her free hand and gave it a squeeze as she laughed and danced in the windswept paradise, pretending for just one moment that it would all work out.

TWENTY-FIVE

As they pulled into the parking lot in Williamsburg an hour later, Layla twisted her red and silver *hijab* in her hands, debating its fate.

Mo shifted the car into park and turned to her. "Do whatever you want, Layla. For once in your life, it's up to you. There's no one to judge you. It's a weekday, and Muslims hardly frequent patriotic historical sites. If you want to be a normal American girl for once, I won't stand in your way."

"I'm not sure. Maybe just this once. It would be fun to try."

Mo's features split into his heartbreaking smile. "Then do it."

"I don't know. I probably shouldn't." Allah might judge her for such behavior.

"Then don't." He made it sound so simple.

Layla bit her lip.

"Layla, I don't want to encourage you to do anything rebellious or dishonorable. In my new belief system, the veil represents oppression, not respectability. To me there is no sin in leaving it behind, but you have to make that decision for yourself." Mo reached out and touched her chest over her heart. "What is this telling you?"

What was her heart saying? No one ever asked her that before. She hardly knew how to determine the answer. She moved the veil toward her head and felt her chest clutch and tense. Lowering it back down, her heart returned to a peaceful patter. Warmth spread through her.

Layla leaned forward and swiped a curl from Mo's forehead. "I'll do it." She tossed her veil over her head and into the backseat. She finger-combed her dark, shiny hair. Then Layla Al-Rai jumped out of the car before she could change her mind. Sunshine glistened through leaves just beginning to change their colors and seemed to kiss her bare head in approval.

"You're brave. I like seeing you this way." Mo offered his hand. "And very, very beautiful."

"Shh. Don't tell anyone. You're not supposed to know." Layla giggled, ducking away.

They walked hand and hand down a pathway to the town center, and as they did, her fear faded. Trees and whitewashed wooden houses lined the cobblestone street along with hitching posts and high-backed benches. No cars defiled the scene. Modern day pedestrians mixed with workers in colonial dress. But not a veiled woman in sight. A tour group walked past led by a gentleman in short breeches and a long frock coat. At one end of the street stood a proud government building in russet brick. "Oh, Mo. It looks like a storybook. Like something straight out of the *Colonial Kids* series I read as a child."

Mo raised his eyebrow. "*Colonial Kids?*"

"Contraband reading material. I was a bad, bad girl."

"You? Never."

Layla breathed in the essence of the historical town. "You'd be surprised."

"You wanted to explore this other side of your heritage."

"My heritage?" Layla turned to examine Mo.

"Sure. This is your country too. Right down at the end of that street the Virginia delegates agreed to sign the Declaration of Independence." He put a hand on her shoulder and pointed to the imposing structure. "Your Declaration of Independence."

"I never thought about it that way."

Mo clasped her shoulder tighter. "Other than the full-blooded Native Americans, every family in the states started as strangers in a strange land. We're not so different, Layla."

She let the picture of the colonial building imprint upon her mind. "I love this culture. Not all of it. But most of it. I love the freedom. I love the sense of individuality. Not just religion. Not just family. But real live people with their own hopes and dreams."

"Don't I know it." Mo ran a hand down the fabric of her long sleeve. "Family and religion are important. But at the end of this life each of us will stand before God and be judged as an individual."

"Mo, let's not talk about God. Let's simply be happy, free Americans and walk through a storybook town." She felt so safe in this place. She didn't care anymore who saw her.

Layla turned and hugged him under an ancient oak tree in front of a clapboard general store. She giggled to herself and buried her head in Mo's muscular chest, wishing this day could last forever.

They strolled hand in hand by an old stone church, a wooden pole fort. Horses clip-clopped past, pulling a carriage full of laughing children. Revolutionary soldiers marched beside them in full regalia with fifes and drums. Layla and Mo browsed through an open-air market with rag dolls, toy muskets, mobcaps, and handmade balls of honey-scented soap. Layla popped on a cap and placed a black tricorne over Mo's curls.

They glanced into a mirror and laughed.

"Look at us. Like real live colonials." Layla adjusted the lace trim and posed.

"We look more like wild Indians playing dress up than proper British colonists." Mo raised one hand. "*Hau?*"

"*Hau!* How dare you ruin my fantasy?" Layla pulled off his hat and swatted him with it.

"Hey, cut that out." He pulled a wooden musket out of a tall barrel. "Freeze or I'll shoot."

Layla grabbed a rag doll and held it in front of her. "I have a hostage."

Mo stared at her and squinted one eye comically. They both broke into hysterics. He stuffed the colonial items back on their stands and dragged Layla into the grass, where he tumbled her to the ground in laughter. Such lightness and giddiness overtook her, as if her veil had been a weight pressing down upon her all these years.

They purchased oatmeal cookies and cider and settled on

the field in the town square. Mo fed Layla piece by piece, his hand meeting her mouth with a gentle graze. After they ate every last bite, Layla lay down on the grass and watched wispy clouds roll lazily overhead against the azure sky. Before them sat the governor's mansion, and she spied a flag of red, white, and blue swaying against the horizon.

She recalled reading the story of Constance Chambers, a young girl living in Williamsburg at the time of the Revolution. She remembered thinking that she and Constance weren't so different deep down. Constance questioned the British oppression in her nation. They shared the same sort of hopes and dreams and ideals. Constance worried about a neighboring slave treated cruelly by his master. Much like Layla worried about Fatima. She wished she could be as bold as Constance and dare to interfere. Layla recalled feeling such kinship with the girl as a child. Such admiration for her.

Today she walked the same streets Constance once tread. She likely passed by the milliner's shop her father had owned, and no one stared or gawked. She wasn't Layla the veiled Muslim woman from the Middle East.

She was plain old Layla.

Just a girl.

And oh, did it feel good.

She sensed no shame at having her head uncovered for all of creation to see. There was nothing to be ashamed of. The only shame would lie in denying her true self.

Her true heart.

Finally she understood.

Mo resisted the temptation to lean over and give the enchanting woman a feather light kiss on her luscious lips. He planted his hands into springy grass. So much for his good intentions to keep things platonic. But never in a million years had he expected Layla to toss her veil into the wind on their very first date. To press herself against him on the wide open street.

He had been terrified as he stood in the hallway waiting for her. So sure she would turn him down. He wasn't positive he could keep his lunch in his stomach. As she walked through the door and saw him there, her face told him everything he needed to know.

Layla so badly wanted to change, but he couldn't rush her. A step at a time. Let her see what life could be like without the veil: without the strictures, demands, and fear of Allah's judgment. Maybe in time, she'd be ready for more. He watched her stare at the stars and stripes. He wanted to tell her about freedom found in Christ. Not freedom in a flag.

But he had to start somewhere.

"So can we do this again?" He brushed a silky raven colored strand from her forehead.

"If we're careful."

"I was hoping we wouldn't have to sneak around. That maybe I could speak with your family."

"I don't want my uncle to know. He doesn't like you very much. He said he'd shoot you if you touched me again." Layla said it dreamily as she smiled into the sky.

Mo stiffened. "I don't even know your uncle. He wouldn't really..."

Layla sat up and placed her hand on his cheek. "No, no. Don't worry. Uncle's all talk. He saw us together that night at the party. He was being overprotective. But he's heard things about you. He said he didn't trust you. I think people are starting to suspect that you aren't so Muslim anymore." A shadow crossed her face.

"I'm sorry. I don't want to make things difficult."

"It's okay. You need to be true to yourself and what you believe. It's beginning to make sense to me." She placed a kiss on the tip of his nose.

He pulled back before he gave in to his desire to return the caress. "Maybe we should cool it with the kissing. Be friends for now. It's safer that way." For so many reasons. He needed to stay focused on his intentions to convert Layla before he let this romance go any further.

"You might be the best thing that's ever happened to me, Mo."

"Or the worst?" He couldn't keep the words from slipping out. He sat back.

"Let's take things slowly and keep them to ourselves for now. I don't want to share you anyway." Layla picked at the grass by her feet. "Mo, do you really think we could make this work? I mean, could we be one of those American families with two religions?"

He tried not to be disappointed by the question. "Let's just take things slowly like you said. Having two religions would be hard. Neither of us takes our faith lightly. The Bible doesn't recommend marrying outside the faith. But every time I try to turn away from you, it feels wrong. I've prayed so much about this, Layla. I want you to have a chance to be the person you long to be. That you dream to be. I can't bear the thought of your parents marrying you off to some traditionalist who will break your spirit. I want to keep you from that."

"You don't have to be my savior, Mo."

"I know. Somehow we'll work it out. And I don't have to make a big deal about my conversion right now. I can keep it quiet for a while longer."

"I don't want you to pretend you're someone who you aren't. I want us both to be free."

"Somehow, someway, Layla, we'll figure it out. We have to." He couldn't bear to consider the consequences if they didn't.

· ∴

TWENTY-SIX

How did the other guys sit around watching this inane spectacle, James wondered as he stared at the television screen surrounded by rancid pizza scraps. Men in tight pants jumping on one another. Patting their teammates on the rear. Dancing in the end zone. What a violent and ridiculous display.

This was an American pastime?

Then he remembered the young father playing football with his sons at the park. Okay, that had been nice to see. James sat alone in an old recliner in the frat house on Sunday evening wishing to be anywhere else.

Well, not quite anywhere. He could hardly go running home while Rain remained so obstinate. Nor did he want to go to the party that most of the frat guys had disappeared to. Booze and babes. Neither held appeal. He didn't want to become the out-of-control person his father was, and he didn't want some cheap bimbo.

He wanted Rain.

His woman.

Intact, the way she was a month ago. Or was it two months by now? He didn't know or care. He just wanted things back to normal. Was that too much to ask?

Derek, a pre-med buddy, walked into the room and kicked the recliner. "Get off your lazy rear, man. I want to take you somewhere."

"Anything to escape this football game. Makes me wish I didn't own a television." James stood and stretched. He'd spent most of the day sulking in the easy chair. Derek was a cool guy, and James needed company.

James followed Derek into the old theatre on the outskirts of campus. A lectern stood on the stage as he might have expected, but the casually clad musicians warming up their drums and electric guitars were a surprise.

"A concert?" He sat beside Derek on the worn cushioned seat.

"Something like that." Derek's grin suggested that wasn't the whole story.

"Who's playing?"

"Just give them a chance."

The room filled with students and a few young families while Derek and James discussed anatomy. The long-haired blond guy on the guitar shouted into the mike with a singsong voice. "Are you ready?"

The audience answered back, "Yeah."

"I said—are you ready?"

The people answered louder this time. "Yeah."

"Welcome to The Gathering. Stand up and join us."

Odd way to start a concert, but James stood to his feet and clapped along. Words flashed on an overhead projector. They were halfway through the first rhythmic tune before the truth struck James upside the head.

"This is a church?" He whispered loudly in Derek's ear.

"Yeah, man. So what? Is it like you expected church to be?"

"No...but..."

Derek grinned at him again. "So give it a try. Think of it as a fellowship. It's better than football. Am I right?"

James closed his mouth and crossed his arms over his chest, stretching his neck against the mounting strain in his muscles. He didn't want to make a scene. He should storm out the door, but Derek was right on every count. He had no desire to go back to the empty frat house and watch the stupid football game shrouded in loneliness.

So far the service didn't seem too objectionable. The music brought him some comfort, and the Bible wasn't completely worthless as a piece of wisdom literature. It contained the finest ancient poetry. He'd stay. Just this one time. For Derek. Maybe this place would give him some clue into what the heck had been going on with Rain.

James took a minute to survey the auditorium. On one side a man who could have been Jesus in jeans and Birkenstocks painted on a large easel. To the other side, a young energetic woman led a group of children in a boisterous circle dance.

This was church? He rubbed his chin as his tension ebbed.

The lyrics about God being great and revealed in creation did nothing for him. He had witnessed again and again the fallacy of that sentiment. However, something in the spirit of the place touched him.

He considered the corollaries between Christianity and his own belief system. Both encouraged a sense of gratefulness and dying to self. Both encouraged love, forgiveness, and generosity. Yet there was too much in Christianity he could never stomach. Beginning with their benevolent God and ending with their long list of antiquated rules.

For the moment, though, he decided to relax, clap along, and enjoy whatever this place had to offer. After a few songs the music slowed. The children went to sit with loving, smiling parents, and several other adults joined the young dancing woman, picking up colorful flags and waving them in worship. He could almost feel the wind of the spirit sweeping across his skin. James understood worship. But not worship directed toward a worthless God.

Either worthless or nonexistent.

No other options remained. Still, the worshippers were beautiful to watch.

The last song of the set repeated simple phrases. "Hallelujah." "You are worthy." "Lord we thank you." James closed his eyes and sang along. Just for the experience. He recalled sitting in a very different church with an elementary school friend long ago, perhaps singing these same words. What was the boy's name? Jim? Joe? Jeff? His home had provided a safe haven for James on many occasions. How had he forgotten?

Jeff. Yes, that was his name.

Jeff's mother had often smiled at him, kissed his forehead, and wiped away his tears. She smelled of lilacs when she hugged him to her soft chest. Almost like an angel sent by some benevolent sort of God. But the memory had been too wrapped up in painful ones, and he had nearly lost it.

Mo sat in the cushioned theatre-style seat. He listened as the young African-American pastor wearing jeans and an oversized polo began his lesson on love, pacing back and forth across the generous stage. I Corinthians 13 was his text. How would Pastor Mike feel if he realized Mo had disregarded his wise counsel and gone out with Layla twice already?

He hid further behind the tall man with the tri-colored hat sitting in front of him. Mo hadn't wanted to be sneaky, but Layla's uncle didn't sound like a reasonable man. Perhaps he could find a way to speak with her father.

"So the goal." Pastor Mike thumped his fist on the podium. "Is to lay down our own desires. Submitting in love to one another. Putting our brother and sister before ourselves."

Mo had tried to keep things in the friendship zone. Really he had.

He listened to the definition of love once again, brushing his fingers over the fresh, crinkly page of his Bible. He shouldn't have taken Layla's hand and held her close. Not yet. That sort of love didn't seem to be what the scriptures referred to at all. He should just be there for Layla and be a friend like he intended in the first place. Could he pull back?

"What greater love has any man than this..." Mike's tone took on a poetic lilt reminiscent of Martin Luther King Jr. "That he lay down his life for his friends?"

Mo was only human, after all. He was doing his best to follow God step by step and day by day, as he had learned in this very place. Had God asked him to be so romantic and affectionate with this girl? Probably not. But he felt certain bringing Layla back into his life aligned with God's plans. And he didn't know how to be with her without loving her. He would keep praying and keep trusting.

God was not too small to fix his mistakes.

He brought the Bible to his nose, drinking in the fresh leather scent that always filled his soul with peace.

Maybe he should talk more with Pastor Mike.

James stared at the worn book in Derek's hand, leaning closer to decipher the words as the man on stage read them, causing the wooden arm rest between them to press against his side. *Love never gives up. Love cares more for others than for self... Love doesn't strut, doesn't have a swelled head, doesn't force itself on others... Doesn't fly off the handle... Always looks for the best, never looks back... Love never dies.* James glanced at the pastor. Warmth shining from the eyes of the young black man lent truth to his statement.

The words swirled through James's head. That was the sort of love he dreamed of, desired his whole life. That was the sort of love Rain showered upon him, yet he failed her so tragically in giving it back. James gave up. James cared more about his needs than Rain's. James strutted with a swelled head and longed for Rain's affirmation of his pride. James tried to force the sweet, caring woman to abort the life inside of her. He assumed the worst. That she had planned it. That she had tricked him. But that wasn't like Rain at all. She was the most honest person he knew. He flew off the handle. He looked back.

But at least his love had never died.

"It takes courage to give this type of love," the Pastor intoned.

James considered the Taoist viewpoint. The words of Lao Tzu were not so different. *Being deeply loved by someone gives you strength, while loving someone deeply gives you courage.*

He pressed his hand to his forehead, massaging his temples

with thumb and forefinger. What was he thinking? Rain could never hurt a living creature. She caught spiders by their long skinny legs and carried them outside. The one time she crushed a mosquito by instinct as it bit her while she stood in the corner of the kitchen, he spied a tear in her eye. And he wanted her to destroy a child. Her child. His child.

Their child.

James still struggled to wrap his mind around the idea. He dragged his hand down his goatee and pulled in a breath, blowing it out in a low swoosh.

Could this type of love the pastor spoke of turn him into the father he needed to be? He had no use for the Christian God, but maybe the faith did contain something of value. James considered himself an open-minded guy. Most of the world's religions held some beauty hidden within. He wasn't above gleaning the good from Christianity. The pastor had mentioned letting go of old wounds.

Maybe if James could change?

Maybe it wasn't too late.

Lao Tzu was also famous for saying, *A journey of a thousand miles begins with a single step.*

TWENTY-SEVEN

"Are you sure you don't want to come with us?" Allie said from the living area.

Rain stood in her kitchenette, filling a plate with pickles for an evening snack. The vinegar scent called her name. She waved to Allie and Layla as they gathered their purses. "No, really, go enjoy the movie without me. I'm pooped. You wouldn't believe the energy this tiny person drains from me."

"Are you sure?" Layla smiled. "My treat."

"I seriously can't. But thanks for dinner. You're awesome. That afternoon at the mall did me in." Rain feigned hobbling to the living room with a cane. "You youngsters go along now and don't worry about these tired old bones. I'll be hitting the hay soon enough."

"Nice." Allie walked over for a hug. "I'm still older than you. You realize that, right?"

Layla did the standard Lebanese set of three kisses against Rain's cheeks. "Fine, get some rest. You do look tired. But call us if you need anything."

The girls headed out the door.

So Rain sat down alone on the couch and ate her pickles. Pickles, of all things. The pregnancy hormones must be kicking in. She held up the sour green spear. What was the appeal? *Oh well,* she thought, and devoured three more. Thankfully, she hadn't experienced much nausea, but she was certainly eating for two, even if one of those two only weighed a few ounces. And she could easily sleep twelve hours a night.

The place was too quiet. She snatched up the remote from

the end table and clicked on the television, randomly flipping to the first mindless sitcom. The smiling Africa-American family on the screen taunted Rain and her empty house.

She clicked the television off and downed yet another pickle.

But she did grin to herself as she recalled Allie's story of her latest scuffle with Andy. That guy was hilarious. Getting all worked up over nothing like that. She had been raised to think physical desire natural and beautiful.

On the other hand, what would Allie and Layla think if she admitted losing her virginity to James at age sixteen in her own bedroom with her parents' blessing? Now that she was about to become a mother herself, the idea seemed strange to Rain as well. She wanted to raise her child with traditional values. What would her parents think? What would James think?

James.

Her plate of pickles sat bare now. Maybe she'd walk to the corner store to get some more. Rain picked up her wallet, dreading the contents. She opened it and flipped through the crisp bills. Three dollars. Pulling the snap to the change section brought no comfort. A few quarters and some pennies glinted from the pocket. That wouldn't pay the rent coming due this week.

She knelt down by the couch to pray as had become her habit, not daring to dwell on her circumstances. Instead she cried her heart out to God. Food, shelter, she could live without. She'd done it before.

But James?

She tried to count her blessings as her mother taught her to do. The dinner Layla had bought for her. The roof still over her head. The promise of a bed at Allie's house if needed. The little life growing inside of her...

Things could be worse.

Right?

James took another sip of his steaming black coffee and

shook his head in wonder. He glanced at the abstract paintings along the wall of the shop. Their randomness comforted him somehow. The man sitting across from him at the small round table seriously blew his mind. Where did this guy come from?

"So we could really use your help at the soup kitchen if you're available." Pastor Mike leaned back in his chair, although his eyes sparkled with enthusiasm.

"Sure thing. I work nights, but I'm off most Thursdays. I'll try to do that. It's harder to find time for helping others now with my school schedule, but I've always had a strong sense of social justice." James took a moment to explain his years spent traveling with Rain.

The girl had been fearless, following him anywhere. She supported him no matter the challenges he faced. Her huge heart overflowed to everyone they came in contact with. Her smile alone spread joy and contentment to those surrounding her. Reaching out to the poor and the needy. Comforting those who hurt. How had he ever let her go?

"I'm right there with you, man. *What you've done for the least of these you've done for me.* I spent five years in Africa digging wells. Boy, do I miss those days." The pastor crossed his arms over a broad chest that spoke of a history with manual labor.

"Ever think about going back?"

"Maybe when the kids get a little older. But I think God wants me here right now." He had introduced James to his wife Serena and their three stair-step preschoolers at the service. James recognized the oldest daughter as one of the children who danced in the back of the church.

Church.

The word still made his head spin, but he was thankful Derek had dragged him there. Maybe the universe had planned it all along.

"So tell me what I can do for you." Pastor Mike reached for his own steaming mug.

"I need to be a good father." James stared straight into the man's deep brown eyes.

"What's stopping you?"

Good question. James considered it a moment before answering. "I don't think I know how to love. Not like you talked about. My father... It has a lot to do with my father. He..." He hated to say more, but if he was ever going to talk about it, he needed to start here and now.

A journey of a thousand miles and all that.

"He beat me. Insulted me. Blamed me for everything."

Pastor Mike shook his head but never turned away. "That's some heavy stuff, man. You sure you're ready to deal with it?"

"It's now or never. If I don't deal with it, I'll lose everything."

"It's gonna be rough." Brotherhood exuded from Pastor Mike, shined from his eyes.

"I know." Not the sort to pull any punches, James had already made certain Pastor Mike understood he had no interest in God or church. The guy was cool, though. No pretense. No pride. No persuasion. He seemed to like and appreciate James for who he was. For a moment James dared to believe that the love Mike preached about might be real.

The pastor leaned forward, elbows on knees. "I could probably arrange for some free counseling with a church member who's working on his PhD in psychology. Do you think you'd be up for it?"

"If you can work it out, I promise to give it a try."

Rain startled awake in her cozy bed, cuddling a warm afghan around her chin. Golden early morning sunlight filtered through the blinds, creating a horizontal pattern across the wooden floor. Hadn't she fallen asleep cold and crying on the couch the night before?

Her eyes darted about the room until she found her answer. On the dining table sat a vase full of sunflowers, her favorites, along with a box of chocolates and a card. She crawled out of bed and tiptoed to the table, as if it were a shrine deserving the utmost reverence.

A memory trickled from the haze of sleep.

James carrying her and tucking her in.

She opened the thick card. A stack of twenty dollar bills fell onto the table. Inside it said, "I love you. The rent is paid. I'm trying to change. James."

Surveying the room again, her stomach dropped as she noted nothing to suggest he had returned. No suitcase. No oversized jacket tossed over the counter. No sandalwood cologne drifting through the air. Other than the flowers, the apartment looked as bare as ever. She clutched the card to her chest. At least it was something. A start.

Rain collapsed into a dining room chair wailing with relief. She placed her hand to her abdomen, cuddling the tiny life in her belly. "We're going to make it. We're going to be okay."

If only she could convince her heart it was true. How much longer could she survive without James beside her?

TWENTY-EIGHT

Allie sat with Rain and Layla in the library Tuesday afternoon pouring over volumes of poetry. She read aloud the verses by Saint Catherine about being enclosed in God, about dwelling in him like the sea in the fish and the fish in the sea.

"Medieval Christian mystics." Allie shook her head. "I can't believe I never heard of them before."

"I know," Rain said. "Aren't they great?"

"The poems are lovely." Layla smiled. "Saint Catherine reminds me so much of our Middle Eastern Rabia."

"Mm, definitely. Rabia's poem about the temple, the shrine, and the mosque dissolving into God, how beautiful was that?" Allie clicked her pen against the book. At first the poem had struck her as heretical, but the more she thought about it, a deeper meaning began to emerge. The poem conveyed such strength of feeling. Such closeness with God. Much like St. Catherine's verses. Amazing that an ancient Muslim had written it.

"Yes, we definitely need to capture some of that emotion in our poem for class." Rain jotted down notes for once.

Allie tossed the book on the coffee table between them. "We have our work cut out for us."

Layla nodded. "This will be the hardest assignment yet. I'm certainly no poet."

"We'll figure it out." Rain spoke with confidence. "How difficult can it be? We'll focus on a central image to represent each of us and tie them together with the deeper quest we have in common. That's why I recommended these poets. I've seen them all together in an anthology of Eastern and Western mystics. Each stresses love and intimate relationship with God. We'll do the same." She clapped.

Allie raised a questioning brow to Layla at Rain's bizarre level of enthusiasm over poetry.

Layla shrugged.

"You're in a chipper mood." Allie leaned back and crossed her ankles on the table, eyeing Rain. "What happened since Sunday?"

"A miracle."

"A miracle?" Layla sat forward.

Rain filled Allie and Layla in on the details of James's surprise visit.

Allie breathed a sigh of relief, tucking a strand of hair behind her ear. Guilt plagued her for weeks. She hated thinking her high ideals had separated Rain and James. However, she didn't feel quite as confident as Rain that things would work out.

"So, when will Mo get here?" Rain's whisper held a hint of conspiracy.

Layla pulled out her cell phone and checked the time. "Soon."

"He really has no idea?" Allie said. She hoped this wasn't a mistake, but Layla had assured them that this was what she wanted.

"I don't think so." Layla twisted her fingers in her lap.

"Tell us more about the beach on Saturday. We got sidetracked last time the subject came up," Rain said.

"Besides the fact that it was surprisingly warm." Allie wiggled her eyebrows at Layla over their shared secret.

"You already told us that part." Layla blushed.

Allie had braved an outing to the oceanfront on Saturday with her family for a picnic. "Not as bad as I feared. It's easier to get along with them when I'm not living at the house. I even did some surfing with my brother."

"Was it fun?" Layla asked.

"Well, he's no Andy...but..."

"Good thing!" Rain pointed at Allie. The hint at Allie's romantic interlude with Andy last week provoked a fresh round of giggles.

"So have you decided yet? Don't you owe him a phone call tomorrow?" Layla asked.

Allie didn't need Layla's reminder. She had thought of little else for days. "I do, but I'm not sure what to say. I'm still annoyed, but I miss him too. It's weird. When I'm with him, it feels so right. But when we're apart, all the old sensations come back. I get this choking, strangled feeling like I did when we were engaged. The ring pinches my finger all over again."

"Hmm." Rain folded her hands and looked at Allie overtop. All she needed was a pair of glasses to play the role of amateur shrink to perfection. "Those are some pretty intense reactions. Do you think you might be holding some sort of grudge?"

Allie squinted, but it gave her no clearer vision into her own soul. "I didn't think I was the type of person to do that, but maybe I am. I certainly haven't been very gracious about the whole church issue. Andy gave me some great advice that's helping me see my mom in a different light. That made it a lot easier to get along with her this weekend."

"Maybe you need to apply that same advice to your relationship with him," Layla suggested.

"That's the problem. He recommended I stop worrying about what my mom thinks of me." Allie tucked up her knees to her chest and leaned her chin against them. "As much as that helps, I don't see how it would work with Andy. The man wants me to marry him. I have to care about what he thinks, don't I? I mean technically, he would be the head of my home someday. I can hardly think of him as a weaker Christian. I still worry that he's judging me. He swears he's not, but he's sending mixed signals. I'm not sure if I'm ready to trust him yet."

"Obviously you can't date the guy if you feel all choked up and panicky when you think about him. I wonder if there's more to it?" Rain pressed a forefinger to her chin.

Should Allie tell them she felt God leading her to give Andy a chance?

The girls dropped the subject at the sight of Mo.

Mo turned a corner in the library, and there she was, sitting between her friends in a soft pink veil and creamy tunic over jeans. The most beautiful girl in the world. They all stared as he approached, but Mo had never minded the attention of females.

"Hi, Mo." Rain stretched out the words. "Long time no see."

"How are you ladies on this fine Indian Summer day?"

"We're great," Allie said. "Especially Rain. I haven't seen her in such a good mood in a month."

"Yes. I had a miracle this week."

"Really." Mo wondered if these girls might share his faith. Maybe they could help with Layla. Maybe they already did. A miracle. He was about to ask for details when Rain cut back in.

"Yes, but nothing like the miracle of Mo and Layla reunited. I hear you're taking her to the ocean today."

Mo glanced back and forth between the smiling girls, wondering what they were up to. "Yeah, it might be our last chance till spring. Layla only got to swim once this year. That should be a crime in Virginia Beach."

"The water's still nice. I'm sure you'll have a great time."

Rain gazed at him with mischief in her eyes.

"Just don't tell my auntie," Layla said. "She'd freak. Lebanese people think anything cold makes you sick. I can barely sneak a pint of ice cream into the house."

"Oh, I imagine the water temperature is the least of your secrets, Miss Al-Rai." Rain winked. "You are quite the rebel these days."

"Not a rebel," Allie said. "Just her true self."

Layla's cheeks tinged the color of her veil. So pretty. Mo longed to kiss her cheek. She reminded him of a timid little mouse. *Fara,* the Lebanese endearment ran through his mind. "I'm so pleased Layla's trying new things."

"Me too," Rain said.

"I like seeing her so free and confident." Allie gazed at Layla with the affection of an older sister.

The color on Layla's face deepened to a berry shade. "Enough, enough. Let's get out of here, Mo, before I die of embarrassment." Layla picked up her bag.

Mo blew her a kiss. "I'll meet you outside. Beware of spies. Bye, ladies. Have a great afternoon."

"You too," Rain called after him. Rain and Allie burst out laughing as he departed the library. What were these girls up to?

Layla took a bracing breath as Mo pulled into the residential area on the deserted side of the beach a few blocks from where they had met at the MSU party. He jumped out and grabbed the supplies from the trunk. "Mo," Layla called out the window. "I need a minute. Can you meet me down there?"

Mo looked at her quizzically. "Sure."

Once Mo disappeared over the sand dune, Layla stepped out of the car. She pushed off her loafers. Unwrapped the soft pink veil from her head. Slid off the creamy tunic. Taking another deep breath, she removed her jeans.

She stood in a cute swimsuit of a pink and blue striped tank top with a pair of blue shorts. Although Rain and Allie helped her choose it at the mall on Sunday, it had been all her own idea. Allie resisted at first, not wanting Layla to rebel against her beliefs, but Layla assured them that this was what she wanted.

Allie confirmed that the swimsuit they selected bespoke modesty and respectability in this nation and was no sin according to biblical beliefs. In fact, Layla feared it belonged on a forty-year-old mother of five. She felt her cheeks flaming, but continued on, convinced that while wearing a swimsuit was new to her, it brought no shame. She stuffed her feet into a pair of flip-flops and grabbed her bag. After one more glance around the empty street, she marched toward the dune in Mo's wake. This felt right in that place deep in her heart. She would not allow her mother's voice in her head for even a second on this beautiful day.

Mo blinked at the vision floating toward him down the wooden walkway. Perhaps floating wasn't quite the right word. Perhaps skittering like the shy mouse he adored. No wonder the girls couldn't contain their giggles. Layla Al-Rai had purchased a swimsuit, albeit the most modest swimsuit he had ever seen.

As she came closer, he saw fear cross her face, but she continued putting one courageous foot in front of the other. At the end of the walkway, she dared to strike a pose. Mo smiled and waved. Layla was too curvy to be an emaciated fashion model. He watched her silken black hair billowing about her shoulders and swallowed down a lump in his throat.

What had he done to deserve such perfection? God had created a true work of art in this young woman.

She stopped beside the beach blanket and fidgeted with the strap of her suit. "What do you think?"

Mo was having a hard time thinking straight at all, so went with the last coherent word to cross his mind. "Perfection."

She knelt down beside him. "It's so strange."

"Do you like it?"

"I think I could get used to it. The sun feels good against

my skin."

"Well, let's get some sunblock on that virgin skin of yours." She brushed her hand over her arm. "I'm too dark to burn."

"When's the last time your arms and legs saw the sunshine?"

"My arms, age twelve. My legs...? I don't know?"

Mo handed her the bottle of sunscreen. Layla slathered it over her limbs, taking a deep whiff of the coconut scent. She gave him the bottle and allowed him to rub it on her back. Mo attempted to focus on the task as his hands slipped over the soft slopes of her shoulders. He came back around to the front of her and swiped a dollop on her nose, spreading it over her sculpted cheekbones with his fingers.

He'd better lighten the moment, and quick. "There you go. Like a regular beach babe."

"Layla Al-Rai. A beach babe?"

"Why not? Let's relax, warm up a little, and let that soak in before we hit the water."

"Okay." Layla leaned back against the blanket and closed her eyes. "The sun sort of tingles, doesn't it."

Mo lay down beside her. "I never really thought about it."

"Hot sun and cold water. Auntie would have a fit." They settled into companionable silence, enjoying the scents and sounds of the sea while baking in the warm fall sunshine. Mo wondered what it would be like to be a Muslim woman who had forgotten the feel of the sun.

Layla perked back up after a few quiet moments spent acclimating to her new swimsuit. This was even better than a *burqini*. And Mo seemed to like it. She turned and sat cross-legged on the sundrenched blanket.

"How many children do you want, Mo?"

"I don't know. Two or three. I could probably be talked into more."

"And you really don't mind if your wife works?"

He laid his hand over hers. "I'm not like that, Layla. My wife and I will decide together what's best for our family. I want a partner, not a servant."

She smiled into his warm brown eyes. She hadn't imagined it. He was the perfect man. "That's what I thought. Ready for a swim?"

He stood and flexed his toned body. "Yeah, I can't believe how hot it is here in October. It'll be snowing soon in Ohio."

"Hmm," Layla leaned back on her elbows, watching him stretch. "Or maybe I should just enjoy the view a while longer."

"Get up, silly girl." Mo pulled her to her feet. They both glanced around once again, but they had the beach to themselves. "Race you."

They splashed into the water side-by-side, gasping at the chilly temperature. When Mo dove head first into a breaker, Layla joined him. Her body streaked like lightening through the water with no fabric to hold it back. Her head split the surface. Cool waves lapped against her skin.

Layla dove back under to enjoy the weightless sensation of gliding beneath the water like a fish. Her body so light and free. So unrestrained. She felt at ease swimming in her bathing suit. Not nervous a wave would knock her over and trap her heavy body. Not worried a breaker would snatch her veil from her head.

Mo continued swimming into deeper water, past where she could touch the soft sandy bottom. Layla had never ventured so far. But she felt like superwoman, strong and capable of anything. And Mo would keep her safe as always. She followed him into the depths of the ocean.

Bobbing beside him over the swells as they tugged her to and fro, she splashed him in delight. Mo. What had she done to deserve him?

"How is it?" Mo finally broke the silence.

"Better than I ever dreamed." Layla tipped to float on her back and rocked atop the ocean like a babe in a cradle.

She may have no idea where they could go from here, but at least she would enjoy the ride until the world came crashing in on her.

TWENTY-NINE

Allie had to call Andy. Her week was over. She sat at her desk late in the evening, pressing her back into the rungs of the hard wooden chair, her eyes glued to the cell phone in her hand. No point in putting it off any longer. She punched in his number and cringed as the phone jangled against her ear.

"Allie?" His tentative voice came over the line.

"Yeah."

"So...how is everything?"

"Fine." She knew she should say more, but she couldn't find the words.

"Which means?"

"I'm not sure, Andy. I promised I'd call, and I called."

"Have you had time to think about things? To pray?"

She brushed some crumbs from the desk. "I guess so." In truth she hadn't prayed much. Didn't really want to know what God might have to say.

"And."

Allie swallowed hard. "And. I do think God wants me to give you a chance, but I'm so scared."

"Scared? Of me?" He sounded sad. Disappointed. Hurt.

"Of you. Of what you represent. Of how I felt when we were engaged. I don't think you realize how awful it was for me."

"Wow."

She didn't want to hurt him more. But she had to be honest. It was their only chance. "And remember what you said about me holding grudges against my parents and the church."

"I don't think I used the word *grudges*..."

"I have held on to those bad feelings. The bigger problem is, I've done it with you too. I'm not sure how to fix that. I mean, I can say the magic words. That's easy. I forgive you, Andy. I forgive you. I can even try it with my eyes closed. Andy, I forgive you. But it doesn't change the way my chest constricts and my throat closes up when I think back to those days." Tears filled her eyes. She wished it could be so easy. She wished some magic spell could make it all go away.

"Now I don't know what to say. I mean...I'm not sure forgiveness is even the right word. Do you want something bad to happen to me? Do you want me to suffer for how I hurt you?"

"No. Of course not. I want you to be happy." Allie swiped at the tears rolling down her cheeks.

"Then maybe the issue is more about reconciliation and trust. You don't trust me."

"I guess not. I don't know how," she whispered.

"Do you have any...plans?"

"This might be something I can talk to Rain about. Her mom was a psychologist, and she's growing close to God these days in her own way."

"Maybe you can find some sort of book." He didn't sound very hopeful.

"Maybe."

He blew out a breath. "I wonder if we could do pre-pre-marital counseling."

"You have to admit, it seems ridiculous to put so much effort into a relationship that died almost a decade ago."

"So why are you?"

She sighed. "I think I'm supposed to. I don't know what else to say, Andy. But I need more time. I'm going to visit some churches this weekend. Maybe if I don't feel so trapped in that awful congregation, I'll be able to see you differently."

"You're sure this is what you need? Time? Space? We've had eight years apart."

Poor guy. Allie wished she didn't have to share this. "I'm not sure of anything, Andy."

"Are you saying that you don't have feelings for me at all?"

"Don't be silly." Her lips tingled at the memory of his kisses. "You know I do. But I still have a lot of negative reactions too."

"Then there's hope." His voice cracked.

"I think so. But I need to get past this."

"I'll wait. I love you."

"I...I care deeply about you, Andy."

"Bye, Allie."

Rain and Allie entered the old theatre on Sunday night. The place certainly didn't fit Rain's expectations. There were no stained glass windows or altars or incense. The place felt casual, homey, and warm. Allie's family church had a stiffer, formal feel to the brown and cream sanctuary circa 1970. This morning they tried Reality Church, but the place had a dark, death metal vibe, which was totally cool, but didn't fit Rain's taste. Allie agreed that it didn't feel much like church to her either.

This place with its worn satin walls and bright red stage curtain exuded a festive mood. While unexpected, the décor seemed to match the purpose of church. The congregants wore normal casual clothing rather than chains and spikes. Rain recognized many students from the university.

Tension seeped into her body at the reminder that James could discover she had visited this church. She pushed it aside, though. The only positive step in their relationship had so clearly emerged as an answer to prayer. Perhaps in a strange way pressing closer to God could bring her closer to James as well, although logically it made little sense.

She still didn't plan to rush into any sort of "commitment." Making Jesus "Lord" of her life struck her as odd. Surely such antiquated ideas faded with feudalism. Why should she need a "savior" to forgive her sins? Rain spent her whole life striving to live in harmony with the universe. She may not be perfect, but she'd never done anything evil.

Allie wore a smile. The place must appeal to her as well.

"There's Venessa." Rain pointed to the young lady with curly, platinum-blond hair hanging out in the back with some small children.

"Good, I was hoping to meet her."

They started in that direction, but stopped mid-stride as they heard their names.

"Allie! Rain!" An enthusiastic Mo rushed over to them. "Wow. Welcome. I'm so glad to see you guys here."

Rain couldn't remember if they were supposed to know about the whole conversion thing or if it was a secret. But since Mo seemed comfortable seeing them, she didn't bother faking surprise. "I'm baby-sitting Allie while she tries out some new churches." Rain nudged her.

"Funny." Allie rolled her eyes. "I grew up in Virginia Beach, but I've sort of outgrown the family church."

"So I guess..." Mo said.

"Layla? No, sweetie, she's not even close to ready for something like this." Rain swept her hand across the room.

"Yeah," Allie said. "She came to my church once for a school assignment. I thought she'd have a heart attack."

"I figured. I just..." Mo took a deep breath. "I'm glad she has you two in her life."

"You can't rush these things." Rain patted his arm. "Trust me. I know."

"Hey. Tell me about your miracle," Mo said.

"Oh, it's a long story. Short version is that I'm pregnant and my significant other doesn't want the child and walked out."

Allie put a supportive arm around Rain's shoulder.

"Man." Shock washed over Mo's face.

Probably not what he was expecting from a churchgoing girl. "You look like Layla did when I told her." Rain chuckled. "Anyway, the miracle is that he snuck in at night to leave presents and enough money to get me through another month. And he paid the rent."

"Yes, I spent a good hour on my knees thanking God for that one." Allie gave Rain a squeeze. "Otherwise she'd be crashing at my place." She winked.

"Shut up." Rain pushed her away. "Dork."

Mo studied their interaction and smiled. "I was going to say, 'Praise the Lord,' but somehow that doesn't fit after 'dork.' They're about to start. Would you ladies like to join me?"

"I want to introduce Allie to Venessa first. Save us some seats."

Rain and Allie headed to the back corner. "Venessa."

"Rain!" The bouncy girl with white-blond curls ran over and hugged her. "And you must be the dancer." Venessa held out her hand. "Welcome to The Gathering."

Allie shook it and gestured to the patterned carpet. "So this is where the action takes place."

"Yes. Hang out back here with me. I'll teach you some Jewish round dances. I'm sure they'll seem really simplistic..."

"No worries. Sounds like fun." Allie's face lit up.

"What about you, Rain?"

"Nah, this is Allie's thing, and I'm tired. I'll go sit with Mo."

"Cool." Venessa picked up a tambourine and handed it to Allie. "I'll take good care of her."

Rain headed back to Mo, glad to be off the hook. She was so exhausted lately. This baby sapped most of her strength. Missing James sucked whatever little she had left. She was in no mood to dance.

Mo scratched his head as he returned to his chair through the long narrow aisle. The girls knew each other for less than two months, yet they behaved like old friends. He wondered if Layla shared such closeness with them. From the stories she'd told him, he imagined she did. Rain's admission had startled him. Not long ago, he would have warned Layla away from such a heathen, but in this church he learned you would never win anyone to Christ by judging them.

People didn't need to clean themselves up. They could come to God as they were. He was more than able to take it from there.

Mo flipped down the theatre-style chair and sat, leaning his elbows on his knees. He still struggled with the concept of grace. In Islam, he had to earn everything himself. He defended Allah with all his might, never understanding that God longed to be his defense. That he could never be good enough through his own works. That God loved him and paid the price long ago.

Moisture came to his eyes as he thought about it, and he pressed his thumb and forefinger to his tear ducts. The ideas still overwhelmed him. If only Layla could understand.

Rain seemed like a sweet girl. Allie didn't say much, but it sounded like she had been a believer for many years. What drew these women together? They had nothing in common.

He scratched his head again. A wave of thankfulness washed over Mo. Whatever the reason, God must have a hand in it.

Rain came to join him as the first song began. "Allie's going to hang with the dancers for a while. I'm glad we came."

"That's right. She's a dancer." Mo watched the slender blond with her ballerina bun as she flowed easily through the steps Venessa demonstrated.

"Yeah, and her family attends this super uptight church down by the beach front. They're always twisting her arm to go with them."

He knew the feeling. "She should put her own spiritual well-being before her family's expectations. And trust me, that's a hard thing for a former Muslim to say. I hope she finds what she's looking for here."

"Are you kidding?" Rain pointed to Allie dancing merrily. "This is exactly what she needs."

Rain looked cautious standing beside him. She glanced around and read the words on the screen. She clapped softly at first, taking everything in. Then her hands began to move with more assurance, and she joined the singing with a strong alto voice.

And what do you need? Mo wondered but didn't verbalize.

He hoped whatever it was, Rain would find it in this place.

THIRTY

After the service, Allie let Rain drive her the few blocks to the bungalow. Allie invited her inside and put on a pot of decaf. She had cleaned up before leaving, and the place looked tolerably neat. "We should have an hour or two before the teeny-boppers crash the place."

"Come on. They're not that bad." Rain sat on a stool at the bar separating the kitchen from the living room.

Allie shot her a look. Rain had witnessed the never-ending slumber party from hell firsthand.

"Okay." Rain admitted. "They are."

"They're so perky and sunshiny. It makes me want to talk about dead kittens just to wipe the vapid grins off their faces." Allie demonstrated by pasting on her phony church smile and smearing her hand over it with a touch of violence.

"You're twisted." Rain smiled. "I doubt I'll make it late enough to see them again. Too bad for me." Rain pouted her lower lip.

Allie rummaged through the cabinets. She settled for a bag of Oreos, arranged them on a plate, and set them down in front of Rain.

"This is how you stay thin?" Rain picked up an Oreo and examined it.

"Roommates. I like to eat healthy, but with as many hours as I put in at the studio, it really doesn't matter."

Rain tried a bite. "Do you think the chocolate's real? I could sure go for a stack."

"Yes, focus on the dark anti-oxidant rich cocoa."

"Excellent." Rain devoured several cookies. "So, you liked it, right? Looked like you had fun."

"I did." Allie thought back on the service. She hadn't danced that way in months. Free and unrestrained. Spontaneous. There was something marvelous about moving from deep in her core. No prescribed patterns. No rehearsals. Allowing the heavenlies, the kingdom of God within her, to flow out her fingertips and toes. She did a little spin in the kitchen as she thought about it. What would Andy think? Could he accept such a thing?

"You looked beautiful back there. I got a little misty eyed." Rain pretended to wipe away a few tears.

"We used to dance that way during our morning devotional time when I was with *Alight*. I felt weird doing it during an actual church service."

"It's a casual place. I enjoyed it. Felt like a celebration. Better than the slam-dancing this morning." Rain reached for another cookie.

"Much. I liked it, but I just didn't feel quite at home. I can't put my finger on it. Maybe I'm stuck in a rut, and I need a more traditional morning service."

"Isn't that what you have already?"

"Not that traditional." Allie stuck out her tongue.

"The sermon was good. I liked the pastor," Rain said. "But I can keep visiting churches with you to hold your hand."

"I'd say shut up, but I kind of need you to."

"It's not like I have anything else to do on the weekends," Rain said.

"At least things are moving in a good direction with James."

"Yeah." Rain wiped her hands on a napkin. "At least." The right side of her lips turned up into a grin, but it didn't quite reach her eyes.

Allie wished she could do more for her. She thought of the vulnerable little life growing in Rain's womb. What a huge responsibility. At least Rain enjoyed the church. Allie had watched her with bated breath during the altar call. Two students went forward, and while Rain smiled her approval, she didn't seem interested in following their lead. Allie didn't want to push her friend. Maybe she'd already made some sort of decision on her own.

The Gathering. Allie loved that name. It had been perfect. So why didn't the place feel like home?

James didn't go to church. He thought about it, but he felt awkward standing in the middle of a congregation busy worshipping a God he didn't believe in. He did, however, sit on his bouncy blow-up mattress on the floor of Derek's room, surrounded by anatomy posters, and read a Bible. He needed to understand more about this Christianity stuff before his first meeting with the counselor. Make sure there was nothing too terrible he should watch out for. So far so good. He'd been thumbing through the different books. Mostly a lot of history and poetry. Some of the topics surprised him.

He thought Christianity was supposed to be all neat and clean from the sanitized versions he'd observed. The Bible had stories of rape, incest, child sacrifice. Of course they were considered evil, but still, he hadn't expected that sort of raw portrayal. And so much violence. Enough blood, guts, and gore to please any horror fan. He thought Christians were naïvely optimistic. Blind to the evil in the world. But at least their book wasn't.

Buzz, nicknamed after his haircut, poked his head through the door. "Oh, no." He pointed to the book in James's hands. "Don't tell me he's getting to you too."

"No, man." He slapped the Bible against his thigh. "Just trying to figure out what makes Derek tick."

"Derek's great. Don't get me wrong." Buzz picked up a small blue ODU Monarchs basketball from the desk and tossed it overhead a few times. "But I do not understand the dude."

"No worries. I'm not about to buy into all this God nonsense."

"Good." Buzz tossed the ball back on the desktop. "Stay true."

James raised his fist as Buzz headed out. "Stay true."

He leaned back against his pillow. How did Christians bring

it all together? Dealing with evil but still imagining a God could exist. It made no sense to him.

And that Song of Solomon book. Sexy stuff. But it made him think of Rain, so he flipped past it.

James looked at the volume in his hand. He could finish the second half tomorrow. He wondered how long the guys would put up with him crashing on their floor. He suspected Derek would do anything to keep him from getting his own place and deserting Rain for good.

Nice guy, that Derek. James would have never guessed he was a Christian. He didn't talk about it, but thinking more, James realized there was a difference between him and the other frat guys. He wondered why Derek even lived here. He wasn't into all the partying. He'd maybe have one beer, but then he'd spend the rest of the night keeping the other guys out of trouble.

Real nice guy. Maybe becoming more like Derek wouldn't be so horrible.

THIRTY-ONE

Layla rested in her favorite cushy chair staring at her laptop with tears in her eyes. The surrounding pink room blurred in a haze. She had spent another two amazing weeks with Mo, and yet her friend Fatima's situation grew worse than she ever expected. What could she possibly do to help? She read the e-mail through for the third time.

> *Layla,*
> *Sister of my heart. Part of me hates to write at all. I have no good news to brighten your day. But as you persist in asking how I am, I must assume that you truly care despite your exciting new life. I fear you are the only one. Who cares, I mean. Even at mosque I stay sequestered on the female side, lost among the women in their long black robes. The women with no faces like me. The women with muffled voices and haunting eyes.*
> *I suppose in a way Father's plan is working. I find myself longing for a husband, a home, children. At least it is something. For now I have nothing. Father's chains grow tighter about me. Squeezing the life from me.*
> *Oh Layla, why must I say such things? Think such things? Even among family I feel lost. The women speak of cooking and decorations, and I care not. I would speak of*

literature, of philosophy, of science, of truth. No one mentions bruises or black eyes, as if a well-prepared meal, an organized home, can wipe it all away. The women hold their parties and chat merrily, dance happily, slap their cards down on the table in delight, far from the prying observation of men, but I cannot. They are forever a shadow over me.

A prison around me.

Perhaps this country is to blame. It has ruined me for my own culture. I long to run away. To hide in your bedroom and hear every detail about your classes. About your new friends.

For now I content myself to read. I download English books as you suggested and learn about the wonders of the world. No one seems to notice. As long as I'm quiet and keep to myself, they are happy to leave me to my little handheld machine. My electronic gateway to an existence beyond the veil. But it opens too many new thoughts, too many new ideas. A pleasant sort of torture. Some days I long to throw it out the window and watch it smash upon the concrete.

And I write. I write my heart.

I'm so sorry, my friend. I did exactly what I swore not to do. I spilled my sorrows upon the page. But you are the only one to tell. The women in my circle are blind to their own bondage. The men simply do not care. As long as we stand quietly by waiting to meet their needs, their whims, why should they?

Surely I can think of something positive to say.

My sister visits often with her sweet little twins. Her husband is kind although highly devout. My mother's health is good. Three years

*cancer free. I've found many novels that make
me smile or cry or both.*

*And Allah is still great. Of that I have no
doubt. It is only the interpretations of men that
leave me to question. We were always the same
in that, you and I. But I see the grandeur of God
each morning as I kneel near my window and
pray. I see him in the sunrise. I hear him in the
birdsong. Someday I shall join him and dance
beneath the striking blue heavens. Someday,
somehow, I will find a way.*

Your devoted friend and sister of the heart,
Fatima

Poor, poor Fatima. But what could Layla do? Clutching at
the soft coverlet, she wondered if Fatima's father would even
let her visit over the holiday break. He had questioned Layla's
influence on Fatima for years. They lived on the same block
and played together as little girls, but since puberty, had been
allowed only limited contact together in Fatima's home.

Although they both lived in the Muslim district, were both
of the Sunni faith, Layla was little better than an infidel to
Fatima's fanatic Saudi Arabian family. Layla had gone to a
moderate Muslim school where girls and boys learned side by
side. Where girls shouted out answers even when boys got them
wrong. Where girls brashly displayed their faces.

Her family attended a progressive mosque, their traditional
faith interwoven with social responsibility and common sense.
Fatima's father did not approve. Would never approve. Only
due to Fatima's pleading had he allowed Layla into her life at
all, but he no longer heeded his daughter's cries.

In this land of freedom and individuality, so many Muslims
turned bitter and jaded. More conservative than ever. They
clung so tightly to the old ways that they could no longer hear
the truth.

And here she was running off to beaches with boys. Quite
a contrast.

Layla lifted a glass of icy water covered in condensation from the coaster on the nightstand and took a sip. A chill shot through her, from the drink or fear for Fatima, she wasn't quite sure. She started a long letter to her gentle childhood friend, her fingers tapping rapidly against the keys. She would write pages and pages and allow Fatima to live through her adventures, to see through her eyes. She would recommend more books and websites. Perhaps Rain and Allie would be willing to write her as well. How could a woman be held prisoner in the middle of this bastion of freedom?

Except by her own traditions. By her own beliefs. By fear. The last thing Layla wanted to do was endanger Fatima's safety. But her friend's mind needed to be challenged. Perhaps she could in some small way encourage Fatima to find the truth for herself.

Layla looked up from the laptop screen and gazed out the window at the blue-gray sky over the sparkling inlet. She recalled the sensation of warm water slipping along her bare limbs. The taste of salt upon her lips.

Truth. She still wasn't sure what that meant. But at least she was no longer afraid to question and to wonder. Over winter break she would introduce Mo to her family. He planned to drive to Detroit to visit relatives. At least that was the reason he would give his family. If only her parents would like Mo. If only they could accept him. Then Layla could continue living out her own newfound freedom without causing upheaval at home.

She could only hope. Hope that perhaps Fatima could find a gentle husband who would understand. Layla had certainly never dreamed of finding Mo. Yet there he was.

Layla was well into typing the third page of her letter when she heard shouting in the kitchen.

Something crashed and fell.

Shattered on the floor.

Auntie shrieked.

Uncle cursed a vile slew of Arabic words that made Layla's cheeks turn warm. For all of Uncle's tantrums, she had never heard him like this. She hit save and ran to investigate the problem.

As she entered the room, Uncle pointed and glared at her. "You...you harlot...you betrayer...you... I have no words!" Which he followed nonetheless with another dramatic string of Arabic curses.

"Tell him," Auntie said. "Tell your uncle it isn't true." Something in Auntie's tone suggested she didn't care what the truth was, as long as Uncle calmed down.

He kicked the cabinets, yelped, and grabbed his foot. "This is all your fault. I should...I should..."

"What's all my fault? What happened?" Layla finally managed to get the question out.

Auntie rushed to her and grabbed her by the forearms. "Tell your uncle you are not dating a boy. How ridiculous. These gossipy women have nothing better to do than make up stories. Tell him. You are a good girl."

"I...I..." Layla's face turned cool and tingly as the blood drained from it. Why hadn't she expected this? How had she let herself forget the dangers? Her situation was not so different from Fatima's after all.

"See. She says nothing. It is true." Uncle threw his hands over his head and stomped to the counter. He banged it with his fist, causing the pots overhead to clang together. Tolling the bells for her relationship with Mo.

Auntie rubbed Layla's shoulder. "You've scared her. I know my darling niece. She would never go out alone with a boy. Ridiculous, I tell you. Lies."

Layla dragged her hand down the side of her face. "I...he... Mo is a nice guy. He's from Lebanon. Our parents have met. We just...we...we spent some time together. That's all. Nothing happened."

"Nothing! Her reputation is ruined, and it's nothing. She brings shame to our family, and it's nothing." Uncle strode toward Layla and shoved his finger in her face. "I told you to stay away from that boy. I told you he was trouble."

Layla backed up toward the counter and arched her back to escape Uncle's attacking finger. It was almost funny. Except that it wasn't. Auntie held her head and moved to the corner in a moaning lament.

"I don't know what to say. I'm...I'm so sorry. But..."

"No buts, young lady!"

"Let me talk, Uncle. I know you expect me to obey you, but I'm an adult woman. This is America, not the Middle East. Shouldn't this be my decision?"

"You are living under my roof. Eating my food. And you will obey me." He pounded the counter once with each pronouncement.

"It's not fair, Uncle." Layla fought back tears. Uncle wouldn't want to see them.

"What's not fair is my niece lying to me and sneaking around behind my back. I never expected it of you, Layla. You've always been an honest, honorable girl. What happened to you?" He shook his fist.

"I'm sorry, Uncle. I'm truly sorry. I didn't know how to tell you. I was afraid."

"You should be afraid! That's the first sensible thing you've said. I've already spoken with your father. It's over. You will not see this boy again. One more stunt like this, and you'll be saying good-bye to Old Dominion University and your degree." Uncle pulled back. "Go to your room. Now! I can't stand the sight of you."

Layla turned to her aunt for defense, but she faced the corner, still groaning. Layla backed out of the kitchen, turned, and dashed for her bedroom.

"*Baba*," Layla cried over the phone to her father through her sobs. She sat curled in her spherical chair in the corner of her room, which suddenly struck her as a Pepto Bismol prison. "You must talk to him. You're the older brother. He'll listen to you."

"Layla, Layla, *habibti. Ya fara zgheyri.*" He called her his dear. His little mouse, like Mo did. The two men were so much alike.

If only she could make her father understand.

"My precious princess."

"Please. I'm so sorry. I'll behave better. I promise. But you can't do this. Mo planned to speak with you over the holidays. His intentions are honorable. You remember his family, don't you?"

"Your mother is having a fit. She wants you home immediately. I'm on your side. I'm going out on a limb to let you stay there at all, but you simply can't see the boy anymore."

Layla groaned. "Why, *Baba*?"

"Why? You brought this on yourself. Sneaking around. Going off alone. I raised you better than that. Don't act like I'm the problem here. Why couldn't you stay in groups? See each other at the MSU? The cafeteria?"

Layla could hardly admit that Mo didn't attend the MSU. The fact would raise all sorts of questions she wasn't prepared to answer. "Well, we can do that now. I'm sorry. I made a mistake. We were just having fun. Playing like we did when we were children. Imagining what it would be like to be a normal couple. Is that so terrible? Truly?"

"Your uncle says he is not a good Muslim. That he does not attend mosque."

What could she possibly say? "He loves God, father. But he's a free-thinker. Like us. Isn't there some way?"

"Maybe if you had asked. Maybe if you had talked to me. But your uncle feels betrayed. I put you in his care. If you want to stay in his house, you must live by his rules."

Layla sniffled and hiccupped. "Can Mo still come meet you? In Detroit? In December? You should see him, Father. He's kind and smart and respectful. He treats me like a princess, *Baba*, like you do. Isn't that what you want for me?"

"I don't know, Layla. You made a huge mistake. Your mother is beside herself. I don't think she could ever accept this boy."

"But it's your decision. Not hers."

"I don't run our house that way. Oh, Layla, this goes much deeper than one boy. Things are crazy. These new shows, new Internet feeds. So many Muslims are questioning, and so many grow harder and more radical. I fear your uncle is drifting in that direction. Please, promise me you won't do anything to upset him."

Layla sat silent for a few seconds, clenching the phone. Perhaps her father understood more than she realized. She normally talked to her mother about such things.

She bit her lip, her teeth pressing deep into the fleshy skin. "Was it so wrong, *Baba*? To want to be a normal American girl for once. To hold hands with a man. A nice, kind man who loves me."

"Wrong, I'm not sure. Dangerous, absolutely. We walk a fine line, my princess. No one quite knows how to hold on to our traditions while still changing and progressing. I'm campaigning actively for reform these days, but how much? I feel adrift. Where's the line?"

"Like me."

"Like you." Father took a deep breath. "Just be good, study hard, and stay out of trouble. We'll see what we can do when you get home. Don't push your aunt and uncle. You need to be grateful for what they provide."

"Of course. You're right, and I'm so, so, sorry." Layla heard her mother nagging in the background. "Tell Mama I love her, and I'll be good."

"Don't you want to speak with her?"

"Are you kidding? Trust me, I heard plenty. I'll talk to her in a few days after she cools off."

"Okay, I'll pass along your message."

Layla and her father said their lengthy string of traditional good-byes, and she sat looking at the phone in her hands. Perhaps her father did understand. At least a little. Perhaps some hope still existed.

So then why did she feel so hopeless once again?

She punched Mo's number into her cell phone for the last time. As she listened to it ring, she prayed he wouldn't push her. That he wouldn't make it harder than it needed to be.

He answered. "Precious, I am so sorry. I heard through the Lebanese gossip chain."

"We made a mistake." And Layla dissolved into tears. She couldn't lose him. She simply couldn't.

THIRTY-TWO

Allie collapsed cross-legged on the floor of the old musty theatre. She blew some escaped tendrils of hair out of her eyes. Jaron and Jenna sprawled over the hard wood after another long, difficult practice. Nothing was going right with the dance piece for Expressions class. The demonstration lurked less than a month away, but they were doomed for disaster. Their music selections didn't mesh, they fought over time allotments, and the choreography felt disjointed. The entire piece was awful.

Shondra held her own as a director, despite having little to work with, but when it came to costuming, she stank. Everything she suggested was wrong, wrong, wrong. She held up a long purple dress made of heavy material and draped in yards of gold braid. "What do you guys think?"

"It looks awfully...royal," Jenna said. "It might work for my piece, but I'd prefer something light and airy."

Jaron just raised a haughty brow.

Allie somehow managed not to roll her eyes. "Seriously, Shondra. There's no way that would work for Jaron's Negro spiritual. And it would look ridiculous for mine too."

"Well, it's not as if Jaron was going to wear the dress. I planned to put him in ripped purple pants." Shondra tossed the costume over a chair.

"Ha!" Jaron spit out the word with disgust. "Not going to happen."

"You don't have to be mean about it." Shondra picked up another outfit, a skintight petal pink concoction with a short, sheer skirt. "What about this one. Jenna, is this more what you were hoping for?"

"It's pretty, but..." Jenna resorted to her nervous habit of stretching into a split and burying her face against her knee.

"I hate it." Jaron leaned away from the offending costume.

Allie decided it was time to pull rank and age. "There's no way that will work for a church. You know what, we have a big dance closet at the studio where I teach. I'll find something."

Shondra shook the dress. "I've got this. It's my responsibility."

"No," Jaron said. "You're fired. Allie, take over the costuming."

Jenna, although twisted like a pretzel, managed to look Shondra firmly in the eye. "I agree."

Shondra stomped her foot and balled her fists. "You can't... you...oh, I hate this project."

A wave of compassion for the younger woman rolled over Allie. She walked to Shondra and put an arm around her shoulder. "Look guys, I know this assignment has been rough. Shondra's trying really hard, but we aren't helping matters with our discombobulated choreography and our mismatched music selections. Maybe we need to rethink this project entirely."

Jenna's graceful jawline dropped into an awkward gape. "But we're almost done!"

"I know, I know. We probably need to pray about this." Allie gave Shondra's shoulder a squeeze. "This is a worship piece after all. Come on."

The others acquiesced and joined hands. As they prayed, a soothing spirit of peace fell over the group for the first time since their initial meeting.

Jaron spoke up. "You know what, I sense this dance is important. We didn't take it seriously enough." He lowered his head. "I'm sorry guys. I've been a cocky jerk."

"Yeah, you have." Shondra giggled and everyone joined her as the tension broke. "Allie, I think you should lead this piece. I feel like God's going to give you something special."

Allie sensed that too. A warm, bright blossoming from deep in her. Jenna gave her hand a little squeeze of approval. Jaron nodded.

Allie entered the costume closet that evening confident she would find something to pull the performance together into a unified whole. However, after nearly an hour searching through rack after rack of dresses and tutus, she slumped to the cold vinyl floor, covered in a pile of stiff tulle skirts. Nothing would work. The project was off from its conception. At least it offered ample distraction from her troubles with Andy.

She should seek God, then and there, amidst the jumble of satin and silk. Allie didn't want to miss this opportunity to minister to Rain and Layla in the manner she knew best. They needed to see what went on deep in her heart, and what better way to show them than through dance?

She crushed down the tulle to a manageable mound and took some deep breaths. This time instead of bowing before his majestic throne, or meeting him at a happy place like a beach or mountain, Allie closed her eyes and remained still, and Jesus came to her. He plopped himself right down on the linoleum beside her and took her hand in his.

Tell me all about it, she sensed he said.

And Allie did. She poured out all the problems and frustrations, ending with, "Oh, Lord. I feel so lost."

Be lost in me, he said with quiet assurance.

Allie looked deep into his eyes. "Lost in you." She had been in that place, danced in that place so many times. A total immersion in the Holy Spirit. That was the true nature of worship.

He echoed her words. *Lost in you.* And they washed over Allie like gentle rain.

"Lost in You." The title of the tune playing in Andy's jeep that day! What better song to dance to? And it was long enough for a full piece. Thoughts and pictures filled Allie's mind. They would choreograph the dance as if each stumbled into the spiritual kingdom from their own time and place on earth. The song featured classic strings, deep drums, and heavy metal guitars

227

all mixed together, as if woven from the foundations of the world for just such a performance.

She felt Jesus give her hand a little tug, sensed him directing her eyes back to the rack of clothing. There hung a collection of loose, flowing white unitards, featuring a variety of diaphanous overlays with rainbow shimmers.

That's it! A rainbow of color. Worshiping God in different shades, in different cultures and contexts, but all from the same heart of worship.

A pair of simple white drawstring pants and a white dress shirt hung nearby for Jaron. As she stared mesmerized by the costumes, Allie saw the new ending in her mind's eye. They would all worship spontaneously, freely, beautifully in their own style. Tears slid down her cheeks as she pictured it.

A few moments later, the ramifications of the revelation hit her like a splash of cold water. She turned to Jesus. "Are you serious? You want me to change the entire piece?"

He offered a wry grin and nodded.

When the images and sensations faded, Allie could only hope and pray that she would be able to talk the rest of the team into tackling the idea. They had a lot of hard work ahead of them.

THIRTY-THREE

"Ugh," Rain said out loud. "How can there be thirty channels and nothing on?"

She clicked the remote and turned off the inane programming. James hadn't even wanted a television, but a well-meaning neighbor offered them an old set for free. They felt too bad to turn it down, and so accepted it and slowly became addicted to the stupid thing. Now that she lived alone, Rain was turning into one of those crazy ladies who actually talked to the odious machine.

Maybe she should get cable. Cable would be good. Or a cat.

A knock at the door startled her out of her ridiculous thoughts. She pressed a hand to her chest. Please let it be James.

Rain stood, straightening her leaf green T-shirt and smoothing her wild curls, thankful she hadn't changed into her holey pajamas yet. She pulled open the door, and there he stood, literally with hat in hand and head drooping like a tree in need of water. Not able to bear seeing him that way, she dragged him inside and enveloped him in a warm hug.

He felt so right in her arms, and once there he responded with his own crushing embrace. She stepped back to examine him, not knowing what to say. Not a suitcase in sight. She looked into the melting chocolate depths of his eyes, hoping to read some hint there.

His gaze turned to Rain's stomach and hers followed. Although it remained flat, she placed her hand on it, an instinctual protective gesture. James laid his hand over top of hers against her womb. Against their tiny offspring.

Could it mean? Might he accept their child? "James, I love you. I do, but...I couldn't."

"I know, baby. I was crazy to ask you." He cast a significant glance toward the corner of the kitchenette.

Rain laughed. "The mosquito incident?" She recalled the day when she crushed a pesky mosquito out of instinct and cried afterward at the mangled carcass left on her palm. James had brushed away her tears.

"Yeah," he said. "I should have known."

Rain fidgeted for a moment. "Come in. Sit down."

James crossed to the couch, and Rain perched herself on the edge of the cushion beside him.

She fussed with a loose string on the upholstery. "So, how have you been? How's school?"

"Good." He crossed both hands behind his head and leaned into them. "I'm getting the hang of homework and schedules again."

Hmm. Not quite what she was looking for. "And work. How's work?"

"Work's okay. I have a lot of free time while I'm there."

Rain resisted the urge to moan. This was going nowhere. Maybe she needed to ask more pointed questions. "Where have you been staying?"

"With some buddies at a frat house."

Images of bimbos in wet T-shirts and erupting kegs of beer flashed through her head. She pursed her lips.

"Don't worry, Rain. None of those sorority girls hold a candle to you. Besides, you're the mother of my child."

She covered her mouth with her hand, but a little moan escaped anyway. A pathetic sound of sadness, relief, and joy all mixed into one. She didn't want to feel helpless without James, but she needed him.

He scooped her to his strong, solid chest and held her close, burying his fingers deep into her tuft of hair. "I'm sorry. I'm so sorry. I'm trying to change. You deserve better."

Despite what she might or might not deserve, she wanted James. Back in her arms. In her home. In her family. James was all she had ever wanted. After a few moments Rain sat up and wiped her eyes. "So, where are we now?"

"I went to a counselor this week. Twice. He suggested I talk to you about some of the issues I shared with him."

"Oh, James. I've wanted you to open up for so long."

"Well, it's not easy to say. And it's not going to be easy to hear, so don't get too excited."

"But will you come home?"

"Maybe. Soon. Not yet. Let's take one thing at a time."

Rain blinked away the tears that threatened to resurface. "Then go ahead. Tell me your stories. We have all night." As James began to share, Rain realized it would indeed take all night. How could he ever overcome such trauma and go on to live a normal healthy life? Burns, welts, bruises, broken bones. And those injuries were nothing compared to the damage his father's words inflicted. Why hadn't anyone stopped it? Why didn't anyone help?

God in heaven, help him now. Help us.

Rain's beautiful golden-green eyes shimmered with moisture throughout the story. James wanted to cry. But he wouldn't. Instead he laid his head on Rain's denim-clad leg, as he remembered doing with his mother so many years ago. He had a hard enough time opening up without bawling like a baby. He felt as if he pulled open his chest and revealed the delicate organ of his heart for Rain's examination. The counselor had removed the faulty stitches he had so carefully sewn the wound together with over the years, revealing a festering mess of infection still hidden inside.

But the skilled professional had soothed the pain as well, with gentle strokes of emotional ointments. Talking about the past drained the worst of the sores. James had not yet begun to mend, but for the first time in his life, healing flickered on the horizon.

Now, here he was, laying his heart bare before Rain. What if she tore it open further, poked yet another hole? The counselor had been a stranger. James could always walk away. He could steel himself against the man. Once he told Rain, there would be no turning back. But if he couldn't trust her, he was doomed.

He closed his eyes. "If it's too much, let me know. I can stop. I know it's a lot to take in."

She stroked his cheek. "No. It's okay. Keep going."

He took her soft hands in his own. Turned them over, studying them. Pressed a kiss against them. They smelled of cinnamon, so he continued. Placing his torn and bleeding heart into her lovely silken palms.

And there it felt safe and at rest.

By the end of it all, Rain gazed down at James, lying exhausted with his head in her lap. Her gaze caught on the dining room table they had lovingly transported together. The earth-toned art deco vase he had purchased for her with his first paycheck. She twisted his dreadlocks absently and leaned forward to kiss the eye his father had once blackened. "You're worn out. We can save the rest for another time. But I'm so glad you told me. I always felt it inside of you. I just never knew exactly what it was."

"You felt it? You knew?" he murmured like a scared child. "I thought it would change everything. I thought you would lose respect for me."

"Of course not. It takes a brave, brave man to share these things. If anything, they make me love you more. I hated that you held part of yourself back. I wanted to know all of you. Now I have a name for the pain. A history to go along with it."

They sat in silence for a few moments. The hum of the refrigerator lulled Rain toward sleep. She tried to fight back a yawn, but the day had been long.

"You're tired, baby." James stroked her cheek.

"I'm always tired these days. Come on. Let's go to bed before we end up on the couch all night."

James shook himself awake. "No, not yet. I'm not ready yet. I need a while to work through this. I'm determined to become the man you need and the father our child needs. Then, and only then, will I move back home."

"But..."

James pressed a large finger to her lips. Drowning out Rain's protests that he was good enough. That she just wanted him home. "No buts. I've made up my mind."

Rain saw his resolve and respected him more than ever for it. He fished his keys out of his pocket and headed for the door.

"But what if you never think you're good enough?" Rain sounded like the scared little child now.

He tilted his head back and let out an extended exhale. "We just have to hope, I guess."

"And pray?"

"It couldn't hurt." With that James walked out her door all over again.

THIRTY-FOUR

The squeals of college students playing Ping-Pong nearby distracted Layla from her misery. Rain and Allie sat beside her in the student center, scratching their pens against their papers, hard at work on the narrative essay due for English class. She hadn't been able to tell them the awful news. Layla stared at the blank white page on her laptop. Each member had to share a significant memory from childhood, and they would link the stories together with transitions, introduction, and conclusion.

This would be the last joint assignment before they moved on to separate research papers concerning one element of their culture they wished to change. Layla's mind kept slipping ahead to that project. Oh, there were so many things she wished to change. Far too many to fit in a five page paper.

Rain looked at her. "Layla. Are you okay?"

"I'm not sure where I want to go with this essay. Sorry. I don't mean to hold you guys up."

"Do you want to brainstorm a little?" Allie sat her papers down.

"No. It's fine. I just need to start writing. It'll hit me."

"Let us know if you want help." Rain went back to work.

Allie shrugged with a quirk of a smile and did the same.

They had earned As on all the assignments so far, but Layla couldn't wrap her head around this one. Instead she opened the Word document from the poem they wrote together and reread the lyrical words.

"All I Really Want"

Another patchwork frock, no patterns, no prescriptions,
A swath of this mottled with a square of that,
Scattered stitches of untried threads.
Will it stand against the wind?
Hold with the strength of an unbroken weave?
All I really want is to be sure.

Bolt of silk about my head, portrait of modest
Respectability. Badge of honor or of shame?
Wraps my neck in a strangling embrace,
Weighs against my shoulders like lead.
A faceless phantom in an endless night.
All I really want is to be free.

Nylon hose squeezing flesh, satin slip masks lines and limbs,
Skirt of stiffest fabric, blouse obscures a curve of breast.
Cram feet into unyielding pointy-toed pumps.
Elevated inches above the human norm.
Sticky hair sprayed to match a pasted smile.
All I really want is to be true.

Her own words echoed through her head in a haunting refrain. *All I really want is to be free. To be free. Free.*

She would hate to let the girls down, but how could she even ponder a significant memory from her childhood? Each one reminded her of Mo or the family and religion that tore her away from him.

Maybe that was it.

She should dive in and tell the story of the buttercups on the playground, linking the memory to the day Mo challenged her entire belief system and whisked her away on an adventure leading straight to heartache. It would be one way of breaking the news to her friends.

She started typing before she chickened out.

Twenty minutes later, the rough drafts were finished. Layla resisted the urge to highlight the pages and hit the delete button. "Maybe we should organize them by age." Allie shuffled her papers into a neat stack. "I'm nine in mine. It's about the day I saw *Swan Lake* and decided to pursue dance as a career."

"Mine's handing out food at a homeless shelter. I was about eight." Rain pushed her chair away from the table with a screech and crossed her legs Indian style. "What about you, Layla?"

"I'm five in mine." Did she really possess the courage to share the story?

"Well, go ahead then," Rain said. "You go first, and we'll see if this order works."

Layla cleared her throat. "My most significant memory from childhood occurred when I was five years old, although I would have never guessed its importance at the time..." She continued, recounting the story of swinging at the playground with the breeze sweeping through her hair, of Mo's declaration of love against the creaky noise of the chains, of how he ran away and came back with a fistful of perfect yellow buttercups from under a shaded tree. He cuddled against her side as she sat in the U-shaped seat and pressed the cool, moist blossoms to her lips. Then he whispered in her ear that he would marry her someday.

When the story flashed forward in time, Layla stuttered over the words. She explained how Mo had met her with those same buttercups once again, and while she tried to give him a chance, her family snatched it away, leaving both her heart and those buttercups crushed and lifeless.

Allie and Rain sat staring. They waited until she concluded. "That's the end."

Rain pulled a chair toward her and hugged her from the side. Layla could no longer hold the tears at bay.

Allie grabbed a tissue from her oversized purse and joined them. "Why didn't you tell us sooner? When did this happen?"

"A few days...ago." Layla hiccupped through her sobs. "I didn't want...to think about it. I...didn't want it to be true."

"You should have called us." Rain stroked her head.

"Uncle...doesn't allow me to see you anymore. He doesn't know...I'm here. He thinks I'm...studying." Layla sniffed and managed to collect herself. She blew her nose into the tissue.

"What can we do?" Allie said.

"There's nothing to be done." Layla stared straight ahead with resolve. Her family was right. She shouldn't have snuck around with Mo. More than that, she could never marry a Christian. Allah came first in her life. Why had she deceived herself?

She turned from Allie to Rain and back again. "Please don't try to fix this. I know you mean well, but don't. As much as this hurts me, I don't see any other option. I was a fool to let things go so far."

Rain sucked in a deep breath, as if pulling back her argument before it could escape. "Well, at least you could let us administer some ice cream therapy."

"Sure, we'll grab some as soon as we're done. I won't be able to hang out as much as I used to, though." Layla wiped the trickling eyeliner from her cheeks.

"That's okay." Allie fished out another tissue. "I'm swamped with this dance project right now. I'm not going to have much free time for a while."

"With James around again, hopefully I'll be busy too. But if you need anything, seriously, just ask." Rain gave Layla's shoulder another squeeze. "I'm always here for you."

"Me too." Allie's gentle blue eyes exuded comfort.

Layla wanted to ask about James. She had heard only the briefest details by phone, but Fatima also weighed heavy on her mind. "Maybe you can help me with something."

Rain leaned forward in her chair, elbows pressing against

her knees, and blinked back her own tears as Layla explained Fatima's situation.

"It kind of puts my problem into perspective, doesn't it?" Layla held up her hands, as if unconvinced.

"It's horrifying." Allie grasped Layla's hand. "And I will definitely write to her. But just because your problem is less dramatic doesn't make it any easier to go through. I think the situations are more similar than you realize. This is your life, your heart, your feelings we're talking about."

Rain wondered about Allie's heart and feelings as well, but remained focused on Layla for the moment. "Yeah, I agree. I mean, Fatima's grown up like this. She never expected any better. It must be confusing for you. You've had a taste of freedom, and now it's been yanked away. That's rough. It's hard on the psyche."

"I understand, though." Allie sighed. "On one hand I think I'm ridiculous to be such a mess over Andy. On the other hand, the awful feelings and sensations I experience when I remember our engagement are too strong to ignore. I guess sometimes it's not so much about the severity of our circumstances, as it is about the severity of our reactions to them."

Glad that Allie brought up the subject on her own, Rain could no longer resist switching the conversation to her second hurting friend. Allie had been in her prayers. Rain hoped her guess was wrong, but she had been struck with a strong impression about the situation, and it aligned neatly with her years of amateur psychology training. "You know, I've been thinking about that. Your reactions seem disproportionate, Allie. And that snake image you told me about, it must link to a really early time in your childhood. Have you ever wondered if something happened that you're forgetting?"

"Actually, the thought's crossed my mind." Allie twisted her lips. "I can't imagine it, though. Not with Andy. Maybe...it has something to do with the church and how my memories of him are all tangled together with that place. Maybe I'm...forgetting something that happened there." Her face grew pale as she struggled through the words.

"You could see a shrink. Or maybe a hypnotist," Rain said. Oops, scratch that. Christians weren't into hypnotists, but Allie, gracious as always, let the faux pas slide.

"I don't know. I need some more time to pray about this. Maybe God could just show me what's going on. I don't really have money for that right now anyway." Rain didn't wish to sound alarmist, but Allie needed outside help. "They have free therapy at the school. James has been seeing a counselor. It might not be a good idea to face this on your own. You never know what you might find. Once you follow that trail of feelings and memories, it's hard to turn back. What if you discover something traumatic? You might need a trained professional there to put you back together."

"True, but I don't even know if he's worth all that trouble." Something interesting flitted across Allie's face. A shadow of guilt perhaps? Or was it desire? Rain studied her more closely. No, she knew that look. Knew it well. Like it or not, Allie was in love. Poor baby.

"Well." Layla seemed to be calming down now. Only red-rimmed eyes and an occasional hiccup gave evidence to her recent outburst. "I think this is something you need to deal with whether you end up with Andy or not. You should consider seeing a counselor as Rain said."

"Everyone has some sort of childhood wounds, Allie. Even people from good families like us. And they affect the way we see things." Sometimes Rain wondered if her own laissez-faire upbringing contributed to her clinging dependency on James. "They can cloud our vision and screw us up. It couldn't hurt to talk to someone."

"I don't think it's anything that serious." Allie drew her legs up onto the plastic chair and hugged her knees. "But I'll consider it."

They sat quietly for a moment.

Allie looked back and forth between Rain and Layla, clutching her paper in her hand as it drooped by her feet. The story on the pages seemed insignificant now. She certainly hoped she wasn't suppressing any traumatic childhood memories. Yet while she wasn't ready to admit it to her friends, she found a part of herself falling deeper and deeper in love with Andy. If only she could get that other portion of her subconscious to cooperate. She needed to get to the bottom of this so she could move forward with her life. But where would she ever find the courage?

Layla's head snapped up. "Wait a minute. What's this about James seeing a counselor?"

Rain smiled. "I didn't want to get your hopes up yet, but he's seeing some doctoral psychology guy at student services. He actually called me 'the mother of his child.' But he won't come back home until he feels confident he isn't going to turn into an abuser like his father. He told me a lot of the details." She shivered.

"Do you want to talk about it?" Allie offered.

"No. He wouldn't want me sharing his private business." Rain swiped a hand down her cheek. "Part of me wishes I didn't know, even though it was important for me to hear. Everything makes sense now. I'm just glad he's getting help."

"Will it be enough?" Layla asked.

"I don't know. Some people never recover from that sort of abuse. It's amazing how such epic evil can exist in the world alongside so much beauty."

"At least he's trying." Layla gave Rain a squeeze this time. "At least he wants to be a good father. I'm sure he'll get there."

Allie thought back to one of their first meetings. They'd come so far since then. "Life is a beautiful mess, remember."

Layla rolled her eyes, which looked oddly vulnerable stripped of her makeup. "I'm ready for a little less mess and a little more beauty."

"You're preaching to the choir, sister." Rain nodded. "I think it's time for that ice cream."

"We're going to need it to get through the rest of this semester." Allie gathered her things.

"Forget this semester." Layla snapped shut her laptop. "I need it to get through this evening. Something with a whole lot of chocolate."

Yes, chocolate sounded good. Allie could use some too. She needed to face these feelings that haunted her. She wanted to get to the bottom of them. Rain was right. Some wound hid beneath the surface. She had to figure out what it was.

Was she forgetting something?

Surely she hadn't suffered any trauma, any abuse like James. Hers had been a happy childhood. But something was off, skewed. She didn't see things properly. Her physical responses didn't make sense. She would follow those feelings to their source and somehow get to the root of the problem. She had to find the courage. Her future was at stake.

"Allie?"

She chuckled into her cell phone at the astonishment in Andy's voice as she drove toward dinner with her family. Scenery of trees, lakes, and houses blurred past her along the side of the highway. The breeze from the open window tickled her cheek. "Hi, Andy."

"How...how are you?"

She couldn't resist dragging out the suspense. "Well, I'm really busy with school work. We decided to start from scratch with our choreography for that dance piece I told you about. Oh, and Layla's family found out about her boyfriend. They were..."

"Allie!"

"I'm teasing. I've missed you, Andy. I have."

His answering sigh of relief came through loud and clear. "You have no idea how glad I am to hear you say that. Can I see you?"

"Not yet. Look, I won't prolong the torture. I just wanted you to know that I'm working on it. Okay?"

"Okay, but—"

"No buts, Andy. I'll let you know when I'm ready. I wanted

you to understand that I'm not blowing you off, though."

"So..."

"Good-bye, Andy."

"I—"

"Andy, say good-bye."

This sigh was not a happy one. "If you insist. Bye, Allie."

The phone clicked, and silence filled the air. A matching echo of loneliness filled her heart. Something was shifting deep inside of her. The positive feelings kept growing and the negative ones diminishing. Andy didn't try to control or convince her as he used to. Instead he allowed her the space and freedom she desired.

Hold on a little longer, Andy. I'm almost there.

THIRTY-FIVE

Allie and Mom actually lingered over decaf after the rest of the family disappeared to sort through the games in the living room. This new camaraderie between them as they sat at the dining table refreshed Allie. For once, she didn't require the scent of vanilla creamer to soothe her nerves, although it tasted nice. Mom may have a different perspective and personality, but she had a lot of maturity and wisdom too.

"Mom, I wanted to talk to you about what's going on with Andy."

Mom threw her hands in the air. "I thought you'd never bring it up. I wasn't sure if you'd get upset if I mentioned him. I know you're sick of me harping on the subject."

"I'm sorry I was so testy. Here's the thing, though. I've come to realize that I'm holding on to some negative feelings about Andy. And please try to understand, Mom. I have forgiven him, but I still experience some very disturbing physical sensations when I think back to our engagement."

"You shouldn't let your feelings..." Mom held up a finger and stopped the sentence short. "Scratch that. I'm trying to understand this whole kinesthetic dancer thing. It seems some people are wired as thinkers and some as feelers. King David was a feeler, and look at all those beautiful Psalms he wrote. God called David a man after his own heart."

Allie smiled. "Thanks, Mom. That means a lot to me."

"You know, Allie." Mom paused and took a deep breath. "I only ever wanted what was best for you. I wanted to protect you. Keep you as far away from evil as I could. Maybe I went too far."

"Mom—"

"No, let me finish. I made some horrible mistakes in my past. Mistakes I'll never be able to fix. I just wanted to keep you safe. I didn't mean to crush your spirit." She focused on her coffee cup.

Andy had suggested there might be something from Mom's past that made her cling so tightly to rules and outward appearances. Why had Allie never known? What in the world could Mom have done? "Do you want to talk about it?"

Mom snapped her head up. "Goodness, no. I can't change it now." She pasted on a smile. "All I can do is press forward. But you...Sarah...you girls have your whole lives ahead of you. I don't want you to mess up like I did."

Compassion surged through Allie. She reached over and squeezed Mom's hand. "I love you, Mom. We'll be okay. You'll see."

Sarah entered with a fresh pot of coffee. "Refills?"

Mom and Allie both took her up on the offer.

Mom blew on her mug. "So back to Andy. Let me ask you this—do you have good feelings about him too?"

"Feelings?" Sarah poured herself another cup. "What do feelings have to do with love? Love should be a decision."

"Well," Mom said. "Ideally both would be good. Let Allie answer the question, darling."

"Fine. I'll keep my opinion to myself." Sarah's face grew tight.

Allie ignored the comment. "Oh, Mom, I have very good feelings for Andy. Feelings so good, I don't want to explain them to you." Heat rose to Allie's cheeks.

"Do you seriously think I don't know about those things, sweetheart? I did manage to make quite a few babies, you know."

Allie covered her ears. "Don't remind me."

"And that's where I exit. I don't need to hear all of this yet." Sarah took her mug and headed to the living room.

Mom waved her away. "You children are too silly. So, let me see if I understand. You do care for Andy, and you do have romantic feelings for him, but you also have these strange reactions."

"Exactly, and sometimes, don't get mad at me for saying this, Mom, I think it's because I associate him so closely with our church."

Mom sucked in a deep breath and waited a minute before she spoke. "I still don't understand why you hate church so much."

"It's not church in general, Mom. It's that church."

Mom contemplated a moment. Apparently she could find nothing nice to say.

Allie decided to dive into the heart of the matter. "Do you think something might have happened there? Something awful? Something I don't remember."

"Don't be silly." Mom's features tensed.

"Please, Mom, don't blow this off."

Mom sat her cup down and pushed it to the center of the table with both hands. "By the way, you heard the big news, didn't you?" Classic Mom maneuver—when backed into a corner, change the subject.

"No."

"Andy was officially voted in as assistant pastor last night at the board meeting."

The cream and beige room seeped to red.

"Pastor Jenkins is grooming him to take over in the next few years."

The sensations struck again. The squeezing. The tightening. Pressure built in Allie's head, pushing against her skull in all directions, threatening to explode.

"Pastor wants to retire soon." Mom continued with her merry chatter. "Isn't that wonderful, honey? Aren't you so proud of Andy?"

Allie snapped. "Pride is a sin, Mother, and if you weren't so obsessed with rules you might know that. No, it is not wonderful. No, I am not proud of him. No, this isn't good news. Why am I hearing this from you? That two-faced, lying, son of—" She clapped her hands over her mouth just in time.

Then she stopped and saw the hurt, the disappointment, the true sorrow on her mother's face and deflated like a leaky balloon. "Oh, Mom. I'm so sorry. I don't know where those awful words came from. I didn't mean them. But can you see? This is what he does to me. I can't marry a man like that. It would be a disaster."

A spark brightened Mom's downcast demeanor. "Marriage? Allie? Are you two talking marriage? Is he the one?"

"I thought maybe he was, but clearly I was wrong. I can't trust him. I certainly can't marry him if he's going to pastor that church. We were talking about going somewhere else if we got together." The last vestiges of hope vanished. It would squelch the life right out of her to attend that church week after week. Be under constant scrutiny as a pastor's wife.

"Um...Allie—"

"Game time," Dad shouted. "All slow-poke coffee drinkers please report to the living room immediately."

Mom stood, leaned against the table, and offered a weak smile.

"What, Mom? What were you going to say?"

"It's nothing, Allie. I was just going to say I'll be praying for you, but I'm sure you knew that. I'm cutting back on the Christian clichés like you requested. Don't be too hard on Andy, though. I finally do see your point, but that boy loves you. Try not to crush him."

Allie reached across and gave Mom's hand another pat. Oh, she'd crush him all right. She'd crush him for good this time, but there was no need to crush Mom in the process.

On the way home, Allie pulled up Andy's number on her cell and jabbed the send button with all the violence she would like to administer to his nose.

"Allie." He sounded happy.

"Where are you right now?" She maintained a level tone.

"I'm still at the church, why?"

Figured. Where else would he be? At least the awful place was only minutes away from her parents' home.

"I'm coming over to see you. I'm ready to talk."

"Thank you, Jesus. Thank you, thank you, Lord." Andy stood watching out the glass entry of the church as Allie's little car zoomed into the driveway. He couldn't stop praising. The moment had finally arrived. His skin buzzed with excitement. He could hardly see straight. Hardly think straight.

Allie slammed the door and rushed toward him in the dim streetlights.

His smile spread from ear to ear as he swung the door wide to welcome her. Then he noticed her stormy features. He barely had time to register the impression.

"You! You two-faced, lying..." Allie hollered, poking his chest with her finger. "How dare you? Why didn't you tell me? Why did I hear this from my mother?"

"I don't..." His heart fell to his feet with a thump.

"Assistant Pastor of the First Church of the Goody-Two-Shoes? Seriously? Seriously!"

Dear God, help. He should have told her. Should have insisted she stay on the phone until he gave her the news. "I would have...I tried to...but you didn't let me..."

"I would have listened to something that important. I thought we were going to find another church together. Don't you think I should have been consulted about this decision? You asked me to marry you." Allie let out a frustrated growl.

Andy tried to breathe steadily. His hand began to tremble. He knew it would be bad, but he never expected this. His future crumbled before his eyes like the twin towers of 9/11. "And you didn't answer. I prayed about this, Allie. I did. I figured since I had no guarantees about our future, I needed to make the decision independent of you. Do you have any idea how long I've dreamed of this? The plans I have for this church? How much good I can do?"

"Well, I hope that comforts you, Andy. Because you'll be doing it alone. We're through!" With that she smacked him on the shoulder, turned, and stalked away.

He wouldn't let her leave so easily. He'd made that mistake before. Rushing forward, he grabbed her elbow and pulled her back around.

"Let go of me!" Wild fear flashed through her eyes, like an animal cornered by a predator.

Why was she so terrified? Of him? "Allie, something's wrong here, and it's not me. It's something about this church. I know it is. There must be a reason you hate it so much. Let me walk you through this place. We need to figure out what happened."

She took a slow breath in and out. Her eyes darted about the foyer. Pain cut across her face, and she winced against it. Something in her resolve melted. "Maybe you're right."

"Come on." Andy wrapped a reassuring arm around her shoulder.

She shrugged it off and began to shiver. *Lord, help her through this.* How could they ever be together if she couldn't overcome this fear? "Is there any place in the building that particularly bothers you?"

Allie gulped. She bit her lip as she turned a slow circle. "Well, it always starts in the foyer."

Andy tried to look at the room through her eyes. The large potted plants next to the swinging doors to the sanctuary. The smell of old hymnals lining the shelf on the wall. The fundraising board. Nothing sinister that he could find.

"I think...I think I remember what happened. There was some deacon or usher who used to holler at me for dancing to the music on the way back from the bathrooms. That's probably all it is."

A worship dancer, practicing her gift, and she got hollered at. But could that alone explain her strong reactions? "I'm so sorry, Allie."

"Yeah, it was a bummer. But it's not all that terrible here. Now that I think about it, I can hardly bear to visit the Sunday school area."

"Okay." He laid his arm over her shoulder again, with all the gentleness he could muster. This time she didn't push him away. "Come on."

As they passed through the building and entered a dark narrow hallway around the back, her steps grew heavy and she shrank into his side, shivering and gasping for breath. He flipped a light switch to banish the shadows. Again he attempted to see it through her eyes. Brightly painted trees and forest creatures covered the walls. The bunnies and squirrels smiled. A dragonfly hovered near a purple flower. The happy images should help.

Instead, she doubled over. She grasped her knees, hung her head low, and sucked in a sharp inhale. When she looked up, her face glowed pale white in the fluorescent lighting. A blue tinge lined her lips. Sweat trickled from her brow.

"I can't." She covered her mouth with her hands then turned to stumble away.

He caught her elbow. "Come on, Allie. I'm here. You can do this."

She snatched her arm back and shrieked. Her face transformed from white to red. She raked her hands into her scalp, pulling strands of hair from her bun. They fell about her face in helpless disarray. "No. You can't make me."

She waved her hands in front of her, pushing back some unseen fiend. "You're always bullying me. Always telling me what to do."

She bit her thumb, garbling a second shriek. "Always trying to talk me into things."

Her eyes focused and stared directly into Andy's.

Her voice fell to a raspy whisper. "Just leave me alone! We're through. I never want to see you again."

With those parting words she flew like a phantom out of the hallway, and out of his life.

THIRTY-SIX

Layla slammed the car door, tension gripping her neck and threatening to cause a headache. She always ended up driving home during traffic on Tuesday and Thursday evenings. The drive that should take forty minutes morphed into nearly seventy.

Note to self, do not take four o'clock classes next year.

Looking up at the stone front mini-mansion turned virtual prison, she thought that better yet, maybe she could talk her dad into letting her find some roommates closer to campus. A few girls from the MSU perhaps. Like Allie and her teeny boppers. Safety in numbers and all that. She didn't know if she could survive three and a half more years in this house, but for the moment, she had no choice.

Frowning, she entered the foyer and heard voices filtering from the living room.

Great. Visitors.

As if the day wasn't bad enough already, now she'd have to smile and make small talk and pretend she wasn't under house arrest.

She tried to slide past for a moment in her room before the torture began, but Auntie caught her out of the corner of her eye. "There she is. Layla, *habibti*, come and join us. There's someone I'd like you to meet."

A tray of sweets sat on the round glass-topped coffee table and caught Layla's eye. At least there were some benefits to hosting guests. No one stood to greet her. Layla further scanned the room and found a handsome young man sitting with his elbows on his knees in an overstuffed chair in the corner near the entryway.

"Hi," Layla said.

"Hi there." The guy grimaced. If the fact he remained seated was not enough to clue her, his perfect English confirmed the suspicion. He wore skinny jeans and a polo shirt in a surfer brand popular on the East Coast. His short brown hair was tousled into a trendy style intended to look like he just rolled out of bed.

Yep. American through and through.

Was Auntie feeding the cable guy again?

"Layla, this is Ryan Hassan. Ryan, my niece, Layla." The first name was American, but the last Middle Eastern.

He found his manners and stood to shake her hand. "Nice to meet you." Then he turned to her aunt. "*Um-Wassim.* I thought you invited me over to try out some new recipes for the restaurant. Naughty, naughty. And from the look on this young lady's face, she's none too pleased with your scheming either."

Layla couldn't help but laugh. So he wasn't in on it. At least there was that.

Uncle held up his hands. "I had no part in it."

"Well, you're here now and dinner is ready, so what's the harm? We eat. We talk. You go home." Auntie bustled in the direction of the kitchen but turned back when no one followed.

Ryan took a deep breath and ran his fingers through his hair. Something about his teasing smile was terribly attractive. "I don't know. I wouldn't want to ruin Layla's evening, but the smell of that food is seriously calling my name."

Layla rolled her eyes. "I suppose it would be all right. Who am I to stand between a man and his dinner? Just let me put my books away and freshen up."

"I will help you," Auntie said.

Layla twisted her face into a confused expression. She was actually quite capable of fixing her own makeup. Ryan laughed. She shook her head and turned down the hall.

Auntie followed her toward the bedroom. She clicked the door closed behind them. "So what you think? Not bad, eh?

Your old auntie, she knows what she is doing."

"My old auntie is nuts." Layla put down her books and headed to the mirror.

"Oh, not so nuts. This is the first time you've smiled in weeks. I cannot stand to see you so heart broken, *habibti*. He is quite a catch, this Ryan. Don't you think?"

"You brought the poor guy here under false pretenses. Recipes? Seriously?"

"Fadi wasn't handsome enough. Bassam wasn't American enough. So I find you a man who is handsome and American, and what thanks do I get?"

"Yeah, what's up with that? He's like totally American."

"His father is from Jordan. His mother is from Virginia. But he is a good Muslim. I've seen him stop and pray during his lunch break at the restaurant."

Layla examined herself in the mirror. Somewhere in the course of dating Mo, her look had transformed considerably. She whipped out a Kleenex to clean a few brown smudges from beneath her eyes but didn't replace the thin, natural line. Most of her earth-toned lip gloss had rubbed off, but it wasn't as if she needed to impress this guy. She straightened her veil and checked her teeth. "So how do you know his parents?"

"I don't."

"You don't." Layla spun away from the mirror and looked her aunt straight in the eye.

Auntie crossed to her and took Layla's shoulders in her wrinkled hands. "I am telling the truth, Layla. For once I am thinking of you. Believe it or not, I do listen. I can't stand to see you hurting."

Layla put her own hands on the woman's arms and gave her a kiss on the cheek. "Thank you, Auntie. That means a lot to me. I don't think I'm ready for a new man in my life, but I promise to be nice."

"He is exactly what you're looking for. And he is in law school. Let this other boy go. He is no good for you."

"I know you're right, but I need time." She had resolved that she must put Mo out of her heart and mind. What choice did she have?

"Time, of course, and in the meanwhile you make friends with Ryan."

"You're incorrigible, you know that, right Auntie?"

Auntie swatted her in the direction of the dining room. "What's that? Some fancy word you learned in college. I assume it is an insult."

"It means you never change."

"Ahh, well in that case, thank you."

After a pleasant dinner, Auntie shooed Layla and Ryan to take a walk on the inlet while she did the dishes and made coffee. Layla hated to admit it, but she enjoyed his company. The sun slipped low in the sky and reflected off the water as they strolled side by side. She looked up into his handsome face.

He turned his head and laughed. "All told, not as bad as we expected. You're cool, Layla Al-Rai."

"I don't know what I'm going to do with that aunt of mine. This is the third time she sprang a man on me like this." And the first time she approached getting it right. Ryan was nearly perfect. Except that he wasn't Mo.

No one would ever be Mo.

"So who's the guy?"

Layla felt her cheeks flush. "What guy?"

"Come on, now."

"Seriously, what makes you think there's another guy?"

He tossed back his head. "At the risk of sounding immodest, most women consider me quite a catch, and you've been sending me the friendship vibe all night."

Layla bit back a smile.

"Don't get me wrong. It's a nice change. I actually got to know you."

"And?" She couldn't resist asking.

"And the crazy thing is, as much as I avoid these awful matchmaking sessions, I kinda like you."

She gave him a sympathetic glance.

"Ahh, so there is another guy."

"Yes. There is."

"What's the story?" He stopped and sat down on a bench. She joined him. "It's complicated."

"Do your aunt and uncle know?"

"Yes."

"They don't approve?"

"Not at all. And they don't even know the whole story. Did they mention I'm under house arrest?"

"My, my, naughty girl. Ah...you do realize you're a grown women, right?"

Layla snickered. "Try explaining that to them."

He tilted his head and caught her eye. "So are you going to tell me about him?"

She looked down at her hands in her lap. "Have you ever been in love, Ryan?"

"Actually, yes." He took a deep breath and blew it out slowly. "She wasn't a Muslim. I thought it would be fine. We both believed in God. Our morals were the same. My mother wasn't Islamic at first."

"How did that work out?"

"She agreed to go to mosque with my dad and over time she started praying and fasting. Eventually she decided she liked it. It was something we did together as a family, you know?"

"Do you live with them?"

"Nah, they're still in Richmond. It was time for me to strike out on my own. Thought it would be fun to live near the beach."

This was exactly the sort of guy she wanted. "Does your mother veil?"

"Only at the mosque. She has blond hair and blue eyes and wears designer clothes. It's kind of comic."

"But it worked out for them."

Ryan nodded. "It did. But Rachel, that was my girlfriend's name, wanted me to leave my faith behind. I just couldn't, Layla. As laid back as I might seem, I have great love and respect for Allah. When I refused, she freaked out. Her parents had been giving her trouble. She was picturing some sort of *Not Without My Daughter* scenario. I mean, do I look like a psychotic abuser?"

Layla examined his hollow cheeks, the cleft in his chin, his soft blue eyes. What he looked like was adorable. In that moment, she could imagine reaching up and ruffling his hair into a new arrangement. "Not at all. She must be crazy to let you go."

"It's taken a while to get over her. But I think I'm about ready to find a nice Islamic girl. I don't want to take the risk my father did. Not after Rachel."

"You're right. I'm coming to that same conclusion. At least I want to. At least I'm trying to want to. Oh, Ryan, if only I had met you a year ago." Before Mo had stolen her heart.

"A year ago I was stuck on Rachel."

"Seems like our timing is off."

He shifted to face her. "I'll tell you what, Miss Al-Rai." He took her hand in his. It fit surprisingly well. "How about for now, we keep in touch. I could use some friends down here. And later, when your heart heals..." He brushed her chin with his thumb. "And it will heal. Who knows?"

She looked into the deep pools of his eyes. Oh, how she hoped he was right. He seemed so certain, but she doubted him nonetheless. She had to find some way to go on without Mo.

"In time...who knows?" She offered him a timid smile. Ryan might not make her heart race, not yet, but he was precisely the kind of man she had dreamed of creating a future with. Precisely the type of man she had thought Mo would be. Now if only she could convince her heart, she just might survive.

THIRTY-SEVEN

Rain had never seen Allie this way before. She had to drag her out of the darn bungalow to church this morning. Allie's head hung low, and she flinched at Rain's embrace, but still Allie hadn't mentioned what was wrong. Venessa had suggested trying the large congregation that planted her small campus church, so Rain stuffed Allie in her little Volkswagen and headed out to try the place.

Surely this one was perfect. Surely Allie could find nothing to take exception with here. The sanctuary managed to balance elegance with warmth. The stage featured banners with scripture quotations, swathes of fabrics in turquoise, orange, and white, even lively greenery. The professional quality worship left Rain convinced she could float to the heavenlies. And while no children frolicked in the back, at that moment trained dancers presented a worship special that gave Rain shivers. Surely this church would please Allie and improve her mood.

She leaned over to whisper in Allie's ear. "Wow. That's gorgeous."

"It's okay, I guess." Either Allie's standards for dance were much higher than Rain's, or the girl was being difficult.

As for Rain, although touched, she found herself questioning this faith filled with "absolute truth" more and more. She desired to open herself to new experiences but didn't wish to be swayed by emotion alone. So many portions of the Bible rang true, yet there were many others she could never accept. Books of laws and judgment and wrath. God's instructions to wipe out entire nations. No one was that sinful. That evil. Everyone deserved the right to live by their own standards.

She clapped heartily as the special concluded.

A young woman stood to give the announcements. Picnics, baptisms, classes. Sure, it sounded benign enough.

But all those sacrifices. Soaked in blood and death. Even Jesus on the cross. Despite his supposed willingness to give his life, Rain kept super-imposing that image over slain lambs bleating in anguish.

Ew! The whole subject made her want to become a vegetarian again.

Rain still had a hard time believing she had done anything deserving such a sacrifice. Her mom's voice whispered in her mind. "People are born good, darling. It's rules and suppression that distort them. Let them live free, and their natural purity will shine through." Yet this religion claimed man was born sinful. She couldn't picture an innocent little baby as evil.

James wouldn't like this one bit. He understood evil, more than anyone deserved to, but evil resulted in consequences, bad karma. He would say we should each be accountable for our own mistakes. How could he ever accept Jesus paying the price for his father's abuse?

Let him come back and try again in another life.

Preferably as a flea.

The thin middle-aged pastor called a pair of missionaries to the front for prayer. "Joan and Eric will be leaving us soon to minister in Kenya. Let's all stretch our hands toward them and plead the blood of Jesus over this family."

There it was again. The blood. And exactly what sort of ministry would these people be doing in Kenya? Convincing the natives how evil they were?

Rain believed in God now. That much she knew for certain. Maybe she should look into some sort of ecumenical congregation. One that took the good from all religions and brushed over the spooky, radical stuff. That seemed more her speed. James might be able to handle a church like that. He was changing.

Truly changing.

She could sense it. She wasn't about to risk their relationship by doing something crazy like getting "born again."

James came first. He always had, and he always would.

When the pastor instructed the congregation to greet one another, Allie turned to Rain and shook her hand. No one at this mega-church seemed to notice they were new. The people around them engaged in their own conversations, leaving the two girls alone. "Whew! We're safe for the moment."

Sure, the place was pretty enough, but given Allie's mood, the bright banners glared against her eyes, and the chatting of the congregants scratched against her eardrums. She wished Rain had let her stay home and sulk. The irony of their role reversal did not escape Allie.

Rain scanned the crowd. "Well, we could always introduce ourselves. I like meeting people. This place seems perfect for you, Allie. You should make an effort."

Allie yanked Rain back around before she could make eye contact. "Not today. I'm not up to meeting anyone."

"True, you might scare them away. What's wrong with you? When are you going to tell me what's going on. Is it Andy?" Rain laid a hand on Allie's shoulder.

Allie resisted her initial urge to pull away. "It's a long story. I'll fill you in later." She had been trying to forget the whole incident. After she drove away from Andy that night, she realized she had made a terrible mistake. She missed him so much already, but how could she ever face that church? Telling Rain would only make it more real. Hopefully she could stall a while longer.

Rain dropped her hand back to her side. "Oh, I will get it out of you on the way home. So what do you think of this place so far?"

Allie blew out a long breath. Dare she mention her mounting suspicion? "I'm starting to have a bad feeling about this whole church quest."

"What do you mean?"

Dreading to verbalize the thought, Allie swallowed hard. "What if God wants me back at my old church?"

"But you hate that place." Rain put a hand on her hip. "Why would he do that to you?"

"Maybe I'm being paranoid. But if I learned one thing on tour with *Alight*, it's that God is more interested in our character than our comfort. I don't expect him to let me take the easy way out."

"Then maybe you need to deal with these feelings. Get your issues resolved so that you can move on. Once you do, it shouldn't matter where you go to church."

"I hope so."

Today would have been Andy's big day. Pastor Jenkins begged for permission to make the announcement and officially pray over him as the new assistant pastor. But that should happen on a Sunday of joy and hope. Not one of devastation and despair. The happy hymn about God's sufficiency playing in the background rang as a travesty in Andy's ears. Like giggles at a funeral. He gripped the curved back of the wooden pew in front of him. Glanced about at the smiling faces raised toward heaven.

No one. No one understood how much Andy sacrificed for this new position. He would quit and walk out the door right now if he thought that would win Allie back, but there was no accounting for her fickle heart.

He let his head fall between his arms and shook it.

She won. He gave up. What else was new? She had been calling the shots for months anyway. Despite his upbringing, Andy had no problem with spouses submitting to one another in love, but for crying out loud, he wasn't even an equal partner in this relationship.

After fumbling around like a lifeless zombie for the last few days, he at least managed to drag himself to Sunday morning service. But he sat far in the back slumped over the pew. He had nothing to celebrate on this day. He had nothing left.

Nothing? Only his dream job. Only God. Only eternal life. Only forgiveness through a cross. He lifted his head. There the symbol hung over the stage. Its transverse angles depicting the most essential element of his life.

Somehow all these years he had been wrong. He had been sure Allie was the one for him. How did he miss God so monumentally? Yes, he wanted Allie, had intended to marry her ever since high school, but more than that he dreamed of this church. God had given him a heart to reach his generation. That's what fueled him throughout the tough times in seminary. What drove him to read book after book about evangelism, postmodernism, church growth strategies. Pinned him to his knees night after night interceding for the lost.

He would reach them. He would reach them right here, from that glass pulpit at the top of the brown stairs. He assumed Allie would come around once she realized what he hoped to accomplish. How stupid he had been to ever mislead her.

Andy moaned. He needed an attitude adjustment. Still in zombie mode, he stood and trudged up the aisle toward the altar, although no one invited. He didn't care what people thought anymore. A soft worship song played in the background, but he couldn't focus on the words. The time had come. He needed to lay it down. He fell to his knees on the bottom stair, clutching his head, and pressed his face to the carpet.

"God, I give up," Andy whispered beneath the volume of the music. "I die to myself. I die to my dreams. I die to my desires. I give you Allie. I lay at your feet our relationship, Lord. Only you can raise the dead. Only you can take the bloody remnants of my cold, dead heart and bring them back to life. I give it to you. I give it all. I place it in your mighty hands. I rest in your steadfast arms."

That's where you belonged all along.

The answer floated up from his heart. He took a few deep breaths.

A strong, gnarled hand clasped his shoulder, and he turned to see Pastor Jenkins kneeling beside him, head bowed in prayer. Warmth flowed through Andy, filling the empty places in his heart. The pastor continued to pray quietly over him. He remained at the altar until the song ended. Then the pastor stood and pulled him into a bear hug. He rested his head on the shoulder of this man who'd been like a grandfather to him. Then Andy turned and moved toward his pew with weighted feet, aware of his surroundings once again. Eyes bored into him from both sides of the aisle. An older man quirked his brow, probably wondering what juicy sin Andy committed that week.

Boy would he be disappointed.

Nothing but despairing. Giving up hope. Dwelling on his heartache and his lost love. Very normal and natural responses, yet sin-filled in their own way. Andy was done. He wouldn't try to get Allie back. He wouldn't beg or whine. He had laid her on the cross, and there she would stay.

He sat down, opened his bulletin, and masked his face behind it, a trick Allie taught him years ago. To the left, in place of the normal platitudes and folksy stories, sat a poem. And not a trite, cliché poem. A real one. How in the world did that happen?

"Beauty for Ashes"

*I bring to him my garden overcome
with thorns and weeds, without order
or purpose, an unkempt riot of color.*

*I bring to him the tangle, the mess,
the mixed up threads I worked so
hard to weave. Only to disappoint.*

I bring to him the charred remains,

261

the smoking mire, the gray ashes of
all I held dear and lost in the flames.

I bring to him the bloody remnants,
torn and shredded, of my cold dead heart,
which once beat with well-intentioned love.

I must die to truly live.
Make me beautiful once again.
Overwhelm me with bouquets
of fragrant roses, petals strewn in joy.

Well, what do you know? Andy's own personal miracle. A word from God sitting right there in the bulletin of the "Church of the Stick-in-the-Mud." With or without Allie, God had a plan for his life, and God would see it through to perfection.

He dared not let himself hope anymore that Allie might be a part.

THIRTY-EIGHT

Mo arrived early to The Gathering on Sunday evening. He pushed open the red metal door and walked into the old theatre. Only a few people mingled in the seats. Musicians warmed up on the stage. The electric guitarist picked through a metal rift, and the lead singer tapped his microphone a few times until the sound man turned it on.

Pastor Mike greeted Mo with the classic male half hug, half handshake maneuver. "Hey, man. How's it going? Any progress with Layla?"

Mo had called him and shared the whole story the day they got caught. Although Mike was disappointed that Mo hadn't heeded his advice and agreed that sneaking around had been a bad idea, he seemed to understand Mo's reasoning as well, and had been there for him ever since. "No. None. She won't even talk to me."

Mike shoved his hands in the deep pockets of his baggy jeans. "That sucks."

Mo liked that about this guy. He called it like he saw it. "It sure does. I wished she'd just walk away from it all. She doesn't deserve this. We didn't do anything wrong."

"Could she? Could she just walk away? Wouldn't that be dangerous?" Mike eyed him warily.

"Maybe. Her parents seem pretty moderate, but I'm not sure. How ridiculous is that, though? This is America. She's an adult. She could take out a restraining order, right? I'm half tempted to pick her up after class, haul her over my shoulder, and drive away."

"Don't do it, Mo. You can't push her. This isn't about the law. It's about family dynamics and personal choices." Pastor Mike caught a small boy as he zoomed by and slowed him down with a firm pat before sending him on his way.

Mo nodded. "Stupid choices. She's choosing to stay trapped in that house. Bound in that culture. I wish I could make her see reason."

"I'm sure you of all people know how complex this is. You don't want to encourage her to rebel and do something she'll regret. You want to lead her closer to God, not push her away from him." Pastor Mike crossed his arms over his chest.

Complex. Wasn't that the truth? Mo's own relationship with his family remained strained. They were still waiting for this "phase" to pass. What would they do if they realized he toyed with the idea of switching schools to study theology?

"And what about her education?" Pastor Mike continued when he didn't respond. "I imagine that's a factor too. Who's going to pay for it if she breaks with her parents?"

"Then what can I do?" Mo hated feeling helpless.

"These bondages are spiritual as much as mental. Keep praying. Don't give up. We're not fighting against flesh and blood, man. If you let me, I'll take this before the congregation tonight and ask them to intercede for her."

"Good idea. But don't mention her name. I don't want to make matters worse."

"Sure thing." Mike dropped his arms. "We need to believe her eyes will be opened to the truth."

Opened to the truth. Mo's eyes had been blind once. He was living proof that nothing was impossible with God. But in the end, Layla would have to make the decision for herself. No one, not even God, could force her into it. Mo needed to accept the possibility that he might lose her for good.

Layla spent most of the weekend in her bedroom pacing her putrid pink carpet. How could it be Sunday again already?

Accepting her situation in no way made it one bit easier. She missed Mo so much, it stabbed like a knife to her gut. Ryan had offered a few minutes of respite, but nothing more. Why couldn't she control her heart? Why wouldn't logic prevail? Would it really be so hard to fall for a sweet guy like Ryan? A handsome, successful guy that her family approved of? What was wrong with her? Why couldn't she just be the good Muslim girl she'd been raised to be? But did she even believe anymore? Deep in her heart? She just didn't know.

Hoping to put things into perspective, she sat in her cushioned sphere chair in the corner to type an e-mail to Fatima before she went to bed.

> *Dear Fatima,*
> *I think of you daily. I have even tried praying for you as I have seen a woman on the television do, and I feel that some God in heaven is listening. I wish so badly that I could snatch you away, hide you beneath my bed, and take you to school with me. I'm learning such amazing things there.*
> *What can I tell you that might brighten your day? I love engineering. And I'm earning good grades in all my classes. I was gaining weight from Auntie's amazing cooking, but I've lost my appetite lately, so I guess that's a good thing. My friend Allie is working on a big dance project. I am looking forward to seeing it. Rain's boyfriend is back in touch with her. That's good news.*
> *I haven't been up to much, really. Uncle doesn't want me around the Americans anymore, and I have little interest in the MSU.*
> *Oh, but Fatima, I must be honest. I've lost my Mo! Uncle caught us and forced us to break up. Forbid me to see him. I hardly leave the house except for classes. My life is not so different*

than yours these days, I fear.

How could I have been so stupid, to let myself get caught up with a man I knew to be Christian? That remains our secret, of course. Mo still wants to meet my father over the winter break, but I can't live a lie anymore. And no matter how open-minded Baba might be, I can never picture him allowing this.

I've been caught up with too many Christians lately. They make me ask too many questions. And that stupid show with Brother Rasheed. Have you seen it? Uncle never misses it, and yet he wonders why I'm changing.

Here's the thing. There's a whole world out there. And we live in a country that guarantees our rights and freedoms. So why do we allow ourselves to remain so bound? So trapped?

I don't know what to do anymore. Auntie was so worried about me that she actually brought a decent guy home for once. His name is Ryan. Can you believe it? But he's not Mo. Who knows? Maybe in time. That's what he said. Maybe in time.

May the God of the universe show us both his truth. His real truth. Not merely the version we were raised to believe. I long for him to open our eyes, so that we shall know him as he really is.

I am done living in fear, Fatima. I am no longer afraid of the truth. I just want to know what that is. I am ready to face whatever this request might reveal. I wish from the bottom of my heart that you will stop living in fear as well.

Always your friend,
Layla

Exhausted from too many emotions roiling inside her, Layla hit send and stumbled to her bed. She pressed her face into her pillow, still wet from the afternoon's tears. The words whispered like a refrain in her mind. *May the God of the universe show us his truth.* But which God? Which truth?

She pulled the silky sheets up to her chin. Rolled back and forth, tossing and turning. Thoughts spun through her mind, one on top of each other. Finally, she fell into a restless sleep.

The next thing she knew, Layla woke in a vast room, surrounded by bright white light. Ahead of her sat a man, a brilliant shining man. He himself was the source of the glow.

"Come, my child," he said. "I've been waiting."

"Allah?" Yet as Layla said the word, it caught in her chest. She knew it was not his name.

She took a step closer, her bare foot pressing against a gleaming marble floor.

"Allah is God in your language. Is it not?" His voice cascaded like heated honey.

"Yes it is." Layla continued moving forward.

"But I think you know the name that I prefer." His indescribable fragrance wafted toward her, a tender, soothing balm.

Layla did know.

The word escaped her mouth as a moaning lament. "Jesus?"

Something shattered to a million fragments deep within her.

Something hard and cold she hadn't known existed. And into its place flowed that pure white light that suffused the room around her. It saturated her full to bursting with brightness and warmth. Spread to her fingertips and toes, to the roots of her hair. Lifted a lifelong weight from her back.

A burden she never knew she carried.

Drawn toward him like a magnet, she ran and threw herself at his feet, anointing them with tears.

"I'm so sorry. I didn't know."

He tugged the white silken veil off her head. "You won't be needing this anymore."

A sharp breeze snatched it from his grasp, and it fluttered away upon the wind. He lifted her face, cupping it with his hand. That hand with its nail-pierced flesh. "I will be your covering. I am the way, the truth, and the life. Will you have me?"

Her breath caught in her throat.

"Yes, Jesus." Her heart overflowed with that radiant white heat, throbbed with new life.

She sank into his ancient arms. Buried her face into his chest. Clutched the fabric of his robe in her hand. Something had changed deep inside of her.

She felt fresh and clean like a babe. Not just on the outside, but all the way to her core.

"Yes, of course. I love you, Jesus. Please make me your own.""

Layla awoke still mumbling the words. "Yes, yes, yes."

She sat bolt upright on her mattress in a tangle of sheets. "It was just a dream. It was only a dream."

But her heart still pumped with that balmy flow. Her skin tingled from his touch. Looking down at her hands, they retained the faintest trace of a radiant glow.

Delight battled with terror in her heart. Could the dream have been from the devil? Did he seek to trick her? To lure her to hell? She must pray to Allah. She must know the truth.

Layla hurried toward her small, adjacent bathroom to wash, but as she twisted the faucet, she realized she could not bear the possibility of losing the glow. Instead she pulled out her prayer rug and fell to her knees on her bedroom floor. But the Arabic words would not come. The prayers did not flow easily from her mouth as they had for so many years. Instead the words of Jesus reverberated in her heart. *I will be your covering. I am the way, the truth, and the life. Will you have me?*

The words from the dream. A dream truer than anything she had ever experienced. And then the realization hit her. The letter to Fatima. What had she said? She dashed to her computer and checked the sent items in her e-mail. Rereading those words she had written before she fell into slumber, Layla knew.

May the God of the universe show us both his truth. The dream was real. Jesus was real. He had answered her cry, and she had asked him into her life.

And in that moment, she wanted nothing more than to confirm her decision with a cognizant mind. Years of tradition told her to return to her prayer rug and fall to her face, yet somehow that did not feel right. Recalling the image of Jesus, she turned her face upward as she had in the dream, and repeated her promise to him. "I love you, Jesus. Please make me your own."

The molten heat flowed through her yet again. She shivered at the power of God's almighty touch. Never in twenty-two years of following Allah had she sensed him within her and all around her like this. Never before had he filled her heart full to the point of bursting.

She curled up in her bright pink chair, and right there, she poured out her heart to God. Talked to him as a real person, an actual friend. Not just some far away being who had set her destiny in stone long ago. She shared her deepest hopes and dreams. Her heartfelt thanks. Asking him for guidance and direction as she set out on this new journey.

Layla could hardly wait to jump online and delve into the Bible. To follow every last Christian link on Brother Rasheed's website. To listen to his lessons again and again. And to *The Muslim Woman* show with Sister Amani as well. What a treasure trove awaited her on the computer.

Jesus would be the most important thing in her life now. She was a brand new person. Allie would be so pleased. And Mo! In all the excitement she had actually forgotten Mo. She and Mo could be together now. The thought brought her great joy, yet it paled in comparison to the bliss of being found by a heavenly father.

Unable to fall back to sleep, Layla poured a glass of orange juice from the refrigerator and took it onto the patio. Sitting in a lounge chair, she sipped the cold, tangy liquid and gazed into the sky. White stars winked at her against the black night, calling to mind the brightness that flowed from their creator. Each one a twinkle snatched from his almighty eyes to illuminate the darkness.

As daylight dawned in a colorful array and her euphoria dissipated to a quiet contentment, Layla began to consider the consequences of her actions. What would she do now? What would her life look like? What would her parents say? Where would she live? How would she support herself?

Uncle had grown so radical of late. She doubted he would hurt her, but she couldn't be certain. Honor killings were on the rise in the Middle East.

No, Layla was not ready to shout her conversion from the rooftops. She wanted a moment to treasure it secretly in her heart before all hell broke loose. Maybe she could tell Mo when the time was right. He alone would understand. She gripped the cold empty cup in her hand and watched condensation drip down the sides.

Uncle stepped onto the patio and stretched. "You're up early. Go wash. Prayers in a few minutes."

"Right. Prayers. I'll go wash." She repeated like a robot.

What would she do? Mutter the words under her breath? Hope Aunt and Uncle didn't notice if she changed a few? Would she attend mosque as if nothing happened? And what about Ryan? He really was a sweet guy. Maybe she could fix him up with someone. Maybe the impish Aisha. She laughed, but the mirth quickly died on her lips.

Now she realized the anguish Mo must have gone through, the sense of being torn in two. She certainly hadn't made things easy on him. No wonder he chose to keep quiet. Avoided mosque and prayers. It all made sense.

But no matter how hard her life might become, there could be no turning back. She had met the God of love face to face. Gazed into his eyes. Felt the touch of his hand. She was forever changed.

THIRTY-NINE

On Tuesday afternoon, James lay on the therapist's brown couch, wrung out like a sponge. As if all the memories had been squeezed out of him like sweat, leaving him numb and exhausted, staring at the dotted ceiling tiles over his head and pressing himself deeper into the soft leather.

"I think that's enough for today. We're making good progress." The doctoral student flipped shut his notebook.

James gathered the energy to sit up and look the man in the eye.

"Have you given any thought to moving home yet?" The therapist slid his pencil behind his ear.

James leaned his elbows onto his knees and let his head droop. "No. I don't trust myself."

"Why not? I trust you."

James's head snapped back up. "You trust me? Why would you trust me?"

The therapist crossed his legs and leaned back into his easy chair, indicating the session wasn't quite over yet.

James sighed, not sure he could take any more today.

"Let me ask you something, James. When you think back on the last few years, when were the times that you felt the very angriest?"

"The shooting, for sure."

"And how did you respond?"

"I don't know. I was busy trying to save Rain." This dude sure did ask some crazy questions.

"You didn't abandon her and go chase down the bad guys?"

"Of course not."

"What about when the hospital denied treatment? Did you beat anybody up?"

James twisted his face in confusion. "I was holding her in my arms."

"So in the moment you were the angriest, you protected Rain."

James saw were this was going, but it wasn't that simple. "What about when she told me she was pregnant? Did I protect her then?"

The therapist tilted his head. "No, you didn't."

"No, I didn't. I turned violent."

"Really? Did you strike her?" The therapist's voice remained steady.

"I threw things all over the room. Broke stuff. Kicked a hole in the wall." James shook his head, his stomach churning at the memory.

"Okay, so you were angry. We've already established that."

"And I hurt her."

"Hurt her how?"

"I jerked her chin up because I wanted to stare her down."

The therapist raised his brows. The first response he had shown since James sat up to face him. "So in that moment when she pushed your worst trigger buttons, stirred your most troubling memories and emotions, ones we've been working on for weeks, the worst you did was pull her chin up?"

"Well...yeah." It sounded stupid when he put it that way.

"Did you even for one moment consider hitting her?"

James thought hard. He had been so angry. His head about to explode. He would have done anything to control her. No... not anything. When he looked into her eyes, he knew from the bottom of his soul that he could never hurt her.

"No. I didn't." James took a deep breath. "But I told her to kill our baby. I would have killed our child."

"You could have beaten her up there and then and gotten rid of the child yourself. Punched her in the stomach. Maybe pushed her down the stairs."

James shuddered. "I...could never." He began to see the situation in a new light. Through different eyes.

"You made a mistake, James. A big one. We both know that. But were you actually thinking of killing a child?"

James took another deep breath and shook his head. "No. I just wanted to be rid of a problem."

"Lean back and relax," the therapist instructed. "Picture a child. A baby with little arms and legs, wrapping its tiny fingers around your hand. Picture it gazing up at you with big, helpless eyes."

James did. The baby had Rain's creamy brown skin and soft green irises. A rush of love flowed through him. Love and joy. The full weight of the revelation sank in. He opened his eyes.

The therapist leaned forward and looked directly at him. "Could you ever hurt that child?"

He twisted his head softly from side to side. His next word came out in awe. "Never."

"You are *not* your father, James."

Rain woke to tapping. She rolled over and spied the clock. Only 7:30 p.m. The sun still shined through the window, streaming in low and golden from the west. Struggling to shake off her pregnancy-induced lethargy, she sat up on the couch.

"I'm coming, I'm coming," she hollered toward the insistent knock, which had grown louder, and stumbled yawning across the cool wooden floor toward the front door. How could a baby who only weighed a few ounces sap so much of her strength? And add so much width to her hips?

Once she got her energy back, she vowed to take up jogging.

She pulled open the door and blinked her bleary eyes, not trusting the vision before her. There stood James, suitcase in hand.

"Baby, I'm home."

"Oh, James." She threw herself in his arms, sucking in a deep whiff of his sandalwood scent.

She pressed her lips to his soft, full ones. They tasted of mint and honey. Honey and streams of water in a desert. She ran her fingers over the rough scruff of his beard, closing her eyes and pressing her head into his neck.

James dropped another feather light kiss on her forehead. "I'm home, and I'm going to be the best dad in the world."

FORTY

Rain arrived early to English class the next morning. She wanted to share the good news in person. Layla sat at her usual desk in the far back corner, but Allie was nowhere in sight. Probably another early morning rehearsal. Rain scanned the hallway full of students jostling one another on the way to their classes. No blond bun in sight. She had hoped to tell the girls together, but didn't think she could wait another moment.

She shouted across the room, "He's home."

Layla jumped up to run and give her a hug. Her silky yellow veil wisped against Rain's cheek. "That's wonderful. I'm so happy for you."

"We're going to be a family, Layla. A real family." They headed back to their seats.

"What changed?"

"He had some sort of breakthrough with his counselor." Rain tossed her oversized sack on the floor. "Can you believe it?"

"Wow."

"I guess this prayer thing works." Rain felt guilty as the words left her mouth, and she sank into her chair. Even as she sent her thanks heavenward last night, she knew James could only add to this wall she'd been building to hold God at bay. The distance was growing. She hardly sensed his presence these days.

Layla seemed lost in her own thoughts for a moment. She gave Rain a serene smile. "Yes, I suppose it does."

"You look happy. Did you figure out something with Mo?"

"Maybe. I think I'm changing. I really don't mind so much anymore that he's a Christian. I mean...we both serve the one

God, maker of heaven and earth. That's what counts, right? Although I'm not sure my father will see things that way."

Layla's pretty features stiffened.

Rain wanted more than ever to drag her friend away from that constraining religion. Maybe she should do something to help get her back with Mo. "You know, I've been thinking about this spiritual stuff a lot lately. There are many paths to God, right? How can anyone say one book, one prophet, one preacher offers absolute truth? Life isn't that simple."

"Well, I didn't mean to imply..."

"Remember our skit. Different paths. Lots of truths. See my point?"

Layla put a finger to her chin. "I didn't really look at it that way. I thought of it more as...we ended up in a place none of us expected, but it was a specific place. A perfect place."

Allie slid into her seat as the bell rang for class. "What am I missing?"

"Rain was illuminating me on the many paths to God." Layla winked.

"Oh?" Allie's brow creased.

"I'm really enjoying all of these churches," Rain said, "but the mentality is too narrow for me. I might try something more syncretistic. James might be into that. James! Allie, James is home!"

Allie and Rain squealed and hugged, meeting between the desks, and stomping their feet rapidly against the floor.

The professor broke through their clamor. "Miss Butler-Briggs? Miss Carmichael?" Humor glimmered in his smile despite the censure in his voice. "I'm glad to see the project has proven such a huge success, but could we start class?"

"Yes, sir," Allie said, holding back a laugh.

"Of course." Rain returned to her desk.

Layla just ducked her head.

"Oh, Rain. That's wonderful," Allie whispered, reaching across the aisle to clasp Rain's forearm.

Yes, wonderful. So, why did something still catch in the pit of Rain's stomach? She had one priceless love back in her life, but to get him, had she pushed away another?

Between keeping busy with dance rehearsals and being furious with Andy, Allie managed to put off getting to the bottom of those wretched feelings for yet another week. But, as Layla pointed out, she needed to deal with them, Andy or not. Coming home late from rehearsal, Allie tossed her dance bag in the corner of her room and collapsed on her bed, rolling onto her back. She felt so weak. So exhausted. So drained. She didn't have the courage to face this.

But no matter how far or fast she ran, she could never outrun God's plan for her life. A plan that involved getting to the bottom of her issues with that church. A plan that involved opening her heart to Andy. Oh, she could turn her back on it. Rebel against it. But what would happen then? She didn't even want to consider the consequences. Tears filled her eyes. Allie so wanted to do the right thing, but she had nothing left.

When you are weak, then I am strong. Was that it? Allie could never do this in her own strength. Had that been the point all along?

And so on that quiet Tuesday evening she folded herself cross-legged on the floor in front of her bed, leaning her head against the pastel comforter, and tuned her thoughts to that inner-kingdom once again. She needed God's light to cast out the darkness that had fallen onto her soul. God's hope to cast out despair. God's joy to cast out depression. She needed to ask him what in the world had happened in the hallway of that church. Ask him to help her find her way back to Andy.

Sensing God gathering her hands into his own, she looked up into twinkling eyes and poured out her heart. And he answered. Boy did he answer. First he confirmed her conclusion that her feelings for Andy were tangled into something deeper. But when she asked what that deeper memory might be, he responded, "Ask your mother."

"You know," Allie said, gazing with a smile into his weathered face. "You have quite a track record here. First it's take another look at Andy. Then it's scrap your entire dance project. Now, go talk to Mom?"

God chuckled. Yes, the God of the entire universe found that funny. "My ways are not your ways."

Yet she couldn't deny the lightness and peace that accompanied God's marching orders. She stood and gathered up her purse. The time had come to get to the bottom of this.

Allie pulled up in front of her childhood home and headed inside. Mom waited with steaming mugs as usual, and they sat down on stools at the kitchen island.

"So what is this big emergency?" Mom blew on her coffee.

"Last week, when we talked, you were about to tell me something, weren't you? And Dad interrupted."

"I don't seem to recall—"

"Mom." Allie cut her off. "I know there's something you're not telling me. Something happened at church that I don't remember."

Mom cocked her head sideways. "Why are you so sure?"

"Because God told me." Allie took a few bracing sips.

"God...told you. Just like that."

She pinned Mom with her eyes, ready to wrestle the truth out of her this time if necessary. "He told me to ask you what happened. I took that as a yes."

"Honey, that's wonderful. I'm so glad you're growing closer to God. Why, the other day I was talking to Judy, and I was saying—"

"Mom." Allie slapped her cup down on the counter. "Stop stalling. There is something, right?"

"To tell you the truth, I hadn't thought about it in years, but when you asked last week, it sort of leaped into my head."

"Why didn't you say anything?"

Mom dipped her chin. "When Dad interrupted, I thought maybe I wasn't supposed to bring it up. I mean, it's been a long, long time. Paul says in Philippians that we should press on toward the goal, not look back. Sometimes the past is best left in the past."

"And sometimes the past needs to be dealt with so that we can move forward. What happened?" She wished Mom would face her past as well. But the woman clearly wasn't ready. Perhaps Allie could serve as an example for her.

"Do you remember Pastor Brody?" Mom tapped her fingers against the counter.

"We had another pastor?"

"He was an assistant pastor. A younger man."

"No, I don't remember him."

"Your dad picked up on something odd in the way he treated you, and I guess without mentioning it, he was keeping an eye on him. Then one day Dad noticed you were taking too long in the bathroom, and he went looking for you. He heard your voice around the corner, and hid to observe what was happening. You were sitting next to Pastor Brody." Mom paused and took a deep breath.

"Go on," Allie prompted.

"Your dad didn't like the way he talked so sweetly to you, the way he was too touchy, but you were a cute little girl. Everyone was affectionate with you. So Dad waited." Mom took another sip of coffee and cleared her throat.

"Then he saw Pastor Brody fondling your hair, reaching around and grabbing you by the neck. About that time, Dad rushed toward you, but Pastor Brody leaned in to give you a kiss."

"What!" Allie's stomach tied into knots, and nausea rose in her throat.

Mom grabbed her hand and rushed on. "Your father hauled him up by his slimy lapels and told you to run and find me. No sooner were you out of his sight, than Dad knocked the guy out cold."

Allie's thoughts swam at all this unexpected information. Cool drops of sweat beaded at her hairline. She gripped Mom's hand tight.

Mom continued. "Pastor Jenkins fired him immediately and took appropriate actions. We asked you enough questions to make sure nothing else had happened. You were so little. You didn't seem to realize anything was wrong. There didn't seem to be any reason to bring it up again."

Allie blinked as her mind struggled to put the pieces together. She always wore her hair tightly secured in a bun. She freaked out completely when Andy became assistant pastor. Pastor Brody must have been the awful usher in the memory that made her gag. The pieces slid together. All told, it wasn't as bad as she might have expected. Allie cracked a half smile. "So Dad really punched the guy?"

"Flattened him."

"Go, Dad. I wish I could remember." She stared into the pool of her coffee, as if the answers might lay hidden beneath the surface.

"Maybe you will with some time. Did I do the right thing to tell you? Will it help somehow?" Mom's lips pinched tight.

"Definitely. It explains why I overreact to certain things. I need to think through it more, though."

Mom came around the counter and placed a comforting hand on Allie's shoulder. "I'm sorry I didn't tell you before. I really didn't see the need."

"It's okay, Mom. Maybe I wasn't ready before. But if you don't mind, I think I'll head home. This is a lot to process."

"Sure, sweetheart." Mom gave her a hug.

Allie clung to her for a moment. "Thanks." She placed a kiss on Mom's cushy hairdo before heading out the door. A part of her wanted to run back and hide her head against Mom's chest where all was safe, but she had put off facing these demons for far too long.

FORTY-ONE

Two hours later, Allie sat on her sagging front porch curled up in a blanket against the nip of the November night, still wishing she could remember. No wonder she couldn't find her balance since she'd come home. Something had been off-center deep in her core all along. She'd been wracking her brain and trying to sort through events ever since Mom made the big revelation. Maybe she needed to relax and stop trying so hard. Rain had said something about following a trail of memories and feelings. Maybe that was the trick. She needed to stop thinking and let herself experience those sensations again.

"God, I have no idea what I'm doing here. Please guide me."

Let yourself feel it, the answer floated up to her mind from somewhere in her chest. Allie pressed her lips tight together, summoning the strength to get through this.

She pictured the snake with its evil hypnotic eyes and gaping mouth. Braced herself as it tightened around her, slithering around her neck, her chest. Choking, binding, constricting. Allie allowed her body to relax into the feeling and found herself back in that foyer, dancing freely.

There she saw him.

She saw the face of the mean usher hollering at her in the foyer. A round face with dark brows and a mustache atop his three-piece suit and tie. Pastor Brody. She remembered him clear as day.

"You're my special girl, Allie," he yelled in a panic. "You shouldn't do such things. You shouldn't tempt me like this. It's wrong. It's bad." He reached toward her, and she dashed into the sanctuary, bile rising to her throat and her stomach clenching with nausea.

She continued to follow the wispy trail of sensations. The Sunday school room, she felt them so keenly there. And she found herself back in that room, pinned in a corner by his presence. Every fiber in her trembled to push past his hulking frame and escape, but he gazed down at her with those bulging hypnotic eyes, pulling her in, alluring her. "Allie, it's okay, my precious. Oh Allie, my pure and perfect little girl." He reached and picked up a tendril of her long, blond hair, letting it slip through his fingers.

Allie pressed herself into the wall. So afraid her teeth chattered. She didn't want him to yell at her again. She didn't want to get in trouble. She wasn't supposed to be here. She didn't move.

His voice grew raspy. "I have a present for you. But it needs to be our little secret. Okay? You can't tell anyone where you got it. Hide it when you get home." He pulled her left hand from her side and slipped a child's ring on her finger.

She stared down at it, frozen, terrified. Her mommy wore a ring like that. Gold with a big shining crystal. The sparkles glinted sharp and painful like knives. She was too little to get married. She didn't want the horrible ring.

"Do you know what this means, Allie? It means that we're special to each other. That we can do special things together. Do you like it? Oh, Allie, I want to bring you more presents, okay? But you can't tell anyone. You wouldn't want me to have to mention what a naughty girl you've been. Bad things might happen. Very bad things."

Allie couldn't take it anymore. She dashed past him screaming. Tore the ring from her finger and threw it in the trash. It was all her fault. She wasn't supposed to wander the church alone. She had been a bad girl.

The hallway. What about the hallway where she freaked out completely on Andy? Then, in a flash, Allie found herself in a dark, narrow, tunnel-like hall, sitting on a spare pew. Animals gawked at her, showing their fangs. The trees mocked her with their gnarled faces. And the man was beside her. His eyes sucking her in. She had been bad again, dancing through the hidden passageways when she was supposed to be in the sanctuary. It was all her fault. This time his words didn't register, only the swirling, confusing draw of his eyes.

She felt the weight of his hand against the back of her neck, his fingers wrapping around. She couldn't breathe. His other hand slithered down her back. She couldn't move. Her head pounded. Her vision blurred. He dragged her toward him, crushing her, pinning her with his eyes, with his huge hands. His gaping mouth descended toward her. Cold, hard flesh pressed against her skin and something wet wedged between her lips. She clenched them together. Vomit rose in her throat. She pressed her eyes shut.

And he was gone. Ripped away from her in an instant. "Run, Allie! Just run. Run to your Mom." She heard her father's voice, full of anger, but she couldn't see his face. Her head swam and her eyes filled with tears. She was in big trouble now.

Allie ran to the bathroom to hide in a stall. She threw up her breakfast in the commode, sank to the floor, and cried.

In that place, in that lonely stall, as if she lived it all again, Allie heard a whisper.

Allie, it wasn't your fault.

The nausea dissipated.

Your dad loves you.

The band loosened from around her belly.

You did nothing wrong.

Her chest felt light and free.

I love you.

She pulled in a deep breath of fresh cool air.

Your parents did their best.

The strangling sensation disappeared.

Pastor Jenkins defended you.

The weight lifted from the back of her neck.

You don't have to run anymore.

The last of the pinching faded away.

It's okay, Allie. It's over. And you're safe.

Allie felt God's warmth permeate the chilly evening. *It's not your fault. It's not the church's fault. It's not Andy's fault. It never was.*

She breathed in his presence. God had been there all along. Truly at peace for the first time in many days, Allie whispered up her thanks, told God good night, and headed to her bed, where she fell into a sound, healing sleep.

In the morning, as Allie brushed her hair in the mirror, somehow the sunlight took on a brighter tint. She decided to wear her hair down for once, and shook it out in a streaming mass of blond waves. Allie couldn't quite explain it, but something had shifted deep within her. The world looked subtly different. Like when she got an updated contact prescription. One day, she would think she could see just fine, and the next she would get her new lenses and realize everything had been hazy and fuzzy for months.

Today, her vision was clear. No wonder she felt uncomfortable when the new director joined *Alight*. He looked so much like Pastor Brody, from the mustache, to the age, to the features, to the three-piece suits. No wonder she had run away. But God had been with her all along. Guiding her. Directing her. Bringing her to this place of healing after twenty years.

She thought of Andy. His handsome face with its smattering of freckles. His warm hazel eyes. The roguish curl of his hair. The tingling wonder of his kiss. It all felt so right. So good.

Pushing herself further, she called to mind the night he asked her to marry him. The ring around her finger. But the memories were benign, objective—stirring a slight sadness as she recalled the incident—but none of the visceral sensations.

Amazing.

And in that moment her last doubts faded away. She and Andy were meant to be together. She simply hadn't been ready to deal with the truth. Now she was ready. Was it too late? She had to get Andy back. She loved him. How could she ever convince him? She applied some pink lip gloss as she devised a plan.

FORTY-TWO

Layla stared at the large flat screen television hanging from the center of the media room wall. Brother Rasheed featured a music video tonight for the topic of discussion. A song about a young Muslim woman, Rana from Jordan, martyred for her newfound Christian faith. Layla's family sat in silence, watching the evocative images and listening to the stirring melody. Even her chatty aunt said nothing. As the girl's father pummeled her head with a rock and thrust a knife into her chest, Layla's eyes filled with tears. She experienced the pounding and the stabbing in her own body.

Would her fate be the same?

But the song assured, Rana ran free now in heaven with Jesus. *She's twirling and she's leaping, not bound by time or space. Wrapped in the arms of Jesus, she'll gaze into his eyes. With no more tears in heaven, no more burdens there, she flies.* Her heart soared along with the young woman as moisture trickled down her cheeks. She swiped the salty liquid away before Uncle could notice.

As a voice on the video chanted, "Fly, Rana, fly," she could hardly contain the beauty and wonder of the words. She had experienced that feeling, so light and free in the arms of Jesus. Joy overwhelmed her, and a sob escaped Layla's throat.

Her uncle turned with daggers in his eyes, every bit as lethal as the one in the video. "You dare to mourn this girl. This traitor. This infidel pig!"

He stood and paced the room, throwing his arms over his head. There was no comedy in his outburst today. He pointed

287

his finger in Layla's face. "Her father was a good man. He did the right thing. He put an end to their family's shame and dishonor. More Muslims should stand up for what they believe in."

Uncle snatched up the remote and turned off the television. "I've had it with the lies. I've had it with that show. The girl, she does not fly in heaven with Jesus, she broils in the pit of hell where she belongs."

He shouted directly into Layla's face. "And her father should be proud to be the one who put her there."

Auntie stood and yanked her husband by the arm. "*Khalas!* Stop it. You're frightening her. It was a sad video. You are overreacting."

"You don't mean it, Uncle." Her eyes grew wide and dry. "Tell me you would never, ever do such a thing."

"I would. I would do it. Any honorable Muslim would. We've heard too much talk of choice and freedom in this land. We grow soft. We let these shows continue. It's too much. The time has come to stand up for Islam. To fight for it, before it is too late."

She saw in his eyes that he meant it. Her loving uncle meant every word. Her stomach fell to the floor. Her heart clenched. She pressed her hand to her mouth to quiet her moan and dashed from the room, as Auntie whispered, "Let her go, *habibi.*"

Layla slammed the door behind her and threw herself on her bed, clutching the comforter and dragging ragged breaths into her petrified lungs. "Oh, God. What will I do?" What if her uncle found out? She hadn't fully grasped the enormity of her decision. Yet she could never turn back. This new existence was everything she ever dreamed of. She was a child of the one true God. She needed help, but she still didn't know who would be safe to ask.

Mo? She could get in trouble for merely speaking to him, never mind the subject matter. It would be just like uncle to press his ear to the door at a moment like this. No, she couldn't make matters worse by dragging Mo into the mix. Uncle was already furious about him. She still didn't believe he could ever kill a daughter, a niece, but after what she saw tonight, she thought he'd be more than happy to wrap his hands around Mo's neck.

Allie? Rain? They would never understand the complications she faced. They'd try to drag her to church, get her to read the Bible. No, she wasn't ready for any of that.

Ryan? He seemed open minded enough, but she wouldn't want to lead him on. She couldn't trouble him over this. She no longer shared his faith, and Mo was the man of her dreams. The man who shared her beliefs and passions.

Her parents? *Baba* might understand, a little, but she'd break her mother's heart.

Fatima? She could always talk to Fatima, and clearly no one monitored her Internet activity, or they would have been in trouble long ago. Layla opened her computer and hit the e-mail icon. Fatima would understand. The tapping of Layla's fingers against the plastic keys soothed her frayed nerves.

As she stood at the counter preparing dinner, Rain took in a deep whiff. The apartment smelled wonderful. Not just the aroma of chicken, curry, raisins, and couscous. The place smelled of James again. His sandalwood cologne, the waxy scent from his dreadlocks, the warm, heady fragrance of a man.

"Dinner smells good." James walked into the kitchen.

Not half as good as he did.

His arm reached around her for the wooden spoon in the pot.

She slapped it away. "It'll be ready in a few minutes. Go watch the news."

"Violence is not the answer, woman." His deep, rich chuckle ran over her ears like silk. "Is it the pregnancy, or do we need to cut back on your meat intake?"

"Funny."

He dropped a quick kiss on her neck. "Call me when it's done. I'm starving."

Rain would have sworn her feet floated inches from the floor. Yet as she glanced over at the rumpled sheets, an odd twinge she barely recognized caught hold of her gut. Her toes landed on the ground.

Conviction? Ridiculous.

She'd spent too much time in churches lately. Her love for James was pure and right. They belonged to each other. It was only natural. She'd had quite enough of Christianity and its repressive restrictions. James belonged in her arms with or without a piece of paper to prove it.

Rain massaged her hands over her belly. And here was the ultimate proof. The product of their love. This little human would bind them together come what may. It would grow, and thrive, fusing their DNA. Living, breathing proof that they were one. Tomorrow she would go for her first prenatal appointment. In a month or two she would see the little face on a sonogram.

Why should she need a ceremony, a license to validate her relationship with James?

But she did miss her time with God. God didn't care about such things, did he? Even in the Old Testament a man took a woman into his tent, and that was that, they were married. Things were much simpler back then.

Christianity had just gotten off track somewhere along the way.

Rain popped the entrée into the oven and wandered over to her notes on the dining room table. Too bad she couldn't do her research paper on what she'd like to change about Christianity rather than what she wanted to change about her own culture. She had much clearer thoughts on that issue. Her culture was so ephemeral. She could talk about a personal God, but surely some New Age hippies out there already believed in that. Her own background had no absolutes, no clear definitions. Wasn't it best that way? To be free and natural with no restrictions? To make your own truth?

But who ever really did? Maybe that's what she could talk about. Truth. Truth found in the eyes of a personal God. Like how she couldn't go through with the abortion no matter what her background might tell her.

She missed her prayer time. Those special interludes with

her creator. She needed to get back into that habit. And in that moment, Layla's face floated through her mind. Something was different with Layla these days. Something other than Mo. She wished Layla would confide in her. Rain wanted so badly to help this sweet girl bound by an oppressive religion. Christianity didn't even come close to Islam in that department.

In fact, this morning in class as Allie shared about her big breakthrough, she sounded downright free. Allie could probably use a few prayers as well before she faced Andy tomorrow.

Rain leaned her elbows against the counter and pictured Layla's face again. Her eyes looked bright and hopeful, yet fear lurked in their depths. Something was wrong. Something was terribly wrong. Was Layla in some sort of danger? If only Layla would talk to her, maybe she could help. Rain folded her hands.

James came back into the kitchen.

She shot him a look.

He held up his palms in surrender. "Just thought I'd set the table."

As he gathered plates and silverware, Rain gathered her thoughts and moved to the stove. "You're so good to me." She picked up the serving spoon and handed him a taste. "Here. Have some."

He took a bite of food and snitched a quick taste of her neck as well. "You are too easy."

Rain grimaced. Maybe he was right.

FORTY-THREE

Andy picked up the nameplate from his new desk in the larger office across the hall from Pastor Jenkins's. ASSISTANT PASTOR ANDREW VARGAS read the gold letters on the black enamel. He set it down and looked around at the framed artwork of seascapes. The church secretary knew him well.

He should be the happiest man in the world. His dreams had come true. Already the pastor was implementing some of his ideas. Only this morning he had clapped Andy on the back and said, "It's time for some new blood around this place. You've done such a great job with the kids. I can't wait to see what you're going to do with the rest of us."

Andy had resisted the temptation to tap on his head and knock out whatever messed with his hearing. Surely Pastor Jenkins, head of Fuddy Duddy Chapel would never say such a thing. He wished Allie had been there to witness it.

And therein lay the problem. Allie. How would he ever get over her? He tried to keep his thoughts away from the girl, but his traitorous imagination would not obey. The best he could do was turn his mental energy to God. Pray yet again, and try to keep himself too busy for his mind to wander.

He picked up Sunday's agenda from his desk. This week would be the formal announcement, and then he would preach to the entire congregation for the first time. There was so much he wanted to say to them. He really wished he could remember what it was. Instead, his eyes drifted back to the seascape, and he dreamed of surfing with Allie.

Focus, Andy! You have a sermon to write. Maybe something

on freedom in Christ. This was his big chance after all. He went to work looking up scriptures and outlining his sermon. A few minutes later, he was interrupted by a knock at the door. Great, the cheery secretary always wanted to talk. "Come in."

The door swung slowly and a figure hid behind it. When she moved into the opening, all he could see for a moment was her shadow against the fluorescent light of the hallway, but the slim silhouette could not belong to the plump, middle-aged Doreen.

Once in the room, the young lady moved toward him with clipped efficiency. "Hello, Pastor Vargas." She extended her hand. "I'm a student from Old Dominion University, and I was wondering if you could answer some questions for me?"

Her hand hung in midair above his desk. He stood and shook it from years of habit, but his head swam with confusion. "Huh?"

"Allow me to introduce myself. My name is Allison Carmichael, and I'm writing a paper for my English class about changes needed in the Christian culture. Do you have a few minutes?"

"Allie, what are you talking about?" His heart twisted.

"I'm talking about a college student who would like to question an assistant pastor. I've heard some great things about your ministry, and I'd like to learn more."

She wore a blazer and fashionable flats with her jeans today, looking the role of journalist. He would play along for now.

"All right, Miss Carmichael." He waved his hand to the chair in front of his desk. "Please have a seat." Settling himself into his new swiveling monstrosity, he blinked a few times, checking his vision again. His pulse sped. Her hair was down and flowing for once. Waving and golden like the ocean at sunrise. He wanted nothing more than to reach out, tangle his fingers through it, and pull her to his lips.

"Tell me about the changes you've made around this place so far."

"Well, up until now I've only had authority over the youth group. My first goal was to make it feel casual. A safe, relaxed place for kids to hang out and share."

She pulled the pencil from her notebook and jotted down some notes. "That doesn't sound too radical."

"It was radical enough to start. When I was a kid we met on Sunday mornings in our ties and skirts before service." He steepled his hands and watched her overtop.

Allie frowned. No doubt she remembered those days. "So moving to a week night must have helped."

"Yes, it did, but I've gone to bat for the kids over things like music and hobbies too. When I was their age, people acted like those were spiritual issues. At some point I realized our parents were driving kids away with that sort of mentality. As you mentioned, a lot of those issues are more about culture than spirituality."

"Must have been quite a shock to the congregation." Her eyes gazed more deeply into his than the comment demanded.

"At first, but I tried to take it step by step. Generally it's not a good idea for a pastor to enter a church hoping to change it, but this is my church, and I understood the needs. I didn't introduce the rock concert idea until two years in." He took a deep breath and caught a hint of her lavender perfume. Good Lord, what was this woman doing to him now?

"But you recently received a promotion. How do you plan to implement changes with the adults?" She sounded like a reporter for WAVY TV 10.

"The same way, little by little. I keep praying and asking God for wisdom with every step. You can't rush people, but many of our members have been hoping to see these changes for a long time. It might be awhile before I can implement some of my crazier dreams like video presentations, performance art, alternate coffee-shop style seating." He couldn't take it anymore. "Allie, tell me what you're doing here."

"Well." She turned her eyes down. "I heard a lot about this innovative new pastor at one of the area's oldest and most traditional churches, and I wanted to meet him."

"Allie," he snapped. "I'm serious."

"We need a fresh start, Andy. We have too much baggage."

"Oh." Not a half bad idea, actually.

"If you don't mind me saying so." Allie lifted her head and grinned. "Allison Carmichael is quite taken by this handsome young pastor. She might be interested in going out for some coffee and getting to know him better. If he wanted to ask, of course."

"And this is how you plan to get reacquainted? Coffee?" He shook his head in frustration. Hadn't he been tempted to throw her onto the hood of his car and make love to her a few short weeks ago?

"Little by little, Andy. Right?"

He stared into her breathtaking face and crystal blue eyes. Maybe she was right. But he had laid her at the cross. Shouldn't he leave her there?

You laid her at the cross, and now I'm giving her back.

He clutched the edge of his desk as the words swirled through his mind. Could it be true? Was it wishful thinking? He looked even deeper into her eyes. He saw no pain. No fear. No resentment.

Instead all he saw was love. And longing.

"Please, Andy."

He shook his head in wonder. Cleared his throat. He ran a finger over his desk calendar. "Ahh, Miss Carmichael, it seems I have some time available right now, in fact. Would you care to join me for a cup of coffee?"

He strode around the desk and offered her his arm.

She stood, wrapping hers through it. Her eyes sought his. "More than anything in the world."

As they walked through the hallway all he could think was, *She's ready to give me a chance. But what about this church?*

FORTY-FOUR

Layla pulled her convertible along the curb, hoping to avoid broken glass. The car alarm gave a quick pulse as she set it and rushed into Rain's soot-stained building, grateful that Auntie and Uncle agreed to let her out of the pink satin prison to enjoy her first real Thanksgiving dinner. Weeks had passed since the Mo fiasco. They couldn't keep her locked up forever. And if she linked the dinner to her English grade, surely that wasn't stretching the truth too far. The theme for the semester *was* multiculturalism.

She hit the buzzer and was caught off guard by the attractive, olive-skinned face of the man who opened the door. For a fraction of a second she couldn't place him in this out-of-context setting. But there they were, the features that had floated behind her eyelids for months.

Her heart fluttered, then fell.

"Mo? Oh no. This was a terrible idea. Rain!" Her muscles tensed and she turned to run, but Mo caught her by the elbow and ushered her inside.

"Relax, will you? Everything's fine." His voice, with its trace of a Lebanese lilt, filled her with heady warmth and dreaded chills all at once.

Rain walked around the kitchen counter, wiping her hands on a dish towel. "So, how do you like my surprise?"

Every muscle in Layla's body still clenched tight. A headache was sure to ensue. "Oh, Rain. You shouldn't have. You don't understand how hard it was to persuade my aunt and uncle to let me come. If they knew this, they'd be furious."

"Why do you think I kept it a secret?" Rain smiled mischievously.

"It isn't funny." Layla's eyes filled with moisture.

Rain's smile vanished. "Wow. You're really scared. I'm so sorry. I figured this way, you'd be innocent."

Mo came and placed a strong arm around her shoulder. "I'm sorry too. I didn't mean to push you. I can go."

"And leave me here with this gaggle of females, man? I don't think so," a deep voice called from the worn couch. Layla turned toward the sound. From Rain's description, she recognized the man immediately. If anything, he was even handsomer than she imagined. "I didn't mean to make such a fuss. You must be James." She crossed to shake his hand as any American girl would do. "I'm Layla. It's so nice to finally meet you. I've heard a lot about you."

"I don't think I want to know what you heard about me. I haven't been on my best behavior these last few months." His rich chuckle belied his words.

Rain threw herself on the couch and snuggled beside James. "You're here now, and that's what matters."

Allie entered from the kitchen, licking mashed potatoes from her fingers. "Andy will be back with the ice any second. You'll be fine, James. But, Layla, I hope you'll let Mo stay. He was telling us the most fascinating stories about life in Lebanon. Did you know he was there during the last attack from Israel when *Hezbollah* kidnapped their soldiers in 2006? He had to be evacuated on an American naval ship."

Layla had been there too, newly arrived, but she couldn't leave her grandparents. Bombs were nothing much to get excited about in Lebanon. Besides, *Hezbollah* rockets had nothing on the bomb ticking away at home.

Rain wagged a finger at Layla. "How come you never want to talk about Lebanon?"

While Mo had broken free of that old lifestyle, Layla still felt pulled in two, as she did at this moment between her family and her friends. But, oh, how she longed to spend a carefree day in Mo's company, and she needed to share with him about her newfound faith. Rain had protected her from lying to her uncle. Layla should accept it for the gift it was.

She placed a hand on his bulging bicep. "I'm sorry, Mo. Please stay. I don't know what I was thinking. I've missed you so much, and this is the perfect opportunity to spend time together. I couldn't ask for better, really."

He took her hand and squeezed it in his own strong, warm one. "We'll be careful. I promise. I've missed you so much I can hardly stand it." Mo turned her and hugged her to his chest.

"Okay." James stood and stretched. "Enough of the sappy stuff. You're gonna make the rest of us look bad."

As if on cue, Andy, entered with the ice. "Layla, hey. I like this boyfriend of yours. He's a real stand-up guy."

Allie took the bag from him and raised her cheek for a kiss. Looked like those two had ironed out their differences. Layla had missed so much.

Why bother fighting it? She curled into Mo's side and smiled up at him, ready to embark on her first triple date.

Rain sat the final dish—steaming sweet potatoes covered in butter, brown sugar, and walnuts—on the table. She straightened the white linen cloth and surveyed the bountiful spread, happy she had gone the traditional route this year. Nothing spoiled Thanksgiving like a vegan Tofurkey. Instead, the scent of real roasted free-range poultry wafted from the table. She took in the gleaming eyes and drooling mouths around her as she seated herself next to the cranberries and lit the tapered orange candles.

"Well." She took James and Allie's hands in her own. The others joined them. "What are we all thankful for this year?"

"Not more sappy stuff." James snorted. "I don't know how much I can take today. How about we just thank the universe for its bounty, and Rain and Allie for their amazing cooking, and dig in?"

Andy spoke up. "I'm thankful that Allie's back in my life." He turned to drink in Allie with his eyes. "It's been eight long years." "And I'm thankful that Layla let me stay." Mo laughed. "I couldn't handle the thought of leaving all this food behind."

"Hey!" Layla swatted him. "What about me?"

Mo caught her hand back in his. "Oh, yeah, that too." He grinned at her.

Rain said, "I think I speak for Allie, Layla, and myself when I say how happy I am to have found such close friends this year, and that for once, all of our men are here beside us."

"Amen to that," Allie whispered.

"Speaking of amens." Andy stood. "Do you mind if I bless the food?"

"Ah—"

Rain clenched James's hand and shot him a warning glance. No need to offend their guests with James's philosophical rants.

"Ah," he continued, "before you do, I want to get serious for a minute and say that I'm very grateful to have Rain and my child back in my life. I don't know what I did to deserve them."

Tingles flowed through Rain as he gazed down into her eyes. "Amen to that," she teased, and kissed him smack on the lips.

"So let's bow our heads and pray." Andy, Allie, and Mo all turned their heads downward and closed their eyes. Rain, James, and Layla looked at one another, questioning. Rain shrugged her shoulders, and closed her eyes as well.

"Lord God, you amaze me day after day with your faithfulness and your love." Andy paused.

Rain bit her lip. Why did that simple sentence bring tears to her eyes?

As Andy continued, he sounded choked up as well. "Oh God, how I love you. How I adore you. Thank you for these friends. Thank you for how far you've brought us this year, for your continued work in our lives. Bless this food and bless the hands that prepared it. In the name of Jesus I pray, amen."

James bristled beside Rain. "Interesting choice of words for such a multicultural gathering. Don't you think, preacher boy?"

Andy turned pink. "Hey, sorry man. No offense. Force of habit."

"It's fine, Andy, really." Layla patted Andy's hand.

Rain ignored the comments and scooped the first slices of turkey onto James's plate. "Allie, turkey?"

"Please. It looks gorgeous and smells even better."

"It's the first one I've ever cooked," Rain chattered. "I tried that paper bag method they always show on television. I hope it's good. It's supposed to be really—"

"What do you think of the prayer, Mo-hammed?" James flicked out his cloth napkin.

Rain stomped on his foot under the table. He grimaced and leaned back in his chair but continued to stare at Mo.

"I thought you knew." Mo offered his own plate for some turkey. "I go to The Gathering. I saw you there once."

Rain's jaw fell. "You saw James...at church?" Her glance bounced back and forth between the two men.

James didn't comment. Instead he piled his plate with trimmings.

"Yeah," Mo said. "Maybe a week or two before you and Allie visited."

James turned his head up and glared at her. Rain just quirked an eyebrow. He had actually gone to church. Would wonders never cease?

"Derek dragged me," James said. "I was crashing on his floor for free. I couldn't be rude. What were you doing there?"

"I've been helping Allie shop around for churches. She's a big wimp about going by herself." Rain shoved a forkful of green bean casserole into her mouth before James could grill her further.

Andy held up his knife. "Mm, this is really good, Rain. So moist."

"Yeah," Layla piped up. "I'm no expert, but it's the best I've ever tasted."

James sent Rain a we'll-talk-about-this-later look.

Andy caught the silent messages flashing between Rain and

James. He popped more of the savory poultry into his mouth. He hadn't lied. The turkey was awesome, but he could barely force himself to swallow it. He supposed he should be thankful it wasn't some tofu, vegetarian substitute, but Allie and he had already shared a meal with her family and his. Holding back a groan, he turned to gaze at her once again.

She seemed unfazed by the tension at the table, and more able to handle this third helping of dinner than he was. No wonder, she'd been rehearsing like crazy trying to get ready for the show.

As he watched her, the words *thank you, Jesus,* floated through his mind. This past week with Allie had been better than he ever dared dream. He draped an arm over her shoulder, amazed at how well she fit in the crook. Unable to resist, he leaned over and placed another kiss on her cheek. The smile she sent him made him shiver.

Boy, had tongues wagged when she sat beside him in her favorite jeans and flip flops and held his hand at church on Sunday. Let 'em wag! Andy had spent eight long years wandering the wilderness. He now stood at the Jordan, looking into the Promise Land. *Oh, thank you. Thank you, Lord.*

He was only slightly embarrassed by his faux pas with the prayer, and he doubted he would have worded it differently even if he had expected the reaction. As always, he had simply spoken the words in his heart. Sounded like Rain and James were long overdue for a conversation anyway.

He decided to probe some more. "So James, since I accidentally shoved mine on you, I'd like to hear about your belief system. If you're comfortable sharing."

James sent him a cool warning look, but Andy didn't back down.

"I believe that people who pin their hopes on a God who would create such a messed up world are..." James paused as a thud echoed under the table and a look of pain crossed his face.

Andy choked back a laugh.

Rain stood. "More turkey?" She began piling plates again. "James, why don't you tell them about what we've been doing for the last few years? I think actions speak louder than words when it comes to what we believe in."

"Yeah," Mo said. "Layla's told me a little, but I'd love to hear more about it."

As James shifted from the role of antagonist to storyteller, the mood at the table shifted as well. Andy sat back and relaxed. James had led a fascinating life. Not many people would give up everything the way James and Rain had. In fact, Andy didn't know many Christians who could match them in that department. Andy offered some of his own stories about taking a group of kids to Africa last summer to build homes and distribute food. James's eyes softened as he listened. Somehow in the process, Andy managed to clean his plate.

At Allie's prompting, Layla shared about her time spent reaching out to poor Muslim street children. No wonder these girls had managed to click despite their varying backgrounds. When Mo suggested that they all go to the homeless shelter together next week to help out the people from The Gathering, everyone heartily agreed. Even Layla felt confident her uncle would approve of her participating in *zakat* with a group of friends.

What you've done for the least of these, drifted through Andy's head, *you've done for me.*

After dinner, Mo sat back against the metal railing of the fire escape beside Layla and moaned. A cool breeze drifted past. He wrapped his arms around her to keep her warm. At least they had a few moments together to talk. But he didn't want to pressure her. "I don't think I've ever eaten so much in my whole life."

"Not true. I bet you ate like this every year after Ramadan finished."

"Yeah, but we're talking salads, hummus, and rice. Never anything as heavy as gravy and pumpkin pie. Ugh. How do they do it?"

"It was fun, wasn't it? Was this your first Thanksgiving dinner too?" She turned her eager face, fringed in a blue veil, up to him.

He longed to kiss the tip of her perfect little nose, but resisted. "Yeah, I guess it was. Although I ate turkey loaf with stuffing in the cafeteria last year."

Layla rested her head against his shoulder.

"Mo, there's something I need to tell you." Her voice trembled as she spoke the words.

"What is it? Is everything okay?" He struggled to see her face, but she had hidden it against his chest.

"Yes...no. I don't know. It's complicated. But look who I'm talking to." She paused.

"Layla?" He tipped her chin up with his fingers to examine her eyes.

"I had a dream."

"A dream?" Mo had a dream. A dream to marry a beautiful girl he proposed to on a playground one day almost seventeen years ago. At the moment, it almost seemed within his grasp.

"Yes. I saw Jesus. He was so real. Mo, I believe now. I do." She bit her full bottom lip.

Emotions roiled within him like the ocean in a storm. Layla accepted Christ? So many Muslims were coming to the saving knowledge of Jesus through dreams and visions these days. He shouldn't be surprised. But what would this mean? He wanted to run away with her. Shield her within his arms where her family could never hurt her. "Did you...?"

She nodded her head, both wonder and fear evident in her eyes. "I gave my life to him."

"Oh, Layla." He pulled her back to his chest. What if he lost her?

She shook against him, thankfully muting his own trembling.

"Who did you tell?" he whispered over her head.

"Only you and my closest friend, Fatima. It's the most amazing thing that's ever happened to me. I've been reading the Bible and learning about the Christian faith in every spare moment. I'm so happy." She swiped at her eyes.

He pressed a kiss against her silken veil. "Oh, Layla." He repeated the phrase. "This is what I've been praying for. I'm so happy for you too, but you're right. It's complicated."

Couldn't he have one moment of joy before crumbling with terror? Blast their culture. Blast their religion.

She looked up at him, big eyes shimmering with tears and hope now. "But we'll figure it out, right? You said, somehow, we would figure it out."

"We will." Mo wished he felt as certain as he sounded. "Do you have any plans?"

"I can't tell my uncle. He'd freak out. When I go home I want to talk to my father. He's such an understanding man. He'll tell me what to do. Right? And you'll come meet him. Won't you?"

"I hope you're right. And I will come." He pulled her more tightly to him. He'd be there and would protect her with his life if necessary.

Would Layla's father blame him? Maybe he was to blame. "If you think that's best. But are you sure? Maybe you should deal with one thing at a time."

"No." Layla shook her head against him. "I just want this to be over."

Over. One way or the other, Mo feared it would all be over sooner than Layla expected. "Don't tell anyone else. I'm sure your friends would mean well, but they don't understand the risks."

"I know. It's been so hard to keep this to myself. I'm so glad I have you, Mo."

Did she? Did she have him? After tonight, would she even be able to speak to him? "How can we communicate until Christmas break without getting you into trouble? We need to talk together. To pray together."

"I set up a private e-mail account my uncle knows nothing about."

"Sounds good." This time it wasn't about sneaking off for frivolous dates. Mo needed to make sure Layla remained safe. He wanted to tell her it would all work out. That it would all be okay. Instead he settled for, "I love you."

FORTY-FIVE

The soup kitchen was cheerier than Andy expected. A blue industrial-style carpet spread over the floor and yellow plastic covered the long rows of tables. One of the ladies from The Gathering had even taken time to top each with a little bouquet of silk flowers. The aroma of simmering stew filled the air. Although it was located in an old mission house in downtown Norfolk, various area churches took turns keeping the place stocked with food and workers.

He smiled at the next face in line as he scooped salad onto a proffered Styrofoam plate.

The shy brown-skinned man with graying hair kept his eyes turned down.

"Ranch or Italian?" Andy asked.

The man indicated the ranch dressing.

"That's the popular choice tonight." Andy poured some over the lettuce. "More?"

The man looked up now and smiled. "No, that's all."

"How about some bread and butter," Allie suggested.

The man made his way down the row as Rain and James filled his plate with beef stew, Layla helped him pick cookies, and Mo poured him a drink. By the end of the table, the man laughed at Mo's joke and chatted for a moment.

Others from The Gathering offered nonperishable food items from a pantry, manned a used clothing rack, and mingled among the diners. In a small room to the side, Pastor Mike ran a prayer station. Since most of their group were new, Mo and James led them through the no-brainer job of serving dinner.

The line had thinned out. A woman with a bright golden tooth passed by laughing merrily. "Oh, I just gots to get me some more of them there cookies. I loooves me some cookies. They're my very, very favorites."

"Did you try the cranberry with white chocolate chips?" Andy pointed to the dessert tray. The pastor's wife had made the cookies by hand.

"Mm doggie. That sure does sound good. I'll have to try them next."

The lady's joy proved contagious, and Andy found himself chuckling along with her. He had forgotten what a mood booster outreach work could be.

Layla held the treats on a napkin when the woman arrived. To everyone's surprise, Layla had opted not to wear her veil that evening, claiming she didn't want to raise questions or upset the guests in this Christian setting. Very thoughtful and generous of her. Andy could certainly understand what Mo saw in the dark-haired beauty. But he felt concern for his new friend too. Dating an unbeliever was never a good idea.

Layla handed a stack to the woman, and when she smiled her face lit like sunlight. No wonder Mo couldn't resist. The situation was complicated.

"Thank you. Thank you so much, sweetie pie." The enthusiastic woman pumped Layla's arm. "God bless you. God bless all of you."

"And God bless you," Layla said in return.

Andy whispered to Allie, "Is that something Muslims say, or is she just being nice?"

"I've never heard her use the phrase before," Allie said. "But I've never seen her without a veil in public either. She's been acting strangely. Jumping from one extreme to another. One minute she's more relaxed and joyful than I've ever seen her, and the next she looks downright terrified."

"Maybe she's considering a major change in her life." Andy studied Mo as the guy refilled a paper cup and then draped an arm around Layla's shoulder. He hoped so for Mo's sake. For Layla's too, of course. But the guy was obviously in love. Andy knew what that felt like. How horrible to be torn apart by your religion from the woman you love.

He turned his attention back to Allie. Maybe he should reserve some of that sympathy for himself. "I want to bring the youth group here sometime. What do you think? Maybe we could take one day a month."

"Are you kidding?" She put her hands on her cute little hips. "Pastor Jenkins doesn't even consider the people who run this place proper Christians. You know darn well he doesn't work with other denominations. He'd be afraid the youth were leading people astray. Goodness, he can barely cooperate with the other churches in our conference. Heaven forbid someone get the credit for his hard work."

As he suspected. For as well as their relationship was going, they still had their own religious differences to overcome. "That's not fair, Allie."

"Really, I attended his congregation for eighteen years. I'm not making this stuff up. I saw it again and again."

Andy blew hair out of his eyes. "I wish you would believe me when I tell you he's changed. Look, I'm not supposed to talk about it, but he went through some really hard stuff about four years back. He almost gave up on his faith. He realized he needed to make a fresh start. That's when he brought me on board."

"I'm sorry that he went through something rough, but I don't see any difference in him." She crossed her arms.

"How many times have you gone to church this fall? Two, three? You haven't given the place a fair chance."

"I went enough times to know that everything's still the same."

"Were the sermons the same?"

"Well...not exactly. They may have improved slightly." She tilted her head in thought. "I guess there was more humility about him. But the music was the same. The people were the same."

"The youth are different. The people are coming around. And I told you we purchased a drum set this week. That's big."

He held his hands wide over his head. "I mean huge."

"I don't know. I'm happy about how things are going between us, but I'm still struggling with this whole church issue. It's such an important part of your life...your calling...your identity. I know you want to improve things, but I can't picture myself as a part of that yet."

Andy leaned against the wall and bumped his head on it. Had they made any progress at all? What if after all this, she turned him down in the end?

"I'm sorry, Andy. I didn't mean to discourage you. I thought it would be better to be honest. I'll keep praying and trying. I'm over my old fears and resentments. Really I am. But I still have concerns about some very real issues at the church." She leaned her head on his chest and wrapped her arms around his waist. He encircled her with his own.

Hoping against hope that he could hold her there forever.

"God bless you." Layla stood behind the table and handed a stack of peanut butter cookies to a teenaged boy with body odor and drug tracks streaking his pale arm. What she really wanted to do was grab him by the shoulders, shake him, and tell him that Jesus could set him free. She didn't know how much longer she could hold her secret inside before she burst and shouted it from the street corners.

What a wonderful feeling to strip off her veil and shove it inside her glove compartment. As much as she still treasured her family and heritage, she couldn't bear the thought of giving the wrong impression to these priceless people. Too many Americans believed there were multiple paths to God. That all religions were equal. That each individual created their own truths.

Layla knew the truth. She had met truth face to face.

More than anything she wished she could talk to Rain. She looked happy enough standing beside James serving stew. Of course Layla was glad to see the makeshift family reunited, but something had dimmed in Rain's eyes since James came home. As if she had tossed a shade over her spirit to keep it from shining too brightly and scaring him away. Rain had come so close in her own quest for God, yet Layla beat her to the finish line.

Who would have guessed?

"I love this, Mo. Can we do it again sometime?" She pressed against his side.

"You know I'd be happy to. But I'm not sure how many risks you should be taking before you get a chance to talk to your dad. I don't want anything to happen to you." He kissed the top of her head.

"I told Uncle I'd be doing charity work with friends. I didn't lie, but I don't think we'll run into anyone from the Middle Eastern gossip chain tonight."

"I know. And I don't want to scare you, but I've been praying for you so much. I can't shake this sense that you're in some sort of danger."

"Of course I am. We knew that all along. That's the risk any Muslim convert takes. That's the risk you take every day. What's gotten into you?" She turned up her head to look into his eyes. In them she spied something she had never found there before.

Fear.

"I know. I know. It's funny how I've never worried much about my own life, but with you it's different. I want to protect you. Guard you. That's hard to do when I'm not supposed to go anywhere near you."

She tapped his chest. "So let's meet here again next week. I'll be fine. I promise. I'm a big girl." Layla hated to make guarantees she couldn't keep, but there was no point in Mo wasting time worrying about her.

What would happen would happen.

FORTY-SIX

A week after Thanksgiving on Friday evening, Allie hopped from foot to foot backstage, keeping warm and expending nervous excitement all at once. Her entire body thrummed with energy. She ran her fingers over the slick rainbow fabric. Wiggled about to watch it flow along the lines and curves of her body like water. She hadn't realized how much she missed performing. They were up next. Theirs would be the final piece of the night.

She peeked around the black velvet curtain. In the front row within the glow of the stage lights, sat Andy, Rain, and Layla, as well as Allie's entire family. Mom had come nearly an hour early to save the seats. Maybe she didn't consider Allie such a failure after all. But what would her family think of the performance? They had seen her dance ballet before, but never anything like this.

Oh well. Too late now.

Allie's hand itched to wave at Andy. Her man. After all these years. She could hardly believe it. She pressed her fingers to her lips in a silent kiss that he couldn't see, longing to press her lips against his instead. They would wait to start all that again, though. The chemistry between them was too off the charts to fool around with.

But what if tonight was the end of them? The very thought made her sick to her stomach. Andy hadn't seen her dance since high school and wasn't terribly happy about it at the time. Would this piece be too passionate? Too unrestrained? What if he put his ministry above hers and asked her not to perform like this again? No matter what she thought she heard from God, she could hardly marry a man who wouldn't support her calling in life.

Come on, Andy, don't let me down.

But she would dance full-out, come what may. She would do it for Rain. Do it for Layla. They needed this choreography. This message. She wouldn't hold back. The lights went out on the ending pose of the piece before them. A tribute to jazz. The dancers a shadowed silhouette of musicians playing their instruments.

"Eek," Allie whispered to her partners. They were all there and ready. She brushed spirit fingers with each of them. The dance had been committed to prayer. Nothing was left but to get out there and live it.

Jaron entered the stage. The first notes of the music spread over the audience as he stumbled about, as if waking from a dream, surprised to find himself in the heavenly sphere. He moved in tempo with strong African stances and kicks, his toned muscles bulging against the white fabric of his costume, feet pressing hard into the ground. Before long, Jenna joined him, floating across the floor on *pointe* shoes, feather light as she spun and leapt through classic ballet shapes. They flowed together in lyrical worship to the first chorus.

Then it was Allie's turn. As she placed her first foot onto the polished stage, bright white light poured from deep within her, charging each cell with power and immediacy. Music coursed through her and burgeoned into embodied praise. And she danced.

Sliding through postmodern patterns. Toes flexed then pointed as the melody demanded. Arms flailing one moment, and curving into a graceful extension the next. Gentle butterfly motions, punctuated by beating stomps. Passion in every curl of her hands, every contraction of her abdomen. She rolled across the floor, succumbing to the weight of gravity, only seconds later to defy it by throwing herself into Jaron's waiting arms. He boosted her high over his head within the warm yellow flood of lamps.

Shondra joined in, adding upbeat jazz in a joyful refrain, and their group was complete. They moved through the unified worship section once again. Then came the hushed interlude. As each knelt to the floor, bowing and worshipping in their own style, their voices rose over the music.

Jaron spoke first, quoting Matthew 11 from The Message translation. "Are you tired? Worn out? Burnt out on religion? Come to me." He stood and opened his arms wide.

"Get away with me and you'll recover your life." Jenna twirled, fluttered, and swooped back to the floor in a relaxed pose. "I'll show you how to take a real rest."

"Walk with me and work with me—watch how I do it." Allie leapt from the floor, throwing back her arms and touching her feet to her head from behind. She streaked across the stage into an asymmetrical position.

They all slid to a new spot on their knees and tapped the floor, rising and falling in an earthy, native tempo and chanting, "Learn the unforced rhythms of grace. Unforced rhythms of grace. Unforced rhythms of grace."

As three of them continued, Shondra stood and wrapped it up with all the sass and flair of a Southern gospel preacher. "I won't lay anything heavy or ill-fitting on you. Keep company with me, and you'll learn to live free and lightly."

At which point, Jaron lifted Jenna over his head in the shape of a cross. He turned ever so slowly in a circle in the middle of the stage. The cross spiraling over them like sunshine lighting the earth, as Allie and Shondra burst into spontaneous worship. Twirling and leaping beneath the cross.

Then all four of them were dancing, moving from deep within. Pouring out the kingdom of heaven onto that stage, into that auditorium. Weaving and circling around one another like human ribbons of praise. Hoping, praying, crying out to God with their very beings. They ended back in the form of the lifted cross, with Allie and Shondra prostrate at Jaron's bare, brown feet.

For a moment, silence fell over the place.

Then the audience exploded into roaring applause. Applause that wafted to the King of kings. Shouts of "Amen," and "Glory," even, "Praise you Jesus" rose over the din.

Allie stood, staring at Shondra in wonder. Jaron lowered Jenna to the floor, and they all grasped hands. Hot and sweaty, their palms joined together. They bowed in unison, not merely to the audience before them, but to their marvelous creator who had given them all things. Including this dance. Jaron dropped their hands and pointed toward heaven. The crowd stood to their feet and thundered their approval once again.

Allie could barely believe it. She had never seen an audience moved quite like the one before her eyes. All the dancers joined them on stage for a final round of applause. Once the curtain settled into place and she congratulated her team, Allie rushed into the crowd.

Her sister Sarah was the first to meet her, teary-eyed as well. "Allie, I had no idea. I never understood before."

"I thought you'd hate it."

"Well...the music I could have done without. But you were incredible."

Mom ran up and crushed Allie to her. "Oh baby, there can't be a prouder mama anywhere in the world than I am right now."

Dad turned it into a group hug, and the rest of the family joined in. "Beautiful, honey. Exquisite. I knew you were a great dancer. But that. I've never seen anything quite like it."

"Ah, Allie." Sarah pointed over her shoulder.

Allie broke away as she saw Andy standing behind the clump of Carmichaels, arms filled with long-stemmed red roses. He passed the blossoms to her and scooped her into his arms instead, swooping her in a circle. "Gorgeous." He planted a kiss on her nose. "And the dance was awesome too."

Her heart could barely handle such acceptance and approval. Is this all it took? Being completely and utterly herself. Becoming a conduit for God to flow through. And she had wondered if it would scare them away.

"You have to do that for church. I won't take no for an answer. They need to see what their future pastor's wife has to offer." Andy gave her another tight squeeze.

Allie's mouth gaped open. She had no words.

"Please, Allie." Sarah actually hopped up and down. "Will you? My friends would love it." What happened to her reserved, heavy-metal-hating sister?

"That's a great idea," her brother Rob agreed.

"Are you all crazy?" Allie shook her head. "Pastor Jenkins would never allow it."

"I think you'd be surprised. Don't worry. I can take care of it." Andy held her hand in the air, twirled her, and dipped her ballroom style.

Allie's head swam.

"It's about time we bring your gifts to the congregation, Allie." Dad crossed his arms over his chest with resolution.

Allie blinked, trying to take it all in but having a hard time. Then she saw Rain and Layla waiting quietly in the aisle. Layla smiled, but Rain was weeping.

She motioned her head in their direction. "I'll catch up with everyone later. Looks like I'm needed right now."

Mom kissed her cheek. "Sure, sweetie. We'll see you Sunday morning."

"Sunday morning and dinner after at your place." Allie held up the roses. "Thanks again for the flowers. I'll see you tomorrow, Andy."

Layla stepped forward to hug her. "It was lovely. I felt honored to watch it."

Rain stood still, staring at her feet.

Allie laid a hand on her shoulder. "Rain, what's wrong?"

Tears streamed down Rain's face. She swallowed hard. "That's what I want. That's what I need. It's what I've been looking for all this time."

"Okay, give me a minute," Allie said. "Let me get my stuff, and we'll get out of here."

Back at her place, Rain sank into the cushiony couch. Allie

and Layla settled themselves on either side and stared at her. She felt sort of silly now. Her emotions had gotten the best of her as she watched that dance. Something about the cross symbol rotating high over their heads tugged at Rain's heart. But the entire piece had been spiritual and moving. Not so different than the New Age dance companies she had seen. Surely it wasn't a big deal. Weeks ago she vowed not to make an irrational decision about this whole religion thing.

She was being ridiculous.

"We should have stopped for ice cream." Rain giggled. "I could use some about now."

"We'll get some later." Allie patted Rain's knee. "Why don't you tell us what happened first?"

"It's nothing." Rain lied, hoping the universe wouldn't hold it against her this one time. "I just got a little carried away."

"I mean..." Allie spoke slowly. "Would you like me to pray with you? I know I pinky swore not to 'make' you get saved, but I don't want to let this moment pass either."

Rain took in a deep breath and smelled James's lingering cologne in the room. Her jeans pressed tight against her expanding belly. She placed a hand on it. "No. Not yet. I don't know what I was thinking. I'm not ready for a commitment like that." Wouldn't getting born-again make her and James, what did they call it, "unequally yoked"? And what about the whole "fornication" thing? They could hardly go back to being celibate after all these years together. No, it was asking too much. It would never work. Her eyes trailed to the queen-sized bed on the far side of the room.

Allie followed her gaze. "You know, Jesus doesn't expect you to come to him all squeaky clean. Just come as you are. Trust him to guide you step by step. You don't need all the answers right now. He's able to handle the messes in our lives and turn them into something beautiful."

But that was exactly the problem. Cleansed from what? Rain still couldn't buy the whole sin and atonement thing. She shook her head and choked out the words. "I don't think I can."

"Are you certain?" Layla said.

Rain jolted. She turned toward her Muslim friend with head cocked to the side and heat welling in her chest. "Seriously, you too? Why would you even care?"

"You shouldn't dismiss your feelings so easily." Layla kept her head downward, staring at the geometric print of the couch. "I saw your face as you watched that dance. Something very real was going on inside of you. You can't ignore that. Not everything can be understood through reason. Sometimes we must take a step and accept things by faith."

"Is this what Islam teaches?" Rain heard the confusion in her own voice.

"Islam?" Layla looked up. "This is what Islam teaches I suppose. Although I never really thought of it in those terms. We're sort of commanded to believe."

"If the performance was so moving," Rain snapped, "why don't you accept Christ?" She regretted the words the second she saw her friend's crestfallen face. "I'm sorry, Layla. I didn't mean it."

"What's wrong?" Allie reached to touch Layla's knee.

"I shouldn't say." Layla covered her face with her hands.

"It's all right." Rain gently extricated Layla's hand and took it in her own. "You know you can tell us anything."

"You must promise me that you won't say a word." Layla took a breath and composed herself. "Not to anyone. And don't get too excited. It's complicated. It will be hard for you to understand."

Goodness, what in the world was going on? "Tell us."

Allie stretched her hand over as well. "Please, Layla."

Layla swallowed hard. "A few weeks ago, I had a dream. In it, I met Jesus. I did accept him. And I am so happy with my decision. But I must be careful. My uncle's been ranting about honor killings and upholding Islam. You don't understand the danger I'm in."

"Oh, Layla," Allie said.

They all fell into a hug.

"But why?" The words fell unbidden from Rain's mouth.

"Because I believe now." Layla sniffled and wrung her hands.

"For so long I've questioned. I've wondered. I loved God with all my heart. Longed to please him. To serve him. But something was wrong. Too much in my Muslim faith did not make sense to me. We might say in the West that Islam is about peace and love. We even try to convince ourselves. Those scriptures are tucked in there somewhere. Mostly in verses undone by ones written later in time. But hate, pride, shame, terror. These are what I've seen in the *Qur'an*. What runs rampant throughout the Middle East where our religion began. So much injustice. So much intolerance. Sadly, most of it modeled by the prophet himself. *Sharia* law crumbles nations from within, and no one dares to speak a word."

She stared Rain directly in the eye, piercing deep into her soul. "But Jesus, he speaks of love and of peace with no contradictions. He lived by these principles. With humility and compassion and sacrifice. He gave his life for me. Me. A woman. I can barely fathom it. But I have felt the touch of his hand. I have seen love emanating from his face. I know it's true. No one can ever tell me otherwise. This is the God I always dreamed of serving. Nothing will make me turn back."

Rain shook off the turmoil rising in her over Layla's passionate testimony. This is what Rain had wanted all along. Sort of. She wanted Layla out of that repressive religion. But what about the consequences? How must Allie feel? Even happier? Even guiltier?

"I long to live, to have a home with Mo. To raise a family. But if I must give my life in return for the gift I've received, I'll do it without regret."

Rain surveyed Allie over Layla's head.

Allie's lips pinched together. She squeezed her eyes shut. When she finally opened them, she said, "Layla, I'm overjoyed to hear you say these things. It's a dream come true. Better than I ever hoped for. But you're right. It's complicated. It's scary too. Where do we go from here?"

"We trust God." Layla clasped her hands to her chest. "He is bigger than our problems. Able to clean up our messes. Turn our lives into something beautiful. That's what you said. Right?"

Why did that sound so much harder when applied to Layla's situation than to Rain's?

Apparently, Allie agreed. She grasped Layla by the shoulders. "Of course you're right. But I think we should pray. I'm afraid the danger is greater than you realize. Satan would like nothing better than to turn this into a tragedy, but we're not going to let him do that."

Allie let go of Layla. "If God's called you to be a martyr, so be it, but I don't think that's the case. I think he has an amazing ministry planned for you and Mo. When I hear your heart, your words, I keep thinking how much you could bless others. How many lives you could change. We're not going to give you up without a fight."

The girls joined hands and bowed their heads. Rain would put aside her doubts and questions. What she didn't doubt was God's reality. That he spoke to his people. That he had the power to protect this beautiful, sweet young woman sitting beside her.

And more than anything, they needed him right now. The next few hours could mean life or death.

FORTY-SEVEN

Layla crept through the ornate front door. She closed it with the faintest wisp of sound. Taking off her shoes, she laid them upon the plush carpet and began her tiptoeing trek through the salon. She had assumed Auntie and Uncle would be at the Lebanese wedding until late in the night, but their car out front said otherwise. Surely she could sneak safely to her room and gather her most important belongings without waking them.

She passed through the formal sitting room and into the hallway without incident. Sidling by their master suite, she slipped into her own dark room, pulled the door shut, and leaned against it. Allie was right. It was past time to move out. A smothering, palpable sensation clung to the air in this place.

How wonderful it felt to share her conversion with Rain and Allie. She had held the secret far too long, but when she heard Rain making excuses and pushing God away, she could resist no longer. Hopefully her confession would be the confirmation Rain needed, but even if not, she needed to make it for herself.

When she clicked on her light, Layla sucked in a gasp. There on the floor in front of her desk was her laptop, smashed into a hundred pieces in the middle of the plush pink paradise. The shards of plastic and metal screamed their warning. Her heart shattered to pieces along with it. *Ya'allah!* The word flashed through her mind before she corrected it. *Dear God, please help me.*

How much did Uncle know? What had he discovered? Surely not her e-mails to Mo. Those were on a secure system. But Uncle had helped set up her laptop. What if he installed some sort of override? And that first e-mail to Fatima had been sent through her normal Google account.

Allie had been right. Mo had known too, but Layla didn't want to admit to herself that Uncle might be capable of this.

Her eyes flew about the room. Dare she throw together a suitcase? Why did it even matter? She wouldn't need her Islamic clothing anymore. And she still had *Baba's* credit card. Whatever she couldn't borrow from Rain and Allie, she could purchase tomorrow. She wouldn't miss this room or anything in it. During the last few weeks, it had grown to be a prison rather than a paradise.

How had Allie known she needed to move right away? Was it too late already? Thank God the girls sat waiting in the circular driveway out front. Oh, but she would miss her aunt and uncle. And what about her parents? They were sure to find out. Maybe they knew by now. Would they disown her? Deny her very existence as so many Muslims did in these situations? She pressed her hand to her mouth as her stomach churned in her abdomen.

She grabbed her smallest jewel box full of sentimental heirloom pieces and slipped it into her purse. Snatched her backpack with school books and supplies from the floor, hoping at least most of what she needed was contained inside. Of course, her computer was dead, along with the start of several end-of-semester papers.

Mourn it later.

No time now.

At least the only loss was an inanimate object.

Scooping a favorite teddy bear by the arm, she headed for her door. Layla tiptoed her way out of the house.

She made it past her aunt and uncle's bedroom.

Not a rustle.

Through the dark hallway.

Back into the salon.

Halfway across.

When a voice spoke through the darkness. "Where do you think you're going?" Cold ice, razor sharp, clung to every word.

A lamp snapped on, flooding her uncle with harsh white light as he sat clenching the arm of an overstuffed leather chair. His glare of pure hatred stabbed her, cutting deep into her chest. "I said, where do you think you're going?"

Layla's reply stuck in her throat. The words wouldn't come. What did he know? How much should she say?

"Out with that boy? Running to your infidel friends? To a church perhaps?"

"What...what do you mean, Uncle? I just went to a performance at the university tonight. I was just—"

"Just what? Headed to the kitchen for a snack?" His gaze lowered to the teddy bear in her hand. "Why you lying..." Uncle slid into a stream of Arabic curses.

Layla's stomach plummeted to the floor along with the bear. She understood the crushing, pinching, breathless fear Allie once spoke of. Struggling to catch her breath, she murmured, "Uncle, I'm sorry. I don't know..."

"Stop talking. Shut your mouth. I will listen to no more lies."

Layla took small sideways steps, one at a time toward the foyer. Surely Rain and Allie saw the light click on. Surely they would come.

"Go to your room. I need to decide what to do with you."

"I...I can't, Uncle." Layla dashed for the door.

Uncle raced toward her, pulling an object from his pocket. Something flashed in his hand. He reached the archway first with a long kitchen knife glinting over his head.

Layla held out her two palms in front of her, reversing directions and backing to the bedroom now. "Uncle, don't. You don't mean it. Please stop."

Auntie emerged from her hiding place, rushed to Layla's side, and shielded her with her own body. "*La, la, habibi.* Don't do it. She is our family. Our niece. You love her."

"Step away." Uncle's voice slapped Layla like an arctic wind. Was this the same man who had held Layla on his knee, singing her songs of barnyard animals and entertaining her with hand gestures?

Hal seesan, the childhood tune ran through her mind. *Sho helween. Click, Click.* She had been Uncle's beautiful little chicky, but no more. Now he threatened to slaughter her like a sacrificial lamb on the altar of honor.

It made no sense.

How could he do this?

Auntie clutched her more firmly to her side. "No, no. You don't mean it. You've gotten so worked up these days. This isn't you. This isn't the man I married."

Slamming the knife into an end table, Uncle let out a roar. "Step away!"

Auntie slunk back. Shivering. Mumbling. "No, no, no." Retreating deeper into the covering of her veil.

Layla fell to her knees and dropped her bags beside her. Held trembling hands before her to keep the furious man at bay. How could his hatred run so deep? He had loved her like a father. "Uncle, look. I'm not leaving. I'm not going anywhere. Please, calm down. Let's talk about this."

"You have shamed our family. You have brought dishonor on us all. You have betrayed the great Allah. There is nothing left to talk about."

"I know you don't mean this, Uncle. How could you ever live with yourself? Do you want to spend your life in prison? Please, don't do it." Would he destroy Layla, himself, and his family with one sweep of the knife?

Quaking with rage, Uncle stepped toward Layla.

Allie clutched Rain as they stood in the entryway. She had begun to pray in the car the moment the light clicked on. But as she saw the tableau played out in silhouette, she and Rain ran for the door without hesitation. Thankfully Layla had left it unlocked, and the uncle's roar drowned out the sound of their entrance. Clinging to Rain now, her chest clenched as they hobbled toward the archway and peered around it. Would witnesses deter the uncle, or make him more determined than ever to complete his ugly task? Layla always said he was such a loving man.

Surely, he would never do it.

Allie stood on the tips of her toes, weight forward, prepared to rush him from behind and hope she could wrestle the knife from his hand if he took one more step toward Layla, who knelt begging on the floor.

But the uncle froze several feet away from her. Allie held up a finger to Rain, indicating they should wait and watch for now. She prayed fervently under her breath. Dear God, was this all her fault? Somehow, someway, they had to save their friend.

"Please don't do it." Layla repeated, still pressing at the air before her with her hands. Her eyes glimpsed Allie and Rain, peering in from the archway. Their very presence seemed to fill her like breath in a sagging balloon. Layla stood back to her feet. Allie watched the labored rise and fall of Layla's chest.

"Come back," the uncle shouted. "Come back to Islam, to the one true religion. It is the only way. Declare there is no God but Allah."

"No, Uncle. Jesus loves me. He loves you."

"Stop it!" he bellowed, brandishing the knife.

Allie bit her lip. Poised to leap on his back. Surely this couldn't be the end.

"He does," Layla said. "He loves you. He died for you. Like he died for me."

"Enough of this. I don't want to hear it." The uncle covered his ears with his hands.

Rain dug her fingers into Allie's arm. She pulled Allie around the archway and forward a few steps.

"You can kill me. Go ahead and do it. It won't matter. I know I will be safe with God in heaven. I have that assurance. What do you have?"

The aunt's terrified eyes darted about the room. She watched as Rain and Allie approached her husband but never uttered a word.

"Shut up, shut up." His voice grew weak and ragged as his shoulders sagged.

"Jesus loves you, Uncle. It's true."

The knife clattered to the floor. Layla's uncle dropped to his knees now, still clutching his head. But the weapon lay within easy reach of his hands.

Allie caught Rain back as she lunged toward it.

"He loves you. He'll forgive you. Just accept him."

"No!" The man moaned. "It can't be true. I can't accept it. I won't."

"It is true, Uncle."

"It can't be. It would change everything." He slumped until his face was on the floor.

Rain rushed forward and grabbed the knife. "Go, Layla. Go!"

"I'll pray for you, Uncle," Layla said as she snatched up her belongings and dashed to Allie's waiting arms. "I love you." Her voice broke. "And I forgive you."

The three girls ran for Allie's car. As their feet pummeled the pavement, the oddest thought surfaced in Allie's mind.

If Layla could take on an armed Lebanese man through the power of the Holy Spirit...Allie could follow God's path and return to Atlantic Community Church in order to help Andy reach the future generation.

How easy that seemed in this moment of clarity.

How surmountable a task.

All she had to do was be herself.

Rain opened the backdoor of the car and shoved Layla inside, hopping in behind her. Allie jumped in the front. Locked the doors. Jammed the keys into the ignition. Turned it, and slammed her foot on the gas. The girls sped safely into the night.

Allie pulled her phone out of her purse and tossed it to Rain. "Call the police."

Rain could hardly hold her fingers steady to press 9-1-1. She held the phone as it rang. In a voice that sounded robotic even to her own ears, Rain reported the incident. "I'm calling about an attempted murder. No. She's fine. We have her with us. We're driving away now." She fought off Layla's hands as the girl roused from her catatonic state and realized what Rain was doing.

"Layla," Allie snapped from the front seat like an army commander. "Stop it."

"What's the address?" Rain turned to Layla and demanded. "What's the address? The police need the address."

Layla glanced back and forth between the two girls. Tears filled her eyes as she supplied the information. "4528 Bay Avenue."

Rain listened to the instructions from the operator.

After she hung up, she removed Layla's restricting veil and smoothed her silken black hair. "You did the right thing, sweetie. I doubt he'll get in much trouble. He didn't even touch you. But it's important to notify the authorities. You may need to take out a restraining order."

"So, are they sending the cops?" Allie tore down the street, jerking the steering wheel hard from side to side.

"To Layla's house. And we need to go to the precinct and file an official complaint." Rain made shushing sounds into Layla's ear as Allie swung the car in a new direction.

What had Rain witnessed in there? Another miracle to be sure. But the calm. The determination. The true belief in Layla's eyes. Somehow that unhinged Rain even more than the knife held unsteadily in the hand of Layla's rotund uncle.

No, Rain did not share that sort of faith. Maybe someday. But certainly not yet. More than anything else, Rain believed in her love for James, in their family, in their need to stay together. It would have to be enough.

Still, something in Allie's assurance, in Layla's quiet confidence, made Rain wish things could be different.

FORTY-EIGHT

"Mm, my two babies. I don't know which I love more."

Rain stood at the sink washing dishes, swishing bubbles back and forth in the water, as brown arms wrapped around her waist and a gruff chin nuzzled her neck.

"You big softie." Rain splashed water over her shoulder.

She could relax and tease again now that Layla was safely settled at Allie's house. Layla's father had been upset by her news, but at least for the moment he seemed understanding and supportive and, most importantly, willing to let her finish the semester.

"Big softie, huh?" James kissed her cheek. "I can't wait to go and hear his tiny, little heartbeat."

"It's amazing. And fast. But how do you know it isn't 'her' heartbeat?"

"A girl? A girl would be cool. A girl with your eyes. How long till we see the ultrasound?"

"A few more weeks." Rain pressed herself against his solid length, drinking in his strength.

"I should get started on a cradle. I want to build one by hand."

"James?"

"Hmm." He rubbed his head against her tumble of hair.

Rain gathered her courage. She'd been meaning to ask ever since Thanksgiving, and she couldn't hope for a better mood. "Do you think maybe we could try The Gathering again sometime? Together?"

When he didn't answer, she continued. "It's not that I buy

all the 'absolute' stuff. But I enjoyed it as a community of faith. I want to raise our child in a place like that. With values and with purpose. You know?"

"We don't need a church for that. They're nice people and all. We'll see them at the homeless shelter, but I don't want them feeding lies to our kids. No matter what pretty package they put it in."

"Oh." He was right. Of course he was. But Rain wilted in his arms.

He hugged her tighter to him. "Maybe we could try some sort of congregation where they honor all faiths. That would be better. Don't you think? I'm sure they have potlucks and fellowships too."

"Yeah," Rain said. "We could try that." But would it fill the emptiness growing inside of her? Would it fill that place she had discovered deep in her heart while staring into the eyes of a personal God?

James picked up the dish towel and started drying. "I'll never understand these religious types. Your friend risking her life to convert. All that fuss. Over what? Some characteristics of God? Some definition of truth?"

"I don't know, James. I admire her dedication. Her commitment. Her strong sense of right and wrong. Sometimes I wish I had more of that." Rain gulped and looked up at him.

"We have each other." James closed his hand over her womb. "That's what matters. We'll always have each other."

She turned in his arms and lifted her head to receive his kiss. James was all that mattered.

Allie tugged Andy through the hallway of the Batten Arts Building and toward the office of her English professor. That slight tinge of mold and disinfectant filled the air. "Over here."

The grades for their research papers were posted outside the door. Only one more week and her first semester would be finished. She ran her finger down the list of social security numbers. "Yes! Got an A on my research paper."

"That's my girl." Andy gave her shoulder a squeeze.

"Allie?" A voice came from around the corner in the office. Professor Robinson stuck his head out the door. "Allie Carmichael. There you are. I've been meaning to talk to you."

"Professor Robinson, this is my boyfriend. Andy Vargas." Just saying the words tickled her lips into a smile.

"Nice to meet you." Andy offered his hand and the two men shook.

Andy pointed over his shoulder. "I can..."

"That's fine," the professor said. "Please stay. I simply wanted to ask Allie how the multicultural assignment went. I get to read the papers, but it's nice to hear from an insider."

"Insider?" What did he mean?

With a smirk, the professor pointed to her shirt, which read, *In him I live and move and have my being.*

Allie looked from the professor to Andy and back again. "You're a Christian?"

"Guilty as charged." He held up his hands in surrender.

"But you never said a word."

"Why should I? You and the other believers in the class had plenty to say."

Allie shook her head. "I thought you were some sort of politically correct agnostic or something. I thought that's what the whole assignment was about."

"God laid that assignment on my heart over ten years ago. I've been giving it in two classes a semester ever since."

"Wow." Andy sounded impressed. "Get them talking and asking questions. That's brilliant. I'll have to remember that."

"I believe that all we have to do is present truth into the mix. People can spot it."

"But you never said..."

"I know, I never said a word. I like to let the literature do the talking for me. Who can see the hopelessness of Hemingway contrasted against the moments of grace in Flannery O'Connor and not get the point?"

Allie shook her head again and searched past his wire-rimmed glasses deep into his blue eyes shining with the love of Christ. How had she missed it? "You are something else, Professor Robinson."

"I'd love to hear any good reports about your partners. I've quietly been keeping track all these years. To date, nearly thirty students that I know of have given their lives to Christ during or shortly after taking my class."

"Wow. Thirty converts in ten years." Andy nodded. "That's more than a lot of missionaries."

"And I bet the people you've ministered to don't even know," Allie said.

"A few do, but that's not important." The professor shrugged. "I do the task God assigned me. That's privilege enough."

"Well." Allie's heart tugged in her chest. "One of my partners did accept Christ. But I'm not at liberty to say who. And the other...she grew closer to God, but I don't think she's ready to make that final step."

"Keep me posted."

"I will. I'm so glad we got to talk." Allie giggled.

"I need to get back to my grading. You take care of this young lady, now." The professor shook Andy's hand one more time before heading into the office.

"That's amazing." Andy squeezed her shoulder again. "Maybe we can have him over for dinner sometime."

"You sound like we're an old married couple already." Allie bumped him with her hip.

Andy turned and took her hands in his. "Actually, I don't want to do anything to rush you this time, but I heard about a big diamond sale at the mall this weekend."

"Rings! No, Andy. Not that again." She tossed back her head dramatically. Then took his face in her hands. Enough sparks flew between them to start a brush fire. "I love you, Andy Vargas, and I want to marry you, even make babies with you. But please, no ring."

"Of course not. I was thinking some sort of pendant."

Tears welled in her eyes. He truly knew her. He understood. "Oh, Andy."

He placed his hands over hers. "I want so badly to kiss you right now. You have no idea."

"I think I do." Allie's lips tingled at the thought. "I guess we need to start planning that wedding."

"Not without some type of diamond. It's sort of a tradition." Andy twisted his face into an apologetic smile.

"Who needs tradition?" Allie wrapped her arms around his middle and proceeded down the hall. "Hey, I know. Maybe I can get my nose pierced. You can get me a stud for that instead."

He leaned down to drop a quick kiss in the hollow on the side of it. "Whatever makes you happy, crazy girl."

"As if the congregation at Fuddy Duddy Chapel would stand for it."

"All I care about is you."

She snuggled into his side and breathed deep his sea-scented cologne. "Actually, I think a pendant would be perfect."

He pulled her tight against him, resting his forehead against hers. "You do?"

"I do."

"God has given me the most precious gift in the world, Allie. And I'm never letting you go."

Layla rested on her own small bed in Allie's room. The white walls and the mix of greens and lavenders in the décor created a refreshing escape from her pink prison.

"Are you sure you don't want to come?" Allie asked from the bedroom door.

"Go pick out jewelry with Andy and be happy. I'll be fine."

"Okay, see you later." Allie closed the door behind her.

A bird sang outside the window, and Layla turned to watch the last fall leaves blowing in the breeze. She sensed God all around her and within her, not hidden far behind the clouds. After spending so many years praying with her face pressed to the floor, it was freeing to speak to him in a relaxed posture.

So God, all my plans are shot to hell. Okay, not hell. Now that I think of it, I guess that's exactly where my old plans were leading me. What I really mean is, what do I do now?

She waited for an answer as Allie had been teaching her during this last week. For that still small voice. For that spontaneous flow of thoughts, impressions, and visions to flow from her heart, but nothing came.

Oh well.

Her laptop chimed, "You've got mail." At least someone had a message for her—she shot the thought heavenward. Was she getting sassy with God? Layla laughed, and somehow felt he laughed along with her.

So liberating.

She opened her computer and found a new e-mail from Fatima.

> *Dear Layla,*
>
> *I have nothing to brighten your day. I shall not for one minute pretend. I wish my computer had a teardrop font. I want to pull out a pen and paper to show you how I feel right now. I know you must be busy, but please, spare a moment to hear the cries of your old friend.*
>
> *Saleem has married and moved away now, and Shadi refuses to take me out in public anymore. I have become a prisoner in my own home. Father doesn't care if I never leave the house again. If I dare to argue, he only hits me. He will beat me into submission, he says. Allah decrees it. Mother does nothing to help. Father calls the Americans a pack of filthy dogs. He wants me to marry someone in Saudi Arabia, where I will be kept safe and pure. But, Layla, this is my home. I do not want to leave, even if I only glimpse it from my bedroom balcony.*

Layla gasped. The raw pain in the e-mail was almost too much to digest. Her own problems suddenly seemed so insignificant.

> *I spend time there each morning calling out to Allah, begging that he will hear my cries and grant me some sort of life worth living. I know Allah is great and he is just, but has he no compassion?*
>
> *There is a young man who walks by every morning mumbling to himself. For weeks I wondered why. He took notice of me crying on my knees at sunrise. He looked right at me. Not with lust like some of the Americans. Not with curiosity. But with sympathy. True heart-rending sympathy. He turns his eyes to me and gazes at me each morning. I'm so used to being invisible, but he stares straight into my heart.*
>
> *After a few days passed, he mouthed the words, "I'm praying for you." The mumbling made sense. The man was praying as I was praying. Every day he whispers up the precious words, "I'm praying for you." Finally I could not resist. I pulled aside my veil to let him see my face, the face of the girl he prayed for. I wanted him to know me. For someone, for anyone, to know the true me on the inside. I whispered back down, "Thank you."*
>
> *Oh, the comfort it brings me to think of my praying man. Yet the terror if father should ever find out. Layla, please pray too, that God will hear my cries before I fall into the pit of despair never to return.*
>
> *The Sister of Your Heart,*
> *Fatima*

And Layla knew.

As if warm oil poured over her head and cascaded down to her toes, Layla felt it. She understood. A new purpose. A new calling was hers. She would give her life helping the Fatimas of the world. Be God's instrument to answer their cries.

Layla considered the timing of the letter, and mirth overtook her. She and God shared another laugh. He had sent his answer via e-mail this time.

Funny.

Who knew God was such a joker?

But as her mind returned to Fatima, her laughter faded. *Oh, God has heard your cry, Fatima.* She typed the simple words. "God has heard your cry. I pray he will speak to you in a dream."

No, Layla did not know what her future would hold. She felt safe enough now that the restraining order was final. Something had broken in her uncle that night.

As for her father, after yelling at her over the phone for several hours, he had finally settled down and relented to let her stay with Allie until finals finished next week. But he made no promises beyond that. And though her mother swore to disown her, something in her father's voice gave her hope, caused her to think maybe, in time, he could come to understand.

And what about Mo? They loved each other so but still had many obstacles to overcome.

All Layla knew for sure was that God held her future secure in his love.

She would rest safe in the palms of his hands.

I have spent the last twenty years married to a Middle Eastern man with a heart to reach Muslims. He grew up in Lebanon with as many Muslim friends as Christian and is still close with some of them today. Because of that, I have always wanted to write the story of a young Muslim woman. The last time I was in Lebanon, a beautiful, stylish young Muslim woman in a bright red mini-dress layered over black clothing caught my eye. She is the inspiration for Layla.

I truly hope that I have accomplished my goal of writing Layla's tale with compassion, respect, and love. I took pieces from a number of different stories of former Muslims I have met, wove them together, and added a good dose of fiction. While I know that I can never entirely understand their experiences, I did my best to capture the essence of what I gleaned from them.

A number of interesting details in the book are real, including the Brother Rasheed show, The Muslim Woman show, and the song about the martyr Rana—which I wrote the lyrics for by the way. Also, Layla's dream is based on the fact that many Muslims around the world are coming to Christ through dreams and visions. Another interesting note is that Ramadan moves every year because it is based on the lunar calendar. Although I kept the time line hazy, anyone who knows Islam well will probably notice that the month of Ramadan in this story doesn't match the publication year of 2013, as I wrote it several years earlier.

Of course I understand that current Muslims will probably not like this story. Please know that it is not my intention to offend, and I certainly don't want to argue. I did my best to be fair, to illustrate that there are many different types of Muslims in the world, and to show that there are many beautiful aspects to their culture. However, there are also many Muslims coming to Christ and facing great hardships because of it. I believe their stories deserve to be told, and I think the thought processes Layla followed are typical of those who convert to Christianity.

That being said, I imagine I managed to offend a few Christians too, and again, that was not my intention. But this book turned into a full examination of cultures, religions, and what draws people to Christ. I think Allie's journey is typical of those who love God but give up on church, and that her thought processes represent those who have been turned away by Christian religiosity. Of all my characters, Rain seems to be the least controversial, but again I apologize if I failed to capture any aspects of African-American culture correctly. I thought a bi-racial character would be perfect to embody the eclectic mix that makes up the postmodern mind set of our current generation.

This book was quite an undertaking. There's a lot of challenging content in here, and maybe I was crazy for attempting it. But this is the story God placed on my heart, and I have to believe that means there are many other hearts out there that will in some way be touched by it.

For more articles on the book and purchasing information about my other novels and my "Cry for Peace" CD including "Rana's Song," please visit my website at http://dinasleiman. com. And drop me a line while you're there. I love to hear from my readers.

ACKNOWLEDGMENTS

My thanks to my husband, his family, and all of his many friends who have been teaching me about Islam and the Middle East for two decades. I think I should have earned an honorary degree in the subject by now. Thank you to Brother Rasheed who allowed me to use his show in the book. And a special thanks to Sister Amani of *The Muslim Woman* show for reading this early and offering suggestions for authentic touches that really strengthened the story.

Thank you to my critique partners, Roseanna White and Christine Lindsay, who taught me so much about writing through this book. Also to my beta readers, Sarah Dolan, Jennifer Gammil, Angela and Amalie Andrews, Christiana Sleiman, Susan Johnson, and Teresa Mathews, who guided and encouraged me through this process, and to the ladies of Inkwell Inspirations who always stand by me and who helped me wrestle the beginning of the book into shape. I hope I didn't forget anyone who contributed, but just in case, thank you to all my friends and family who support my writing in so many ways.

I also want to thank Juliette and Robert Alston, who taught me so much about inner-healing and helped me to find my own place of healing and peace. And thank you to Rob and Bev Stevenson, who for the last twelve years have blessed me with a church where I truly fit. Rob, you are loved and missed.

Oh, and thank you to the U.S Marines who rescued me from Lebanon that time when I got stuck there in the middle of a war between Hezbollah and Israel, and to the navy ship that whisked my family away. You guys rock!

Finally, thank you to my agent, Tamela Hancock Murray, who believed in this crazy book and to WhiteFire Publishing who was willing to take a chance on it.

Discussion Questions

1. The book opens with Layla stepping into a very new experience. When is the last time you faced a new experience? How did you react?

2. Do you have cross-cultural friends in your life? Are you familiar with the three cultures represented by the main characters in the book? What questions do you have about their cultures at this early stage?

3. Rain has lived a wild and adventurous life, but secretly she longs for structure and stability. Which do you value more and why?

4. Layla has fought long and hard for something she wanted. Are you willing to fight for what you want in life? Are you willing to wait and be persistent?

5. Allie has had some bad experiences with church. Have you? What sort of Christians are most difficult for you to get along with and understand?

6. Allie's honest searching seems to draw the other girls to Christ rather than push them away. Why do you think that is?

7. When Layla meets Mo, they share an instant connection. Do you think God has a perfect match for each person? At what point could that concept contradict a Biblical view and lead to problems later in marriage or life?

8. Something from James's past makes him unable to accept his child. Has anything from your past held you back from something good? Have you overcome it, or do you still struggle in this area?

9. Andy regrets how he treated Allie the first time around. Have you ever been haunted by regrets? How did you deal with them?

10. What do you value most in a church? What sort of church culture best fits your needs and personality? Is your current church a good fit for you?

11. All three of the girls learn about hearing God's voice in this book. Are you able to hear God's voice for your life? Did you learn anything from their experiences that might help you in the future?

12.   Allie struggles with the price that both Rain and Layla might have to pay to come to Christ. Have you ever had to give up anything significant for Christ? Have you ever honestly contemplated what others might have to give up for Christ?

13.   Both Layla and Allie struggle with reconciling their feelings for the men in their life with what they believe to be God's plan for them. How does each girl solve this dilemma? Have you ever struggled in this area?

14.   Mo decides to continue seeing Layla even though typical Christian wisdom says that dating an unbeliever is a bad idea. Do you think he made the right decision? Why or why not?

15.   Rain seems to have her own sort of relationship with God, although she has not yet accepted Christ. Do you think this is possible? At what point do you think God would expect her to make a decision?

16.   Allie and James both find inner-healing—but in very different ways. Do you think both of their experiences are valid? Can you think of any reasons their experiences might have been different?

17.   How did you feel when Layla came to Christ? How did you feel when her life was threatened? What can you do to be a blessing to both current Muslims and to those who come to Christ?

18.   Were you surprised by Rain's final decision concerning James and Christ? Why do you think she made that decision? What do you think she might need in order to take that final step?

19.   When Allie lets go of her resentment and fully embraces who God has made her to be without shame, she finds that those who truly love her accept her as well. Who has God truly called you to be? Are you living in freedom in that area or still struggling to find your place?

20.   Layla's story is left somewhat open ended. How would you write her future?

And now a preview of the second book in the
Deep Within Series!

dare
from DEEP
WITHIN

This is killing me!

Curling deep into a corner of the worn couch, Layla Al-Rai
blinked away tears and read the text message from her ex-
boyfriend one more time: *This is killing me!* Then she hit delete.
She needed to put Mo far from her mind. Forget about what
she couldn't have and focus on what she could.

Somehow forget that this was killing her too.

Swiping newly cut black bangs from her eyes, Layla surveyed
the cozy living room of her little bungalow. She searched out
her friends gathered in the well-lit kitchen and honed in on
their smiling faces. Allie and Rain had been her strength and
comfort throughout the tumultuous first semester of college.
These returning students, both independent women in their
mid-twenties, showed her what life could be like beyond the
veil.

Surely miracles did exist. If anyone had told Layla six months
earlier that her Muslim parents would allow her to share a house
with a group of Christian college girls, she would have cracked
up laughing. Yet here she was. Not only sharing a home, but a
new Christian believer herself.

"Coffee, Layla?" her roommate Allie called from the kitchen.

"Sure. Plenty of cream and sugar." Coffee. Another thing to
be thankful for. Nice light American coffee wafting through the
air, not her auntie's syrupy Lebanese version. Layla took a deep
breath and attempted to ignore the stab of longing in her chest.

As if a caffeinated beverage could replace the love of her life.

Layla's good friend Rain plunked down on the arm of the rust-colored couch, pregnant belly and all. Rain didn't live with Layla, but she folded her legs Indian style and wiggled an indentation for her burgeoning rear as if she did. Hugging an oversized coffee mug to her chest, she took a hard look at Layla's face in the dim lamplight. "Hey, we're happy tonight, remember. No more tears."

"I'm not crying." Layla grimaced.

"Then what's that wet thing on your eyelash? You should know better than to try and fool me. The wise, all-knowing Rain sees everything." She took a sip of coffee before hollering into the next room. "Allie, we might have to break out the big guns. Any ice cream in that fridge?"

As if Rain needed ice cream. Layla's lips quivered into a grin. The all-knowing, New-Age hippie guru evidently didn't *see* that she was about to break the couch. Although Rain looked prettier than ever with her café-au-lait skin, corkscrew brown curls, and fern green peasant blouse, she needed to slow down on the weight gain if she wanted to continue perching herself in such precarious positions.

"Never mind, Allie. I'm fine, really. Rain has no idea what she's talking about."

Allie and her little sister Sarah came to join them. Sarah, wearing a long beige skirt and turtle neck sweater against the winter chill, settled herself primly on the edge of an overstuffed chair. Meanwhile Allie handed Layla a steaming mug of amaretto-scented coffee and plopped onto the couch, stretching her bare ballerina legs onto the glass-topped table.

Could the sisters possibly be more different? Despite their matching blonde coloring, Sarah represented everything Allie had left behind from her ultra-conservative past. But at least they were getting along these days. Hopefully Allie could help Sarah unwind a bit before she snapped.

"I'm all for ice cream." Sarah brushed her twill skirt down flat. "I don't need an occasion."

Allie took a long sip and sighed. "You'll all have to be content with amaretto creamer tonight. The teenyboppers wiped out the fridge. I swear those girls swarm like locusts."

Layla nodded. "A real life Biblical plague." Allie's nickname for their roommates certainly fit. Those four freshman girls bopped in and out all hours of the day and night. "At least we have some peace and quiet for the moment."

"I don't know how you guys do it." Rain shook her head. "They give me a migraine."

"They aren't so bad once you get used to them." Allie laughed. "Besides, I only have to put up with them until summer. Save your pity for Layla."

Layla didn't need pity. Truly, she was still overwhelmed by the wonder of it all. "The girls are kind of fun. You can't imagine how amazing it is for me just to be on my own."

No Auntie watching over her every move. Attending a real live church. The joy of praying when and where she pleased, and feeling like someone actually listened. After twenty-two years in a restrictive culture, Layla was finally free. The constant, nagging fear of Allah gone from her life. Surely giving up her boyfriend Mo was a small price to pay.

"Yeah, I guess surviving a murder attempt puts everything in perspective." Rain placed a warm hand on Layla's.

"Oh my goodness." Sarah's blue eyes grew big and round, all the more obvious beneath her tight chignon. "I forgot about that. You must have been terrified."

The last thing Layla wanted to talk about tonight was her uncle's botched honor killing. "It's over, and I'm safe now. That's what matters. I doubt he would have gone through with it, but I'm sure you can understand the teenyboppers look pretty good to me after all that."

"And things are okay with your parents? They didn't disown you?" Sarah sat up a bit taller and leaned in.

Layla couldn't help but feel sorry for the girl. Unlike Allie and Layla's friends at her new church, Sarah looked quite bound by religion herself.

"No, thank goodness," answered Layla. "They didn't disown me. I still can hardly believe it. My mom wouldn't speak to me for a while, but my Dad's moderate in his beliefs. He's all for religious reform. I mean, they aren't happy with me, but for now they're paying the bills. So my dream of an engineering degree is still alive. And they've dropped the subject of an arranged marriage, which is way more than I expected."

"Yeah, but she's not supposed to tell anyone. And they made her give up her boyfriend in exchange for tuition. Which totally sucks." Rain slammed her cup down on the end table, causing the lamp to shake. "I swear, Layla, you're a grown woman. You should find a job and be done with them."

Rain wouldn't understand. She'd been living with her significant other, James, since she was eighteen, her parents off on perpetual safari somewhere in Africa. But Layla needed her family. She loved them. Longed to honor them in whatever way she still could.

Sarah tilted her head and tightened her lips. "We're supposed to honor our parents, Rain. The Bible says so. Layla's doing the best she can in a hard situation. Besides, this is not the right time in her life for a boyfriend. She should focus on God."

Somehow hearing her thoughts filtered through Sarah's judgmental mind made Layla question her own reasoning. "Mo was a huge part of why I came to Christ. So it's not that simple. Without Allie and Mo, I might never have found him. That has to count for something."

Sarah gazed at her sister skeptically. Layla knew the women well enough to decipher the look. *How could a heavy-metal loving, short-shorts wearing, so-called Christian lead anyone to Christ?* Layla stifled a giggle.

Not so successful at restraining herself, Rain snorted. "How about you, Sarah? Any hot guys in your life?"

Red crept up from the edge of Sarah's high collar to tinge her entire face. "No guys at all, hot or otherwise." She patted her fastidious hairdo. "I have no need for men right now. 'Awake not love before it pleases' and all that. Really, Layla, your parents are doing you a favor. I have no intention of dating. After college I'll consider courtship."

Despite Layla's new appreciation for the Bible, Sarah's habit of spouting scripture left a bad taste in her mouth. She took another sip of amaretto coffee to wash it away.

"Courtship!" Rain laughed out loud this time.

Heat emanated from Sarah's face, but she had no way to stop it. They probably figured she was embarrassed by all this talk about guys. Better they imagine her a pious fool than suspect the truth. Jesse's seductive smile flashed through her mind along with his searing eyes that turned her to melted butter. Tingling in places she shouldn't at the mere memory, Sarah gulped and attempted to steady her breathing as guilt washed over her in torrents.

Allie cleared her throat and looked to be choking back a giggle. "So have you decided on a school yet, Sarah?"

Thank God, a change of subject. Although, on second thought, Sarah doubted God deserved any credit for her relief at the moment. Surely he was standing on alert to zap her with a lightning bolt. She smiled her appreciation to Allie. "I've been accepted here at Old Dominion University and also at a Christian college near Roanoke. But I'm leaning towards ODU. I plan to study languages, and they have a great Arabic department."

Allie twisted to recline her long legs over the back of the couch behind Layla's head. How did Allie do it? Looking relaxed and happy as she lounged in her minuscule hot pink dancer's shorts. Somehow at peace with God and suddenly engaged to the assistant pastor of Sarah's own conservative church in Virginia Beach. Surely Allie was delusional. Kind-hearted but nuts.

Things just didn't work that way with God.

"Wait a minute." Layla seemed to shake off the funk she'd been in all evening. "Did you say Arabic? *Hal tatakalame Alarabiya?*"

"*Naam ya habibti. Ftakartic betaerfi,*" Sarah answered.

Rain threw up her hands. "Translation please."

Layla sat forward. "I asked if she spoke Arabic. She said yes. She thought I knew. But I had no idea. How'd this happen?"

"I go to a high school for international studies. I hope to be a missionary someday."

Rain sucked in a sharp breath.

Layla glanced from Allie to Rain and back again.

Allie just shrugged her shoulders.

The heat returned to Sarah's face. Did they suspect she was nothing but a sham? A failure of a Christian? She had planned to be a missionary for years. She wasn't ready to give up her dreams over one little stumble.

"You know, Sarah." Layla smiled encouragingly. "You could learn a lot from Allie in that department. The way she was just herself and open about both her faith and her struggles meant a lot to me when I was searching for the truth."

"Yeah." Rain contentedly rubbed her protruding belly with her ringless left hand. The woman had no shame. Sarah should be glad Rain chose life, but still. "I'm not into all that Christian stuff like Layla, but Allie definitely gave me a better perspective on it. She really changed my ideas about God."

Oh, so they didn't think she'd be a good witness. Not as good as Allie. No matter how hard she tried, never as good as Allie. A heavy lump filled Sarah's stomach.

After eight years gallivanting the globe, living life on her own terms, Allie had returned home to the proverbial fatted calf. Okay, so she was on a dancing "mission" trip and not quite the prodigal child. But after Sarah killed herself to be the perfect daughter and meet every last one of her parents' high standards, it stung to see her free-spirited sister accepted so easily back into the fold. They even bought Allie that zippy red Mini-Cooper, while Sarah had no car of her own.

Well, she'd show them. She'd show all of them.

"Hey, Sarah," Rain said with an evil grin, "if you end up going to school here, you could take Allie's bed after the wedding. I'm sure she'll be occupied in a much warmer mattress."

"That would be fun." Layla nudged Rain, otherwise ignoring the inappropriate innuendo, and perked up even more. "I'd love to share a room with you. I could help you with your Arabic."

"Oh, my gosh." Sarah blinked vapidly a few times and squealed in imitation of Allie's eighteen-year-old roommates, wiggling her fingers beside her head. "Like, I so totally get more of Britney and company than I can stand at church every week. Like, I might just die or something."

"That is so her." Rain clapped in delight.

Although only eighteen herself, Sarah had no need for a bunch of immature, boy crazy roommates. This recent incident was just a blip on the radar. She'd get things under control soon enough and had no desire to surround herself by such worldly influences.

"Look, there she is now!" Allie teased.

Sarah turned to the dark window. A shadowed figure stood on the sagging front porch, barely discernible against the soft glow of the street lights. Her heart sped. But surely it wasn't Britney. The person was alone, and Britney always had a posse in tow.

A soft knock rapped against the door.

Allie stood and shot a questioning glance to Layla. "Too quiet for the teenybopper crew. You expecting anyone?"

Layla just shrugged.

Allie called, "Who is it?"

"Help me, please." A pleading, accented voice filtered through the crack. Its broken timber tugged at something deep in Sarah's being.

Allie shot a questioning glance around the room. Rain hurried to stand behind her, cupping her shoulders.

"Let her in," Sarah whispered.

Allie opened the door. Through it stumbled a slight figure shrouded in black.

"Layla? Is Layla Al-Rai here?" emanated the familiar voice from the black fabric.

Layla jumped from the couch in response. "Fatima? Is that

you?"

A sob broke through the slit of the *niqab*.

The poignant sound rang all too familiar in Layla's ears. A cry she had heard far too often. She ran to her dearest childhood friend, picked up the heavy hem of the full-body veil, and threw it over the woman's head—revealing a golden-haired beauty, stunning despite a split lip and the purple smudge rimming one of her hazel green eyes.

CPSIA information can be obtained at www.ICGtesting.com
Printed in the USA
BVOW08s0449271113

337471BV00001B/12/P